Praise for
EDGE OF THE GRAVE

"Powerful and moving . . . Morrison's portrait of Glasgow and its denizens—both the vicious and the virtuous—is superb."
                                                            —*Literary Review*

"A highly evocative novel with a strong sense of place . . . Morrison brings to dark life this time period in an engaging and mesmerizing way."
                                                            —*Crimesquad*

"The atmosphere Morrison conjures is so captivating it's hard to believe this is his debut crime novel . . . You should grab *Edge of the Grave* at the soonest opportunity. Without doubt the most evocative and engaging Scottish crime novel we've come across in a very long time."
                                                            —*Crime Fiction Lover*

"This deftly plotted novel is a more than worthy successor to William McIlvanney's Laidlaw novels: the title is a homage to them. I am very glad that this book is the first in a projected series."
                                                            —*Historical Novel Society*

"Mesmerizing. Early gangland Glasgow with the gloss razored off."
        —PETER JAMES, bestselling author of the Roy Grace series

"Wonderfully gritty, violent and nasty in all the right ways."
    —JAMES OSWALD, bestselling author of the Inspector McLean novels

EDGE OF THE GRAVE

ROBBIE MORRISON

EDGE OF THE GRAVE

A JIMMY DREGHORN MYSTERY

BANTAM BOOKS
New York

A Bantam Books Trade Paperback Original

Copyright © 2021 by Robbie Morrison

Published in the United States by Bantam Books,
an imprint of Random House, a division
of Penguin Random House LLC, New York.

Bantam Books is a registered trademark and the B colophon
is a trademark of Penguin Random House LLC.

Originally published in hardcover in the United Kingdom by Macmillan,
an imprint of Pan Macmillan. Published in the United States
by Bantam Books, an imprint of Random House, a division
of Penguin Random House LLC, in 2023.

The epigraph quotation is taken from
The Papers of Tony Veitch by William McIlvanney.

ISBN 9780593723319
Ebook ISBN 9780593723326

Printed in the United States of America on acid-free paper

randomhousebooks.com

2 4 6 8 9 7 5 3 1

Book design by Fritz Metsch

To

MY PARENTS, MARIE AND HAMILTON MORRISON,

*who instilled in me a love of reading and writing,
and gave me the freedom to follow those occasionally
precarious dreams for myself.*

And

IN MEMORY OF MY GRANDMOTHER, ANNIE
(1917–2017)

"Read on! Read on!"

"It was as if Glasgow couldn't shut the wryness
of its mouth even at the edge of the grave."

—WILLIAM MCILVANNEY, *The Papers of Tony Veitch*

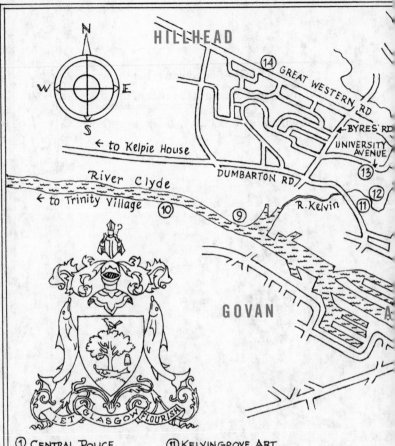

N
W E
S

HILLHEAD

GREAT WESTERN RD

⑭

BYRES' RD

UNIVERSITY AVENUE

← to Kelpie House

DUMBARTON RD

⑬

River Clyde

R. Kelvin

⑫

⑪

← to Trinity Village

⑩

⑨

GOVAN

A

LET GLASGOW FLOURISH

① CENTRAL POLICE HEADQUARTERS
② BRIDGETON CROSS
③ MERMAID BAR
④ GLASGOW MORTUARY
⑤ COURT HOUSE
⑥ NECROPOLIS
⑦ CENTRAL STATION
⑧ THE GORDON CLUB
⑨ PAGAN'S SHIPYARD
⑩ LOCKHART'S SHIPYARD

⑪ KELVINGROVE ART GALLERIES & MUSEUM
⑫ KELVINGROVE PARK
⑬ GLASGOW UNIVERSITY
⑭ GREAT WESTERN TERRACE
⑮ HAMILTON PARK AVENUE
⑯ ROYAL INFIRMARY
⑰ CATHEDRAL
⑱ CITY CHAMBERS
⑲ GEORGE SQUARE

GLASGOW

0   ½   1
MILES

Forth & Clyde Canal

COWCADDENS

CASTLE ST

SAUCHIEHALL ST

ST VINCENT ST   BUCHANAN ST

DENNISTOUN

⑯
⑰ ⑥

GYLE ST

⑲ ⑱

⑧

ERSTON

⑦

DUKE ST

TRONGATE
SALTMARKET

JAMAICA ST

CALTON

GALLOWGATE

④

①

⑤

HIGH ST

LONDON RD

②

LONDON RD

GORBALS ST

CROWN ST

GLASGOW GREEN

③

BRIDGETON

MAIN ST

GORBALS

River Clyde

~HEMESH ALLES~

EDGE OF THE GRAVE

Sparks rage through the darkness, then slowly fade. The smoke and ash are thick and cloying. I move through twisted metal and shattered bodies, the uniforms making them seem like one great, ruptured mass.

He stares up at me with a faith I find touching. I say words that bring no comfort, powerless against the screams and moans, the roaring flames and desperate prayers.

He is fair and beautiful, his skin smooth, his body opened up below me, insides wet and glistening. Flakes of ash fall on him, fading into his blood.

I run a hand through his hair, smoothing it back into place. "There, there," I say, and lean forward to kiss his brow, the flesh cold and damp.

Our eyes meet and his fear, his innocence, fill the emptiness within me. I cup his face in my hands and kiss him again, gently pushing my tongue past dry, cracked lips.

At first, there's little more than cigarettes and whisky and blood, but then, slowly, I begin to taste his life, almost as if it's my own. A birth in a squalid little tenement room, a woman's cries. A mother and father old beyond their years, working and breeding, breeding and working, pieces of the human machine. A childhood of struggle and hardship, but little complaint, just acceptance. Brothers and sisters in the same crowded bed, pissing into a chanty near overflowing by morning. Football in the streets with a ball of crushed newspaper. A job lined up, same trade as the father, the child becoming the man, the pattern unbroken but for a patriotic call to arms and the embrace of a far crueler machine.

I pull back, the early morning air cool on my face. The faith and innocence in his eyes are gone. I take out my revolver and fire it into his beautiful face.

I move on to the next one—he is older, not so trusting. He tries to crawl away, but his legs are ruined. Another explosion shakes the earth. All around us, shots ring out.

"There, there," I say.

GLASGOW

1932

Bandit country. That's what they call it. When civilization dims with the daylight and the gangs come out to play.

From Castle Street, as you pass the Royal Infirmary and approach Glasgow Cathedral, the Necropolis is visible on a low hill to the east. Gazing upon the tombs and monuments inspired by the Père Lachaise Cemetery in Paris, you'd be comforted, reassured; surely any city that honors its dead so grandly must treat its living with equal respect. A common misconception, but you'll learn.

Castle Street joins High Street, which in turn leads to the Gallowgate, where they used to hang people for stealing potatoes and other heinous crimes. Here you might pause to say a prayer for all the poor souls who danced in mid-air, nooses around their necks, to entertain the crowds in the days before the pictures.

If you're of a religious persuasion—and in Glasgow it's hard not to be—a certain flexibility is an advisable survival instinct. Staying true to your faith might get you killed when those age-old questions, known to every child in the city, ring out: "What school do you go to?," "What team do you support?," or more bluntly, "Are you a Billy or a Tim?"—a Billy being a Protestant and supporter of Rangers Football Club, and a Tim a Roman Catholic and fan of the rival Celtic FC. Part of the fun, for the interrogator, is not letting on which side they themselves favor. Of course, you might encounter a nutter, who'll declare himself in the opposite camp to whatever you answer just because he wants to hurt you.

Turn onto Garngad or London Road, and you're entering areas patroled by some of the biggest Catholic gangs in the East End: the San Toy, whose name comes from some obscure slang for "boys"; the Kent Star, from the teeming tenements of Kent Street; the Calton Entry, who ensure no one sets foot on Calton Street without their permission; and the Cheeky Forty, who number more than forty and whose idea of cheek is a slash across the face, not the sort of witticisms delivered by comedians at the Empire.

A gallus strut, a Celtic scarf, and a half-decent selection of Irish rebel songs might help you navigate this fiefdom, if you hold your nerve.

However, even if you do pass through unscathed to continue along London Road toward Main Street, you'll hear the drum of boots on cobblestones and the strains of a song that will chill your newfound Catholicism to its core:

> *Hello, hello, we are the Billy Boys,*
> *Hello, hello, you'll know us by our noise,*
> *We're up to our knees in Fenian blood,*
> *Surrender or you'll die,*
> *For we are the Brigton Billy Boys.*

Bridgeton Cross is the heartland of the Billy Boys, named after William of Orange, whose victory at the Battle of the Boyne in 1690 ensured Protestant rule in England, Scotland, Wales, and Ireland. This is where you'll need the panache of a quick-change artiste, tearing off the Celtic scarf before it becomes a noose, and whipping out a Rangers scarf or a sash of the Orange Order.

Then a quick change back to the Celtic scarf as you encounter the Norman Conks, self-styled conquerors of Norman Street, who have a penchant for pick-shafts in addition to the usual blades, hatchets, and sharpened bicycle-chains.

If you've made it this far unscathed, you're probably growing in confidence. But that would be rash, because after the Conks, faiths jump back and forth with alarming alacrity—the Catholic Nunney Boys of Nuneaton Street. The Protestant Sally Boys of Salamanca Street. The Savoy Arcadians—Catholic—named after the row of shops they congregate outside on Savoy Street. The Baltic Fleet—Protestant—who patrol Dalmarnock Road with the determination of the Great War naval convoys they take their name from.

To stay safe, you have to switch religious allegiances with bewildering speed. Celtic. Rangers. Rangers. Celtic. God save the King. God bless the Pope. God, get me out of here . . .

But continue along the Saltmarket, cross over Albert Bridge into the Gorbals, and the religious divide becomes blurred in a melting pot of cultures, forced to live cheek by jowl by poverty, persecution, and political circumstance.

The Gorbals gangs are composed of Catholics, Protestants, and Jews, so religious beliefs give way to blunter interrogations, such as "Who are you?," "Where do you come from?," and "Who are you looking at?"

The Beehive Boys view themselves as the aristocrats of this underworld, connoisseurs of housebreaking and armed robbery, the South Side Stickers are content to booze, brawl, and stick a knife in you, while the Nudie Boys of Mathieson Street—if they lived up to their name and braved Scottish weather in the buff—should be the hardest gang in the city. In fact, they were once led by a short bandy-legged seventeen-year-old named Mary Mooney.

And that's only two areas you've visited. What about the rest of the city—Plantation, Anderston, Govan, Kinning Park, Maryhill?

Bandit country.

Watch your step.

1

When Jimmy Dreghorn was twelve years old, Rab Hunter held a cut-throat razor he'd stolen from his older brother Billy to Dreghorn's neck, causing him to pee himself in front of at least three lassies that he fancied—Dreghorn liked to keep his options open back then, when he was young enough to think he had any.

Six years later, as they lay trapped together in the mud and blood of the Somme, Dreghorn would watch Rab Hunter die and wonder where all the hate he'd once felt had gone. "Fuckin' hell, Jimmy," Rab would say in a child's voice, and then fall silent, staring without seeing, his eyes never leaving Dreghorn's.

The girls who'd been there that day in the no-man's-land between their schools were Ina Beattie, Louisa McCallum, and Rachel McAdam. Ina, not the brightest or the prettiest, who ingratiated herself with the so-called hard men of both schools with whatever else she had to offer, pointed at the puddle and laughed, which cut Dreghorn almost as keenly as the razor.

Louisa had been scared and tearful; only two years later, she would be dead of TB. But Rachel had stood up to Rab as if he wasn't twice her size. She didn't even flinch when he motioned with the razor as if to cut her, boasting that this was the blade that had given Matt Johnstone his big braw smile.

A few weeks earlier, Dreghorn, kicking a ball on his way home, had turned the corner into Ballater Street to see Johnstone on his knees, whimpering, hands covering his face, blood seeping through his fingers, and Billy Hunter standing over him with the open razor in his hand.

There was a girl with Johnstone, pretty, frozen with fear. Billy touched the handle of the razor to her chin, forced her to look him in the eye.

"It's your own fault," he said, "going with a worthless wee shite like that when you could've had me."

He lowered the razor, wiped the blade gently on her breasts, turning the white of her blouse red. "Too late, now, though," he said. "No' after he's been up you." He closed the blade with a snap and sauntered off.

Dreghorn often thought of Rachel and the sympathy she'd shown after Rab had let him go. He'd just stood there in his wet trousers, unable to look her in the eye. Afterward, although he developed an easy charm and humor with other girls, whenever he saw Rachel he was back in that moment, weak and embarrassed in front of the last person he wanted to see him like that. That was partly why, years later, on his last night in Glasgow before shipping out for France, he found himself up a close with Ina, kissing hungrily, as they pulled at each other's clothes while the rain teemed down outside. She laughed at his fumbling the way she had when the razor was touching his throat, and he drove himself into her hard, not caring, wishing she were someone else.

It was a sin, Father Nolan would say; though not, he figured, as much of a sin as taking cold, careful aim at an enemy soldier stumbling blindly across the mud, or driving a bayonet into a man's belly over and over again, or splitting open a skull with the sharpened edge of a shovel.

All of which Jimmy Dreghorn had done before he turned eighteen.

2

A face; pummeled beyond all recognition. An open tenement door, darkness within, blood smeared across the cold stone floor. Dreghorn wanted to lift the woman from where she lay, but was scared to move her in case he made her injuries worse.

Archie McDaid leaned against the wall, head bowed. Usually, Dreghorn went in first, a quiet understanding between them, never talked about. This time, McDaid had gone further in, baton drawn, as Dreghorn had rushed to the woman. He'd stumbled straight back out, stunned. A glimpse was enough.

"Just a boy," he'd said, voice cracking.

The woman whimpered, and Dreghorn's stomach tightened. He knew what she was asking, but couldn't answer, not the truth. He spoke softly. "Don't worry, hen, I'm the polis. There's an ambulance on its way. You're going to be all right." He hoped he sounded like he believed it.

He got to his feet. McDaid looked up, tears in his eyes, clearly thinking of his own children, and Dreghorn felt a rush of affection for the big man.

He brushed it aside. It didn't do to show weakness or compassion, not in their position.

"Fuckin' pull yourself together," he said.

The house was the same as the one Dreghorn had grown up in, one room and kitchen to hold an entire family. An overturned table, a shattered chanty, the torn curtain of the alcove box-bed hanging by a single hook, the imprint of a small body on the mattress. Further into the darkness was the range, the big oven that should have been the heart of the home. The fireplace below contained only ashes. He gazed around, sensed the horror in the corner, daring him to look.

At first, he hoped the sticky matter on the edge of the range was spilled food, but the sad little form on the floor told another story.

The lights of a passing tram shone briefly through the thin blanket pinned over the window. The boy was wearing only a simmit, his skinny limbs startlingly white in the shadows. About six years old, Dreghorn reckoned; hard to tell with the malnutrition that stalked the tenements.

He visualized what had happened, in shaky black-and-white-like newsreel footage. The mother bludgeoned to the ground, the chanty emptied over her and smashed. The curtain ripped away in a frenzy to reveal the terrified boy in the alcove. His little body, weighing next to nothing, swung against the iron range again and again.

Dreghorn had seen a lot of corpses, dead from natural causes or the brutalities of warfare, but he was glad when the tram light faded.

There was a commotion on the landing. McDaid was questioning the neighbors who'd finally found the boldness to emerge, ordering them to bring blankets and tea for the victim, to show some of that community spirit the tenements were famous for.

A shape blocked the light, an ambulance man in the doorway. "See to the woman first," Dreghorn said, his voice pulled from the depths. "Nothing you can do here."

He went out onto the landing. McDaid angled away from the crowd, speaking low. "Victim's Peggy Bryce. Her man's one Thomas Bryce. Runs with the Billy Boys, supposedly, though he's nobody

I've heard of. He was out drinking. Came back raging, yelling his head off. Nobody bothered too much. A regular occurrence."

Dreghorn scanned the neighbors gathered on the landing and hanging over the banister above, saw a woman watching forlornly as the ambulance men eased Peggy Bryce onto a stretcher. She held his gaze for a moment, then a man—her husband, presumably—drew her away. She pulled free, went to say something, but stopped as the door behind her opened, and a little girl about the same age as the Bryce boy came out blinking in the light. The woman swept the child into her arms and hurried inside. The husband strutted after her, giving Dreghorn a smug look. The door echoed like that of a prison cell as it swung shut.

Outside, the tenements loomed high on either side, the walls the color of dried blood. Dim light emanated from some of the windows, others as black as sin. Above the rooftops the sky shimmered red, the furnaces of Dixon's Blazes ironworks raging through the night a few streets away.

One of the ambulance men stayed inside the vehicle with Peggy Bryce. His colleague shut the doors, nodded to Dreghorn, and climbed into the driver's seat. Another ambulance had arrived, but it wouldn't be heading to the hospital, and was waiting only for the police photographer to finish at the crime scene.

In the squad car McDaid was relaying information to Central Police Headquarters in Turnbull Street via the radio. It was still a novelty; the only lifeline on their early beats was the Acme Thunderer whistle that street bobbies still carried. He had surreptitiously turned on the engine to keep warm. For a man of the islands, he was a big girl's blouse when it came to the cold.

"You'll maybe be needing this, no?" Dreghorn turned to see the woman from the landing holding out the jacket that he had taken off and put under Peggy Bryce's head. "You'll catch your death," she said.

"It'll have to catch me first." He smiled, the warmth and sincerity surprising her, and gratefully slipped on the jacket. "Is your wee yin all right?"

"She's fine, still half-asleep. Bit of luck, she'll think she was dreaming."

"She's about the same age as the Bryce lad?"

"Aye, went to the same school. They used to play together. Don't know what I'm going to tell her."

"What was his name, the boy?"

"Tommy. Thomas."

"After his old man?"

The woman snorted. Dreghorn took a pack of Capstan Full Strength from his pocket, offered her one. "Listen, Mrs. . . . ?"

"Logan. Lizzie." She took the cigarette, didn't meet his eye. "Somebody should've done something. Your lot. This lot." She nodded at the tenement, dark and oppressive. "That poor wee boy's life was a misery."

Dreghorn raised the windbreak of his Ronson Princess as he lit her cigarette. "Mrs. Logan—Lizzie—what he did to Peggy was bad enough," he said, "but what he did to the boy—it was hatred, sheer hatred. It was like he was trying to destroy him. Why would someone do that to their own son?"

She glared fiercely at him. "Because he didn't think Tommy was his son!"

Dreghorn lit a cigarette of his own, allowing her to smoke in silence, gradually calming as she realized what she'd said. "You don't have to say anything else," he told her. "You're the one who has to live here."

She stepped back as the second ambulance crew came out. The stretcher passed between her and Dreghorn, the covered form in the center small enough to break the hardest heart.

Lizzie inhaled deeply, breathed out as if getting rid of something that had resided in her for too long. "Peggy and me grew up together on Muirhead Street. Her mother died when she was wee and her da' took to the drink." She took a final draw, flicked the butt onto the cobbles. "He wasn't bad, he just wasn't there much, left Peggy and her brother alone a lot of the time. In the street, folk said that they went together—you know what I mean?"

Dreghorn nodded. There were always rumors of incest in the slum districts, the proximity in which people lived, brothers and sisters sharing beds through childhood and puberty, often only leaving the family home when they got married.

"Was it true?" He suspected the rumors were exaggerated, that such things weren't as widespread as was claimed. He and his brother were always sent out or told to turn their backs when his mother and sister bathed or undressed for bed. Most families followed similar precautions to maintain modesty.

"Does it matter? Folk believe what they want to believe, don't they?" Lizzie Logan said bitterly. "Things were fine when they first got married. I mean, he was aye acting the big man, trying to get in with the Billy Boys, but nobody took much notice, just humored him, really. After the wean was born, though . . ."

"Some of his so-called pals must've known the stories about Peggy, started slagging Tam about it, saying the boy wasn't his, that Peggy and her brother were still at it. He started knocking her about, stopped her going out." Lizzie started as the ambulance door slammed. "The sad thing is, Tommy would always run to his da' whenever he got home. Tam would ignore the wee yin or push him away, stare at him as if he'd trodden in something."

Dreghorn thought about his own father, the man's emotional recalcitrance and reluctance to engage, as if, consciously or not, he was preparing his family for abandonment.

"Peggy's brother," he said, offering her another Capstan. "Is he still around?"

* * *

The warmth of the engine was dissipated by the withering look of piety that McDaid gave Dreghorn as he got into the car, a look inherited from a long line of God-fearing islanders. McDaid was a long way from the Isle of Skye, but he liked nothing more than to affect an air of moral superiority over Dreghorn.

"Have you no shame?" he asked.

"For questioning a potential witness to the crime? There are more ways to conduct an investigation than dangling a suspect off Jamaica Bridge."

"Gets results." McDaid nodded at the windshield. "She's still there, by the way. The Merry Widow'll be getting jealous—"

Dreghorn glanced back. Lizzie stood at the tenement entrance, still smoking. The glow as she inhaled illuminated her face. Pretty once, but fading, worn away. Whether she was looking at Dreghorn or her life in general, it was hard to tell. She flicked her dowt away in a small shower of sparks and turned back into the shadows.

"How is the Merry Widow anyway?" McDaid asked.

"A lot merrier than she'd be if I wasn't around. And I'm paying for the privilege, remember?"

"Mairi worries about you, y'know."

"Big Bonnie Archie's the one she should be worried about. All those bridesmaids having a peek to make sure you're a true Scotsman."

The car creaked as McDaid shifted his bulk uncomfortably. He didn't mind "Bonnie" when it was used innocently, but grimaced when colleagues bandied it about sarcastically.

Donald Archibald McDaid was the biggest man on the Glasgow Police Force, winner of the bronze medal for wrestling in the 1924 Paris Olympics and Scottish Police Heavyweight Boxing Champion 1928. All of which, he reckoned, ought to earn a man a measure of respect, even if his belly had expanded somewhat beyond its championship peak. The soubriquet "Bonnie" referred specifically to the fine figure he cut swaggering along Sauchiehall Street in full Highland dress, bagpipes under his arm, toward some wedding or police ceremony. In truth, he wasn't the greatest piper in town, but he looked the most impressive, a mountain of tartan and silver buckles, towering over proceedings and drowning out all conversation when he played.

Dreghorn, his mood darkening, reached for the Morse code transmitter and tapped a message. The car radio, specially manufactured by EKCO for the Glasgow Police, was only powerful enough to receive verbal messages. Responses or requests from the vehicle crew had to be made via Morse code or telephoned in from a police signal box.

He asked headquarters to locate an Allan Kerr, possibly resident in Miter Road, Scotstoun. "Peggy Bryce's brother," he explained, and repeated what Lizzie had told him.

"You know," McDaid said when he had finished, "growing up on the islands, you couldn't wait to get to the big city. Jobs galore, the bright lights, the dancing, the women. You thought it was all happening here."

"It is," said Dreghorn. "All the shite in the world's right here."

3

If the Mermaid Bar bore any resemblance to its namesake, it was to one that had been bludgeoned to death in the net by superstitious fishermen. They were parked on James Street, almost directly opposite the Mermaid, having first cruised past the bandstand at Bridgeton Cross, where the drinkers inside would have loitered earlier. It was now past closing time, but a dull glow oozed from behind the drawn curtains, and the murmur of voices drifted from the locked doors.

Bolts rattled. A shaft of light cut through the darkness and drifting smoke, and a bulky shape silhouetted in the doorway waved a reluctant goodbye. The door closed, and under the streetlights the silhouette coalesced into a moon-faced police officer, who straightened his helmet and walked off unsteadily.

"Know him?" asked Dreghorn.

"Aye, useless big lump," McDaid said. "His name'll come to me."

They got out of the car, closed the doors quietly, and crossed the road. McDaid thumped the door with his fist. A long silence, and then the sound of footsteps approaching the other side of the door. "We're closed. Last orders was hours ago. You no' got a hame to go to?"

McDaid remembered the errant policeman's name and lowered his voice, pushing the tell-tale islands singsong out of his accent. "It's Stew. Let me back in, it's Baltic out here."

A pause. Then the door seemed to sigh wearily as the bolts were drawn. Exasperation turned to shock on the barman's face as he saw plainclothes detectives and not a uniformed officer. Involuntarily, he moved to close the door, but McDaid was already shouldering his way in.

The pub was a fug of smoke and hostility, glowering faces watching them. Someone spat loudly onto the scuffed floor. The walls were the color of stale urine, painted with nicotine from smokers' lungs and adorned by grimy pictures of sportsmen from another age, and romantic paintings of hills and lochs as foreign to the clientele as darkest Peru. A photograph of King George behind the bar was the only thing that looked as though it had been polished this side of the war.

"Stew told us to call in if we fancied a dram," said McDaid. "Some man, Stew. Tells us all the gossip, doesn't he, Jimmy?"

It wasn't true, but the next time PC Stewart shirked walking the beat in favor of a fly drink, his welcome might not be so warm. It might even earn him a pasting some night in a dark street, the streetlamps switched off to save money by the Corporation, the local government body responsible for running the city. Into the ground, most people would say.

"Did he now?" A granite-faced barrel of a man turned from the bar, drinks in hand. "Still blowing the pipes, Archie?"

"I've got a pipe he can blow," said a voice, loud enough to be heard, but not for the speaker to be identified.

McDaid smiled. As far as derogatory comments went, it was among the wittier ones he'd had hurled at him. He leaned against the bar, looked down at the man. "Weddings, mainly. And funerals. I'd happily play yours for free, Peter."

"Dance on my grave and all, I bet."

"No' me. Jimmy's the hoofer."

Dreghorn nodded at the man: Peter MacLean, housebreaking, drunk and disorderly, grievous bodily harm; not the worst record, though he hadn't been caught for everything. "Is Billy in?" he asked.

"He's busy."

McDaid said, "We're no' asking permission."

MacLean looked them up and down, snarled at the barman. "Couple of whiskies." He picked up his drinks and nodded for them to follow.

"No' the firewater," McDaid told the barman. "The good stuff."

The barman gave him a dirty look and reached for a bottle of malt. Then they pushed through the throng to where MacLean waited in a private snug, the windows either frosted or so filthy the effect was the same.

Billy Hunter's eyes were always smiling; that's what you noticed, no matter what the rest of his expression said. Sometimes that inner smile was cruel, sometimes calculating, occasionally warm, sometimes even genuinely amused, but it was always there, shifting and sliding so that you never quite knew where you were with him. Dreghorn had seen the smile often: as a boy at the Ballater Street slashing; in the trenches, just before they went over the top; on the streets, as Hunter drilled the Billy Boys like soldiers on parade or led them in a heartfelt rendition of "God Save the King" under the bandstand; and in police cells, breezily denying involvement in some beating or robbery.

About three different shades of smile shifted through Hunter's eyes as he looked at Dreghorn. "Jimmy," he said.

Piles of coins and a small stack of notes weighted down with a glass were lined up on the table in front of him. A nervous-looking man, spectacles held together with gaffer tape, was finishing the count, stacking the final coins with pedantic precision.

"Gregor, beat it," Hunter told him.

Dreghorn took the man's stool, McDaid flopping down on the

bench as if to test its strength. MacLean remained on his feet, closing the door and leaning against it with deceptive laziness.

Dreghorn nodded at the money. "The Depression's not treating some people too badly."

Hunter waved a hand. "Just the boys paying their monthly dues. We're like a social club, you know; there're expenses."

"Very industrious of your lads to rustle all this up, especially when they're no' working," McDaid said. "Bet there's a few shopkeepers light on their takings today."

"Times are tough for everyone," said Hunter, the soul of compassion.

"How's your mother?" Dreghorn asked. "I heard she wasn't keeping well."

Hunter's inner smile hardened. "Keeping her chin up. Always liked you 'cos of what Rab wrote in his letters home. Shame you're a Tim, she used to say."

"Accident of birth."

"Accident, my arse. No contraception? Your man, the Pope, he's got a plan. Everywhere these days, you lot. Aren't they, big man?"

McDaid ignored the question. "We're looking for one of your lads, Tam Bryce."

"Never heard of him."

"Funny, he was seen in here drinking with youse earlier." Dreghorn didn't know that for a fact, but figured there was a good chance.

Hunter glanced at MacLean, who said, "He maybe hangs about on the periphery. No' really one of us, though."

"Periphery, Peter?" McDaid sounded impressed. "That's a big word. Where'd you learn it?"

"From your wife." MacLean leered. "She likes to keep her hand in at the old teaching, offers us ruffians a wee bit of extra education. Learns a thing or two herself, I bet."

Dreghorn downed his whisky, slammed the glass loudly onto the table before McDaid could retaliate. A waste of a malt to knock it back in one, but he was losing patience, and a wretched little corpse was lying cold and stiff on a mortuary table. "This isn't the usual shite," he said. "Bryce went home drunk, started knocking his wife about."

"Maybe she was asking for it. Lot of nagging wives out there. They don't understand how hard it is on a man, no' having any work, no' being able to provide." Hunter himself wasn't averse to dishing out the odd domestic backhander, but when the police had intervened, his wife laid a uniformed constable out cold with a right cross of her own.

"He beat her half to death and then started on his boy, except he didn't stop halfway. Caved the wee yin's skull in against the range. What age, Archie?"

"Six or seven tops." McDaid knocked back his own whisky, as if trying to wash away the taste of the words.

Dreghorn continued, "No' the sort of man I'd want in any social club of mine. Story like that could sully the reputation of the Billy Boys."

"You want us to find him for you?" asked Hunter.

"Any useful information, you pass it on."

"Grass? Be a clype?"

"We're no' playing games now. This isn't about gang etiquette. A wee boy was murdered."

Hunter shared a grim look with MacLean.

Dreghorn noted it, leaned over the table. "And he doesn't just disappear either." He gestured at himself and McDaid. "We get him. He gets arrested. He goes to trial. He faces the death penalty. If I hear any stories about the Billy Boys carving him up and throwing him in the Clyde, doing the job the police can't do, then I'll make sure every polis in the city makes it his job to break the Billy Boys.

I'll knock your toy soldiers down as if you were walking into the German guns again."

He flicked the nearest pile of coins, toppling the stacks like dominoes.

Hunter watched the coins pool together on the table, turned his laughing eyes on Dreghorn. "You're aye so passionate, Jimmy," he said, like it was a weakness. "Sergeant Dreghorn always could fire up the men with some patter, make them follow him over the top." Then his eyes stopped smiling. "No' so good at bringing them all back again, though." Leaning back, Hunter spread his arms expansively along the back of the bench. "We'll keep our eyes open for the bastard." The inner smile ignited again. "Fine upstanding members of the community like us? Wouldn't dream of doing anything else."

Dreghorn and McDaid got up as MacLean opened the door.

"Mind you," said Hunter over the murmur of the pub. "Wouldn't hold out too much hope. Like Peter said, he's no' really one of us. Wanted to be, but only the *crème de la crème,* know what I mean?"

MacLean followed them out. Dreghorn put money on the bar for their drinks. The barman waved a hand. "On the house."

"No, they're not."

McDaid snorted. "If I'd known you were paying, I'd've had a large one."

Dreghorn turned to find his way blocked by a skelf of a lad, eighteen maybe, almost the height of McDaid, who glared at him.

"My brother's in the Bar-L because of you," Skelf accused.

"If he's in the jail, it's because of himself, not me," Dreghorn said.

"You put him there."

"It's my job. I'm no' bad at it either. Do you want to get out the way?"

"What're you going to do if I don't—arrest me?"

"Paperwork, courts? Too much bother for a scrawny bawbag like you."

"You'll no' be saying that when I fuckin' do you, wee man." Skelf loomed over Dreghorn, expression fierce, his breathing growing heavy, like a maddened bull's, then burst into a contemptuous grin and stepped aside as if taking pity on the detective.

"I'll let you off, wee man," he said. "Looks like somebody's already gie'd you a good kicking the night anyway."

Dreghorn glanced at the dark stains on his jacket. The sleeve rode up as he raised his arm; Peggy Bryce's blood was smeared across the white of his shirt cuff. He turned back on the boy, heard a small sigh behind him as McDaid started to say his name, quickly stopping himself. The move had been made. Nothing to do but back it up.

"I'm telling you, I'll fucking do you!" Skelf said again, twitching like a bag of nerves. He glanced around quickly, yelled, "C'mon, let's get into them."

Nobody moved.

Dreghorn cocked his head impatiently; *I'm waiting.*

The boy cursed, fumbled in his inside pocket, then drew his hand back out with a flicking motion.

Dreghorn grabbed Skelf's wrist with his left hand, drove the heel of his right into the boy's knuckles, pushing the wrist violently in on itself. The bone snapped easily, hardly any sound, and Skelf howled as if an electric current had passed through his body. The cut-throat razor dropped from his hand and landed at Dreghorn's feet, and he head-butted Skelf—not enough to break his nose, just enough to send him dribbling down the side of the bar like spilled beer.

McDaid tutted in exasperation, scanned the wall of hostile faces. "Anyone else?" he asked.

There was a moment when it could have gone either way, but it passed. Cigarettes were lit, men gravitated toward the bar, ignoring the lad on the floor.

Billy Hunter was standing at the door of the snug, shaking his head.

"Gang problem?" he laughed. "The biggest gang in this city's the Glasgow fuckin' police."

Dreghorn watched McDaid walk toward his house—not much more salubrious than the sad slums they'd visited earlier—and marveled at the speed of the change in him. A shrug of the shoulders, a loosening of the collar, a roll of the neck, and the big man's whole body seemed to become softer, less imposing. Some people could switch themselves on and off like a peep of gas, shutting out whatever the city threw at them. For Dreghorn, it was always there, pulled taut, an inner tripwire.

Dreghorn imagined McDaid creeping around with the grace of a baby elephant, looking in on his weans cooried up in the same bed, lowering himself slowly, springs creaking, into his own bed, reaching out tentatively to test the mood, and receiving an elbow to the ribs in response.

He smiled as he started the car. His own domestic arrangements were more spartan.

He drove through the night, feeling disconnected from the city, a stranger judging it with a fresh eye, his headlights reflected in the rain-washed streets. As he crossed Jamaica Bridge, the Clyde seemed to pulse like a living thing under the rainfall, winding into the distance where eventually it joined the sea, opening Glasgow to the world.

He turned, passing under the Hielanman's Umbrella. The glass-walled railway bridge, that carried the platforms of Central Station over Argyle Street, had gained its nickname as a gathering place for displaced highlanders who had made their way to the big city, forced from their homes during the notorious Clearances by landowners who reasoned that sheep were more profitable than people. The Hielanman's Umbrella, offering free shelter from the inclement weather, became a place for them to meet and test the limits of camaraderie, musing nostalgically on a lost way of life that was hard at best and fucking miserable at worst. Strangely, it's not just the good things people miss.

Dreghorn should have returned the car to the garage at Turnbull Street, but it was late, the trams finished for the night. He drove along Sauchiehall Street, still jumping with drunks singing and eager young men desperate to get a lumber at the end of the dancing.

On Kelvin Way, his headlights illuminated the greenery of Kelvingrove Park, the Gothic outline of Glasgow University looming above on Gilmorehill. Other dalliances would be taking place there. A few months earlier, the San Toy had thought they were on to a winner by using their prettier gang members to attract homosexuals who frequented the park at night, whereupon they'd beat the hapless men black and blue and rob them, safe in the knowledge that their victims wouldn't complain to the police, sexual activity even between consenting male adults being a criminal offense. The scheme backfired when they encountered a group of officers using the same strategy to boost their arrest records with a few easy indecency prosecutions.

Dreghorn finally drew to a halt on Hamilton Park Avenue. He had lodged in the West End since returning to Glasgow, preferring to maintain a certain distance from the beats he patroled. McDaid joked that it was because he was indulging his airs and graces.

His room was comfortable and civilized—double bed, washbasin, table by the window, chair by the fire, bathroom along the corridor, breakfast and evening meals included, though he rarely made it back for them. The townhouse belonged to the Pettigrew family, but Mr. Pettigrew had died in 1929, leaving the property to his widow who, to make ends meet and save for their children's education, rented out rooms, mainly to academics at the university. Dreghorn was the black sheep of her flock.

He moved through the darkened house as silently as on a trench-raid. The room was cold, but the first thing he did was strip off his stained jacket, vest, and shirt. He filled the sink with cold water, splashed his face and arms, and washed off Peggy Bryce's blood.

He poured a whisky, threw it back, winced at the comparison with the malt at the Mermaid. Honest men never could afford the best alcohol. But one more and he wouldn't notice the difference. Or care.

A gentle knock made him reconsider. She was so close to the door that she was inside before he'd finished opening it, a satin robe pulled snugly but chastely around her full figure.

"Mrs. Pettigrew," he said.

"Inspector Dreghorn." They never addressed each other by their first names, a playful affectation of propriety, but also maintaining a certain reserve.

"Everyone's in bed," she said, as though there was nothing else for it.

"Best place, this time of night." Dreghorn was tired to the bone, could sleep for Scotland, but suddenly felt the need to touch her, to take a warm soft body in his arms and chase away the memory of Peggy Bryce shivering on tenement stone.

He pulled Mrs. Pettigrew toward him, loosening her robe as the door closed.

4

1910

After the razor incident, Jimmy's uncle found him sitting under the kitchen table, scoring one of the legs with a bread knife, damp underwear itching like a rash, his lip petted with rage.

"What's up, Jimmy? How come you're no' outside? It's a braw night."

Jimmy didn't answer, drove the blade into the table leg with more force.

"Jimmy, you don't have that much furniture that you can start chopping things up for the hell of it." Joe Dreghorn hunkered down on his knees, nodded at the knife in Jimmy's hand. "Give me that."

Jimmy shook his head, stabbed again. A splinter of wood sheared off and fell onto the lino.

Joe reached for the knife, but Jimmy jerked it away too fast, the blade slicing across a callused palm. His uncle straightened up with a grunt, kicking the table as Jimmy scrambled out from under it. Joe moved toward him, fist clenched, blood visible between the fingers, and he dropped the knife. "I'm sorry, Uncle Joe. I'm sorry, I didn't—"

Joe pushed the boy aside, stepped to the sink, and ran cold water over his hand. Not a bad cut, but swinging a riveting hammer over a ten-hour shift would only make it worse. Three days until Sunday, no chance for it to heal, and no way he could afford to take time off.

Jimmy apologized again and tried to explain, about the razor at his neck, about wetting himself.

"What's Billy Hunter got to do with you?" The Hunters and their propensity for violence were well known in the Gorbals.

"No' Billy," Jimmy said, "Rab, his wee brother. It was Billy's razor, but Rab stole it."

"So you thought you'd get yourself a bigger knife? You think that makes you a hard man? Anybody can carry a knife, Jimmy."

"They were all laughing at me, Uncle Joe!"

"Who was laughing at you?"

Jimmy's mother had entered the kitchen, as quiet and knowing as ever. He glanced uncertainly from her to his uncle, trying to read the signals, to understand the silent language that often passed between adults.

Joe smiled at his sister-in-law, reassuring. "Me and some of the lads were having a laugh on the way to work, winding the wee yin up. Don't worry, he gave as good as he got. Though he used a couple of words I bet he didn't get from you!"

Jimmy's mother gave Joe the same look she gave her children when they were telling stories. She drew his hand out from under the tap and examined the cut.

"It's nothing," he said, trying to charm her. "A wee accident. Thought I was Dougie Fairbanks for a minute."

"Aye, right." She looked scathingly from him to her son. "The one and a half musketeers." She squeezed Joe's hand, causing him to flinch and try to pull away. "How're you going to work tomorrow?"

"Maybe my big sister'll bandage it up for me?"

"I'm no' your sister."

"More of a sister than he was a brother."

Jimmy noted the exchange but pretended he hadn't heard or didn't understand. They were talking about his father, the shadow over their family. Jimmy's mother glared at Joe for a moment, but the sentiment behind his words won her over.

"You big sook," she said. "Keep it under the tap for now."

Joe did as he was told. He was Jimmy's favorite uncle, full of fun, but clever with it and not touched by the fierce temper they still said his father had possessed, even though he'd been gone for more years than Jimmy had known him.

"Has the wee yin got a clean simmit and shorts?" Joe asked when she'd finished with his hand. "Said I'd take him to the Green for a kick about."

"What's wrong with the street?"

"The Green's better, like a proper football pitch. And there'll be none of his pals around." Joe winked conspiratorially at Jimmy. "I can show him a few wee tricks to run rings around them."

After some humming and hawing, his mother relented and Jimmy skipped happily along, until he realized they weren't heading in the direction of Glasgow Green. Joe refused to answer his nephew's questions, his stride strong and purposeful.

The boxing gym was upstairs at Morris Greene's Dancehall, the murmur of tall stories, political discussion, and drunken singing in the adjoining pub a constant undercurrent to the rhythmic impact of gloves on leather, the swish of skipping ropes and the explosive exhalations of breath as jabs, crosses, uppercuts, and hooks were thrown.

Jimmy stood apart, wary and awkward, watching as the fighters moved around the spartan hall in a disciplined circuit—floor exercises, practice on the bags, sparring in the ring. His uncle talked in hushed conspiratorial tones with an older man, Dougie McGinn, small and wiry in a goalkeeper's jersey, a burnt-out roll-up between his lips. Every now and again, they glanced at Jimmy and his wariness increased.

McGinn approached, Joe hanging back, and told Jimmy to put

his hands out. Jimmy adopted a clumsy boxing stance, feet side by side. "Out, not up," McGinn spoke softly, but there was authority in his voice, a hint of humor which Jimmy figured was at his expense.

The old man unfurled a roll of bandage and started to tape up Jimmy's hands, tight across the knuckles, weaving the material nimbly between the fingers. He selected a pair of worn gloves, the insides stale with sweat, from a cardboard box, shoved them over Jimmy's hands, and laced them up.

"So, you fancy yourself as a fighter?"

Jimmy didn't know what to say. The gloves looked huge and ridiculous at the end of his skinny white arms. He felt as though everyone was watching him.

They put him in with another sliver of a boy, perhaps two years younger than he was. They touched gloves, Jimmy gaining confidence as he looked down on his opponent.

McGinn struck a bell and Jimmy threw a glance at his uncle as if to say, "Watch this." Before he could move, the boy was on him with impish enthusiasm, a blur of movement. He winded Jimmy with a combination of body shots and followed up with a straight right jab that struck him full on the nose, bringing tears to his eyes.

After that, it was all Jimmy could do to keep the boy at bay. He tucked his chin into his chest and locked his forearms into an approximation of a defense, stumbling around flat-footedly as the imp continued the barrage.

Jimmy, thinking that simply staying on his feet would be a small triumph, looped an arm around the boy's neck, trying to wrestle him off balance. The imp responded by driving a short hook into Jimmy's groin. He fell to his knees, hunched over, gasping for breath, head touching the canvas.

The low blow raised a bark of disapproval from McGinn. Through his third set of tears that day, Jimmy saw his uncle's sympathetic wince turn into amusement.

The imp closed in on him, his ferocity fueled by overconfidence. Jimmy backed away, shifting his feet into the same stance as the imp, moving around instead of slumping like a big lazy lump waiting to get hit. He threw out jabs, clumsy but enough to keep the younger boy at bay and spoil his combinations.

McGinn and his uncle were leaning on the ropes, focusing on the bout, instead of chatting and laughing as they had before Jimmy went down. The trainer gave out encouragement—"Keep your distance. Use the jab. Nice footwork"—and Jimmy realized that it was being offered to him, not his opponent. The imp was growing frustrated, his attacks becoming ragged, his guard slipping as he tried to make contact. Jimmy hit him with a right, the first solid blow he had landed. The boy rocked backward, a hurt look on his face, his youth suddenly apparent. Jimmy lowered his hands in concern, blurted out an apology.

By way of thanks the imp hit him twice—one-two, right in the face—and Jimmy was immediately back against the ropes, buffeted by an onslaught of stinging punches.

McGinn told them to break and the imp flashed a friendly grin, touched Jimmy's gloves respectfully, then skipped across the ring to gulp down some water. Jimmy nodded dazedly after the boy, remaining on the ropes. The rage and humiliation he'd felt about Rab and the razor had vanished, replaced by something calmer, an awareness of his own potential, of what he could do to prevent similar humiliations in the future.

It hadn't just been about survival; he'd enjoyed the thrill of the fight, the power he felt when he landed a clean punch, even if it was his only one. And he'd gained a respect for the skill involved.

"No' bad, wee man," McGinn said as he unlaced the gloves. "Although, when you hit someone, don't say sorry—hit him again."

"Did you used to box, Uncle Joe?"

"Your da' and me did a bit when we were wee." Joe sucked air into his mouth to cool the fat chip he'd just thrown into it. They'd got chips from the Central Café as they walked home, a whole bag each, not one to share. "Dougie, the old boy back there—I served my time under him in the yards."

"Aye?" Jimmy tried to appear casual; older members of the family rarely mentioned his father and he was scared that looking too keen would cause Joe to clam up. "Were you any good?"

"Nah, I used to muck about and have a laugh, and your da' didn't have quite the right attitude."

"Did he muck about too?"

"No, he just wasn't the sporting type." Joe looked his nephew in the eye. "D'you like it? Want to keep going?"

"Do you have to pay?"

"You don't get much for free in this world, Jimmy. Don't worry, I'll cover it. Your ma doesn't need to know."

Jimmy finished school the next day with a defiant swagger, playing the inevitable fight in his head like a newsreel. Rab would reach for his razor, but Jimmy would be on him, fists like lightning, dropping him to the ground like a sack of totties, the entire school erupting into a cheer that would reverberate all along Clydeside and cause his Uncle Joe to pause, hammer raised, and smile proudly.

As it was, nothing happened. Rab slunk sheepishly by when their paths crossed, a bigger bruise than any Jimmy could have given him covering one eye.

Billy Hunter had claimed his blade back.

5

MONDAY, 3 OCTOBER 1932

"It's all go this week, eh? Two bodies in as many days," McDaid said with singsong enthusiasm, as if he'd been asked to dance by Madeleine Carroll and Marlene Dietrich and was having a hard job choosing between them. "No' had as much fun since the war."

A rare and beautiful sunrise had broken over the city, but Dreghorn and McDaid were in deep shadow, a half-built ocean liner looming over them, a mountain of iron and steel. They were crouched staring down into the darkness between the jetty and a tugboat, and could hear the lapping of the river through the narrow gap.

"See anything?" Dreghorn asked. He took a final draw of his cigarette, and flicked it with remarkable accuracy into a puddle of vomit on the cobbles behind them.

"Uh-uh. Could've all been in his mind," McDaid said. "A bit of timber or some rubbish. Did you catch his breath? Smelled more like a brewery than a shipyard."

"Aye, one whiff and I've got a hangover."

McDaid turned to a white-stubbled man in disheveled clothes sitting dejectedly on a bollard. A uniformed constable stood over him, brooking no nonsense.

"Hey," McDaid yelled, causing the man to shudder. "Are you sure it wasn't a pink elephant you saw, out for a moonlight swim?"

The man grimaced as if swallowing bile. Bobby Tranter was the night watchman of Pagan's Yard, the only job he'd found that allowed him to legitimately avoid his wife six days a week, sleeping soundly during daylight hours and doggedly patrolling Glasgow's industrial heartland at night, fortified by hearty nips of cheap whisky. McDaid set about getting the story out of him.

Embarking on his early morning rounds, Tranter had stopped at the edge of the jetty and unbuttoned his flies to relieve himself. The stream of urine spattered off something solid. He glanced down, expecting river detritus. Instead, the lapping water offered him a man's body, face down in the Clyde.

When he returned after telephoning the police from the shipyard offices, the corpse had drifted further, becoming jammed between the jetty and the starboard side of a berthed tugboat. The tug listed closer to the jetty, crushing the body against the slimy walls, and Tranter heard the slow cracking of bones. His already churning stomach decided enough was enough and, with a great heave, he deposited the contents into a surprisingly neat pile on the cobbles, which McDaid had trodden in earlier.

"If the bosses find out I was drinking, I'll be out on my arse," said Tranter, lip petted like a child.

"Away and swallow a couple of gallons of black coffee," McDaid said impatiently. "If anybody asks, we'll say you had a few nips from my hip-flask to calm your nerves."

Tranter nodded gratefully and headed for his bothy. "Make some for everyone while you're there," McDaid yelled.

"Jimmy, Archie, I've got something!"

Dreghorn walked to the bow of the tug, where a smaller boat floated as close to the jetty as it could get. Benny Parsonage, Chief Officer of the Glasgow Humane Society, was on his feet in the boat, balanced with the deftness of a tightrope walker, pulling a rope slowly through the water.

"A body?" Dreghorn asked.

"Feels like it." Parsonage nodded. "Depending on how long it's been in the water, getting crushed against the wall, like your man up there said, would've expelled any gases, made it sink."

"Need a hand with that, short-arse?" McDaid grinned. "We've no' got all day, y'know."

"Away and bile your big baw-heid." Parsonage maintained a steady pull on the rope, careful not to jar loose whatever was under the water. The rope was attached to a four-pronged steel grappling hook, with which Parsonage dredged the bottom of the river, searching for bodies. Over the years, he'd become expert at gauging what the hooks ensnared, weight and water resistance alerting him to whether the object was made of wood, steel, or flesh and bone.

Founded in 1790, the Glasgow Humane Society was dedicated to rescuing people, whether from accidents or suicide attempts, from the River Clyde. One of Parsonage's other duties was the recovery of bodies from the murky depths or otherwise inaccessible riverbanks; his house on Glasgow Green, overlooking the river, was the police's first port of call on receiving reports of such. He was only five foot one, but Dreghorn had seen him dive into the Clyde without hesitation to haul a drowning man the size of McDaid to safety.

"Nice and easy, but quick and gentle; if you stop pulling, the current will catch it and the body could float away." Satisfaction broke across the river man's face. "But no' the day."

The corpse broke the surface of the water gently. Parsonage eased it toward the boat, freed the grappling hook, and, as respectfully as possible, pulled it aboard. It was a sad sight. The head hung forward, hiding the features. Other officers approached, watching silently as Parsonage rowed toward the nearest loading bay.

It had been seventeen years or more since Dreghorn had been in a shipyard, not long out of school, getting caught out by tricks like having his tin cup welded fast to a bench. Shipbuilding, like other beasts of heavy industry, had been badly hurt by the drop in production after the war ended in 1918 and beaten almost to death eleven years later by the start of the Depression.

Pagan's had fared better than some firms, but was a shadow of its former self, the vast emptiness of the dry docks eerie and unsettling. Further along the Clyde, on the opposite bank, the morning sun silhouetted the cranes of Lockhart's, the shipyard Dreghorn had worked in as a youth. Lockhart's order books were noticeably fuller, a testament to the old man's business acumen. The clash of steel and workers' banter as they started a new day drifted across the water, stirring his memories.

Dreghorn told himself that he hadn't thought of the Lockhart family for years, though he then heard one of his mother's favorite sayings in his head: "I believe you; thousands wouldn't."

McDaid gestured at two younger officers as Parsonage moored his boat. "I did more than my fair share of humphing bodies around when I was in uniform," he said. "See this suit? Detective. That means it's your turn."

The officers lifted the dripping body from the boat. One of them gagged, but managed to maintain control, the other was focused and composed, trying hard to impress in front of superior officers. "Do people drown often in the Clyde?" he asked.

Parsonage threw a glance at Dreghorn before answering. "No, son, just the once."

"And this poor soul didn't drown," Dreghorn said as the officers lowered the corpse onto its back.

At first, the body put Dreghorn in mind of a flatfish, a bloater maybe. The head looked like it had been deflated, the flesh sagging, the skull cracked by being ground between the tug and the jetty. Yet even in that condition the dead man looked well-heeled and manicured, with a pencil mustache of the kind Ronald Colman used to charm the ladies, but which came across as a sleekit affectation off the silver screen. He was the best-dressed corpse Dreghorn had ever seen. His suit, sodden and stained with river-muck, was expensive, the fine cut of the waistcoat and jacket hardly spoiled by the fact that the wearer's ribcage had been crushed as efficiently as the bones of his head.

While the post-mortem injuries might cause problems for the police surgeon, the actual cause of death would not. The man's throat had been slit, a gaping wound that had bled out and been washed clean by the river, allowing the surgical precision of the attack to be admired more easily. The tendons and windpipe had been severed almost to the spinal column. With a little more dedication, the murderer might have taken the entire head off.

Dreghorn and McDaid hunkered down on either side of the dead man. "Cut himself shaving, d'you think?" said McDaid, failing miserably to lighten the mood.

"Take a lot of force to do that with a razor. I'd say a knife of some sort, a big blade."

"Gang-related?"

"Doesn't look the type to move in those circles."

"Robbery, then. They jumped him, did him in, chucked him in the Clyde."

Dreghorn hooked a finger under a small gold chain that trailed from the corpse's waistcoat pocket and lifted an elegant pocket watch into view. "No mugger worth his salt would leave that peeking out their victim's pocket. Most expensive thing he's carrying, more than likely."

He patted down the wet cloth of the man's suit, came up against an obstruction. He fished a handkerchief from his pocket to cover his fingertips, lifted the flap of the jacket, and pulled out an expensive calfskin wallet. He flipped it open: business cards and sodden pound notes, easily more than he and McDaid made in a month.

"Look at that," Dreghorn heard an approaching voice say.

"Nimble-fingered. You can tell a lot about a man's character by the way he rifles through somebody's pockets."

The speaker might have been trying to smile, but it was hard to tell beneath the weight of the huge ginger mustache that hedged his upper lip. The squat man beside him was smiling, or, more accurately, leering, displaying smoker's teeth that weren't so much stained with nicotine as blowtorched black. Detective Inspector Strachan and Sergeant Orr reminded Dreghorn of Laurel and Hardy, except their idea of slapstick involved a truncheon or pickaxe handle. It wasn't laughter that would split your sides.

"Cheers for holding the fort, lads," Strachan continued. "We'll take it from here."

"We took the call." McDaid made no effort to step aside, blocking their access to the body. "Finders keepers."

"Where do you think you are—the playground?" Orr shambled forward, craning his neck to speak around McDaid. "I'll have that."

Nothing about Orr seemed to fit properly. His ears were too big, his eyes too small, his arms too long, his legs too short. On his own, he was a bit of a clown. Strachan was the one to watch.

Dreghorn ignored him, continued to examine the wallet.

"Why the big hoo-hah?" McDaid went on. "A body in the Clyde's like a jobbie in a swimming baths. Everyone wants rid of it, but nobody wants to claim responsibility."

"Just doing our duty," said Strachan. "The Vicar assigned us personally."

Deputy Chief Constable Sydney McVicar had been passed over by the City Council for the top police job. Ostensibly loyal and supportive of the new chief constable, he was still a member of the old order, a politically aware pillar of the establishment keen to protect those he saw as his own kind.

"What about Sillitoe?" McDaid shifted his weight, forcing Orr to step back or risk toppling into the river.

"What about him? Why would he say anything different? We're all on the same side, Archibald. Mostly. But we have different specialities. We're the Crime Squad; you're the Heavy Mob. A case like this needs brainpower. The only time you need to use this"—Strachan tapped a finger to his temple—"is when you're sticking the heid on somebody."

Dreghorn was surprised to recognize the name on the cards, if not the association with power and privilege that it carried. He looked at the corpse—the fine clothing, the expensive watch, the handmade shoes—and thought of wee Tommy Bryce's skinny body tossed into a corner of an icy room. The Glasgow Police would be directed to pursue the killer of this well-dressed man with the utmost dedication, but who would offer the shattered Bryce family such care and attention?

"Nothing to say, Jimmy? Not like you." Strachan stroked his mustache with thumb and forefinger, almost as if doing so gave him some small erotic charge.

Dreghorn tossed the wallet to Strachan as if glad to be rid of it. "I'm just entranced by that 'tache of yours, Boyd," he said. "Can't work out whether it looks like an orang-utan's oxter or Ginger Ella's big hairy bush."

Ginger Ella was a lady of the night so ubiquitous and notorious that she could only be an urban myth. Her name—along with those of Clatty Bella and Sweaty Betty—was bandied about town in bawdy apocryphal tales, passing from pub to pub like a bad cold.

Strachan caught the wallet with a heavy swipe of one hand. "Ha-fucking-ha. Don't believe all that Untouchables shite they say about you in the papers."

Orr gave a death rattle of a laugh. "More like the wouldn't-touch-them-with-a-bargepole," he said.

Dreghorn tipped his hat to Parsonage who nodded back sagely, and walked off, McDaid following, his reluctance palpable. Strachan bowed with mock deference as they passed, gesturing to show them the open road. Orr smiled smugly, puffing out his chest like a Charles Atlas advert.

"You're standing in puke," McDaid told him.

They walked away past piles of timber and angle-iron, stepping over rails and ropes, and didn't look back, although the sound of Orr cursing as he balanced on one leg and tried to scrape vomit from the sole of his shoe made it tempting. When they were out of sight behind a warehouse, McDaid snatched the fedora from Dreghorn's head and peered inside it.

"Jimmy, are you in there? There's a wee man out here says he's you, but I'm no' sure. He gives up awful easily. Just handed over a perfectly good case to the two biggest fannies on the force."

"You'll thank me for it later." Dreghorn ran a hand through his hair, rubbed the back of his neck, not entirely comfortable with his decision to back off.

"So, who was he?" McDaid planted the hat back on Dreghorn's head. "I know you had a fly look at his wallet."

"Charles Geddes," Dreghorn answered. Then, seeing McDaid's blank look, "Sir Iain Lockhart's son-in-law."

"*Lockhart* Lockhart?" McDaid nodded toward the yard on the far side of the river.

"Get dragged into that and everything else'll be down the Clyde without a paddle. You want Bryce to slip out of the city while you're hobnobbing with the bosses and the papers and a family that's got more money than sense? Who'll care about that wee boy the other night next to this?"

"We would. We could've handled it. I can do more than two things at once, you know." McDaid flexed his muscles melodramatically. "Olympic champion, me."

"So you keep saying. Surprised you don't have it pinned on your chest."

At the wrought-iron entrance gates of the yard, closed to keep workers out while police secured the crime scene, a harassed constable waved them through. Other officers had drawn their truncheons and were warning the disgruntled shipyard workers to keep their distance. Voices were raised, swearwords rife, scuffles developing. The shift should have started over half an hour ago and they feared their wages would be docked through no fault of their own, their pay diminishing as the minutes ticked by.

They surged forward as the detectives emerged. A burly older constable prodded them back with his truncheon. "Hold your horses," he snarled. "Some poor bastard's just been pulled out the Clyde, stone cold dead."

"Aye? He'll no' be the only one if we don't get some work and a square meal soon." Many of those gathered were former employees, laid off months or years ago, but driven to turn up day after day in the forlorn hope of getting some casual work.

The years since the Great War had passed remorselessly, each one bringing another wave of disappointment and disillusionment. The hopes the workers had in 1924 were dashed when the first Labor government, led by Ramsay MacDonald, lost power after less than a year. The Red Clydeside union movement still fought for their rights, but it seemed a losing battle. A second Labor government, crippled by the recession, was swept aside by a Conservative-dominated National Government in 1931. Still led by MacDonald, now pilloried for betraying the Labor values that had gained him power in the first place, the coalition embarked on a brutal austerity program to cut public expenditure, including unemployment benefit. In protest, the National Unemployed Workers Movement had organized a Hunger March to London, the first contingent of which had left Glasgow the previous week.

The constable had little sympathy. "How come you're no' on the march, then?"

"Too fuckin' hungry—I'd be deid before Dumfries!"

For a moment, the hostility was palpable, but resignation quickly set in and the crowd parted grudgingly to let Dreghorn and McDaid through. Dreghorn thought he recognized some of the men, faces weathered, old before their time, but gave no indication of it and received none in return.

Whatever his sympathies, he was no longer one of them. In his suit and hat, with his warrant card and detective's baton, he wasn't even a representative of the law to them, just another tool of the bosses and the government that was failing them.

Dreghorn understood their resentment of him. Maybe he even shared it.

6

The most helpless Archie McDaid had ever felt was sitting on the cold stone steps outside his house listening to the cries of his wife as she gave birth to their first child.

Peggy Bryce, twenty-six years old, howled in the same way when she learned that her son had been ripped from her life forever. She'd not long recovered consciousness when the detectives arrived at the Royal Infirmary to take her statement, and it was the first thing she'd asked. McDaid didn't get further than a faltering "I'm sorry," before she started crying. In her heart she already knew.

They watched awkwardly as the nurses tried to comfort her. One of them said Peggy's brother had been in to see her earlier, before she'd woken up. They'd had to ask him to leave, even threatening to call the police—"In a right state he was, shouting and swearing his head off."

Dreghorn and McDaid backed off, informing the ward sister that they'd be back later.

"Lovely," she said with a sour smile. "Right ray of sunshine, you two."

A radio alert came through as they returned to the car, a disturbance in the Garngad Road, details sketchy, possibly gang-related. Dreghorn tapped back to say they were responding.

They pulled up behind a large black Austin Twenty, parked outside the address they'd been given. Voices bellowed from within the tenement. The detectives took the stairs, Dreghorn two at a time, McDaid three.

Two men in identical suits stood on the second floor, one battering a door with his fist, the other hunched over, nursing one hand. He looked up as Dreghorn and McDaid reached the landing.

"Lost your key, pal?" McDaid flashed his warrant card.

"There's no problem here, officer." The second man, obviously the sharper of the pair, nodded at the offending door. "All perfectly legal. Their menodge is due."

"No problem?" The first man raised his hand, the fingers swollen, bruising rapidly. "The old cow clouted me with a shovel. It might be broken." He yelled at the door. "Hear that? It's the polis. I could get you done with assault."

The second man shrugged with embarrassment as if the detectives were fellow professionals cursed with the company of rank amateurs. Dreghorn ignored the attempt at complicity, shouldered the men aside and rapped on the door. "Police. Open up."

The door was unlocked after a long pause and left ajar. Dreghorn entered and immediately raised his hands in surrender. An old woman, barely five feet tall, with a face like Popeye the Sailor Man on the ran-dan, glowered at him, brandishing a fire shovel with Amazonian ferocity.

"Steady on, missus." Dreghorn tried to keep a straight face. "What's the score?"

"Those bastards from the menodge!" she cried. "They'd steal the food from my grandweans' mouths."

The concept of the menodge may originally have been born of honorable intentions, but capitalism invariably steamrollers honor into the ground. Derived, more educated men than Dreghorn surmised, from the French *ménage,* a menodge enabled poverty-stricken families to acquire essentials like clothing, furniture, and household goods via a credit system. Considerate businessmen allowed customers to open an account into which an agreed sum was paid weekly, enabling them to purchase goods on credit. Extortionate interest rates were factored into the prices of the items, which cost far more than from normal retailers. Few people ever fully paid off their menodge book, trapped in a cycle of escalating debts and never-ending payments. Miss a payment and the menodge men would terrorize victims to make sure they paid next time, a chilling warning to other potential defaulters.

Dreghorn drew the story out of the woman, Mrs. Fredericks. She lived with her son Bernard—her expression beatified when she said the name—and his wife, whose name wasn't mentioned. Laid off from his job in the garment trade, Bernard had fallen behind with his menodge—just a couple of weeks, mind. A conscientious lad, he was out seeking employment as they spoke. An absence, Dreghorn noted, that conveniently coincided with the menodge collection day. Her daughter-in-law was also out, delivering neighbors' washing that she'd taken in to help make ends meet. The menodge men had attacked Mrs. Fredericks, a helpless old woman all on her own.

"Helpless!" the first man bellowed incredulously, waving his ballooning fingers in the air. They had, he claimed, attempted to gain entry to seize goods to the value of what was owed. He'd stuck his foot in the door to stop her closing it and reached in to undo the chain. Mrs. Fredericks, with remarkable speed, had brought the shovel down on his toes with the force of an executioner's axe, and then pummeled his fingers to loosen their grip. He looked around, expecting sympathy, further confirmation that he was in the wrong line of work.

"Only sheriff's men are legally allowed to distrain property. Sounds to me like you were overstepping the mark." McDaid drew to his full height, folded his arms sternly.

"Almost as good as breaking and entering," agreed Dreghorn. "Whose name's on the book?"

"Her boy's." A hint of defensiveness from the second man. "But he's registered at this address."

"So, you're putting the frighteners on a poor wee woman who's not even responsible for the debt you're pursuing?" Dreghorn raised his voice to Mrs. Fredericks. "You seem a wee bit hard of hearing to me, missus, is that right?"

"Eh?" Craftiness shone in Mrs. Fredericks' eyes. "What's that you're saying, son?"

"Didn't even know what you were saying." Dreghorn tutted. "The two of you at her door dressed like a couple of Chicago gangsters? No wonder she screamed murder, polis. Get back to your warehouse and let them know there are genuinely mitigating circumstances involved and that you're giving the Fredericks a fortnight's grace on their payments. And if you're not feeling graceful, we'll put it about that you got hammered by a wee old wifey who's no' the size of tuppence. Won't do your reputation any good. Might make other folk think they can get away without paying, then the whole house of cards'll fall down. Who do you work for?"

"Universal Stores, Cathedral Street," the injured man muttered.

"Names?" McDaid removed his notebook, licked the tip of his pencil. David Jessop, the injured man revealed huffily; Kenneth Brodie, the other admitted with a touch of defiance.

McDaid finished writing, eyed the door. "On your way." He followed them out onto the landing.

Jessop limped down the stairs, cradling his hand. Brodie, following, gave McDaid a look. "This isn't how it works," he said.

McDaid stared back. "It is today."

"We showed them, eh?" Mrs. Fredericks cackled gleefully.

"Not really, they'll still want their money eventually," Dreghorn said, willing her to understand. "If things are that bad, maybe your son should think about going on the Parish."

"The Parish!" She snorted with outrage, displaying that curious mix of pride and working-class snobbery. The Parish Councils that had administered poor relief had been replaced by the Department of Public Assistance in 1929, but the old phrase had stuck, tainting those that needed help. Even in the poorest areas, there was a hierarchy of deprivation; some people would risk everything rather than admit how far they had fallen.

"At least God doesn't send round the angels to stamp on your son's head," he said, but she'd already slammed the door in his face.

"She's my sister, for Christ's sake!" Allan Kerr thrust forward, almost lunging off the bunk. "What do you think we are?"

"Nobody thinks anything, Mr. Kerr," Dreghorn said calmly.

"No? Then how come I'm in here and he's still out there? He's the one who—" Kerr's voice cracked and he slumped back against the cell wall. The outburst had opened a cut at the corner of his mouth. He wiped blood away with the back of his hand.

McDaid was due to give evidence in the High Court that afternoon—a stabbing, though the victim survived and the evidence against the accused was weak. Dreghorn wanted to write up some paperwork while his partner was in the dock, so they had returned to Turnbull Street. Shug Nugent, the desk sergeant, had informed them that Peggy Bryce's brother was in the cells, in a bad way due to "resisting arrest."

"Who brought him in?" McDaid asked.

"Big Willie Stewart."

McDaid grunted. The officer they'd seen leaving the Mermaid.

After visiting his sister, Kerr had gone to Bridgeton, heading for Billy Hunter's house. Armed with a chisel, he'd yelled up at the tenement, demanding that Hunter tell him where Thomas Bryce was hiding. Hunter had opened a window and, by all accounts, tried to persuade Kerr to go home.

As Kerr continued to rant and rave, Hunter's wife Agnes pushed her husband aside. She hurled a basin of dirty water over Kerr and threatened to "shove that chisel where the sun doesnae shine" if he didn't make himself scarce pronto.

Kerr flung the chisel in retaliation, but it struck the windowsill and fell back to the pavement. He bent down to retrieve it, and PC Stewart, having concealed himself in a nearby doorway until the safest possible moment, stepped in, clubbed Kerr to the ground with his truncheon, and handcuffed him.

Dreghorn said, "Billy Hunter's refusing to press charges for attempted assault."

"Big of him," Kerr remarked.

"To be fair, he's not known for his compassion. That just leaves disturbing the peace. In the circumstances, I think we'll drop that."

"Who's playing the big man now?"

"C'mon, up you get." McDaid took Kerr's arm, helped him to his feet. His hostility seemed to fade as they led him through the station.

"I should've been there more," he said. "I knew what was happening, but the wife doesn't like me seeing Peggy. We've got a wean on the way ourselves. Our first. She didn't know the stories when we first met, but these things spread. She says she doesn't believe any of it, but once a lie gets into your head, I don't know—it's like people find it easier to believe the worst of you than the best. Twisted, eh?"

The detectives said nothing, walked Kerr to the door. He stopped halfway down the stairs, said, "It's no' true. None of it," but didn't look back. He'd no more faith in them than anyone else.

Dreghorn flopped into the chair with an explosive sigh, rolling back on its castors, placing his desk out of reach. He was still for a moment, legs splayed out in front of him. The squad room was empty, McDaid in court, the others on patrol, or sloping off for a fly dram.

He flicked through that morning's *Daily Record*. A report on the progress of the National Hunger March. Sir Oswald Mosley, the former Conservative and Labor MP, had founded a new party—the British Union of Fascists, inspired by similar political movements in Italy and Germany. A scandal about James Tinsley and George Meakin, the signalmen responsible for the 1915 Quintinshill rail disaster, who had been re-employed by the rail company after serving their manslaughter sentences, prompting suspicions of a cover-up. In the sports pages, Mancunian boxer Jackie Brown was preparing to fight World Flyweight Champion Victor Perez at the end of the month. Dreghorn recalled the promising flyweight he'd seen box recently—a young Gorbals lad named Lynch.

Eventually, he gripped the edge of the desk and pulled himself back into position with the enthusiasm of a condemned man mounting the gallows. He fixed a report sheet into the typewriter, and stared at the expanse of white like Scott surveying the Antarctic. He thought about everything that had happened in the last forty-eight hours, tried to translate it into the dry staccato facts the courts required. Eventually, he tore the sheet from the typewriter, leaped to his feet as if the chair beneath him had burst into flames, and headed for the main desk.

"Shug, any news on the body found at Pagan's Yard this morning?"

Nugent raised his head from a logbook, frowned. "The deceased's wife's in with Strachan and the Vicar the now," he said. "Fancy, she is too. Chauffeured to the front door and coiffured up to the nines." The twinkle in his eye was unusual. Shug Nugent was a grumpy, glowering, taciturn presence behind the reception desk, his thick sandy hair, sideburns, and mustache resembling a lion's mane. But he was the best desk sergeant in Glasgow, so fierce that only those who were genuinely in trouble would dare approach him. Time wasters would be eaten alive.

Two uniformed constables were manhandling a dazed drunk in through the heavy entrance doors. Before they swung shut, Dreghorn caught a glimpse of a big car outside, a Rolls-Royce or a Daimler, and an uppity-looking chauffeur wiping bird shit off the bonnet.

"The Vicar came down to meet her himself. I'm telling you, even he looked as though he'd happily give up the sainthood when he clapped eyes on her. Sinful thoughts all round." Nugent nodded over Dreghorn's shoulder. "See for yourself—here they come now."

Police stations were bastions of manhood. The few women who worked in them—a handful of constables, their duties severely restricted, police matrons, and secretarial staff—had built up their defenses to the attitudes and advances they endured, maintaining a business-like coldness or giving as good as they got. Otherwise, they were criminals—prostitutes and disorderly drunks, swearing, struggling, offering sexual favors for leniency—or victims; timid, distraught, or outraged, depending on the crime.

Isla Lockhart was a world away from them, utterly out of place, yet so confident within herself that it was the environment around her that seemed wrong. She entered the reception room ahead of Strachan and McVicar, as if she was leading them. She was slim and strong, a knowing humor in her eyes, her Titian-red hair cut short and sharp like the film star Louise Brooks. She wore a slim-fitting woolen day suit, belted around the waist, a cloche hat, and heels that brought her up to Dreghorn's height, more or less. She apparently took no notice of the quiet attention of the men, but was clearly aware of it.

"A shocking and upsetting experience," the Vicar was saying, the superiority of his usual I-smell-shite demeanor softened to obsequiousness. Isla gave a little wave of her hand, gently dismissive, but also letting him know how touched she was by his concern.

Dreghorn could have looked away, could've turned his back, hunched over the counter and pretended to be in a momentous case-breaking conversation with Nugent. That's what he told himself at least.

"Thank you, chief constable," Isla said, turning to McVicar, who neglected to inform her of his proper rank. "You've been most kind. I'll be sure to pass your regards on to my father. This will come as quite a shock to—James?" Her smile washed over Dreghorn, warm and genuine.

"Miss Lockhart." He stepped forward and shook her hand, though for a moment he wondered if she expected him to kiss it.

Her hand held his a heartbeat longer than necessary. "It's Geddes now." She seemed to remember herself. "Or at least it was, if what your colleagues tell me is correct."

"Aye, I heard. My condolences."

She gave a bittersweet smile.

McVicar interrupted, asserting his authority, "Inspector Dreghorn was on the scene, assisting Inspector Strachan with the recovery of the body."

"Good. Then he can take me to do your identification." The matter seemed decided as far as she was concerned.

"With respect, Mrs. Geddes." McVicar put on his sermon face. "Inspector Dreghorn has other duties to attend to. Inspector Strachan is in charge of the investigation."

Isla moved closer to Dreghorn. "Of course, chief constable—and no offense, Inspector Strachan—it's just . . ." She seemed suddenly near to tears, exuding an appealing fragility. "This is all so distressing that I really think I'd feel more comfortable with someone I know. And James—well, James is an old friend of the family."

After a moment's thought, the Vicar assented with avuncular understanding. "Very well. But Inspector Dreghorn's to report to Inspector Strachan immediately afterward."

Strachan was bristling with quiet fury under his mustache.

Isla slipped her arm through Dreghorn's, the vulnerability gone as quickly as it had appeared, and led him toward the exit as if they were off on a summer picnic. As the door swung shut behind them, he glimpsed Shug Nugent silently mouthing *Jammy bastard.*

7

"You take me to the nicest places."

Isla cocked her head in Dreghorn's direction as she spoke, but kept her eyes on the covered shape on the mortuary slab. The mortuary attendant stood on the far side of the slab, head bowed respectfully. She took a deep breath, steeling herself. Dreghorn nodded to the attendant, raising a hand level with his chin, indicating how far to lower the sheet.

Charles Geddes looked almost serene; his eyes closed to spare his wife the lifeless stare that had met Dreghorn when the body was pulled from the water. Isla let out her breath in a half-sob, glanced quickly at Dreghorn and nodded. She looked back at the body, stroked the still-damp hair.

"I used to think he was the most handsome man I had ever seen," she said, "always preening himself. He used to love that little fiddly mustache." She glanced at the attendant. "When you've finished doing whatever you have to do, be a darling and shave it off for me, will you?"

She raised two fingers to her mouth, kissed them softly, touched them to her husband's cold lips, then turned and strode away, her heels echoing on the ceramic floor. Dreghorn followed, keen to leave the white-tiled cellar, escape the smell of alcohol and decomposing flesh. They ascended the stairs in silence, Dreghorn trying not to look at her ankles and calves, the curve of her thighs as the material of her skirt stretched over them, step after step.

They came out onto the Saltmarket. Dreghorn lit them both cigarettes. The mortuary reminded him of a wartime bunker, a single
story high and built to withstand punishment, though few people
would be likely to break in, even fewer to break out. It adjoined the
corner of the High Court and faced Glasgow Green, the parkland
view wasted on its clientele.

"I wouldn't have thought anything could make the air around
here seem fresh," Isla said, staring over the park to the Clyde.

"Not quite the bonnie, bonnie banks, is it?" said Dreghorn.

She appraised him as if taking in his presence for the first time.
"You look well, James."

"Anyone who's walking and talking does after a trip to the mortuary." He breathed out smoke, gave her a small smile. "So do you."

"For a grieving widow, you mean? Practice makes perfect."

The chauffeur had parked further along, but she seemed in no
rush to return to the car.

"Daddy never liked him," she said. "Partly the point, I suppose.
Hard to believe I was ever that keen myself." She stared back at the
mortuary, as if reliving the sights and smells within. "I need a drink."
An order more than a statement.

He flicked the butt of his Capstan into the road. "I hear Miss
Cranston's Tea Rooms is the place to go."

"I said a drink. And I'm not particular where or what."

"Worse than the mortuary?" Dreghorn asked, sipping his whisky.

They'd walked along the Saltmarket to Argyle Street, the Daimler rolling slowly behind them, bypassed the Old Empire and Co-
gan's Coat of Arms, then turned onto Brunswick Street for the Miter
Bar, which Dreghorn thought might offer more privacy. Not that
Isla seemed concerned about her reputation.

"It has a certain rough charm." Isla raised her glass in a toast and
knocked the contents back with a vengeance. She glanced at Dreg-

horn's glass. He laughed, threw back his own drink, and said, "I'll get us another."

She was already on her feet. "No, I will. All's fair. We have the vote now, you know."

Dreghorn nodded. "I was all for it—'Trust in God; she will provide' and all that."

He watched as she walked to the bar, caught her amused backward glance, and felt the weight of the intervening years since they had last sparred. She returned with two more whiskies. Large ones, he noted, and cursed himself for having only ordered normal measures.

"Bravo." Isla raised her glass in a sarcastic toast. "Let's drink to your progressiveness. You were on all the marches?"

"In spirit. Couldn't make it over from the other side of the world." Sincere now. "Your mother would be proud of you, carrying on for her."

"She'd have said it was just the start. She never stopped; sometimes, the cause seemed to be more important to her than anything else, especially after she was arrested. My father could easily have used his influence to have her sentence quashed, but did nothing. He's ever so keen on teaching harsh lessons."

Lady Jane Lockhart had been a prominent campaigner for the women's suffrage movement. Sentenced to three months in jail for leading a protest against Winston Churchill at his Dundee constituency in 1909, she went on hunger strike and was force-fed by the prison authorities, resulting in permanent damage to her health. Dreghorn had read of her death in 1923, five years before women were finally granted the right to vote.

"You didn't continue boxing?" Isla asked, keen to move on.

"Lost my sporting instincts in the war."

"It couldn't have been easy without sponsorship."

"I'd have carried on if I'd wanted to. With or without your father's patronage." He was surprised at the tetchiness in his voice, annoyed by it. "How is he?"

"Glowering at the world for all he's worth. It's amazing how communicative you can be with nothing but a grunt and a glare."

"What do you mean?"

"He's in a wheelchair, unable to talk. Had a stroke about, oh, eighteen months ago. We kept it out of the newspapers as best we could. Business is stable—surprisingly so compared to other shipyards—but Daddy didn't want to unnerve the shareholders. He's still very much in charge, for the moment at least. The mind's as sharp as ever, but trapped in a leaden body. He can write notes or telegrams—blunt, terse little ditties that allow him to dispense with niceties, something I think he's secretly quite happy about."

"I'm sorry." Dreghorn found it hard to think of the formidable figure he'd once known living as she'd described. "He was good to me in his own way."

"Did you a favor?" It was hard to tell if she was genuinely offended or simply being sarcastic.

"He did *you* a favor. I'd have done the same in his shoes. I wouldn't have approved of me."

"And now you're a policeman. Very proper. For some reason, I wouldn't have expected that." She leaned back, crossed one leg over the other, slow and elegant. "Rory told me you'd left the country."

"For a wee while."

"Somewhere nice, I hope."

"Shanghai."

"Lovely. The Paris of the East. Or the Whore of the Orient." She lit a cigarette, the fire playing in her eyes. "I can imagine which you'd prefer, though there are two sides to every story."

"Three," said Dreghorn. "Yours, mine, and the truth."

"If I'd known, I'd have looked you up. Spent a week in the Astor House Hotel on my honeymoon."

"First or second?"

She admonished him with a raised eyebrow, but also gave a small smile. Despite his feigned indifference at the station, he'd revealed that he'd kept abreast of her life since they had last met.

"First. A city like Shanghai would've been the death of Charles." A shadow passed over her face. "You know the Astor?" A hurried attempt to lighten the mood.

"Arrested a man in the bar one night. One of their best customers. If they could've barred me, they would, but I was with the Shanghai Municipal Police."

"It's a long way to go, and not, I imagine, an easy place in which to uphold the law. Couldn't you have joined the police here?"

"Didn't go to the right school."

"I thought all that had changed under the auspices of brave new Chief Constable Sillitoe. A clean sweep."

Dreghorn shrugged. It wasn't listed as an official job requirement, but the majority of Glasgow's police officers were Protestant. The few Catholics that did slip into the uniform were usually guaranteed the worst duties in the roughest neighborhoods, with precious little hope of promotion. Thanks to Sillitoe, an outsider, Dreghorn was the first Catholic police inspector in the city, though the archbishop wouldn't be cheering him on as a pioneer. Dreghorn was about as far from a practicing Catholic as you could get; his faith hadn't so much lapsed as been exorcized.

"Well, I'm in there now," he admitted. "Though I daresay I'd be struck down by a bolt of lightning if I ever set foot in a church."

"So your face isn't on the Vatican's recruitment posters?"

"Only if they say 'Wanted: Dead or Alive.' " He sipped his whisky. "I thought your father was grooming Rory to take over."

"He was. And he is. Or he's supposed to be, but you know Rory."

"Not for a long time. Where is he these days?"

"Somewhere in the middle of the Atlantic, on top of the waves, I hope. He's on the *Lion Rampant,* the ship my father co-funded with Sir Thomas Lipton before his death, sailing back from America with all possible haste to take up his responsibilities. Or so he said in his last letter, but that was weeks ago. He was competing in the America's Cup. Daddy insisted he finish before returning."

Dreghorn's commanding officer for almost the entire duration of the Great War, Rory Lockhart, Isla's older brother, had in the years since become a member of what certain international publications had named "the lost generation." Not lost in the sense of friends and family cut down in the killing fields of France and Belgium or on the dusty plains of Africa, but the lost generation of dissolute expatriates who moped about Paris and other exotic locales, drinking absinthe, falling in love with prostitutes, writing novels that mythologized their own lives, and blaming the louche emptiness within them on the war.

No one Dreghorn knew had the luxury of such aimlessness. They were too busy surviving to ponder the nature of that survival.

The man he had served under was an expert marksman, a fair-minded and pragmatic officer who asked nothing of his men that he wasn't prepared to do himself, and a relentless hunter on the trench raids they carried out. Since the war, he had embraced a life without responsibility, a playboy existence of romance and adventure—international yacht races, expeditions to climb unconquered peaks, Hollywood screen tests, high-profile love affairs, brushes with scandal. It was as if he was trying to distance himself from the man he'd been on the battlefield, the actions he was capable of. The last Dreghorn had heard was of Rory's engagement to an American actress, Lily something-or-other, but that was before the Depression.

"How did Charles die?" Isla was staring at Dreghorn with a business-like coldness now.

"What did Strachan tell you?"

"Not much. That a body had been found, that they had good reason to believe it was my husband, and that foul play was involved."

"They were being diplomatic. He was murdered. I'm sorry."

"How?" Dreghorn could see her mind racing. She'd done well to maintain her composure—part of her upbringing—but shock was slowly seeping in.

"A wound to the throat."

"Do you have any idea who did it?"

"That's what they'll ask you," said Dreghorn gently. "I'm not part of the investigation, so I don't know anything beyond the basic details. The police surgeon hasn't examined the body yet, so it's early days. They need to establish time and place of death, piece together his movements, find out whose company he was in. When did you last see him?"

"It's been a few days; I'm not sure exactly. I've been spending most of my time at Kelpie House recently, helping Daddy with his affairs. Between that and the Trust . . ." She acknowledged his frown. "The Jane Lockhart Educational Trust—it offers further education, secretarial training to women and girls who wouldn't otherwise have the opportunity. Mummy set it up years ago—a condition of agreeing to marry Daddy, she told me. It became more important after the war, when we'd proved that we could do most so-called men's jobs just as well as they could. Mummy was keen for that to continue, but it's slow progress—one step forward, two steps back.

"I've been in charge since her death—I sometimes wonder if it was a cunning ploy to make sure I didn't become some fancy-free dilettante without her influence. Daddy would've preferred that." She sipped her whisky. "Anyway, Charles and Daddy don't—didn't—get on. He stayed at our townhouse, Great Western Terrace."

Dreghorn felt a twinge of irony. They were almost neighbors, not that he let on—Isla in palatial luxury, he in his rented room with the shared bathroom along the corridor.

"We spoke regularly on the telephone, but days could go by without us seeing each other."

"What did he do?"

"He was a businessman, in that he collected businesses as if they were going out of fashion, but didn't actually succeed at any of them. He trained as a solicitor and was briefly involved with Lockhart's, but it wasn't a success, so he returned to his old practice, property dealings mainly."

"Why wasn't it a success?"

"You'd need to ask my father. I didn't think it was my place to inquire. To be honest, perhaps I didn't want to know."

"Did Charles have any enemies? In his professional or personal life?"

"Not that I'm aware of. He was a very easy man to like. Charming, witty, the life and soul."

"But your father didn't think so."

She took a drink before answering. "Charles lacked substance, as far as Daddy was concerned." The bitterness in her voice was astringent. "My first husband, John, was what my father wanted. Strong, dependable, successful in business, from a good family. Came through the war without a scratch, on the outside at least. Inside, he was clawed to shreds, but we just couldn't see it."

John Ferguson, Isla's first husband, had killed himself in 1922, only a few months before Lady Jane's death. A good man by all accounts, there had been no hint of shellshock or psychological damage until the moment he cleaned and loaded his service revolver, put the barrel in his mouth, and pulled the trigger.

"You have a daughter, don't you, from your first marriage?"

"No. Catriona's Charles's. He was a good father, at least." The implication being that he wasn't good in other respects. "John and I . . . we found out that we couldn't have children."

Isla was crying now, unable to hold back the tears. Dreghorn made a show of searching for a handkerchief, but knew he wouldn't find one. She wiped the tears away, drained the last of her whisky, and got to her feet, running her hands down her thighs, smoothing out her dress. "I should go. My father needs to know what's happened."

Dreghorn opened the door, followed her out. After the war, he had tried to pretend nothing had changed. He returned to Glasgow determined to rekindle the spark he had shown as an amateur boxer. Possibly with Rory's encouragement, Sir Iain Lockhart had agreed to finance Dreghorn's turning professional, until he became aware of his daughter's blossoming and potentially scandalous interest in the noble art.

The money stopped dead. So did Dreghorn's contact with Isla; he never learned what threats or inducements had quelled her usual single-minded drive to do whatever she wanted. He'd subsequently read about her engagement to John Ferguson in the paper. The following page featured a recruitment advert seeking "men of strong character and military experience" for the Shanghai Municipal Police Force. The other side of the world had suddenly seemed like an attractive place to be.

A misty drizzle was in the air, refreshing to the skin after the alcohol and the stuffy warmth of the pub. She put her head back, savored the rain.

"Where were you last night?"

She fixed her eyes on him, a flash of disappointment. "Am I a suspect, inspector? I thought this wasn't your case."

"Sorry, force of habit." He felt cheap, as if he'd just delivered a low blow to a better fighter. "Strachan'll be in touch tomorrow to take your statement. It's what he'll ask."

"Then I'll tell him the truth. I was at Kelpie House, attended by a full complement of servants."

The chauffeur was parked a short distance away. He stepped out, started to open an umbrella, but Isla gestured to say it wasn't necessary.

"I do go through them, don't I? Husbands. You were lucky."

"I was never in the running."

She kissed him on the cheek, lingered for a moment, her breath on his face, her hip brushing against him. He moved back slightly, and she smiled. "Despite the circumstances, it's been good to see you," she said with, he thought, the sort of affection reserved for pets who every now and again attempt to bite their masters.

He said something clumsy and inconsequential as she walked toward the car, but she gave no indication of having heard, and he wished he'd stayed silent.

When Dreghorn got back to Turnbull Street, it was like walking into a strange pub, all eyes turning to stare at him. McDaid stood at the counter, bolt upright, arms folded as if he'd been waiting for all eternity.

"What're you doing, standing about like a cigar-store Indian?"

A slow sidelong glance from the big man. "People have been telling tales about you."

"Aye? Always knew you were a big sweetie-wife. The slightest bit of gossip—"

"How in the name of the wee man do you know a high-society flapper like Isla Lockhart?"

Dreghorn leaned his elbows on the counter. "She's an old friend."

"Aye, right, pull the other one."

"I used to box for her father. Sometimes she'd come and watch."

"Ah." That explained it. "The sight of you getting knocked on your arse would be hard to resist."

"Won every fight, big man. If you ever want to slip on the gloves . . ."

McDaid snorted with exaggerated derision.

"How'd you get on, anyway?" Dreghorn asked.

"Case was thrown out of court. The witnesses decided it was in their best interests not to turn up and the victim withdrew his statement and dropped the charges. Said he was confused with the drink, made a mistake. He wasn't stabbed. They were just larking about and he caught himself on a rusty nail."

"Didn't know they made nails that big."

Shug Nugent emerged from the back office to assume his position behind the desk. He gestured at Dreghorn's elbows.

"Uncooked joints off the table," he said. "And by the way, do I look like a secretary to you?"

"No' a very bonnie one. Why?"

"Phone call for Inspector Dreghorn!" Nugent announced like a hotel page-boy. He pulled a crumpled scrap of paper from his pocket and read, "Drew Scullion. Said he'd meet you tomorrow, two o'clock. Said you'd know where."

"Did he now?"

"Another old pals' reunion?" McDaid asked.

"I hope not," Dreghorn said. "Drew Scullion got his brains blown out by a German sniper on Christmas Day, 1915."

8

1913

Jimmy visited Morris Greene's gym every chance he got, and his mother did know about it. But Joe and his wife had no children of their own, so she let her pride rest for once and accepted their generosity, watching with exasperation as her son danced about interminably, shadow-boxing a succession of invisible opponents.

"I'm going to be Heavyweight Champion of the world, Ma! I'm going to be Jack Johnson!"

His mother continued wiping the kitchen table. "The Dreghorns aren't built that way, James."

"Don't be daft, Ma." A mischievous smile. "You don't have to be black to be champ."

She raised an eyebrow sternly, then with a smile of her own, threw the wet cloth at him. He impaled it with a straight right, the material slapping loudly around his fist.

His mother was right, of course. He would never be Heavyweight Champ. By the time he was sixteen, Jimmy had already reached his full height, five foot eight at a stretch, and was bantamweight at best, although he would fill out over the years to reach welterweight.

When he started work, the school gates releasing them and the shipyard gates opening to welcome them without pause for breath or contemplation, Jimmy joined his Uncle Joe in the black squad—the boilermakers and caulkers who sealed the hulls with oakum and pitch to make the ships watertight. It was hard work, dirty work, but they took pride in the leviathans that rose along the banks of the Clyde and powered across oceans, opening up the world.

Jimmy loved the camaraderie, the banter that rung out rapid-fire amidst the beat of riveting hammers and the roar of welders' torches, though as the newest recruit, a fifteen-year-old virgin at that, he was often the target of those comments.

Encouraged by his uncle, he foolishly affected a worldly-wise air of what he hoped was sexual nonchalance to begin with—'course he'd had his hole, probably got it more than they did, married old farts. But the squad had heard it all before and the act was quickly discredited, leaving his cheeks glowing with embarrassment like a well-skelped arse. Joe Dreghorn was a patter merchant of the highest order, hilarious or exasperating, depending on whether or not you were in the firing line; if anything, the family connection made Jimmy a bigger target.

The ring remained his passion. In the three years since he'd started boxing, Jimmy had won a number of amateur medals, a fact Joe wasn't shy about bringing up, seeing as he was responsible for introducing his nephew to the sport. "Finest wee boxer I've ever seen," he said. "Going to be champ one day; buy his family big houses along the seafront at Gourock. Nobody in this place could lay a hand on him. Like lightning, I'm telling you."

"You talk a lot of shite, Dreghorn." Malky Clarke had a reputation for getting mad with it when he drank and wasn't much less belligerent when he was hungover. "One punch and I'd knock his block off."

"You'd need to hit him first, big man. Think you can manage that, a big lump like you?" Joe slipped an arm around his nephew's shoulders. "Five bob says you can't touch him. Not a fight or anything. He'll just stand there, you try and hit him."

"Aye, that'll be right," Jimmy, uncomfortable with his uncle's boasts at the best of times, was even less comfortable at being booked into a fight with the biggest man in the yard.

"Don't worry, Jimmy, you could cook and eat a clootie dumpling in the time it'd take him to throw a punch."

"You're on." Malky raised his left hand reassuringly, as if to keep everything friendly, then swung with his right, an open-handed blow that gave Jimmy little time to react. He rolled narrowly under the shovel-like palm, the bunnet brushed from his head.

"Best out of three." Malky wasn't for giving up.

"Cost you another five bob," Joe said. Jimmy glared at him.

"Your arse it will." Malky tried another slap but Jimmy, ready now, dodged with ease. The next attempt was a straight jab that passed over his shoulder as he sidestepped.

It was afternoon break and the black squad, smoking and drinking tea, gathered to watch as Malky lumbered after Jimmy with clumsy jabs and wild swings. Jimmy danced lightly despite his workboots, evading everything, playing to the gallery of blackened faces.

Ducking a wide back-fist, he stepped into a clinch, grabbing Malky's wrist, slipping an arm around the big man's waist and twirling him around in a couple of pirouettes, as if they were the oddest couple on the Albert dance floor.

He immediately regretted it. As he released Malky, the big man, already off-balance, slipped on a patch of oil and crashed heavily to the ground. Jimmy lowered his guard and offered him a hand up. "Sorry, Malky, I didn't mean to—" The squad's laughter made him tail off awkwardly.

Malky, glowering, gripped his hand, then swept Jimmy's feet out from under him. Jimmy caught the words "Jammy wee prick" as he hit the ground and then felt the weight of Malky's knee trap him there. He heard his uncle yelling that it was only a bit of fun, other voices agreeing, and wasn't sure whether to expect a beating or just some minor indignity.

A sharp whistle sounded, accompanied by urgent footsteps on the cobbles, and the weight on Jimmy eased. He got to his feet to find the hat man in charge of their shift—foremen and managers sported bowler hats instead of the regular pieceworkers' bunnets—raging at them, and trying to look authoritative in front of a group of well-dressed men across the yard.

Joe, quickest to speak, made sure the joke was still on Malky. "He doesn't have much luck getting a lumber at the dancing. So we're giving him a few lessons to make his footwork fancier."

"By rolling around the yard scrapping?" The hat man had been talked round by Joe before.

"Is there a problem, foreman?"

The tallest of the strangers looked like an undertaker, Jimmy thought, apart from the colorful Paisley pattern of his waistcoat and the combativeness in his eyes; a man used to the respect of others. He scanned their ranks like a judge gauging the accused before pronouncing sentence. "If you work hard, I have no objections to you playing hard," he said, "as long as there are no hard feelings."

Joe and the others were surprisingly deferent—no hard feelings at all, sir. Malky even tousled Jimmy's hair.

The man gave Jimmy a look that was unreadable, glanced at his pocket watch. "Take another ten minutes on your break. No wages docked."

"Who was that?" Jimmy watched the group continue their tour, the hat man leading the way obsequiously, though the tall man appeared to take little notice of him.

"Sir Iain, the high heid yin." Joe puffed on a nipped roll-up to relight it. "Your boss."

The second largest shipyard on the Clyde, Lockhart's was widely regarded as the best to work for. A dedicated capitalist, cut-throat if necessary, Sir Iain Lockhart was nevertheless a compassionate employer, fairer than most when it came to compensation for accidents or fatalities and less strict on maintaining sectarian divisions. The head of a shipping dynasty that embraced all aspects of the industry, from construction to running cargoes across the oceans, he had the sea in his blood.

Jimmy didn't expect to ever see him again, let alone stand awkwardly in front of him a few days later after receiving a summons from the yard.

"Young Dreghorn." Sir Iain didn't look up from the ledgers on the enormous desk before him. "No more dance lessons at breaktime?"

"No, sir." Jimmy risked a quick glance around; dark oak paneling, shelves of perfectly aligned books, a conference table laid with charts and drawings, glass display cabinets containing scale models of the great ships Lockhart's had constructed. The rug was deep and soft under his feet. For a moment, he hoped he'd trailed muck across it, to remind the man who hadn't deigned to look at him where his wealth came from.

"Probably best to have an opponent who's in the right weight division, no?" Lockhart looked up, his gaze direct, but without arrogance or superiority.

"It might help, sir, aye," Jimmy replied, relaxing a little.

Lockhart leaned back in his chair, the leather creaking luxuriously. "I'm told you box, Dreghorn. That you show promise. Dougie McGinn, your trainer, keeps me apprised from time to time." The tone became blunt. "Do you? Have promise?"

Jimmy shrugged, the standard approach. Admit to nothing.

"Don't be shy, boy. If you've got a talent, accept it. Use it. It might be all you've got. Do you have promise?"

"Yes, sir." Jimmy nodded, determined to prove himself now. "I'm good. I think I am."

"I've seen promise before, Dreghorn. I've seen it wasted by drink or tossed away by needless brawling in the gutter. Are you in a gang?"

"No, sir." Jimmy thought about Matt Johnstone, kneeling in the street, trying to hold his face together.

"Your family approves?"

"Well, my ma doesn't like the idea of anybody but her skelping me, but otherwise, aye."

"And your father? He works here, doesn't he?"

"No, that might be my uncle you're thinking of. My da used to work in the yards; he was a riveter. He was with the finishing squad on the *SS Maori*, bound for Australia." It was not uncommon for workers to travel on a ship's maiden voyage, dealing with snagging or uncompleted work that came to light during the journey. "Never came back."

"He jumped ship?" Sir Iain seemed suspicious, as if irresponsibility might be hereditary.

Jimmy shrugged again. "My mother says he was killed in an accident on Sydney Bridge, but people talk, you hear things. Either way, she brought me, my brother, and sister up herself."

"Not an easy thing to do, in these times, this city. You'd do well to take more after her in terms of character than your father."

Jimmy, growing resentful of the right Sir Iain obviously felt was his to pass judgment, said nothing.

Sir Iain pushed his chair away from the desk and swiveled round to look out of the large window behind him. Jimmy followed his gaze, the dark waters of the Clyde visible through the skeletons of the ships.

When he first entered the yards, the scale of the works had overwhelmed him. He found it hard to believe the hulls of the ships that towered overhead like cliff-faces could ever have been built by human hands. From the boss's office, however, a few stories up, the sight was different. Here, Jimmy imagined, it felt as though you'd mastered the world.

"I sponsor a small stable of athletes from a variety of disciplines,"

Lockhart said. "I'd like you to become one of them, subject to a trial period. You'll have to be dedicated. There'll be weekend training camps, as well as regular sessions after work, with a small stipend to cover expenses and equipment." He swiveled back to face Jimmy. "Are you interested?"

"Yes, sir!"

"It won't be easy, Dreghorn. I don't stand for shirkers. Neither do the people I employ."

"No, sir."

"Good." Sir Iain seemed pleased, his tone softening. "You'll need to juggle training with work. If you're successful, we may be able to find something easier for you to do."

"Thank you, sir, but if I can, I'd rather stay where I am, in the black squad." The idea of preferential treatment didn't sit right with him.

"The black squad? Good work, but dirty, sometimes dangerous. You could damage your hands."

"Might just toughen them up," Jimmy said cockily.

For a moment, Lockhart said nothing. His expression was unreadable, but Jimmy felt as though he had failed some small test.

Lockhart nodded toward the door. "My secretary will send you a letter with all the details. Good luck, Dreghorn. Don't let me down."

Jimmy tried to conceal his excitement as he returned to the yard, only telling his Uncle Joe the news on the walk home. He told no one else. He didn't want them to think there was something different about him, that he was no longer part of the gang. He may have been uneasy with the thought of preferential treatment, but in truth, the view from Sir Iain's office had allowed him a glimpse of other horizons, other possibilities.

He took the job more seriously when he saw the injuries, understood the dangers Sir Iain had alluded to. An eye burnt out by the misjudged toss of a red-hot rivet from the furnace to the platers. A foot crushed by the relentless wheels of a transport carriage loaded with steel. Fingers torn off by a spinning drill-head. All injuries that could destroy a man's fragile livelihood and leave his family dependent on the Parish.

Smaller injuries were commonplace and Jimmy, with his steady hands and controlled precision of movement, gained a reputation as an eye man. Workers were often struck by sparks that leaped out from under a welder's torch or riveter's hammer, tiny fragments of hot metal that lodged painfully in the eye. Jimmy developed a knack for turning the eyelid with a sharpened matchstick and deftly extracting the shard while other workers watched, their eyes streaming with water at the thought. Ironically, the first man he tended to in this way was Malky Clarke.

9

On Christmas Day, 1914, an unofficial truce had descended like an autumn mist on Loch Lomond. The troops of both sides climbed gingerly out of the trenches and met in the limbo of no-man's-land. They shook hands, exchanged cigarettes, compared photographs of loved ones, and played a game of football, before drifting inevitably back to their respective sides.

On Christmas Day, 1915, with no officers in the vicinity, Drew Scullion tried to encourage the Hun to lay down their arms again and join in a festive rematch. He started playing keepie-up, kicking a ball repeatedly into the air so that it could be seen from the German lines, rising and falling over the parapet of the trench. Receiving no response, he slipped off his helmet and began heading the ball instead, sending it higher into the Germans' line of vision, his head bobbing rhythmically up and down, higher and higher . . .

Dreghorn was warning him to stop when the shot rang out. A few soldiers rushed toward the body, but Billy Hunter stayed leaning against the trench wall, smoking. "One nil to Fritz," he said.

The Necropolis held few Great War graves, and those were mainly drawn from the officer classes. To commemorate the courage of Glaswegian troops in the conflict abroad, and to earn some positive press in the midst of rent strikes and unrest at home, the Corporation had arranged the repatriation of a common soldier's body, to represent all his fallen comrades. Thanks to the timing of his death, Drew Scullion, possibly the worst soldier in the British Army, was buried with full military honors.

Crouching, Dreghorn rubbed away the accumulated dust and moss of years, making the name on the gravestone legible. Andrew David Scullion, born in the same year as Dreghorn, their birthdays only a few days apart, if he remembered correctly. A handful more years, and Dreghorn's life would have lasted twice as long as Scullion's.

"Why, sergeant, you do care?" Billy Hunter appeared on the far side of the stone, collar up, bunnet low, making his identity difficult to discern for any onlookers. Not that the Necropolis on a damp, dreich afternoon was much of a draw for the crowds. "Think anyone'll be as conscientious at your grave?" he asked, eyes smiling as usual.

Dreghorn rose stiffly, as if the coldness of the stone had seeped into his body. "I'll be past caring."

They were silent for a moment, Scullion's gravestone separating them, grander tombs and monuments surrounding them like the soldiers of some lost army frozen to attention. At this distance, the tenements in the streets below didn't appear much different—dark and grim, life entombed within them.

"Wee Drew Scullion, eh?" Hunter said. "Head full of broken bottles, face like a bag of spanners. Good laugh, though. I liked him. Even if he was a left-footer."

"What do you want, Billy?" Dreghorn asked, in no mood for reminiscing.

"I've been thinking about that wee boy. Awful business."

"That's the kind of man attracted to your crowd."

"Told you, he's no' one of us." Anger in the eyes. Hunter hawked loudly to clear his lungs and then spat onto the grass. "Have you found him? Bryce?"

"You know we haven't."

"How close do you think you are?"

"Are you looking for tips for when it's you we're after?"

"Me? I'm a law-abiding citizen. And you're the law. I'm only trying to help."

"Stop fucking about and tell me where to find him, then."

"Oh, I've no idea where he is the now." The smile became cunning. "But I might know where he'll be tonight. Just maybe, y'know."

"What, Billy Hunter turning informer?" Dreghorn's disbelief was real, the world shifting in ways he hadn't foreseen.

"That'll be fuckin' right. This is a once-in-a-lifetime opportunity, Jimmy."

Dreghorn took his time lighting a cigarette, didn't offer Hunter one. "What're you after? Money? Thought all your wee schemes were paying off better than that."

"You want to find somebody? So do I."

"Who?" Dreghorn could imagine what state anyone he delivered to Hunter would end up in.

Hunter didn't answer. He seemed reluctant to take the next step. Finally, he said, "My sister."

"No bother; she lives up the road from you."

"Don't be a prick, Jimmy. No' Janet. My wee sister, Sarah."

Dreghorn had vague memories of Hunter having a younger sister, but nothing more. He smoked and thought. Neither of them looked away.

"If I agree to help," Dreghorn said slowly, "you'll hand over Bryce?"

"No, no, I won't hand over anybody, 'cos I'm no' hiding anyone. But I might have heard a little whisper about his whereabouts."

Dreghorn nodded cynically. "When did you last see her?"

"Eighteen years ago."

"Long time. Any idea if she's still in Glasgow? Still in Scotland?"

Hunter shrugged sullenly, reluctant to impart more information than he had to. Force of habit.

"This isn't an interrogation, Billy. She could've left the country, changed her name. If you want my help, I'll need details—date of birth, photographs, anything you've got."

Reaching into his inside pocket, Hunter produced an envelope, handed it to Dreghorn.

Dreghorn weighed the envelope in his hand. "No one in your family's in touch with her?"

"No."

"They might not be telling you."

Hunter bristled. "You think I don't know my own family? No one's seen her for years."

"Why? How did you lose touch with her?"

"I was in the jail, eighteen months, first stretch. Rab, Janet, my ma, none of them told me at the time, didn't want to worry me."

Dreghorn examined the contents of the envelope as Hunter spoke.

"Sarah got herself into trouble—a wean. My da was a cunt, simple as that. I can only imagine what he'd have said and done. If he hadn't died just before I got out, I'd have been straight back in the jail for helping him on his way." He sighed, curbing his anger. "My ma was working every hour she could, trying to hold things together. Janet was married and had her own family. And Rab, well, you knew him; he wasn't the sharpest."

"You wouldn't catch him running his own gang, no." Dreghorn looked at what Hunter had given him. Sarah Catherine Hunter's birth certificate, a handwritten sheet giving details of her height, the color of her eyes and hair, and a photograph. A family portrait, the Hunters in their Sunday best, the mother and father seated, the children around them, a model of dignity and decorum. None of them were smiling except Sarah. Her expression was hopeful and optimistic, unaware of the heartbreak to come, Dreghorn thought.

"So Sarah was pretty much on her own," Hunter continued. "Must've met someone, though he couldn't have been up to much. Did a runner soon as he found out she was pregnant. They didn't see him for dust. Ma said she never knew who he was, and Sarah refused to say. Tell the truth, my ma wouldn't have told me if she did know. Said I'd just got out the jail, and she didn't want me going back in for something worse if I ever got my hands on him. They wanted Sarah to go away somewhere, save the family the shame. Managed to get her into Trinity, where she could have the baby and then have it adopted."

Trinity Village, a purpose-built late-Victorian hamlet in the Renfrewshire countryside about thirteen miles outside Glasgow, was a charitable institution set up for the education and maintenance of orphaned and abandoned children. One of the village's facilities allowed unmarried women and underage girls to deliver their babies safely and discreetly, the children often being put up for adoption afterward.

"They came up with a story that she'd developed TB and had been sent up to the Highlands to recover." Hunter paced around Scullion's grave as he talked. "Sarah went along with it, didn't argue, until the day before she was due to leave. She took a few things and slipped out in the middle of the night. Must've been planning it all along." He looked at Dreghorn. "None of us have seen her since."

"When was this, do you know the date?"

"June, 1914, I think. I'd been banged up since the previous November, so . . ." Hunter shrugged, nothing else to offer.

"Who was Sarah closest to?"

The bitter humor in Hunter's eyes was replaced by something unreadable. "We were all close, it was us against my da half the time. But Janet and Sarah—they talk more, don't they, sisters?"

"Did anyone look for her at the time?"

"The polis were informed, but it wasn't as if a crime had been committed. They looked for her, but"—he paused—"nothing. I wanted to try and find her myself when they told me, but I didn't get the chance. I was granted early release on condition that I joined up immediately and went to war. They'd have thrown me back in the jail if I'd gone off after her. My ma said it'd be all right; I could look for her when I got back."

"Well, it was going to be over by Christmas."

"Aye. Right bunch of mugs, weren't we? When I got back, well, it was like a lifetime had gone by. You could almost fool yourself into thinking that she'd never been there."

"Why look for her now, after all these years?"

"You said it the other night—my ma's no' well, might no' have long left. She talks about Sarah more and more lately. 'I ruined that poor lassie's life,' that's what she says. I'd like her to see her daughter again—maybe her grandchild—even if it's just the once, before it's too late."

"Can I speak to her? Your mother."

"Why would you need to do that?"

"She was there. She knows what happened. She might remember something important, something that could help. With you, it's all second-hand."

"If you have to, I suppose. But I'd need to be there as well, right?"

Dreghorn said nothing. He took a final draw, dropped the cigarette, crushed it underfoot. He glanced around, searching for signs of movement among the tombs. He'd refused to let McDaid accompany him, but wouldn't have been surprised if the big man, concerned for his safety, had sneaked in.

"It's been a long time, Billy," he said. "I can't guarantee anything. And I need whatever you have on Bryce now. I'm no' playing a waiting game."

"I know." The humor ignited in Hunter's eyes once more, as if he'd just been dealt a winning card. "You wouldn't do me any favors and you'd fight as dirty as anyone if you had to, but something like this? I trust you. If you say you'll try, you'll do your damnedest." He extended a hand, asked in a measured tone, "Do we have a deal, sergeant?"

They stared at each other for a long moment, warnings, threats in their eyes. Dreghorn, extending his own hand, said, "You stab my back, I'll stab yours."

10

"And you trust him?" McDaid was flabbergasted.

"About as far as I could throw you," said Dreghorn. "But being associated with someone who murdered his own son doesn't look good when you're meant to be a local hero, so right now—aye."

"You don't think we should've brought more men?"

"Away, you big jessie, it's only Bryce, Ally Reid, and his wife."

"Wee Sadie's a handful on her own. Still, if that's what your new pal says, it must be gospel."

Tam Bryce was hiding out with Alistair Reid, a low-ranking member of the Billy Boys whom Billy Hunter didn't much care for and suspected of siphoning money from the gang's fund-raising activities. According to Hunter, Bryce had scraped together enough cash to pay Reid to help him out of Scotland. In the early hours of the morning, a friend of Reid's who worked for Caledonia Breweries would arrive in the firm's delivery truck and drive Bryce to Stranraer to catch a ferry to Belfast, where he had family. From there, he hoped to board a ship with an unscrupulous captain and work his passage to America.

Dreghorn had told McDaid that Hunter, in return for confidentiality, had passed on this information because Bryce's crime was so heinous that it crossed the traditional divides between them. He hadn't mentioned Sarah Hunter, the other part of the arrangement.

They'd parked on Anson Street, around the corner from the

third-floor tenement house on London Road that Reid shared with his wife Sadie, the daughter of a once-notorious local hard man, and fond of a good scrap after getting mad with the drink herself. They lowered their voices as they approached the landing. Laughter and conversation emanated from behind Reid's door. They drew their detectives' batons, which were shorter and less imposing than uniformed officers' regulation truncheons. Gripped in his meaty fist, McDaid's looked about as menacing as a lollipop stick.

Dreghorn battered his fist against the door, yelled, "Police! Open up!"

There were curses and panicked movements from within. McDaid kicked the door, his full weight behind him. The lock tore free with a crunch of splintering wood and the door flew inward as if driven by a piston, striking someone on the other side, judging by the loud thud and cry of pain that followed.

Dreghorn surveyed the room as he entered, baton at the ready, McDaid at his back. A typical tenement house, identical to the one in which they'd discovered Tommy Bryce's body—one window, alcove bed, range cooker, sink, table, and chairs. In contrast, gas mantles bathed the room in a warm orange hue and the range was fired up. Steam rose from a large pot of soup, a black-leaded kettle heating on another ring beside it.

Tam Bryce was the only one seated, his dark eyes unreadable, one hand on the table, close to a chopping-board and small paring knife. Ally Reid sat on the floor behind the door, holding his bloody nose, swearing incoherently. Sadie Reid stood by the range, hatred in her gin-baby face.

There were two other men in the room, one of whom Dreghorn recognized: John Watson, drunk and disorderly, assault and battery, another charmer. The other he didn't know, a big bruiser with pitted skin like the surface of the moon or congealed porridge.

McDaid gave Dreghorn a quick scathing look. Obviously arithmetic wasn't Billy Hunter's strong suit. Dreghorn shrugged back with his eyebrows, then pointed his baton at Bryce.

"Thomas Bryce, you're under arrest for murder," he said. "You are not obliged to say anything—"

"What're you waiting for?" hissed Sadie. "Get into them!"

Watson and Crater Face exchanged wary glances. Reid clambered to his feet, leaning on a rickety chair. Bryce stayed still, staring at the knife on the table. A high-pitched whine was rising in volume, the kettle approaching the boil.

"But," Dreghorn continued, "anything you say may be used in evidence."

"Aye, and the rest of you will be getting huckled for aiding and abetting a fugitive," McDaid added. "Though that could become accomplices to murder, depending on how good a mood you keep me in between here and the station."

Reid grabbed a dishtowel off the table, dabbed his nose in outrage. "How do you know we weren't about to hand him in?" He waved the bloody towel at Bryce.

The whine of the kettle changed tone, becoming a whistle, as Sadie shifted from one foot to the other, her head circling like a cobra about to strike. "Fuckin' bunch of shite bags!" she shouted at her husband and his friends, spittle spraying. "Call yourselves men?"

McDaid gave Reid a sympathetic nod. "No wonder you keep getting yourself arrested, Ally. Anything for a bit of peace, eh?"

Sadie snatched the pot from the range and hurled a steaming slurry of carrots, turnips, and potatoes at Dreghorn and McDaid. "Whoa!" McDaid yelled, turning his back, the soup spattering his shoulders. Dreghorn, closer, had less time, throwing up his arms and ducking his head. Boiling liquid seared his right hand, forcing him to drop his baton.

Fearing his wife more than the police, Reid lifted the chair and thrust the legs at McDaid like a circus lion-tamer. McDaid fastened a fist around one leg of the chair, held it fast. Reid pulled frantically, virtually wrenching his arms from their sockets. The chair didn't shift an inch in McDaid's grasp.

Crater Face lunged at Dreghorn, who raised his guard to block and counterpunch, only to be struck from another direction entirely, McDaid's elbow smashing into the side of his face as the big man swung his baton. With seven people in the cramped room, you couldn't swing a cat, let alone throw a punch. "Watch where you're going, will you?" he heard McDaid exclaim with zero sympathy.

McDaid demolished the chair with two swings of the baton. Reid sidestepped frantically and McDaid hit him with a solid, almost disdainful jab, which spread Reid's already bloody nose across his face and dropped him onto his arse as if his legs had turned to water.

Dreghorn covered up as he staggered back from McDaid. Crater Face barreled into him, pummeling away for all he was worth, already breathing hard. Dreghorn drove two short uppercuts into Crater Face's belly, smelled cheap whisky on the man's breath as he grunted explosively, and followed up with a left jab, putting distance between them.

Out of the corner of his eye, he saw Sadie swing the empty pot. He ducked to the side, the pot sailing by his head, and gave her a shove that sent her sprawling to the floor behind McDaid.

Crater Face, bouncing back, walked straight into a right cross. He collapsed onto the table, limbs flailing, shattering crockery, then rolled to the floor.

Bryce was on his feet now, the knife in his hand.

"Aoww!" Dreghorn heard McDaid yell, but kept his attention on Bryce. Sadie had leaped on the big man's back, sinking her teeth into the crown of his head. McDaid pointed at Bryce, yelling, "Do you know what that bastard did?" But Sadie fish-hooked him, clawing her fingers into the corner of his mouth.

Watson, the fourth man, had been holding back, waiting for a chance to have a go or to run, whichever seemed the best bet. He smiled at McDaid's distress, snatching an empty beer bottle from the table.

McDaid threw his weight backward, crushing Sadie against the shelves of a dresser, crockery falling onto his shoulders, as Watson's first swing narrowly missed his temple. Watson started to swing again, but McDaid kicked him in the groin, a brutal blow that doubled him over, wheezing. He sank to his hands and knees, the bottle rolling across the floor.

The shriek of the kettle filled the air, drowning out Sadie's curses. Twisting his head, McDaid bit her fingers, tasting onions and rolling tobacco. He reached over his shoulder, gripped her by the scruff of the neck, and pivoted forward, throwing her over his shoulder. She landed on Watson, smashing him to the floor, and lay writhing and moaning, semi-conscious.

Dreghorn's eyes flicked from Bryce's face to the knife in his hand and back again. It all depended on whether Bryce knew how to use a blade, stabbing straight or slashing unpredictably.

"Fuckin' come on, then," Dreghorn said. "I'm no' a wee boy."

Madness flared in Bryce's eyes. He lunged at Dreghorn, his arm extending as he thrust the blade at the detective's chest. Dreghorn slipped to the side, chopped the edge of his hand into Bryce's forearm, pushing the blade away, and gripped the man's wrist. He wrapped his other arm around Bryce's elbow, started to apply an arm-lock, but stumbled on the rolling bottle that Watson had dropped, almost losing his grip. Bryce threw an arm around his throat. The point of the blade turned toward Dreghorn's face, still in play.

Steam was shrieking deafeningly from the boiling kettle. Dreghorn forced Bryce's hand into the scorching jet, felt the man buck against him with a desperate strength. In his head, Dreghorn saw Tommy Bryce's body, broken and icy cold in the darkness.

Bryce screamed, and the knife fell clattering onto the range. Steam seared Dreghorn's face, blurring his vision. He maintained his grip on Bryce's hand. The kettle shrieked on.

"Jimmy! Stop!"

A sudden impact knocked Dreghorn's head to the side. He shook it off. Wee Tommy Bryce wept and screamed and begged his father to stop. Bryce wept and screamed and begged Dreghorn to stop. Another impact, harder this time. Blood in his mouth. His vision cleared.

McDaid loomed over him, glaring, one hand raised to hit him again. But his voice was gentle when he spoke. "Enough. It's over, all right?"

The world came flooding back in. Dreghorn released Bryce, who fell to the floor whimpering, and stared down at the man's burnt hand, the flesh already blistering. McDaid lowered his hand onto Dreghorn's shoulder and gave it a light squeeze.

Dreghorn looked around at the broken furniture, the prone bodies. He picked up the tea towel, shifted the kettle off the heat, and nodded at Sadie, still sprawled on top of Watson.

"Not very gentlemanly of you," he said.

"Wasn't very ladylike of her." McDaid put a hand to the top of his head, where she had bitten him. His fingers came away bloody. Sadie twitched and grunted, like she was having a bad dream.

McDaid, alarmed, started patting his pockets. "Quick, get the cuffs on her. I don't fancy our chances if it goes to Round Two."

11

1931

Glasgow, second city of the Empire—though you'd have to fight Liverpool, Manchester, and Birmingham for the title. And Edinburgh might be tempted to knife you in the back when you're not looking. It, after all, is the capital city of Scotland.

It's claimed that the name Glasgow derives from two Gaelic words meaning "dear green place," though this is a romantic interpretation. It's a city of grime and grit and graft, an industrial giant whose foundations of iron and steel are slowly corroding.

In its heyday the city was a leader in industries from chemicals and textiles to iron and steel, unrivaled in the field of mechanical engineering. A fifth of the world's ships were Clyde-built, a quarter of its locomotives manufactured north of the city in Springburn. The name of Glasgow was synonymous with strength and progress.

The twentieth century brought a change in fortunes, although it began well with the wholesale transfer in 1906 of the yards, boiler and marine engineering shops of Yarrow and Co. from the Thames to the Clyde, a seismic shift in industrial power and prestige.

Shipbuilding was at full stretch when war with Germany was declared in 1914, turning out new warships for the Admiralty, cargo and passenger vessels for the Mercantile Marine. Despite the horrors and hardships of warfare and Spanish Flu, the relentless influenza pandemic that followed the conflict, industry leaders remained bullish. Imperial arrogance, however, had given way to complacency. The technological gap between Britain and other nations had been bridged—and bridged more cheaply. Soon France, Italy, Sweden, and even Germany were sending Britain quotes to build ships instead of orders to buy them, while the likes of India and Japan made advances in other industries, increasing competition and driving prices down. Britannia bristled, then hung her head sheepishly, humbled by commerce rather than conflict.

The government called the economic shift a slump to begin with, until a nudge from the United States in the form of the 1929 Wall Street crash forced them to admit that the slump was in fact a Depression so severe that it required a capital letter for emphasis.

The most congested and overcrowded city in Britain, Glasgow was struck harder than most. The majority of the poverty-stricken population lived in four-story tenements, the walls blackened by decades of pollution, with little in the way of sanitation, let alone dignity. Alcoholism, sectarianism, and discontent were rife, fueling climates of fear, cycles of violence.

Mass immigration had brought an unwanted flood of cultures to Glasgow—Jewish, Italian, Russian—but perhaps the greatest enmity was directed at the country's closest neighbor, and fellow Celts at that. From the eighteenth century onward, attempting to escape famine and political strife, the Irish, largely Catholic, had traveled to Glasgow in their thousands, to be met with resentment and suspicion by the Protestant majority in an already teeming city. A sectarian war of attrition had been fought ever since, communities forging their own strongholds with little integration, hatred and bitterness descending through successive generations.

And that was before the war, before the Depression, when the good times were still rolling. When hard times came to town the veneer of respectability shattered. The gulf between rich and poor didn't yawn so much as bare its teeth in a vicious snarl. Unemployment soared, as did the influence of gangs in the worst-hit districts, offering solidarity of sorts to their members and an outlet for anger and resentment.

Glasgow's street gangs had long been a dirty secret within the city, but growing newspaper attention and lurid headlines—*RAZOR GANG RAMPAGE, GLASGOW GANGSTERS TERRORIZE SHOPKEEPERS, GLASGOW'S REIGN OF TERROR*—made it a national concern. Crime, it was claimed, was out of control, the slum areas virtually lawless, controlled by razor-wielding outlaws who indulged in armed robbery, housebreaking, and protection racketeering, and battled constantly for territorial and sectarian supremacy. Honest citizens feared to walk the streets. The "dear green place" had turned red with blood.

The London press was especially scathing, imbued with a sense of arrogance and southern superiority, real or imagined, that incensed the Glasgow Corporation, responsible for the political and municipal administration of the city.

But what about the "polis," those champions of law and order? The target of mutual enmity by the gangs, the Glasgow Police were also distrusted by the general public, seen as a blunt instrument to batter the working classes into submission, or better yet, contain them in their ghettoes to fight among themselves.

This resentment had festered since 1919, when police used batons to clear George Square of strikers who were otherwise picketing peacefully, causing a riot that required armed troops and tanks to enter the city the following day. It didn't help that the barbed strands of religious bigotry that divided the gangs also ran through the force. Graft and corruption were tolerated, even encouraged with a nod and a wink and a Masonic handshake. It was said you couldn't even get a job as a public lavatory attendant without kissing the right arse adoringly.

When the post of Chief Constable for the second largest force in the country became vacant, the Glasgow Police Committee felt radical action was necessary to salvage the city's tarnished reputation. The candidate they decided upon was not a yes-man or a slacker; he had radical ideas and few qualms about making enemies among those who wished to preserve the status quo. Most importantly, he proposed a blunt and pragmatic approach to dealing with the violence of the gangs and the terror they wreaked on the streets.

There was only one problem.

He was English.

"There is only one way to deal with the gangster mentality. You must show them that you are not afraid. If you stand up to them and they realize that you mean business, they will soon knuckle under. The element of beast in man, whether it comes from an unhappy and impoverished background, or from his own undisciplined lustful appetites, will respond exactly as a wild beast of the jungle responds—to nothing but greater force and greater firmness of purpose."

Despite the posh English accent and vaguely philosophical musings, Chief Constable Percy Joseph Sillitoe's first address to the new Special Crime Squad on 22 December 1931 passed through their ranks like an electric current through Frankenstein's monster.

"For too long, this city has been preyed upon by the gangs that stalk its streets. Glasgow will endure their swaggering arrogance and terrorizing tactics no longer. We, ladies and gentlemen, will put an end to it."

They were standing to attention in the City Hall, dutiful and respectful, but with a certain lack of engagement that implied they'd heard the speeches before, thank you very much, sir. As Sillitoe spoke, though, Dreghorn could see his new colleagues come to life, sparks of interest in their eyes, nods of approval, a sense of change in the air.

"You have been specially chosen for this squad because of your physicality, and because of your attitude. You are not merely chappers of doors or pullers of padlocks. You are men who wish to make a difference. You have, each and every one of you, shown no disinclination to play the gangsters at their own game, a characteristic that has, on occasion, not earned you the respect you deserved from your superiors. Rest assured, you will have my respect and support.

"If a gang, or any other criminal element, threatens you or a member of the public, you will meet their violence with the strong arm of the law. If, in so doing, you are forced to dispense greater violence in return, then I expect you to view that as your duty—to the force, to the law-abiding population of this city, and to yourself."

Sillitoe cast his gaze over the squad, meeting the eyes of each man in turn. He nodded, satisfied. "Gentlemen," he said. "See it through."

To cut bureaucracy and raise finance, the new chief constable had reduced the police divisions from eleven to seven. Profits from the sale of redundant premises funded his grand plans elsewhere, including an expanded motor division to increase the mobility of the force. The Corporation balked at the cost of the vehicles, but Sillitoe made them a condition of his appointment after witnessing their speed and effectiveness on a research trip to the United States.

A network of police boxes and telephone pillars was constructed throughout the city, allowing the public to contact Divisional Police Headquarters directly about crimes. The police boxes also acted as miniature station houses, where duty constables could write reports and conduct interviews. Some even contained a small holding cell.

Sillitoe was also a great believer in scientific detection, and had insisted upon an overhaul of Glasgow's facilities, especially the Fingerprint and Photographic Branch, the contents of which looked more like a children's finger-painting class than criminal identification files. The Forensics Laboratory too received funds to upgrade equipment and hire extra staff.

But Sillitoe's first and most important action as Chief Constable was the formation of a fast-response anti-gang division. Affiliated to the Robbery and Murder Squads, Special Crime was a plainclothes department. A dozen of the biggest police officers Scotland had to offer—and Dreghorn—were paired and sent to patrol the most notorious districts in the new radio-cars Sillitoe had ordered.

Special Crime weren't just the biggest; they were the fittest and, more importantly, the toughest. Many, like McDaid, originally hailed from the Highlands and Islands, hewn from the harshest of landscapes, where the practicalities and satisfaction of rough justice held more attraction than the bureaucracy of arrest reports and the legal shenanigans of courtroom appearances. They were men who had earned a reputation for bloody-mindedness, happy to use their fists—a couple of them, Dreghorn suspected, only too happy.

The romantic notion of Sillitoe's squad venturing into the badlands of Maryhill, Possilpark, and Bridgeton like Wild West sheriffs to take on marauding bands of outlaws fired the imagination of the press. The *Glasgow Herald* described them as a "flying squad," swooping through the streets in search of crime like birds of prey. In the *Evening Times* they were "the Heavy Mob" or "the Heavies." The *Daily Record* added Hollywood glamour by naming them "the Tartan Untouchables," after the elite unit put together in Chicago by FBI agent Eliot Ness to target the gangster Al Capone in the twenties.

Keen for his officers to achieve larger-than-life status and become the formidable public face of the new police force he was forging, Sillitoe encouraged this mythologizing. Step out of line and the Heavy Mob will be on you like a ton of bricks.

Whether in a rare flash of mischievousness or through some deeper insight, Sillitoe paired Dreghorn and McDaid—the shortest and tallest members of the squad—together, their little and large silhouettes an unmistakable, even comical, sight under the street-lamps at night.

Despite his junior rank, McDaid, two years older than Dreghorn at thirty-six and—he exaggerated with delight—"two feet bigger," got great mileage out of their height difference. That first day he had looked down on his diminutive partner with bemusement. "Did they change the regulations or something when I wasn't looking? What's the minimum height these days?"

"Five feet eight," Dreghorn said.

"You must've been on your tiptoes."

"Always got a spring in my step when I need one."

"Will you be wanting a cushion to reach the steering wheel? And how's a wee featherweight like you meant to survive when Percy starts this new jiu-jitsu program?"

But Dreghorn could hold his own: "Easy, that's how. You'll be Mc*Deid* when I'm finished with you."

The banter became grudging respect on their third patrol, when they received warning that two gangs—the Baltic Fleet and South Side Stickers—had arranged a square go on the South Portland Street Suspension Bridge, a pedestrian walkway across the Clyde.

Arriving in advance, Dreghorn dropped McDaid on the south side of the bridge, and drove to the north side. When the gangs swaggered up, full of booze and bravado, he followed the Baltic Fleet as they crossed, meeting the Stickers in the middle. Tremors thrummed along the iron structure as the gangs argued and brandished their weapons. Dreghorn noted a snooker cue, a bicycle-chain, a hammer, and beer bottles still being drained. Not as many blades as he'd expected.

'Is this a fight or a night at the dancing?" he asked. "I'm no' sure whether to arrest you or ask if I can cut in."

They turned to face him, rivalries forgotten. One of them, already sporting a fetching black eye that was turning yellow, yelled, "And who do you think you are?"

"We're the Heavy Mob, son," said McDaid behind them, flashing his warrant card. "And you lot are lightweights at best."

"Ten of us and two of youse?" Yellow Eye pointed his hammer at Dreghorn, figuring the smaller officer for the easiest target. "We'll duff you up and leave you for deid." He was the most gallus of the pack, eager to kick things off. The least troublesome was a tall skinny lad who was being buffeted by the crowd, unsure what to do and wishing he was elsewhere.

"You're all one big happy family, now?" Dreghorn asked.

"We are when it comes to dirty polis cunts like you."

"Get into them!" a Sticker shouted, shoving the skinny lad toward McDaid who, tutting wearily, shoved back with considerably more force.

The skinny lad, probably half-cut, staggered across the boards, gangly arms flailing like the tentacles of a rubber octopus in a B-movie. He slammed hard against the railing, his upper body folded over the top of the railing, and his legs snapped up to follow with the ferocity of a sprung mousetrap.

McDaid lunged after him, grabbing the skinny ankles just before they slithered out of sight, and pinioning the boy's knees over the top of the railing with his forearms. The dark waters of the Clyde surged past below. "I cannae swim," the boy whispered as if it was a secret. "I cannae bloody swim!"

McDaid rolled his eyes. "Typical." He looked over his shoulder, expecting some help, to see two Baltics rushing at him, one twirling a snooker cue as if he was leading an Orange Walk. He glimpsed further movement behind them, other gang members overwhelming Inspector Short-arse presumably.

"Do you want me to drop him?" McDaid yelled.

"Fuckin' right, the big skitter!" And the snooker player swung the cue at the detective's head. McDaid tightened his grip on the lad's ankles and braced himself for the impact.

It never came. There was a scuffle and a sound like a gong being struck for dinner in some posh country house—not that he'd ever been a guest at such a shindig. He looked up to see the Baltic's head bouncing back off the railing after being slammed into it by Dreghorn, who had also relieved the man of his snooker cue.

McDaid heaved the skinny lad back over the railing and plonked him down. His companions were bolting into the night, frantic footsteps rocking the bridge. Yellow Eye was flat on his back, arms outflung, his face turning into one giant bruise. A Sticker lay curled on his side, cradling his testicles in his hands, taking in great gasps of air. The snooker player was on the deck as well, semi-conscious, hands clasped to his forehead, lamenting incoherently.

McDaid folded his arms sternly, his eyes fixed on the boy. "Name?"

"Wullie, sir," the lad stammered, his lip petted. "William Patterson."

"Go home to your mammy, William. You're no' cut out for this malarkey."

Patterson muttered heartfelt thanks and hared off as quickly as his legs would take him, darting wary glances over his shoulder as though he expected Dreghorn to hurl the cue after him like a spear.

"Seems like a nice lad, all things considered," said McDaid.

"He's lucky he didn't take a trip doon the watter." Dreghorn pushed his fedora back. "Ca' canny next time, eh? Don't know your own strength."

That night was also the first time Dreghorn encountered Mairi McDaid, who rose from her bed in annoyance after the big man insisted they go back to his for a celebratory dram. McDaid quickly excused himself and nipped out for a pee, either ignoring his wife's mood or too tall to recognize it from eye contact.

A teacher before she married, she gave Dreghorn a look that made him feel as though he was back in school shorts.

"Bit old not to be married, aren't you," she said.

"Didn't know there was an age limit." Dreghorn smiled; bittersweet memories. "There's been a couple of close calls." The smile became mischievous. "If you've got any friends . . ."

"I'd tell them to run a mile." She nodded after her husband. "Take care of him. He's got a family, no boozing the nights away in pubs. He can be easily led."

"Have you seen the way he looks at you? It'd take a battleship to lead him astray."

She finally allowed herself a smile. "Crawler."

Glasgow loves a good story. Embellished shamelessly, the tale of the Suspension Bridge stramash snaked through busy pubs and bounced from street to street, achieving legendary status. The newspapers reported it as the turning of the tide against gangsterism. The police, delighted to buff up their tarnished reputation, portrayed it as a major incident. Even the gang members who'd been beaten into submission wore their bruises like badges of honor, proud to have been pounded upon by the Tartan Untouchables.

The only ones who tried to play it down were Dreghorn and McDaid, even now, nine months later, a target for every bampot in town who wanted to test his fighting prowess. Still, it was the job they'd signed up for, so who was the biggest bampot?

12

WEDNESDAY, 5 OCTOBER 1932

"And what do you call this?"

"Rain, sir."

Chief Constable Sillitoe glanced over his shoulder. His expression said that in a previous life, in a less civilized part of the Empire, he had possessed the authority to order a flogging for such an insouciant response. He gestured at the window, the gray sheen of the damp city beyond reflected in the glass. "You Scots have more words for rain than Eskimos do for snow. I was referring to the particular variety."

"Sir," said Dreghorn. "In that case, drizzle."

"Drizzle," Sillitoe repeated, as if it was some native phrase from his wartime days in Rhodesia that it would be useful to learn.

"Aye, not quite full-blown rain, but not a smirr either."

"Smirr?"

"Like a fine mist."

"I like smirr," McDaid said with a philosophical air. "It's refreshing."

Deputy Chief Constable McVicar cleared his throat politely; not for him a great howking cough that filled the mouth with phlegm. "You must be settling in, sir," he said to Sillitoe. "The weather's one of the keenest topics of conversation in Scotland, but we have other matters to discuss. Allegations of police brutality—not the first we've received since the formation of the new unit."

Sillitoe turned from the window, looked at the report on his desk. The detectives stood opposite him, McDaid to attention, Dreghorn more relaxed, dismissive of the claims. The Vicar was seated to one side of Sillitoe, as close to the chief constable's desk as he could get without actually sliding behind it, as if the power was shared.

They were in Sillitoe's office in Central Police Headquarters, Turnbull Street, although the chief's duties more often than not stationed him in the political arena of the City Chambers at George Square. The office was spartan, with little to give a clue to the chief constable's character. A picture of his wife sat on the desk next to his cap, turned pointedly to face him. A framed photograph on one wall showed Sillitoe as a younger man, squinting in the Rhodesian sun and seated awkwardly between two native constables, each displaying the enormous tusks of a pair of elephants the young lieutenant had shot. An original cartoon from the *Yorkshire Telegraph and Star* showed Sillitoe in his previous job as Chief Constable of Sheffield, his lean frame, long face, and wavy hair comically exaggerated. He beckoned readers sternly with one finger, dangling a set of handcuffs in the other hand, and the cartoon had been reprinted widely in the Glasgow press on the announcement of Sillitoe's appointment.

Sillitoe flicked perfunctorily through the report. "It might have been an idea to call more men before you made the arrest. I won't abide shirkers, but I'm no admirer of recklessness or unnecessary risk. A cohesive and cooperative force is what we strive for—no place for show-offs or lone wolves."

"Anonymous tip-off, sir," Dreghorn said; McDaid remained impassive. "Could easily have led nowhere. By the time we'd confirmed the suspect's presence, we had no choice but to attempt an arrest."

"This Bryce fellow—he murdered his own child and put his wife in hospital. There's no doubt?"

"He's already confessed."

"The flesh was nearly scalded from the man's hand." The Vicar sounded appalled, as if he'd never heard the like before. "He'd have confessed to being Jack the Ripper after that."

Sillitoe glanced at the report again. "He attacked you with a knife?"

"Sir." Dreghorn nodded.

"Bryce's accomplices are the ones making the complaint, yet they themselves assaulted you both with chairs, bottles, and"—a touch of amusement—"a pot of hot soup."

"Tasty it was too," McDaid noted. "Shame we ended up wearing it."

"You could ask Sadie for the recipe," Dreghorn suggested.

"Oh, aye, with added arsenic, if she had her way."

"Gentlemen!" The Vicar was almost strident. "You're on duty, not in the Old Empire Bar!"

"By the standards of gangland, my officers patrol the streets unarmed." Sillitoe slid the report across the desk to Dreghorn with an air of finality. "If you threaten a man with a knife, or any other weapon, you cannot complain should he thereupon knock you down with his fists."

Dreghorn tucked the document under one arm. He and McDaid each gave a single nod, marking their understanding.

"I'll attend the trials, of course," Sillitoe addressed McVicar. "Once convictions are secured, I'll give evidence on behalf of the prosecuting solicitor about the menace of the gangs and the frequency of their crimes, and petition for exemplary punishments." Sillitoe had employed the same tactics in Sheffield. By doing so, he shifted part of the responsibility for sentencing, as well as any threat of reprisals, from the magistrates onto himself. "This other matter, the Geddes murder . . ."

Dreghorn felt a creeping wariness. "That's Inspector Strachan's case, sir."

"The Lockhart family has requested that you be put in charge of the investigation, inspector." McVicar's expression was that of a man who'd just detected a particularly noxious fart. Even though Sillitoe was the younger of the two, he was more assured and possessed greater natural authority than the Vicar, who was more politician than policeman.

Sillitoe said, "You have some prior relationship with the family, Dreghorn?"

"I was part of Sir Iain's stable of athletes before the war, and served under his son during it."

"Boxing?"

"Aye. When we got home, I had a notion to take it up professionally. Sir Iain invested financially to help with my training, find a manager, but it all wound down fairly quickly. His interests shifted in other directions, and"—Dreghorn thought of himself as a boy, dancing about the ring, full of promise, full of the joys—"well, my sporting instincts weren't quite as keen as they were before the war."

"They trust you, then?"

"Wouldn't presume to say, sir; it was a long time ago. Tell the truth, I'm surprised they remember me." He and McDaid shared a brief glance, sarcasm in the big man's eyes. Sometimes the sergeant's understanding of rank and seniority were tenuous to say the least.

"I advised against it, of course, but the family are most insistent," said McVicar. "Their importance to the fabric and welfare of our city can't be overstated, so we should respect their wishes to some degree. I propose that we allow Dreghorn to join the investigation in a liaison capacity, but that Inspector Strachan remain in charge."

Sillitoe brushed some fluff off the brim of his cap. White scar tissue was visible on the back of his hand where, it was said, a leopard he'd raised as a cub in Africa had bitten him after being startled awake. Dreghorn wondered if that was how Sillitoe viewed the officers under his command, as predators who'd been tamed, but whose savagery could be unleashed upon his command.

"Too many cooks, Sydney," Sillitoe said. "I prefer decisiveness over debate. Dreghorn will take the case." He raised a finger to cut off McVicar's protests. "It's early days, so it won't cause too much disruption. Strachan will pass on any relevant information."

"So, homicide comes under your flying squad's remit now?" said the Vicar, a touch huffily.

"Whatever police work I deem necessary comes under their remit. You've seen his file. He's more than capable. He's already delivered one murderer this week, and he has the confidence of the family. It's the right decision and I'm glad you brought it to my attention." He turned away from McVicar. "Dreghorn, McDaid . . ."

"Sir." The detectives straightened to attention.

Sillitoe gave them a curt nod of approval. "See it through."

13

"Gives me the heebie-jeebies every time, this place."

McDaid tried to stifle the shiver that rolled from the small of his back to the nape of his neck. He exhaled, breath misting in the unnaturally cold air. "Brrrrr!" The sound echoed and he brightened as a thought came to him.

"Mind you, good acoustics. You think they'd let me practice in here?" He filled his chest with air, tightened his lips, and blew with all his puff, emitting a sound somewhere between the roar of a constipated stag and a chorus of schoolchildren blowing simultaneous raspberries.

Dreghorn said, "Well, if anything could wake the dead, it's you playing the pipes."

"Piped through the pearly gates? That's what I'd call an entrance."

"The way you play, it'd be part of the torment for the ones headed downstairs."

"What do you know? All that shite you listen to. What is it again—jizz?"

"Jazz."

Dreghorn surveyed the white-tiled tomb of the mortuary: the wall of heavy, coffin-shaped doors behind which the refrigerated bodies were stored; a pair of fresh corpses, waiting to be tagged and processed, thankfully hidden under sheets; bloody instruments in a tray by the sinks from an earlier autopsy, still to be cleaned and sterilized; a full-size skeleton suspended upright on castors like some sinister coat-stand. Two visits in almost as many days, a grim reminder of mortality. He wondered if Tommy Bryce's body was still behind one of the doors.

"They could do with some windows in here," McDaid noted.

"Not a bad idea. We could charge, come post-mortem time. It'd be better than the pictures."

"I'm serious; I need somewhere to practice. Mairi goes mental when I do, says it's a dirge. I think the neighbors might've complained."

"Your neighbors, your street, the city, the population of Timbuktoo . . ."

A door closed in the corridor beyond the autopsy room, echoing eerily. Everything echoed in the mortuary. Not the place for an overactive imagination.

A man in a dark suit with a faint gray pinstripe entered, carrying documents. He was trim and handsome, about ten years older than Dreghorn, though it didn't show much, and his quick eyes were filled with a lively humor that erred on the gallows side. A straight white streak ran through his dark hair where, Dreghorn knew, a German bullet had creased his temple on an East African battlefield during the war.

"What're you playing at over there, musical murders?" he asked. "Strachan almost had a hairy fit when I called about the post-mortem report, said you two were in charge of the case now."

"For our sins." McDaid nodded at Dreghorn. "Well, his."

Dreghorn shrugged. "I think Percy was playing a bit of office politics."

"Politics. A mug's game, though give him his due, your boss seems good at it. Suppose he has to be." The medical man opened a fridge door and slid out the pale naked body that Benny Parsonage had fished from the Clyde.

"How come it's you?" asked Dreghorn. "I'd've thought a corpse of this caliber would go straight to the high heid yin."

"Daresay it would have, but Glaister's in Cairo, visiting his son, so I'm team captain for now."

Professor Glaister, the Chief Police Surgeon, was responsible for the wellbeing of 2,248 police officers and of criminals being held for trial, and carried out post-mortems where deaths were thought not to have resulted from natural causes. But today Dr. Willie Kivlichan was in charge.

More than most, Kivlichan understood how to navigate the divisions and fault lines of Scottish society, whether class-related, religious, political, or, as was often the case, a mixture of them all. Born in Dumfries, he was signed as a striker for Glasgow Rangers at the age of seventeen. When they discovered that they'd got their homework wrong and he was a Catholic—anathema to their vigorously denied unofficial policy of only signing Protestant players—they worked frantically to squirm out of the situation and save face. The embarrassment intensified when he developed into one of their best players, even scoring memorable goals against Celtic, the team he naturally supported. He loved the game and he loved to play, placing that well above any bias or bigotry.

Eventually, in a rare example of détente, Rangers swapped Kivlichan for Alex Bennet, a Protestant who'd been playing for Celtic. Kivlichan had a glorious career with Celtic, studying for his medical qualifications at the same time, before serving in the war, which effectively ended his playing days. In addition to his own practice and assisting Glaister as Police Surgeon, he was also the Celtic Club doctor and, the previous September, had treated John Thomson at Ibrox Park after the accidental collision that cost the young Celtic and Scotland goalkeeper his life. Thomson's death rocked Scottish football, and some forty thousand mourners attended the twenty-two-year-old's funeral, many of them walking the fifty-five miles from Glasgow to Cardenden in Fife.

"Victim: Charles Edward Geddes," Kivlichan said. Geddes' corpse had undergone an autopsy, his chest and stomach opened up, ribcage pulled apart, his skull sawn open, his internal organs removed. He had been stitched back together, and a ragged scar of pinkish flesh ran from the tip of his breastbone to just above his pubic hair, where his pallid gray penis lay like a wilted mushroom.

McDaid said, "I wish you'd put breeks on them."

Kivlichan was folding his shirt sleeves up. "Modesty's the least of their concerns."

"It's no' them I'm bothered about."

Kivlichan handed his report to Dreghorn and began pulling on a pair of surgical gloves.

"Charles Edward Geddes," he said again. "Age thirty-eight. Extensive post-mortem injuries to the head and chest, sustained when the body was trapped between the boat hull and the harbor wall, as accounted for in the eyewitness statement. This also caused internal injuries, detailed in the report, but largely irrelevant to your investigation." He gestured at the corpse's throat. "Cause of death is fairly obvious and definitely suspicious. A massive trauma wound to the throat, severing the carotid artery, slicing through the windpipe, and virtually cutting all the way through to the spinal column."

Dreghorn examined the wound. "It's a clean cut."

"Almost surgically precise. A large blade, I'd say."

"Not a razor, then?"

"Unlikely. I'd be looking for a hunting knife of some sort, a machete, a bayonet perhaps."

"Until we establish where the body went into the water, we don't even have a crime scene to search."

"We should speak to Benny Parsonage, see if he can help us," said McDaid.

"He could still have been killed elsewhere and then transported to the river. Time of death?" Dreghorn asked Kivlichan. "That might give us some idea of how far the body could have drifted."

"Taking into account that the water will have cooled the body quicker than normal, I'd hazard a guess eight to twelve hours prior to discovery, but—" Kivlichan broke off, disappointed by his own vagueness.

"So, possibly between ten o'clock Sunday night and two o'clock Monday morning." Dreghorn scanned the post-mortem report without much optimism.

"Blood tests show that there were high levels of alcohol in his system," Kivlichan said.

"He was pie-eyed?"

"Inebriated, certainly." The doctor was silent for a moment. "It might not be related, but the bruising here"—The flesh on either side of the autopsy wound, from the armpits down to the groin, was a patchwork of purples and yellows—"concentrated around the ribs, the abdomen, the groin, and the kidneys. The patterns are about a week old, beginning to fade. He'd have been in a great deal of pain, urinating blood for a couple of days."

"But nothing on the face, the head? No visible marks?"

The doctor shook his head. Dreghorn and McDaid glanced at each other.

"Professional beating," McDaid mused. "Somebody gave him a right good kicking about a week ago, then came back to finish the job?"

"No guarantee it was the same person. What was used?"

"Can't be certain after this length of time," said Kivlichan, "but judging by the bruise pattern and the extent of the injuries, I'd say fists as opposed to a blunt instrument."

Dreghorn noted that the doctor seemed uncomfortable, disturbed, not a good sign in someone who'd just dissected a body without qualm.

"Another thing . . . the angle of the cut on the throat seems wrong. Unusual at least. It might be nothing, but—"

Something about it had been nagging Dreghorn as well. "Go on," he said.

"We were all in the war, we had training. The best position to inflict a wound like that"—he gestured at the gash, red and raw—"would be from behind. You'd creep up on the enemy, then clamp one hand over his mouth to stifle any cries . . ." He mimicked the action, making sure the detectives followed his reasoning. "And then you'd bring the knife in, curling your arm almost around his neck . . ." He sliced an invisible blade through the air above the corpse with enough violence to make McDaid step back involuntarily. "An assault from that position would result in the entry point of the wound starting around here." Kivlichan placed a finger below his earlobe.

"Wouldn't it depend on the heights of killer and victim?" Dreghorn exercised caution.

"Assuming there's not too much of a difference." Kivlichan kept his finger in place. "So, coming from behind, the way I've described, the cut would curve across the victim's throat"—the doctor drew his finger slowly across his throat as he spoke—"almost like a smile, a smirk, if you want to be particular."

"You paint such a pretty picture, doc."

Kivlichan acknowledged Dreghorn's sarcasm with a humorless smile. He moved closer to the corpse's head, following the line of the slit throat with his finger. "But if you look at this, the cut's straight across, which means the killer was probably standing in front of him." He stared at Dreghorn across the mortuary slab. "Closer than we are just now." Kivlichan reached out to draw an invisible blade across Dreghorn's throat. "Once. Twice. Three times, maybe. It's a deep cut."

"You're saying they were face to face?" McDaid shook his head as if to dispel the images in his mind. "But the blood, the killer must've been—"

"Drenched."

"So he watched." Dreghorn drew his eyes away from Geddes. "He cut his throat, then stood and watched him die."

14

If Detective Chief Inspector Monroe was unhappy about Dreg-horn's and McDaid's secondment to the Geddes investigation, he didn't show it. He'd held the position of head of CID for less than six months, promoted from another division when Sillitoe forced the previous DCI, a widely acknowledged blusterer who cruised along on the arrest records of his team, into retirement. Prior to Monroe's appointment, DI Strachan ran investigations as he saw fit and re-sented the fact that Monroe actually took a professional interest in proceedings. It was an open secret that Strachan disliked sharing his fiefdom and believed that he should have received the promotion, not Monroe.

On the first morning of the official investigation, Monroe ad-dressed the detectives and WPC Duncan, there for secretarial and administrative support and to aid with the questioning of female witnesses or suspects.

"By the nature of who he was, the investigation of Charles Geddes' murder is likely to attract undue press coverage, and pres-sure from the Corporation for a quick result."

"Always the same when it's one of their own," said Detective Constable Brian Harvie, who habitually stated the obvious with the gravity of a scientist announcing a major breakthrough. "Toss the rest of us into a pauper's grave, but when it's a toff that's been topped . . ."

"Cheers for that insight into the class struggle, Brian," Strachan said patronizingly.

"Regardless of social standing or outside pressure, I expect every crime to be investigated with the same dedication," Monroe continued. "To that end, Inspector Dreghorn and Sergeant McDaid from Special Crimes are being drafted in to help. Inspectors Strachan and Dreghorn will jointly lead the investigation. I'll remain in overall command."

A chorus of complaints: "What?" "Fuck that for a game of soldiers!" "No chance!"

Orr, his big arse flopped over the edge of a desk, couldn't hide his glee at the reaction. "A Tim in the Lodge?" he exclaimed, then nodded at WPC Duncan. "There'll be women detectives next!"

"Do a better job than you," Dreghorn heard her say. Her eyes were quick and bright, missing nothing. They briefly settled on Dreghorn, daring him to see something in her that the others were too ignorant or too mired in the trappings of a man's world to notice.

"Have a go if you want, hen." Orr shrugged. "Two sugars in mine first, though, eh?"

Monroe spoke over the din. "This is a direct order from Chief Constable Sillitoe."

"Spiffing idea, old bean," said a detective Dreghorn didn't know in a mocking English accent. "Absolutely top-hole."

"Daft big bastard," Harvie muttered. "Put a Sassenach in charge and look what happens. Hell in a handcart."

"You'll be on a charge, Harvie, if you don't show some respect." Monroe was becoming irate.

DS Lewis Tolliver rose slowly from behind his desk, his bald pate and hooked nose reminding Dreghorn of F. W. Murnau's *Nosferatu*. Tolliver didn't smoke, didn't drink, didn't swear, and probably didn't fornicate either, but no one could bear to ask about his private life to make sure. University educated, he was a Reader in the Church of

Scotland, and, to a man, the other detectives longed for him to leave and become a fully fledged minister so they wouldn't have to listen to his interminable lectures on morality. To him, police work was a calling from God, though not a calling that Roman Catholics, with their loose morals and wildfire breeding, were worthy of.

"Detective Chief Inspector Monroe," he said, drawing out the words. "I must protest. This *imposition*"—his eyes darted toward Dreghorn and McDaid—"is at best a slur on our ability to do our job, and at worst, a craven attempt to curry political favor."

"Hey, we're all polis here, aye?" Strachan spread his arms with affable authority. "Whether you hang to the right or the left, we're one big happy family. Let's work together to give Inspector Dreghorn the welcome he deserves." He gestured magnanimously at Dreghorn as he finished, mustache expanding to follow his sleekit smile.

Dreghorn said, "Happy days are here again, eh? Working with you lot of soor plooms isn't exactly the pinnacle of my life's ambition either. Tell the truth, I'm no' sure if it's a promotion or a demotion." That one rankled, which was his intention. "But we've got a job to do and it's the job that's important. If you don't agree, there's the door. Step on gaily, off you go."

He was silent for a moment. There were no changes in expression, no chinks in their armor, and no one moved. Dreghorn held up a folder. "Copies of the post-mortem report on Charles Geddes. Examine it closely. Any thoughts or observations—speak up. We're interested in every angle here."

WPC Duncan stepped forward instinctively, but Dreghorn thrust the folder toward Orr. "Pass these out, Gordon," he ordered.

Orr bristled, looked to Strachan for guidance, received none, so did as he was told, though he made a meal of it, handing out the documents with exaggerated politeness.

Dreghorn continued, "Geddes was found dead in the Clyde by Pagan's Shipyard shortly before six on Monday morning. We don't yet know where he was killed or where he went into the water, assuming it's the same place. Lockhart's Yard, Geddes' family business by marriage, is a short way down the water; we'll conduct a search in case that's the crime scene, but nothing suspicious has been reported by workers, so it's probably a long shot.

"Benny Parsonage analyzed the tides between estimated time of death and discovery. Within that period, he estimates that the furthest point Geddes could have entered the water would be Dumbarton, although it could have been far closer."

"A bloody big search area," Harvie pointed out. Not that it needed saying.

Strachan agreed. "And the glorious Scottish weather is not favorable to the preservation of forensic evidence."

"If he was killed outside," Dreghorn said, "there was little in the way of mud or countryside debris on his shoes or clothing. Dr. Kivlichan thinks it's more than likely that he met his death elsewhere and was transported to the river afterward."

"Could've been washed off," Orr said smugly, parking his backside back on the desk. "He did have a nice long bath in the Clyde."

Dreghorn ignored him. "It's crucial that we piece together Geddes' movements on the night of the murder and in the days leading up to it. His car was found in the Botanic Gardens Garage on Vinicombe Street, where he leased a space, apparently unused on the night of his death. That means he walked, took a taxi, or traveled by tram, so taxi firms and Corporation Tramways will need to be contacted. Geddes had also given the house staff the evening off, so they've no idea as to his actions that night. Whether this is of any significance, we don't know."

"Geddes was a bit of a ladies' man," Strachan piped up, "so he may have been entertaining and didn't want the staff running to his wife and telling tales on him."

"Either way," Dreghorn said, "interview his neighbors to see if any of them spoke to him that day, saw him receive visitors, or thought he'd been acting out of character. He ate what the surgeon describes as a light meal, but had copious amounts of alcohol in his system. We need to establish where and with whom he spent his final hours. Hopefully, Mrs. Geddes can tell us which clubs and bars her husband frequented."

DS Tolliver gripped the post-mortem report as if about to deliver a sermon. "Seems a rather sinful individual for a man of his standing."

"We're not here to judge, minister," said Dreghorn. "And if you check your bible, murder's a bigger sin than shagging, or so they used to tell me at school."

Tolliver took a deep breath, nursing his outrage. WPC Duncan bowed her head to conceal a smile.

Dreghorn waved his copy of the post-mortem report. "Geddes was a solicitor, so we need to examine the legality of whatever he was working on. Duncan, talk to his secretary."

Duncan's head popped back up in surprise, expecting the usual mundane admin tasks to be slid her way, not actual participation in the investigation. "Sir." She nodded keenly, enjoying the skeptical glances and disdainful mutterings of the male detectives.

"Get her to give you his client list and appointments book. Check for associations with known criminals. We'll also need company accounts and bank statements. I want to know the state of his business affairs." He turned his attention back to Strachan and the others. "The post-mortem showed that he received a severe beating a week or so prior to his murder. Whether the two are connected is something we have to work out. Ask around, apply a little pressure—or a lot—to your sources, see what you can dredge up."

There was silence among the detectives, but Dreghorn detected glimmers of interest in some of their faces, a desire to unravel the mystery, to get to the heart of the crime.

"We'll reconvene after Archie and me interview the Lockhart family. The victim's identity won't be released to the press until then. Anything you want to add, inspector?"

"That'll do, I suppose." Strachan's mustache was like a fat ginger slug on his upper lip, draining his features of all emotion. "For now." He let the comment hang in the air, then turned to his colleagues with a what-are-you-waiting-for look and started issuing commands. "Brian, supervise the search of Lockhart's Yard. Tolliver, you can preach to Geddes' neighbors . . ."

Dreghorn watched as Strachan delegated tasks. Finally, he placed a hand on Duncan's arm, spoke in soft avuncular tones too low for Dreghorn to overhear. The hand lingered for longer than Dreghorn thought proper, and she gave a quick glance in his direction as if to confirm it.

He felt McDaid step closer. "If that'd been a first night at the Empire," the big man said, "they'd have been throwing coins."

"You think it went that well?"

"I meant at your head."

The rest of the day had been mundane: fruitless inquiries about Charles Geddes and his affairs; a drive along the Clydeside to see if anything related to the murder caught their eye; intransigence bordering on hostility from their so-called colleagues in the Lodge; politely intimidating telephone calls from the Lockhart family's legal advisers stressing the need for discretion; and the compiling of official reports on Tommy Bryce's murder, with a trial date set for the following week.

The chill of the mortuary and Kivlichan's dark musings hung over them throughout their shift, so the welcome suggestion of a wee libation at the Old Empire was made in unison.

"The Yanks are going to have a right old shindig if Roosevelt gets in," McDaid said. He was referring to the upcoming American presi-

dential election, and candidate Franklin Delano Roosevelt's promise to repeal Prohibition, the alcohol ban that had been enforced
since 1920, if he won.

"Get them blootered legally and they might not notice the
world's falling apart." Dreghorn raised his glass, slurred jokingly,
"Depreshion? Whit depreshion?"

They swallowed their whiskies in one gulp and set the glasses
down loudly to alert the barman. Dreghorn sipped the accompanying half-pint of beer; McDaid swallowed most of his without even
noticing. A "hauf and a hauf"—a half-measure of whisky and a half-
pint of beer—was a Scottish staple, the drinks order of choice, if you
could stretch to it.

"Same again, please," McDaid said. Then he turned to Dreghorn.
"Patroling the streets, cracking heads, dishing out a few slaps around
the ear, at least you feel like you're doing something, y'know, but
this? Feels like you're flailing about in the dark, and you don't know
if what you're looking for is just out of reach, or if you're miles off."

"But you know it's there, don't you? So you keep going, because
some poor bastard's dead before their time and maybe you can make
it right. Except you can't, not really. Not for the dead, or the living
they leave behind. But you've got to try, because if you don't, all
that's left is that darkness you were talking about."

"Just as well we're happy drunks, eh?" McDaid nursed his drink
for a few seconds. "What Sillitoe said, about you being capable?
You've been in a murder squad before—in Shanghai?"

Dreghorn thought about Shanghai—his old mentor in the
police, who'd been like a father to him; the opium lord who'd put a
price on his head; the woman he thought he'd loved, and still wondered about even now. He'd been sent back in '29, just in time for the
Depression, only retaining the rank of Inspector because the Lord
Provost of Glasgow owed the Chairman of the Shanghai Municipal
Council a particularly delicate favor.

"Another time, eh, big man?" he said.

McDaid pretended he didn't see the flicker of sadness in his partner's eyes. "Fair enough. I should be going anyway. What I was saying about driving Mairi round the bend with my pipes was true. Half the time I get home I expect to find she's put a knife through them. Got to practice, though. Piping's a cut-throat business."

"So's everything, these days. Ask Charles Geddes, the man who should have had it all. One for the road?"

McDaid held up a hand in a stop signal, fixed his homburg onto his head at a rakish angle. Acquired when he graduated to plainclothes, he felt the hat granted him a statesmanlike air, unlike Dreghorn's fedora, favored headgear of gangsters in Hollywood flicks. He nodded at the empty glasses. "Stay fighting fit for tomorrow, eh? It's a jungle out there."

Dreghorn ordered another hauf and a hauf. He'd told McDaid that he wanted nothing to do with the Geddes murder or the Lockhart family. Seeing Isla again had made him wonder how true that claim was. And whether any interest now was strictly professional.

He surveyed the bar; a few nods, but no one spoke to him. Probably just as well. The old anger was stirring restlessly within him. The killer had watched Charles Geddes die. Dreghorn had seen people die as well, too many, but had only watched one death. Watched with horror and fascination, wracked with guilt about being unable to help because he couldn't move and thought he was dying himself.

"Fuckin' hell," a voice said somewhere behind him, and for a moment he thought he glimpsed Rab Hunter's frightened eighteen-year-old face reflected in the mirror behind the bar, hovering over his shoulder. He didn't look round, threw back another whisky, and the moment passed.

Eventually he stopped ordering beer and chased the whisky with more whisky.

15

WINTER 1913

It was the horses Jimmy kept telling his mother about after his first trip to Kelpie House, the Lockharts' country house on the banks of the Clyde. Not the vast grounds of the estate or the house itself, bigger than a block of tenements. He was hardly unfamiliar with horses; mounted police patrolled the streets on their Clydesdales, and Black Bob, the coalman's foul-tempered cart horse, had bitten him on the scalp once, tearing free a clump of hair and munching it like hay.

It wasn't the thoroughbreds in the stables that fired his imagination either, some of them highly favored racehorses. No, the horses that thrilled Jimmy weren't even flesh and blood. Two huge coal-black lead stallions reared up as you drove through the entrance gates. Their hind legs stood atop two great stone pillars, their front hooves touching to form an archway over the drive.

More breathtaking still was the grand fountain, centerpiece of the carriage sweep in front of the house. Water erupted like a geyser from the central plinth, and marble horses formed a circle around this churning, frothing column, like racehorses surging for the finish line. It was like something out of ancient Rome. Or Hollywood.

Many wealthy families, aristocrats, and industrialists financed their own stables of sportsmen—no time or respect for sportswomen—to participate in competitions around the country. These stables were sources of pride for patrons who enjoyed the reflected glory of their lads' sporting prowess, while smoking cigars, quaffing port, growing bloated with gout, and laying gentlemanly wagers with their rivals.

One perk of Sir Iain's stable was attending training camps at Kelpie House. Jimmy sat in the back of the rickety old tarpaulin-covered lorry, squeezed in among Sir Iain's other athletes—boxers, runners, swimmers, gymnasts. Bums numbed by the wooden bench, they bounced along the bone-shaking coast road, through Clydebank and Old Kilpatrick, turning off after Dumbarton to Sir Iain's estate. Jimmy had bagged a seat at the rear of the truck, and peered out at Glasgow as it receded into the distance, and at the Clyde which seemed to go on forever, teeming with tugs, steamers, dredgers, and ferries.

He leaped out excitedly, kitbag over his shoulder, as the truck scrunched to a halt, and turned in a slow circle, taking everything in. Some of the others had been there before and shrugged the sights off, laughing at him as if he was some teuchter arrived from the wilds.

Kelpie House was the kind of structure Jimmy visualized when he read Robert Louis Stevenson or Walter Scott; a castle, he'd have called it, full of potential for intrigue, romance, and adventure.

Not that they were staying in the big house—a bothy with dormitory-style bunks had been renovated for their use, and a barn as a well-equipped gymnasium. Sir Iain and his son Rory, two years older than Jimmy, had, however, descended the grand front steps to greet them.

Where bosses were concerned, the art of speaking only when you're spoken to was a working-class caution Jimmy hadn't quite mastered. He started to comment on the horses in the fountain, but Rory interrupted. "They're not horses, they're kelpies. That's where the house gets its name from."

Jimmy had no idea what he was talking about, but nodded blankly. To spare his embarrassment, Sir Iain said, "Kelpie isn't a common term, Rory."

"Kelpies are mythical water-spirits that haunt the rivers and lochs of Scotland, and prey upon humans," Rory explained. "They take the form of a beautiful black horse that seems so tame no one can resist trying to ride it. But once you climb on its back, it'll plunge back into the water, drown you, and devour you, spitting your bones back out onto the bank."

Jimmy glanced at the horses in the fountain. "Nice one," he said dubiously.

"Some people even claim that kelpies can take human form—a handsome man or beautiful woman, naked in the water, tempting you to join them for what would be the last dip you ever had."

Gravel scrunched under Sir Iain's foot as he stepped down beside Jimmy. "What do you say to that, young Dreghorn?" he asked.

Jimmy realized he'd been holding his breath. "Glad I forgot my swimming trunks."

Sir Iain laughed, slapped him on the back like a black-sheep uncle. "All nonsense, of course, but a wonderful story to terrify guests with." He pointed toward the rear of the house. "As for swimming, you'll have no time for such larks. Once the coaches put you through your paces, you'll be so exhausted you'd sink like a stone."

He wasn't exaggerating. The fitness regime was punishing, the ex-military coaches, Captain Ross and Sergeant Robertson, relentless in their quest to push the athletes to their physical and mental limits.

They were woken at six, warmed up with stretches and resistance exercises, and then sent on a six-mile run, with intermittent sprints that had their lungs burning. It was late December, but they were lucky with the weather—bright and cold and crisp, with frosted grass crunching under their feet.

Jimmy loved it. Whether it was the sense of freedom he derived from being outside the city or the great gulps of fresh air that energized him, he felt as though he could run forever. He overtook other runners, ducking under branches as they weaved through forest paths. They eventually broke the cover of the trees, emerging onto a rocky shoreline, the shingle shifting treacherously, the water lapping close to their feet. Jimmy kept a lookout for sinister equine shapes under the surface.

The biggest breakfast he'd ever eaten—bacon, eggs, sausage, beans, fried tomatoes, clootie dumplings, tea, and toast—was dished up in the servants' hall. Afterward, bellies bursting, they had an hour to wander the estate before the real training started.

Jimmy slipped away, smoked a fly cigarette, a habit it was hard to avoid in the yards, and walked around Kelpie House, marveling at its elaborate grandeur.

Piano music drifted from somewhere inside, a phonogram, he presumed at first, but then he realized the notes were too clear. He stepped off the gravel path onto the grass verge so he wouldn't be heard, and risked a keek through the window.

A slim schoolmarmish woman was playing a piano with intense concentration, occasionally barking instructions, not unlike Sir Iain's coaches. Furniture had been shifted in the huge room, a rug rolled back to clear a space on the polished parquet floor.

A girl danced in front of the piano, her movements graceful and elegant, otherworldly almost. Ballet. He'd seen pictures of ballerinas in a book once, so figured that's what it was. The girl was about his age, maybe slightly younger, her dark hair pulled back from her face. Beautiful, he thought. She was dressed in a black leotard and tights that followed the lines of her small breasts and strong slim thighs, as she rose onto her toes and pirouetted. He felt uncomfortable about watching, but couldn't take his eyes off her.

The pianist suddenly crashed her fingers onto the keys, a crescendo of discordant notes. She stood up, gesturing angrily, criticizing the girl's attitude or technique. The girl didn't seem in the slightest bit bothered, her insouciance making her even more attractive.

The woman rolled her eyes, tapped her hand on the piano. The girl sauntered over in response, lifted one leg languorously, placing her heel on the piano lid. She straightened the leg and stretched slowly over it, touching her forehead to her knee. She stayed like that while the dance teacher continued to lecture her. She was so still that Jimmy almost thought she had fallen asleep, until she raised her head a fraction, looked right at him as if they shared a naughty secret, and winked.

16

The horses were still there, but it seemed to Dreghorn now that, instead of rearing up to salute visitors, they intended to crush the skulls of unwelcome guests. Maybe it was his view of the world that had changed.

McDaid leaned over the steering wheel to examine the sculptures as they drove under them. "A wee bit ostentatious, do you not think?"

"If it was me," Dreghorn said, spreading his hands like an artist describing a canvas, "I'd have had scuddy women wrestling."

"Much more tasteful. And they say the aristocracy look down upon the *nouveaux riches*. Just as well you're skint."

They continued along the drive, the car buffeted by gale-force winds, dark clouds scudding across the sky, until they came to the crest of a hill.

"In the name of the wee man," McDaid exclaimed, 'is that what they call a house?"

Kelpie House was primarily Tudor Gothic and Jacobean in style, with so many turrets and towers that you'd think it had ambitions to be a castle rather than a simple grand baronial mansion. The grounds had been expertly landscaped to conceal its full grandeur until the last possible moment.

Years ago, after his first visit, Dreghorn had read about the history of the estate at the library. "'Built in 1868 for Alexander Aitkin, a Glasgow wine and spirits dealer, who obviously had more money than sense,'" he recited. "'The locals called it Whisky Castle—poor taste, considering he eventually drank himself to death. The Lockharts have owned it since 1901.'"

McDaid circled the fountain and drew to a halt. The water was turned off and the horses had been carelessly maintained in recent years. The marble had taken on a gray, dirty pallor and the fine detail of their musculature was fading, worn away by the unforgiving Scottish weather. The door opened as they mounted the grand entrance steps. A young footman ushered them into a large hall, where a sour-faced butler cut Dreghorn off mid-introduction; they were expected. He gestured for the footman to take their hats and overcoats as if they were soiled rags.

Electric lighting had been fitted, but did little to pierce the gloom, as if Kelpie House was doing its best to resist progress. Framed by scagliola Corinthian columns, a vast hardwood staircase faced the entrance vestibule, drawing the eye to arched stained-glass windows on the landing that depicted scenes from Celtic mythology and were rumored to be the largest in any private house in Britain. The walls were hung with portraits, family presumably, that looked down upon them with as much disdain as the butler. Somewhere, faintly, Dreghorn could hear jazz music being played on a gramophone and wondered if it was Isla.

They were led into a library that was about the size of the municipal swimming pool Dreghorn had visited as a child. Bookshelves lined the walls, the books stacked so neatly that a spirit level might have been employed. A fire blazed in the hearth, sofas and a low table around it.

"The family will be with you shortly," the butler informed them, backing out of the room like an undertaker leaving clients with a deceased relative.

McDaid warmed his backside by the hearth. "If we had a fire this big in my house, we'd need to call the fire brigade. You've hobnobbed here before?"

"Servants' quarters only."

McDaid skipped over to an antique cabinet filled with crystal glasses. A decanter of amber liquid sat on a silver tray. The crystal chinked delicately as he lifted the stopper, sniffed and sighed, intoxicated by the aroma.

"The water of life," he said. "And this, to my not-inexperienced nose, is the best of—"

The doors opened with an urgency that would have appalled the butler's sense of decorum. McDaid jumped as Isla Lockhart strode into the library, doing everything he could to look innocent, short of putting his hands in his pockets and whistling a jaunty tune. She gave him a dazzling smile. "Good afternoon." She didn't wait for an answer, her expression growing colder as she reached Dreghorn. "First things first," she said. "I didn't ask for you. Not this time."

Before Dreghorn could respond, his mind flitting between sarcasm and respect, a voice bellowed with parade-ground authority, "*Attention!*"

Dreghorn caught himself before instinct kicked in, but in the corner of his eye he saw McDaid spring bolt upright. Years since they'd left the military, but it was all still there, under the surface. The man who'd spoken strolled into the library, smiled, and raised his hands apologetically. "Sorry, couldn't resist."

It was rumored that Rory Lockhart had taken Hollywood screen tests while in America, and he certainly had the looks for a romantic lead. At the front, the press had loved Captain Lockhart—witty, charming, self-deprecating, never failing to praise the courage of his men above his own, and, of increasing importance, wonderfully photogenic. Out in the darkness of no-man's-land, on trench raids that became long dark nights of the soul, Dreghorn had witnessed a less gentlemanly side to the captain. In truth, Hollywood would have bored Rory. He'd already lived a more exciting life than any actor, and Dreghorn couldn't imagine him submitting to some contract that gave the studio the power to tell him what he could and couldn't do.

Rory was almost as tall as McDaid, but slimmer, though he had filled out from the twenty-year-old officer who'd commanded men on the Somme. In contrast to his sister's Titian red, his hair was blond, slicked into a neat side parting. "You look as though you're still fighting the war, sergeant," he laughed.

Dreghorn smiled wearily. His right eye was bruised, his lower lip split from the fight in Ally Reid's flat. A light bandage, compliments of Mrs. Pettigrew, covered his right hand, burnt by a combination of boiling soup and steaming kettle.

"In some ways, I am," he said.

"The war on crime," McDaid proclaimed, trying too hard and sounding comically pompous.

Rory nodded as if impressed, glanced back at Dreghorn. "You should come and work for me. It might not be much safer, but it'd be a lot more fun."

"Doing what?"

"I don't know. Same as you did in the war?"

"That sort of thing would get a fellow arrested in peacetime."

"Oh, we'd soon buy our way out of that. You policemen love a good bribe." Rory raised his hands toward McDaid again. "Only joking! Dreghorn and I go back a long way, Officer . . . ?"

"Detective Sergeant McDaid," Dreghorn introduced his partner.

Rory shook the big man's hand. "Good to meet you. Lockhart, Rory Lockhart, the deceased's brother-in-law. McDaid?" A spark of recognition. "Archibald McDaid? Bonnie Archie McDaid? Bronze medal, freestyle wrestling, Paris Olympics 1924?"

Compliments about past glories never failed to make McDaid

suck in his belly and puff out his chest. "Aye, sir, that's me. How did you know?"

"How could I not know?" Rory slapped McDaid manfully on the back. "I'm something of a sports fanatic. It runs in the family. And you should've had the silver at least. You beat the Estonian fair and square."

"It's been said before."

Isla indulged their camaraderie with bemusement. Sitting by the fireside, she crossed one slim leg over the other, her dress riding up slightly, her cream stockings taking on the shimmering hue of the fire. Not that Dreghorn was taking any notice.

She smiled sweetly. "Please help yourself."

McDaid realized that he was still holding the stopper of the decanter. Flustered, he rushed to replace it, then stood to attention again. "Thank you, ma'am. Not on duty."

"In that case, would you be a darling and pour me one? Just a dash of water."

McDaid murmured an awkward, "Of course," and reached for a glass.

"Mind pouring one for me, while you're there?" Rory asked. "A large one."

Isla gestured for Dreghorn to sit opposite her. "What about you, inspector? Are you being dutiful too? Some tea, then?"

Dreghorn told her that would be fine, his responses growing curter, pushing them toward the reason for their visit. Sensing his intention, she rang for the butler, whom she addressed as Naseby, and asked him to bring tea.

McDaid handed Isla her whisky. "I'm sorry for your loss, Mrs. Geddes," he said, and sat beside Dreghorn, sinking deeper into the cushions than he expected.

She nodded solemnly, sipped the drink, gave McDaid the warmest of smiles. "Perfect!"

"When did you get back, sir?" Dreghorn asked Rory.

"Arrived at the Royal Clyde Yacht Club last night." Rory sipped his own whisky, leaning an elbow against the chimneypiece. "Sailed into a storm the moment we left New York and it kept us company for the entire journey. Took such a battering that we had to stop at the Royal Ulster Yacht Club in bloody Bangor, of all places for a few days of repairs. Bit of a nightmare all round, actually. Next time, I'm taking the *Queen Mary*. At least then you can indulge in the trappings of civilization."

A low, deep rumble sounded, alarming the detectives. Dreghorn could have sworn the room shook. Rory laughed. "Don't worry; it's not the Boche. We're not back at war. Yet."

"They're doing some exploratory blasting at Dumbuck Hill," Isla explained. "We're looking into the possibility of opening a quarrying operation there."

"I intended to stroll over and watch the big bang, but—" Rory's eyes drifted toward the door.

Isla stood up. "Daddy," she said, an edge to her voice.

Even though Isla had warned him, Dreghorn was shocked by the sight of the man being wheeled toward him. The tall, stern figure from his youth had been twisted into a gnarled husk. His entire body seemed tensed in fury, as if the man he'd once been was trying to break free of the creature he'd become. Sir Iain Lockhart's eyes focused on Dreghorn, but it was difficult to discern any recognition in them. Dreghorn was reminded of soldiers he'd seen wounded in action, maimed by bomb and bullet, limbs missing, faces destroyed and rebuilt into scarred semblances of the men they once were. Whatever bitterness he'd felt toward the old man evaporated immediately.

A nurse who took care not to meet anyone's eyes wheeled Sir Iain through the library to the end of the table. A folding tray had been fitted to the chair, a notepad resting upon it. A child's crayon was gripped in the old man's fist like a dagger.

Isla nodded for the nurse to leave and crouched beside her father. "It's James Dreghorn," she said, her enunciation exaggerated to a patronizing degree. "He's with the police now, here to talk to us about Charles."

"Good to see you again, sir," said Dreghorn. "Sorry it's under such difficult circumstances."

Sir Iain's eyes remained locked on Dreghorn. His right hand moved, the crayon carving into the paper, the effort tremendous. The windows rattled as the wind outside strengthened, and rain spattered the glass. It seemed to take forever, but eventually Sir Iain relaxed, the point of the crayon slipping off the notepad.

Isla tore off the top sheet, read the message, and handed it to Dreghorn. A child's scrawl, jagged and spiky: *NO PITY.*

Dreghorn met Sir Iain's unwavering gaze. "No, sir. Of course not."

They returned to their seats, and Dreghorn introduced McDaid, eliciting a cursory glance from Sir Iain. A maid arrived with teapot, cups and saucers, and a plate of dainty cakes on a tray. The cakes seemed an odd accompaniment to murder as a topic of conversation, though McDaid eyed them with interest.

Dreghorn said, "Charles Geddes was murdered on the night of the second, most likely between the hours of ten and midnight. Cause of death was a severe wound to the throat, delivered by a blade of some description."

Isla poured tea while he spoke. The detectives pretended not to notice the trembling in her hands.

"Was he robbed?" Rory was pouring himself another generous whisky.

"Not as far as we can tell," McDaid said. "His wallet was intact, and there was an expensive pocket watch still on his person."

Dreghorn continued, "His body was found floating in the Clyde and fished out at Pagan's Yard, but Lockhart's isn't far upriver. We'll have to search the premises in case that's where the attack occurred."

"Charles had nothing to do with the family business," Rory said. "No connection whatsoever."

"No, but he would have had access to the yards."

"Not officially."

"Unofficially, then. I'm not saying that's what happened, but the locations are too close to discount it. It's a murder investigation—we wouldn't be doing our jobs if we didn't examine every possibility."

"I'll arrange authorization."

McDaid reached for his tea, the tiny china cup like a thimble in his hand. The island lilt made his voice soft, sympathetic. "Mrs. Geddes, would you by any chance know your husband's whereabouts or movements on the night of the second of October?"

"Not in the marital bed, obviously." Rory raised an eyebrow at his sister, sipped whisky.

Isla smiled at him without humor. "Please venture forth and fuck yourself, Rory."

A sharp sound cut the air as Sir Iain pressed his crayon into the tray in rage, snapping it. McDaid, aghast, sipped tea tentatively, trying not to slurp.

"Excuse me, I apologize for my foul tongue," said Isla, more sarcastic than sincere. "My husband and I had been living apart for some months. Nothing sinister, just one of those things that happen from time to time. Between that and my father's condition, it's been something of a strain"—a barbed glance at Rory—"on those of us who were here. So, no, I have absolutely no idea where he was or what he was doing."

"He was living in Glasgow, while you were staying here?" asked Dreghorn.

"Myself and my daughter, yes."

"We'll need to search your townhouse and his place of work."

"I'll inform the staff. I intend to return there over the next few days anyway."

"I wouldn't advise it, ma'am. No keys were found on your husband's body—house, office, whatever. We have to assume the murderer took them. If the killer's someone with a grudge against the family, then you'll be safer at Kelpie House. For now, at least."

She had poured tea but reached for her whisky instead. "Thank you, inspector. I'll take it under consideration."

"For the record," Dreghorn said to the Lockhart family, "I have to ask your own whereabouts that night."

Sir Iain snorted as if finding the question ridiculous.

"Easy." Rory eyed his glass, considering a refill. "I was in the middle of the Atlantic, either hanging on for dear life on the crest of a wave or heaving up the contents of my stomach over the side. You can check the ship's log or, if necessary, speak to the crew."

"Here," Isla said, "having a cozy night in with Daddy."

"Can anyone corroborate that?" McDaid placed his teacup on the table.

"Twenty-one household staff; not all on duty, but a good few."

"Of course." McDaid seemed to be having trouble with his cup. He sat back, nodding solemnly, and cradled the empty cup in his lap.

Drawing his eyes off his partner, Dreghorn asked, "Did your husband have any enemies, Mrs. Geddes?"

"Not that I know of. Certainly none that would want to kill him."

"You're sure? A week or so before his death, Mr. Geddes was the victim of a severe assault. The marks were still visible. Two attacks, approximately within a week of each other, one of which killed him, suggests a pattern. It could be the same culprit, but perhaps not. Either way, it would seem Mr. Geddes' actions caused at least one person to view him with a less-than-friendly eye. Did he seem worried about anything? Problems at work? A legal dispute? An employee with a grudge?"

Isla's eyes were bright, tears reflecting the firelight. She shook her head, blinked them away.

"Had he been acting oddly recently, developed any new habits, started deviating from his usual behavior?"

"Any contact we had was purely for the sake of our daughter. He lived his life. I lived mine."

"But you've no idea how exactly he was living that life?"

Before Isla could respond, Sir Iain shuddered, grasping for another crayon. He was faster this time, but Isla made no effort to retrieve the note when he had finished. It was Dreghorn who tore it free.

The same angry scrawl: *DRINK*.

Dreghorn passed the note to McDaid. "I assume you don't mean Iron Brew," he said.

Lockhart, ignoring him, was already writing furiously again. *GAMBLER*.

He immediately began scrawling once more. Isla rolled her eyes in exasperation, but this time snatched the top sheet almost before her father had finished. *WHORES*.

"My father didn't hold Charles in high regard," she said drily.

The crayon moved again, the effort clearly taking its toll on the old man. *NOT WORTHY*.

"He's the father of your only grandchild"—Isla gave Rory a disdainful glance—"that we know of."

The crayon was painfully slow this time. *BETTER OFF NOW*.

"Really?" She looked accusingly at her father and brother. "Well, perhaps one of you would like to tell Catriona that the reason she can't see her daddy is because he's had his throat cut. But not to worry, he was a drunk, a gambler, and a whoremonger. She's far better off without him."

"You know that's not what we mean, Isla," Rory said.

Dreghorn spread the notes across the table like a poker player revealing his hand. "If we could stick to the facts," he said. "There was a high amount of alcohol in his system. Did Mr. Geddes have a drink problem?"

"There's a depression on—half the world's got a drink problem," Isla said. "Charles lived as if it was still the Roaring Twenties. I don't know if he genuinely didn't notice the roar had dropped to a whimper or just ignored it."

"Could you give us a list of drinking establishments he favored, clubs he belonged to?"

"The Piccadilly Club, the Palais, the Locarno, probably others I'm not aware of. Not that I'm being critical. At one point, before Catriona was born, I was even more of a socialite than him."

Dreghorn touched a finger to WHORES, shifted it slightly on the table.

"I have suspected him of seeing other women over the years. Rumors and stories would sometimes reach me, and there are signs, of course. Whether they were ladies of a professional persuasion or casual affairs, I couldn't say."

"Any names?"

"Is it relevant?"

"Cuckolded husbands certainly have a motive for murder," McDaid replied.

Dreghorn met Isla's eyes. "So would a woman whose husband had been unfaithful."

She raised an eyebrow, humoring him. "I think I'm rather beyond that sort of thing. Perhaps I should've felt more insulted, but I was content with our living arrangements. Our marriage was over. With hindsight, it was a mistake. I needed Charles, or someone like him, at a certain point in my life, not for an entire lifetime. I'm sure he sensed the change in me. Not fair on either of us, really. Or Catriona.

But as long as he didn't embarrass or humiliate us, I was happy to avoid the so-called scandal of a divorce."

"What about the gambling?"

She steeled herself, the subject uncomfortable. "A few years ago, not long after Catriona was born, a man approached me outside our house in Glasgow. He wasn't threatening, just asked after Charles's health, remarked on what a beautiful house we had. He asked me, very politely, to tell Charles that he'd called, but when I asked for his name, he simply walked away as if he hadn't heard.

"I told Charles that evening. He broke down, confessed that he'd run up gambling debts—the man was a bookmaker to whom he owed money. He couldn't pay and the man was applying pressure, threatening to hurt him and by extension, I suppose, Catriona and me. I made him promise that it would never happen again and agreed to pay. A substantial sum; you almost had to admire his sense of abandon."

Dreghorn asked, "What was the bookie's name?"

"Charles refused to say. He tried to convince me that it would be safer that way. And anyway it was all over. He was never going to bet again."

"Did he keep his promise?"

"A few months later, he came back with the same story, no tears this time. I even wondered if it was simply a story concocted to relieve me of money. This time, I involved my father. In return for paying off the debts, Daddy insisted Charles give up any future claim to our joint assets—property, shares, everything. A solicitor drew up a contract. Signed and sealed. A hard bargain, perhaps, but you have to protect yourself. And I had Catriona to think of."

Sir Iain's eyes warned he was still capable of driving a hard bargain.

"I arranged for him to have a generous monthly allowance in addition to whatever income his practice gave him, and heard no more about his gambling habits. I'm not naive enough to imagine he stopped entirely, but I hope he exercised a little more caution."

Dreghorn flipped his notebook shut with a snap. "I think that'll do for now. We'll be in touch if there's anything else. Likewise, if you think of something relevant, please don't hesitate."

He placed a couple of business cards on top of Sir Iain's accusatory notes as he stood up. The old man cocked his head at Dreghorn as if seeing him for the first time. Isla smiled and nodded, but didn't rise from her chair. Rory indicated that he'd see them out. As they entered the hallway, the footman appeared as if alerted by some servile sixth sense, carrying the detectives' coats and hats.

Dreghorn glanced back into the library. The warm glow of the fire washed over Isla and her father, but all he could sense was the chill between them as they sat in silence.

"The gambling didn't stop," said Rory. "My father bailed Geddes out on two more occasions at least—considerable sums. We corresponded regularly while I was in the States, so I know more than Isla thinks. Frankly, I'm surprised Daddy indulged him, but I suppose he was thinking of Isla and Catriona. Geddes tried again after the stroke, same story. Perhaps having been so close to death changed his attitude, but this time my father refused to pay. In fairly blunt terms. That was the last time Geddes set foot in Kelpie House."

They stopped at the entrance. A slurry of rain flowed down the stained-glass windows.

"Isla played down the womanizing as well," Rory continued. "I didn't say anything to spare her embarrassment, but it was a compulsion. Geddes was an acquaintance of mine—not a friend, but someone in the circle at a certain point. I even used him as a solicitor for a couple of property investments. Isla first met him at a leaving do of mine, before I went off on some adventure or other. They announced their engagement just before I got back. Rather blame myself for the whole affair."

He extended a hand toward McDaid, but the big man, backing toward the door, tipped his hat instead. Rory turned to Dreghorn. "We should meet, talk about the good old days."

"Maybe when the investigation's concluded, sir."

"Of course." Rory offered Dreghorn his hand. "You'll keep us informed of any progress?"

Dreghorn's grip was firm. "I don't report to you any more, captain. I'm my own man these days."

Rory laughed. "You always were, inspector. That's why I asked for you."

"No' putting your coat on?"

They were walking down the front steps of Kelpie House, sheltered by the balcony above. Dreghorn was buttoning his coat; McDaid had his over his arm, as if overdressed for a summer's day.

"You're all right," McDaid said. "It was gey stuffy in there. I fancy a wee bit of fresh air."

Sheets of rain sliced across the grounds ahead of them like some elemental guillotine, the wind shuddering their car. McDaid removed the keys from his pocket. "Do you mind driving, sir?"

The deference of the big man's tone made Dreghorn suspicious. He snatched the keys and charged into the downpour, clamping his hat onto his head. He slammed the door shut, thought about starting up and forcing McDaid to run after him for a bit, but leaned over and unlocked the passenger door.

McDaid clambered in, shaking off water like a dog after a bath. "I'm droukit!" he exclaimed, piling his coat on his lap.

Dreghorn started the car, switched on the windshield wipers, which made little headway, Kelpie House blurring in and out of focus. "What did you make of that?" he asked.

"Not a lot to go on. You think they're hiding something?"

"Probably just being cautious. They might not be too bothered about us finding the killer in case it drops them in the middle of a big juicy scandal."

"Wouldn't want to get on the wrong side of old man Lockhart—he could do you some harm, if he'd a mind to."

"Like what—run you over in his wheelchair?"

McDaid became serious. "A man like that? Money no object? Some bastard treating his daughter like shite? A word in the right ear and there's no telling what he could arrange. You know the Lockharts paid the Billy Boys to act as strike-breakers during Red Clydeside?"

"Probably Rory. He was Billy Hunter's captain for a good chunk of the war."

"As well as yours? And I thought I was the one who came from a small town . . ."

Dreghorn could contain his curiosity no longer. "Why didn't you want to drive? And why did you avoid shaking hands with Rory?"

" 'Cos he'd have thought I was trying to steal the family silver!" McDaid pulled his hand out from under his coat. The handle of the teacup he'd been drinking from was stuck fast around his index finger. "It's stuck. I can't get it off. I've been trying like mad."

"Don't be daft." Dreghorn wrenched the cup.

"Whoa! What're you trying to do? Take my finger off?"

"We might have to. It's probably worth a bob or two—more than your finger, anyway. Why didn't you say something?"

"Aye, right. Oh, hello, Mrs. Geddes, before we track down your husband's murderer, could you maybe teach me how to use a cup and saucer properly? We'd have looked like the bloody Keystone Cops!" McDaid tried to pull free of Dreghorn's grip. "They'll get it back. When I get home, Mairi'll ease it off with some butter or lard. Then I can post it to them or something."

Dreghorn's face became as grave as a hangman's. He produced his handcuffs and deftly snapped one of the manacles around

McDaid's wrist. "Donald Archibald McDaid, I arrest you for theft," he said, locking the other handcuff around the steering wheel. Then he shifted into gear, tried to keep a straight face as he drove off. "It's the Bar-L for you, sergeant. No one's above the law, not even the Untouchables."

Flabbergasted, his mouth opening and closing, McDaid rattled the cuffs against the wheel, the teacup tinkling on the chain. "We'll see how untouchable you are, if you don't get these cuffs off me . . ."

17

"It's all about the wider picture. Some people think they see every-thing, but usually they're full of shite and can't see the forest for the trees. Other people are just dunderheids and don't see anything at all, or only focus on one thing at a time—usually the wrong thing. The real trick, Archie—"

"Sergeant McDaid to you, wee man." McDaid resisted the urge to look over his shoulder. The wee man's left eye stared McDaid straight in the face with a sincerity he didn't believe for a moment. The right was skew-whiff in the extreme, peering behind the detective as if watching someone creep up on him. Crooked was the word that sprang to mind whenever he met Bosseye. Crooked in one eye and crooked by nature, so incorrigibly crooked that you could see him constantly calculating the odds to work out exactly what he could get away with.

Bosseye accepted the reprimand with a grateful smile. "The real trick, *sergeant,* is to see everything, but let them think you see noth-ing." He tapped a finger conspiratorially against his temple, as if at-tempting to knock the wayward pupil back into place. "You don't miss much either. That's why, of all the polis in town, the ones I like to work with are you and Inspector Dreghorn."

"It was either that or the jail, Bosseye."

"True, but you were always the odds-on favorite. How can I help?

Unless you're here for a fly flutter behind the inspector's back? If you're after tips, I've got a couple of stoaters."

"And I've got a couple I could give you." McDaid stepped closer, accentuating the size difference between them, a battleship looming over a dinghy.

"Something tells me I might not like them." Bosseye did the eye trick again, but McDaid's glare didn't waver. He knew fine well that many an officer had glanced off to follow Bosseye's squint, while the bookmaker bombed it away down one of his many escape routes.

Despite murmurings about legalization from a government seeking extra tax revenue, gambling remained illegal apart from licensed bookmakers at racecourses. Placing a bet, let alone accepting one, was a criminal act, which was why most bookies remained mobile, frequently switching "offices" so that only their runners knew their whereabouts on any given day. Bosseye's office for the day was a tenement backcourt in Florence Street. Its cobbles were dark with mud and spilled ash; flies buzzed around the overflowing midden. An optimistic wifie had hung out washing to dry in a brief gap between the rainclouds scudding past overhead, and sheets, shirts, and underwear fluttered blindingly white against the dark walls.

Hamish "Bosseye" Balfour was the most elusive street bookie in Glasgow, the crafty spider at the center of a web of runners who ferried punters' bets to him from all across the city. These runners, unemployed and eager to earn a bob or two, would hang around pubs and street corners, taking instructions. The gamblers would disguise their identities with colorful pseudonyms; if the police did get hold of a bookie's betting slips, they were hardly likely to issue arrest warrants for Baldy Bain, Big Bahookie, or Fanny Magnet.

Bosseye was the perceptive gambler's bookie of choice, due to his prodigious memory, remarkable head for figures, sociable nature, and reputation for honesty, albeit in a dishonest profession. He rarely resorted to the tactics of menace that were an undercurrent to many bookie operations and resisted the temptation to become a moneylender. If pressed, even McDaid would admit that Bosseye was difficult to dislike—especially in comparison to the rest of Glasgow's underworld.

"Charles Geddes," McDaid stated. "Know him?"

"Shipbuilding Geddes? Never had the pleasure. Didn't they just dredge the poor bastard out the Clyde?"

"How do you know that? The details haven't been released yet."

"I see and hear things that nobody else sees or hears, sergeant. That's why you like me."

"Tolerate you. We heard a rumor that Geddes had a gambling habit, racked up major debts."

"And you think he came here? Oh, aye, we get all the bigwigs round here. We've got Winston Churchill, Harry Lauder, and Greta Garbo queueing up around the corner, waiting for us to roll out the roulette table. But Geddes?" Bosseye dropped the sarcasm. "A wee bit out of my league."

"Goes without saying, but you see things that nobody else sees, hear things that nobody else hears. So, I'm sure you can find out who he was in hock to."

"You think some bookie killed him? Doesn't make sense; a live punter's better than a dead one, especially if said punter is plugged into big money like the Lockhart family." Bosseye walked and talked, weaving among the clothes flapping on the washing line. "No offense to my customers, but there are people and places that cater for a better class of gambler—and they won't be jumping for joy if they catch somebody sniffing around their business. No' everybody's as nice as me."

McDaid swept aside a pair of bloomers, looked down on Bosseye with mocking sympathy. "If any of the big boys call you names, pop into the station and tell your Uncle Archie about it. Just make sure you've got the information I'm after."

"If I'm ever seen with you, it'll be me getting pulled out the Clyde. A polis station's the last place I'd be safe, with all the bribes that bounce about this town."

McDaid clasped a hand to his heart as if in shock. "Are you saying our fair city's police force might be corrupt?"

"From top to flaming bottom. I'm amazed they haven't wangled some way of getting rid of you and Dreghorn yet." Bosseye checked his pocket watch. "Do you mind? The eleven o'clock at Ayr's due to start and I'm expecting a last-minute rush."

McDaid raised a fist thoughtfully. "Want a wee jab to make it look like I've been interrogating you? It'll no' hurt much. Promise."

"Very kind of you, but no thanks, not today."

"Just trying to be of help, Bosseye." McDaid tipped his hat as he turned to leave.

The bookie let him take a few steps, then called out, "Hey, Archie, most of the boys just call me Boss these days. For short, you know. You can do the same if you want."

Even Bosseye would have refused to give odds on how succinct McDaid's response would be.

"That'll be the fuckin' day."

18

Turning off Kilmacolm Road, Dreghorn followed the narrow winding road through farmland, crossed over the River Gryffe, then turned onto Faith Street, the main thoroughfare. He passed Love Crescent and Hope Gardens, before turning onto Peace Terrace.

Trinity Village wore its heart on its sleeve. By the time Dreghorn drew to a halt he felt morally and spiritually deficient, all the old Catholic guilt stirring.

Trinity had been designed more along the lines of a traditional English village than the pragmatic Scottish norm. Here, deep in the Renfrewshire countryside, grand houses nestled within parkland and gardens. Untouched by the blackening pollution of the city, the sandstone walls retained their original golden hue. The fresh air was also something of a shock to the system and Dreghorn immediately lit a Capstan on stepping out of the car.

Two chauffeur-driven vehicles that had been on the road ahead of him were now parked outside a large building inexplicably constructed along the lines of a French chateau. The other visitors emerged from their vehicles, the men portly in hand-tailored suits, the women more attractive in elegant dress suits, cloche hats, and fur stoles. They reeked of wealth, but Dreghorn figured them for industrialists, not old money.

"Morning," he said, tipping his hat to the ladies. "Wonderful place, isn't it?"

The nearest woman's brow furrowed with compassion. "Wonderful, yes. Such a worthy cause."

"The noblest," Dreghorn gestured at a couple of toddlers playing in one of the gardens. "They are the future after all."

"With the proper guidance." The woman's companion seemed less altruistic. "A firm hand, that's what's needed—boy or girl, man or woman." His mustache quivered and Dreghorn took an instant dislike to him.

"Good morning!" A short, bottom-heavy man in a tweed suit had emerged from the hall and was walking toward them, accompanied by a tall rake of a woman whose severely pinned curly hair reminded Dreghorn of an overly coiffed poodle. "For those of you who haven't met me already, I'm Alasdair Dalrymple, Director of the Trinity Institute, the charitable body that runs the village, and our other operations throughout Scotland. A pleasure to have you here."

Dalrymple shook hands with each of them in turn, smiling obsequiously. He frowned as Dreghorn took his hand, but said nothing, not wishing to jeopardize the congenial mood he was cultivating. His head was almost pear-shaped, growing wider and rounder from the cheekbones down, and his flesh was pallid, like wet potter's clay waiting to be molded into a more appealing shape. "This is Miss Taylor, headmistress of our small but—we like to think—perfectly formed school."

Miss Taylor nodded primly, hands clasped with the air of someone who might burst into prayer at any moment.

"Speaking of our facilities, I suggest we embark on a tour while the weather holds, and then return to Summerton Hall"—he gestured at the chateau—"afterward for refreshments."

Dreghorn realized that he had inadvertently joined a group of potential donors.

"Trinity Village," Dalrymple began, "was founded in 1869 by William Olyphant. At the time, most orphanages were inhumane institutions that offered little in the way of stability or comfort. Mr. Olyphant dreamed of creating a homely environment far removed from the dirt and degradation of towns and cities, of giving Scotland's lost children the opportunity to build themselves a new life. With the help of philanthropists such as yourselves"—he almost genuflected before them—"he bought this beautiful tract of land and Trinity Village was born.

"Each cottage houses twenty children, four to a room, under the supervision of a house mother or father. There are no external walls or fences in Trinity—no barriers of any kind. The last thing we wish our children to feel is that they're being locked away to spare the blushes of society. This is their home. Today, we have twelve hundred children in our care."

The cottages were grand affairs to Dreghorn's eyes, separated by what to a child would be vast expanses of greenery. A far cry from the single-end and soot-blackened cobbled streets he'd grown up in, happy family or not.

It had taken twenty years to build the village in its entirety, a firm of Glasgow architects offering their services for free. The original patrons had been given a say in the architecture, resulting in an eclectic mix of styles—Gothic, French, Scottish Baronial, Italianate. As they walked, Dalrymple proudly pointed out workshops, a general grocer's store, a working farm, a fire wagon "manned by volunteers in the event of an emergency," a swimming pool, a sports hall, and Trinity Church, which rivaled Greek Thomson in design and was grand enough to serve a town, let alone a village.

"Trinity is Church of Scotland, but we open our doors to all denominations—Protestant, Roman Catholic, or Jewish. William Olyphant viewed sectarianism as a divisive blight on Scottish society, and was determined that Trinity remain free of it."

There were murmurs of agreement among some of the party, telling silences and quivering mustaches from others. Olyphant's idealistic concept was, if anything, perhaps more radical now than it was in 1869.

Miss Taylor quickly changed the subject, pointing out two larger buildings on the other side of the river. One was a TB sanatorium, the first in Scotland—Olyphant had watched a younger sibling die from tuberculosis when he was still a child himself. Sadly, it only opened a year after his death in 1906, but since then had been offering tuberculosis patients treatment in the fresh country air.

Adjacent was a maternity hospital, serving the local communities of Linwood, Houston, Bridge of Weir, Kilmalcolm, and Langbank. It was also, Dreghorn knew, a haven for women who had got pregnant out of wedlock, offering them a safe place to give birth; many of the babies were then put up for adoption. Miss Taylor didn't share these details, perhaps concerned that some potential donors would find it difficult to fully embrace Olyphant's magnanimous morality.

"And now for Miss Taylor's pride and joy," Dalrymple said as he led them along Hope Terrace. "Trinity School."

"Thank you, Mr. Dalrymple." A formal smile. "We are a fully approved educational institute, following the national curriculum to the leaving age of fourteen, but also teaching vocational skills in our workshops—technical training for the boys to aid employment in heavy industry; secretarial and domestic skills for the girls."

A squat man in a dark caretaker's suit and cap emerged from the school as they approached, ringing a hand-bell up and down, an Edward G. Robinson scowl on his face

"Lunchtime!" declared Dalrymple.

There was nothing coincidental about the timing of their arrival at the school. Dreghorn knew when he was being played; he'd been made to look a fool as a youngster by veteran piss-takers in the shipyards, had been lied to and manipulated by officers and politicians in the Great War, and had been targeted by fast-talking con artists as a rookie policeman in Shanghai. This time, at least, it was for a good cause, not that he had anything more than a pittance to offer.

Laughter, high-pitched voices, and chairs scraping on polished floors could be heard from inside the school, rising to a crescendo as the children flooded out into the schoolyard. The girls were identically dressed in long white dresses with frilly collars, while the boys looked like miniature versions of Dalrymple, though their tweed was no doubt a less expensive variety. A select group of pupils gathered around the donors, bowing and curtseying as if meeting royalty. Dalrymple, who'd been casting sidelong glances at Dreghorn during the tour, took the opportunity to approach him.

"Forgive me if I'm being rude, but you are accompanying our guests? In their employ, perhaps?"

Dreghorn flashed his identification. "Inspector Dreghorn, Glasgow Police; I've got a few questions for you." He cocked his head at the tour. "Sorry, I thought the information might be useful."

"I hope you found it enlightening." Dalrymple's congeniality had curdled. "Questions about what, inspector?"

"A woman and child who were in the care of the school some time ago."

Dalrymple thought for a moment, then called out, "Miss Taylor, could you show our guests in for lunch? I'll be with you shortly." Gesturing for Dreghorn to follow him, he said, "My office," as if the detective were a misbehaving child.

Dalrymple's office was in a building on Faith Street. He said nothing further until they were inside and he was tucked safely behind the barrier of his desk.

"Forgive me if I don't offer refreshments," he said, "but I have other guests to take care of. Trinity exists through the generosity of its patrons, so it's vital we make a good impression. It's the children who will suffer otherwise."

Dreghorn glanced around the office; he doubted the children's rooms were so expensively furnished. He nodded at the large wrought-iron Chubb and Sons Fireproof Safe that rested against one wall. "Very security conscious."

"School funds and confidential adoption records." Dalrymple sniffed. "It would be remiss not to take every precaution."

Dreghorn knew a couple of safecrackers who could blow it in the blink of an eye, but kept it to himself. "I'm looking for information about a woman who was sent here," he said. "Young, pregnant, unmarried; the father abandoned her. It was some time ago, about twenty years. You might not have been here then."

"I started as a teacher before the war and was fortunate enough to return afterward. I took on the position of House Father as well and was eventually made Director." A pious smile. "It's not a job; it's a calling. You're sure this woman came here?"

"I checked with council and medical records. Hunter. Sarah Hunter. Born in 1899. She was an inmate here in 1914."

"An *inmate*?" Dalrymple scoffed, pushing his chair away from his desk. "We're not a prison, inspector." He unlocked a wooden filing cabinet, starting flicking through the files.

Dreghorn had first checked the registry of births in Glasgow, and then expanded the search to the surrounding Paisley, Renfrew, and Inverclyde districts, eventually finding a birth registered to a Sarah Hunter in June 1914. At Trinity Maternity Hospital. Fearing Billy's reaction, the Hunter family had, as Dreghorn suspected, been economical with the exact details of Sarah's disappearance.

Dalrymple removed a folder and read silently for a moment. "Yes, a Sarah Hunter was admitted to the hospital in May 1914, registered address Bridgeton, Glasgow. She gave birth on the second of June. A baby girl, it says here, no complications."

"What happened to mother and child after that?"

"The child was put up for adoption—babies and toddlers are

more popular, easier to settle. The mother, I presume, went back to her family."

"They haven't seen her since." Dreghorn noted the tight grip Dalrymple kept on the file.

"Oh. I can see that must have been distressing, but I'm not sure how we can be of help. It's kindest for mothers to make a clean break once adoption has been decided upon. It's heart-breaking enough for these poor women without prolonging the agony by making them watch their babies being given to new parents. We rarely have any further contact." Dalrymple shut the file abruptly. "So, this is a missing persons investigation?"

Dreghorn didn't answer. "The baby was adopted, then? Who were the adoptive parents?"

Dalrymple slipped the file back into the drawer and locked it with a quick flick of his wrist. "That information is confidential. Children and families involved in adoption cases have a legal right to privacy and protection."

"This is a police inquiry, Mr. Dalrymple." That was stretching the truth; he was a police officer and he was making an inquiry, but it was far from official.

"Has someone made a complaint against Trinity, inspector? Against myself or members of staff?"

Dreghorn stood up, gave Dalrymple a hard stare, but knew that things were slipping out of his control. "Not as such, but we are talking about a concerned family."

"So concerned it's taken them the best part of twenty years to ask after her? Many of these children aren't here because they have no families, they're here *because* of their families. Drunkenness, cruelty, violence . . . You're a policeman; you must have seen almost everything there is to see. Forgive me if I put the welfare of my children above the concerns of families that should perhaps have taken better care of them in the first place." He smoothed down his jacket. "Now, I'm afraid I've neglected my other guests long enough. Without their financial contributions, we may have to put the children back on wartime rations."

"Thank you for your time, sir. I'll be in touch if I have any other questions."

Dalrymple raised an eyebrow. "Name's Dreghorn, isn't it? Chief Constable Sillitoe has expressed interest in becoming a patron, you know. I think I'll be having a chat with him about the underhand manner in which you conducted this interview."

The children must have wolfed down their lunches in no time; as Dreghorn walked back to his car, the playground was mobbed, the boys playing football, the girls skipping or bouncing balls off the walls. For some reason, he found the carefree sound of their play comforting.

A tennis ball flew over the railings, bounced in the road in front of him. He skipped to intercept it with his foot and caught it in one hand as it rebounded into the air, pleased at his reflexes. The sight of him pursuing the ball like a wean chasing rolling coins at a wedding scramble would not have done much for his natural authority.

A little girl ran out of the gates, and slowed to a timid halt.

"Yours?" Dreghorn bounced the ball off the road.

She nodded quickly, caught the ball as he tossed it gently to her, but made no move to return to the playground. "Are you one of our uncles?"

Dreghorn frowned. "I'm a policeman."

"Are you going to take Robbie to prison?"

"Has he done something wrong?"

"He calls me names."

"That's not very nice."

"And he hits me and pulls my hair."

"That's not very nice either."

"It was him that threw my ball over the fence."

Dreghorn followed her gaze toward a boy with sticking-up hair and a head so big that it would take him until adulthood to grow into it. The boy glowered guiltily through the railings, gripping the bars as if in practice for a future career in penal incarceration.

The detective crouched down to the girl's level, tilted his hat back on his forehead. "Y'know," he said, "sometimes lads aren't very bright. Sometimes when they do things like that, it's because they like you, not because they don't like you."

She shook her head vigorously. "He does it to all the girls. And some of the wee-er boys."

Dreghorn nodded gravely. Out of the corner of his eye, he could see Dalrymple standing at the door of his house, talking to the bell-ringer, both looking at him.

"Well, then, I think it's all right for you to call him names back. You said he was called Robbie? Maybe you should call him Robbie the jobbie."

The girl started, thrilled at hearing an adult say such a rude word.

"That might teach him a lesson." Dreghorn noticed the scowling man walking toward them. "And if that doesn't stop him picking on you, then bang him right on the end of his nose with this." He tapped the heel of his right hand with the fingers of his left, and winked at her.

"Morag," Dalrymple's man called the girl. "It's almost time for the bell. Back inside."

"Yes, sir, Mr. Bell." She winked back at Dreghorn and ran off.

"Mr. Dalrymple said to ask if there was anything else we could help you with before you go." The man's scowl grew more pronounced, as if his face were trying to curl itself into a fist.

"She asked if I was one of her uncles. What did she mean?"

If the man thought there was anything untoward about Dreghorn's question, he didn't show it. "Some of Trinity's patrons like to remain anonymous; others like to be more involved. They help out with events and organization, visit at weekends. We encourage the children to call them uncles, as a gesture of affection, appreciation. Or aunts. They have a great many aunts as well."

"And you are . . . ?"

"Arthur Bell. I'm a house father for some of the older boys and I supervise security around the village. You can never be too careful where children are concerned."

"Ex-army?"

"I fought, aye." He seemed annoyed that Dreghorn had read him so easily. "But not in your one."

"Boer?"

"Steel plate in the head to prove it." He rapped his knuckles against his skull as if he expected it to ding like the bell he'd rung earlier. "Shall I walk you to your car?"

"No, you're fine." Dreghorn straightened his fedora. "Wouldn't want to run over your toes."

As Dreghorn walked away, he caught a glimpse of Morag and Robbie, the big-headed bully, in the playground. The boy was dancing around in tears, hands clamped to his bleeding nose. Morag and a couple of other girls were pointing and jeering. The bell to end playtime started ringing, but Dreghorn could see her mouthing the words "Robbie the jobbie, Robbie the jobbie" over and over again.

A small blow for equality, he thought. If only Isla Lockhart had been here to see it.

19

WINTER 1913

When the girl winked at him, Jimmy ducked faster than if Bombardier Billy Wells had launched a haymaker. He crouched low and ran, frantic footsteps crunching into the gravel. All they'd seen, he hoped, was a white shape haring off into the distance. He slowed to a stroll as he reached the athletes' quarters, where they were being split into groups to start specialized training programs for their different disciplines.

Jimmy worked as hard as he could—penance for his indiscretion—the rhythm and rigor taking over, flooding his awareness. Skipping. Speed ball. Heavy bag. Shadow-boxing. Sparring. Keep going until everything is instinct, the mind clear and sharp, thought and action becoming one. A peak of awareness where you can almost predict the opponent's next move. Slip the punch before it's thrown. Step inside his guard. Uppercut. Hook to the temple. Jab. Jab. Cross. Exhaustion gone. Adrenaline surging. Cross. Cross. Cross.

"Jimmy, Jimmy! That's enough." Sergeant Robertson, the boxing coach, voice strident.

Jimmy skipped backward. He had no idea how much time had passed. His opponent, Charlie Currie, three years older and two weight divisions heavier, tried a little bravado in an attempt to show he hadn't been rocked by Jimmy's onslaught. "No' bad, wee man," he said as he came off the ropes with a friendly mock punch to Jimmy's jaw.

They showered, put on their best clothes, and trooped back to Kelpie House for their tea. "It's called dinner here, not tea," Captain Ross corrected Jimmy as they filed into the servants' hall again. It was an even more lavish affair than breakfast. Mrs. Muir, the cook, a matronly woman who seemed to take a shine to Jimmy, made sure his plate was piled high.

"Do you cook for everybody in the house?" Jimmy asked, munching enthusiastically.

"Upstairs and downstairs," she said proudly. "Breakfast, lunch, and dinner."

"Well, it's the best I ever had!"

"Oh, you big sook!" She threw a meaty arm around his neck and hugged him playfully.

Charlie Currie glanced over, Jimmy's face pressed against her ample bosom. "Watch out," he said. "If you fall down there, we'll need to send a search party."

Jimmy blushed, but Mrs. Muir took it in her stride, and skelped the smart aleck around the ear. "No pudding for you, Currie."

Later, Jimmy took a pile of dirty dishes into the kitchen, where Mrs. Muir was supervising an assistant's thoroughness at a sink of soapy water.

"Does Sir Iain have any other children apart from Rory?" he asked innocently. "I thought I saw a young lassie through one of the windows when we were out running."

"Oh, you did, did you?" She gave him a sidelong glance to check for ulterior motives. "That'd be Miss Isla, I suppose. You'd do well to steer clear of her, not that she'd take any notice of you lot. And if she did, she'd wrap you round her little finger like she does everyone else. Sharp as a tack that one, and gallus with it."

Ross and Robertson pushed the athletes even harder next morning. As the run wound back to Kelpie House, they heard unexpected noises—dogs barking excitedly, laughter and educated voices, the clink of glasses raised in a toast. Jimmy cleared the forest to see riders gathered on horseback around the fountain, the men dressed in white breeches and red coats, brandishing riding crops like swords, the women in riding habits. Sir Iain was addressing the group, Rory on a horse beside him. Hounds milled around the horses, straining against their leads.

Jimmy could see Isla on the front steps, saying goodbye to a woman he assumed was Sir Iain's wife. Jimmy's mother was a huge admirer of Lady Jane Lockhart who, against her family's wishes, had studied medicine at Glasgow University and served as a doctor in the Edinburgh Hospital and Dispensary for Women and Children. Titled by birth, her marriage to Sir Iain, the prominent shipbuilding magnate, had been portrayed as a fairy-tale romance by the press, but was in reality somewhat more pragmatic—reluctant duty on her part; ambition on her suitor's. This was before Sir Iain had been granted his own honors, and the marriage had become increasingly strained due to Lady Jane's position as one of Scotland's leading suffragettes.

Sir Iain raised a horn to his lips and blew the signal to release the hounds. The pack moved off and began to cast around for a scent, and the riders hurriedly handed their glasses to tray-carrying servants and set off after them.

Isla sprang onto her horse unaided, dismissing the groom, and wove elegantly through the other riders to lead with her father. She was wearing breeches like the men and didn't ride side-saddle. The other women were staring at her askance. She glanced indifferently at the athletes as she passed.

Currie said, "Awful lot of bother to go to for a poor wee fox."

"Aye," said Jimmy. "I know whose side I'm on."

Training unfolded to the accompaniment of baying hounds and huntsmen's horns, sometimes distant, sometimes alarmingly close.

Jimmy hoped the fox would escape, but when he stepped outside for a break, he saw the whole hunting field approaching.

The savaged corpse of a fox hung from Sir Iain's saddle, a sad excuse for a trophy as far as Jimmy was concerned. He felt his stomach turn, and Lockhart's patronage shone a little less brightly.

Before dinner, Jimmy strolled the grounds, heading for the stables. The horses regarded him with little interest as he entered, heads peering over the doors to their stalls. He'd have talked to them, but he wasn't sure he was allowed to be there, so he kept quiet. As he patted one horse's head, he heard a noise a couple of stalls down, a whimper.

He took a few more steps and saw someone in the empty stall, only the head and shoulders visible. They seemed distressed, trembling, breathing heavily. It took Jimmy a moment to recognize Rory Lockhart, still in his hunting garb.

"Mr. Lockhart, sir? Are you all right?"

Rory turned and stepped quickly to the door of the booth, staring over it. He was smeared with blood, as if some mad artist had dipped a brush into a bucket of slaughterhouse offal and slapped it gracelessly over his face.

"I've been blooded," he said.

Jimmy gripped the top of the door, alarmed. "I'll fetch Sir Iain."

Rory clamped a hand over Jimmy's. "He was the one who blooded me."

Jimmy was lost for words. "We should get you to a doctor, sir. It might be best."

His voice seemed to take a long time to reach Rory, who blinked as if waking up, a thread of blood stretching from the lashes of one eye.

"Don't worry, it's not mine," he said. "It's what they do. Tradition."

Jimmy stared blankly, pulled his hand out from under Rory's, blood smeared across his knuckles. Rory smiled reassuringly, opened the door, and stepped out, his breeches splattered with mud.

"It's tradition for a new rider to undergo an initiation ceremony," he explained. "Just an excuse for another drink really, but the fox's blood is smeared over the recruit. Blooded, you see? I first had the honor when I was four, trotting along on my pony, but it's been years since I hunted—boarding at Fettes, and frankly trying to avoid it—so Father thought I needed another blooding."

"And I thought posh people were meant to be all cultured and civilized."

"We just get away with more. Mother thinks it's nonsense. Secretly, I suspect Father does as well, but it's good for business relationships and social standing. Dreghorn, isn't it? The boxer? Father says you show great promise, perhaps enough to turn professional."

"Sir Iain's been very good to me. I mean, this is great." They had started walking toward the stable entrance. "Coming here, the training. Knackering, though."

"Father doesn't invest rashly, in business or in people. Do your best and who knows what you might achieve?"

Rory suddenly fired a couple of playful jabs at Jimmy, who skipped backward, half raised his guard. The young Lockhart had a solid stance and the punches looked decent.

"We should spar one day. Do a bit myself, you know."

"I don't know, sir; maybe no' a good idea."

"You're thinking you'd have to let me win? Boss's son and all that."

"It'd be a mug's game if I started playing it like that, sir."

"Exactly! And I wouldn't expect it of you." Rory dropped his fists. "I've been tutored in all the gentlemanly pursuits—fencing, boxing, shooting. My father likes strength and independence, likes to build character."

Rory had a lazy athleticism about him; he was taller than Jimmy and positively glowing with good health, even under a grimy coating of fox blood. Jimmy got the feeling the young Lockhart would excel at just about anything.

"It's the same with my sister, though she's directed toward more feminine pursuits."

"I know; I saw her dancing yesterday." Jimmy immediately regretted his admission.

Rory glanced at him, a sudden flare of interest, excitement even. "I think we'll make that our little secret. I'm not sure Father would approve."

"No, I was walking in the grounds and saw her through the window. It was an accident. I mean, I wasn't—"

"Did I imply anything untoward? Don't worry, my sister would be outraged if she wasn't the center of attention." He looked at the blood on his hands. "I should get myself cleaned up; I smell like an abattoir. If I stay out here much longer, the hounds will be after me next." He strode away, calling, "Good to talk to you, Dreghorn," without looking back.

Sunday was the final day. The coaches pushed them hard again, but they knocked off early and were allowed a stroll along the shore before getting ready for the Kelpie House Christmas ceilidh.

The dance was an annual affair, held in the grand hall, for the Lockharts' domestic staff and estate workers and their families, similar to the summer trips "doon the watter" to Helensburgh or Largs that Sir Iain arranged for yard workers' families. Some claimed those trips were a patronizing sweetener to promote goodwill among a gullible workforce, but most employers offered no such perks. Jimmy had enjoyed the trips as a wean, until his father jumped ship and was taken off the workers' roster.

At school the boys had mucked about when Scottish country dancing was taught, so Jimmy's mastery of The Dashing White Sergeant and The Gay Gordons was basic at best. He noted, however, that women liked a man who could dance, so he threw himself into the occasion with gusto. The older women were delighted to swing him around the dance-floor, their eyebrow-raising innuendoes camouflaged by the music.

Lassies his own age gravitated toward the older of Sir Iain's "boys," some of whom, Jimmy knew, were engaged or even married, not that they let on. When Mrs. Muir nipped his bum and roared with laughter Jimmy figured it was time for some fresh air and pretended to flee in terror, adding to the hilarity.

Outside, he leaned against the wall and lit a cigarette, feeling the thrum of the music through the stone. Looking out across the silent darkness of the estate, he realized wistfully that he would never own a tenth as much; it was a life he was being allowed a glimpse of, nothing more.

The noise inside grew louder as the door opened, and Isla Lockhart stepped out, wearing a glamorous fur jacket that ended just below the waist. Light flooded from the doorway, making her dress translucent, showing the outline of her hips, her legs.

"Are you allowed to do that?" She nodded at his cigarette.

"It's good for you, clears the lungs. Says so on the posters."

"That must be why people who suffocate to death in fires look so well. Can I have one?"

"Are you old enough?"

"I'm bold enough. And if you don't, I'll tell my father you were spying on me." Amusement in her eyes, a challenge too.

Jimmy swithered.

"You could have been doing other things as well. Naughty things. He wouldn't like that. Not one bit."

He smiled in submission, reached for his packet of cigarettes.

"No, I'd like that one." She skipped forward and plucked the cigarette from his mouth. He half expected her to cough as she took a draw, but she exhaled with ease, finishing with a couple of smoke rings. "I steal them from Mummy all the time. She thinks it's Rory. What's your name?"

Suddenly "Jimmy" seemed immature, a child's nickname. "James Dreghorn."

"You moved quickly when I saw you the other day. Almost thought it was my imagination. Are you scared of me, James?"

"No chance. I've been in the ring with some really scary folk. And I wasn't spying on you; I was—"

"Admiring?"

"That stuff you were doing, ballet? I've never seen it before."

"You liked it?"

"I liked watching you do it." She wasn't the only one who could be bold.

"Then your artistic appreciation is obviously in your arse, because I'm hopeless."

"Not in my book. And I liked the way you were being cheeky to that old trout teaching you."

"That old trout is my mother."

Startled, Jimmy stammered out an apology. But Isla laughed, and he realized she was teasing him. "That was Madame Zelazny, my ballet teacher. You absolutely must have an exotic name to teach ballet. It's the law."

Jimmy became aware of how close they were, wasn't sure which of them had moved. She was staring at him, intrigued, like he was something fresh and new. Someone inside the hall gave a high-pitched whoop as they danced. It was how he felt inside.

"You can kiss me if you want," she said. "You do know how to kiss, don't you?"

"Seen them doing it at the pictures," he said. "Sure I could give it a go."

"You think you're funny?"

"Not much of a boxer if I can't handle a punchline." He slid an arm around her waist, rested his hand on the small of her back, his mind telling him to stop.

They kissed, her hands sliding under his jacket. Everything else faded, the cold, the ceilidh, the cries of the dancers, until there was only the rich fabric of her dress against his fingers, the body beneath it, her lips against his, her tongue tentatively touching his. He felt himself growing hard, and so did she, subtly pushing against him.

She must have been more aware than him, because she was already moving as the door opened, stepping into the shadows. Jimmy leaned back against the wall, reached nonchalantly for his cigarettes.

Charlie Currie poked his head around the door. "There you are," he said. "I've got two wee birds wanting a dance. I don't fancy yours much, but mine's a stoater. Come on! We're in there."

"Aye, all right, hold your horses." He waved Currie away, implying that he'd follow.

Isla stepped out of the darkness, a sly smile on her face. "Sounds like an offer you can't refuse."

"No' interested," Jimmy said. "I'd rather you came in with me."

She shook her head. "I'm not supposed to be down here, not under any circumstances."

"When will I see you again?"

"Maybe never. Ships passing on the Clyde." The look on his face caused her to soften her expression. "Or maybe when you budding athletes come for your next training camp." She stepped to the door. "Of course, by then I could be on the stage—elegant and graceful, a prima ballerina. Then I might not even look at you."

She rose up on tiptoes, lifted her hands over her head, and pirouetted through the doorway with a mischievous giggle. He rushed after her, but when he got inside she was gone. He went back to the ceilidh, danced some more, and winched the lassie Charlie Currie had set him up with, but his heart wasn't in it. His head was filled with images of the other girl who'd danced into his life.

20

FRIDAY, 7 OCTOBER 1932

She found him in her bedroom, which could have been embarrassing, but fortunately he wasn't raking through her underwear drawer. In the past, their relationship had been under Isla's control, with him little more than a puppy eager to please. Dreghorn cringed at the memory. Part of him took satisfaction from the fact that she now had to accede to his authority. All it took was a murder.

"Not quite your color," she said, nodding at the fur coat dangling from a hanger in his hand. He had removed it from the wardrobe so he could search around for anything hidden in the dark recess at the back.

"You don't think it makes me look like some exotic Russian aristocrat, exiled after the Revolution?"

"More like one of the revolutionaries."

He laughed, hung the coat back up and closed the door.

"Please, don't mind me." Isla waved a hand. "Charles's room is on the other side of the landing, last door on the right."

"I've been through it. Separate bedrooms?"

"Separate lives. Did you find anything?"

"Suits and shoes. A lot of suits and shoes."

"All handmade. You're welcome to help yourself if anything takes your fancy."

"No, thanks." Even if the arse was hanging out of his breeks, the last thing he'd do was stoat about the city in Isla Lockhart's dead husband's cast-offs.

The search had turned up nothing, a considerable waste of time, taking into account the size of the townhouse. Designed by Alexander "Greek" Thomson in 1867, Great Western Terrace wasn't completed until a decade later, two years after the architect's death. The grand columns and balustrades associated with Thomson's work, not far removed from those of the Parthenon or Coliseum, were now, in the sleek art deco age, regarded as vulgar and ostentatious, though Dreghorn liked them, if not the mercantile wealth ruthlessly amassed through tobacco, sugar, shipping and slavery that they represented.

Number 10, home to Charles and Isla Geddes, had four reception rooms, eight bedrooms, two bathrooms with showers, a kitchen and pantry in the basement, and servants' rooms in the eaves. Inside, the decor and furniture were highly contemporary, a riposte to the severe exterior and the prevailing gloom of the Depression.

On the night of his murder, Geddes had given the staff the evening off. They weren't suspicious when he didn't appear for breakfast; once or twice a week, he didn't return home, although they didn't comment or speculate out of respect for Mrs. Geddes. They had no idea where he stayed, possibly some gentlemen's club. He belonged to a few, or so they thought.

"He claimed it was good for business, meeting new clients," Isla said, "but I doubt that would stand up in court if you looked at his books. Have you checked his study?"

Dreghorn nodded. "Nothing suspicious that I could see. It was locked, but your maid found a key soon enough when I said I'd get Archie to put his shoulder to it."

Something glinted at him from under the bed. He crouched and drew out a child's battered teddy bear, stuffing leaking out, the single remaining eye catching the light. "Been in the wars," he observed. "I know how he feels."

"Catriona's—she's been asking after it." Isla took the bear, held it to her chest with surprising affection. "I saw your sergeant downstairs, peering into cupboards as if he expected something to jump out and bite him. He was a little embarrassed, I think."

"Archie doesn't like the skulking around that goes with police work. He'd rather someone just pointed out the baddies so he could go and fight them and throw them in jail. He likes to think all the problems of the world can be solved with a good hard punch on the nose."

"What about you?"

"I'm a deep philosophical thinker. You have to consider the problems of society—the poverty, the deprivation, the gulf between rich and poor, the religious divisions, humanity's baser instincts . . ."

They looked at each other, laughed, and said together, "And then punch them on the nose."

Dreghorn's smile became wistful. "Be nice if it was that simple. Good people sometimes do bad things; bad people can do good things. Try and find the truth, that's what you have to do."

They had left the bedroom and were walking toward the staircase. Dreghorn asked, "Are you still planning to move back here?"

"I am back. I dropped Nanny off at the Botanics with Catriona to get an ice cream."

"It's still a bad idea. I told you, there were no keys on your husband's body."

"It's my home," she said. "I won't run. Besides, I've got you to protect me. And Sergeant McDaid—there aren't many who would threaten him."

"We can't be here all the time, Isla. I can make sure officers patrol regularly, maybe station someone outside for a couple of days. And I can give you telephone numbers to contact me. But promise you'll get the locks changed at least."

She agreed as they descended the stairs; McDaid was waiting in the hallway. The front door was open, staff ferrying in luggage from Isla's car which was parked outside, behind the detectives' vehicle. Dreghorn instructed the big man to radio headquarters for an officer to stand guard outside until further notice.

He followed Isla into a reception room off the hall. She lifted unopened letters from a holder on the mantelpiece, reached for an opener. She sat in an armchair, sighed as she flicked through the envelopes.

"Anything wrong?" Dreghorn asked.

"An avalanche of correspondence," she said. "Since I started helping with my father's affairs, I've been overwhelmed by the dullest pieces of documentation in the world." She tossed the envelopes onto the coffee table one by one, deducing the contents from the sender's monograms on the flaps. "Kilmacolm Golf Club, no women allowed; the Merchants Guild, women allowed very reluctantly; the Shipbuilders' Association; Trinity—"

"Trinity Village?"

"My father's a patron, has been for decades. Why?"

"Another case."

"There's something going on there?"

"Not as such, I don't think. They weren't very helpful, and it's not entirely a police matter. Not yet anyway."

Intrigued, she sliced open the envelope, then tutted. "An invitation to their annual charity ball, tomorrow night. I already RSVP'd the one they sent to Kelpie House, though it's not as if I don't have a good excuse to cancel." She pointed the letter-opener at him. "You should come with me."

"No, I shouldn't."

'As my bodyguard. You said it yourself—I could be in danger. You'd only be doing your duty."

"I'm not sure that's how people would see it."

"Who was unhelpful—the Director, Dalrymple? Unctuous little

prick. I'd like to see his face if you walked in with me. He'd be helpful then. My father's very generous."

Dreghorn havered at the thought, recalling the uneasiness, the suspicion he'd felt in Dalrymple's and Bell's company.

Playfulness in her eyes, the years falling away. "Please, James, what harm could it do?"

The little girl and her nanny were coming up the stairs as he left. He introduced himself, and the nanny, in her early twenties, smiled and gently urged Catriona to say hello. The little girl stared solemnly at him.

"Someone told me you've just been for ice cream," he said, crouching to her level. "Lucky you. Did you have raspberry on it?"

Catriona looked at her nanny, who nodded at Dreghorn for the girl to respond.

"My Daddy's gone away," she said.

"Aye, I know, hen. I'm sorry."

"Mummy says he's gone to God's house. But she says he'll be happy there. And that we'll see him again one day."

"I'm sure you will, aye." Dreghorn was also sure the things that made Charles Geddes happy were off the menu in most visions of Heaven. He ruffled Catriona's hair, lost for words, and stood up.

"She doesn't really understand," the nanny said. "Probably best that way."

Dreghorn gave a non-committal nod, tipped his hat to her.

"Done!" McDaid exclaimed, as Dreghorn slammed the door. With his hulking hands, the successful transmission of a Morse code message was always a minor victory.

"You want a medal?"

"Got enough, all the good they do. A dram would be better. Oh"—McDaid nodded at the radio—"a wee laddie dropped a note in to Shug Nugent—somebody wants to see us."

"Who?"

McDaid looked at Dreghorn, went skelly-eyed. Dreghorn waved at the adjacent expanse of Great Western Road.

"Lead on, McDaid."

"Are youse bastards trying to get me killed?"

"Wasn't part of the plan," said McDaid, "but if it was a by-product of the process . . ."

"Like slurry . . ." Dreghorn shrugged as if to say, that's life.

Bosseye glared at the detectives, outraged. "A wee bit of respect, please. I'm your fountain of information. Without me, you'd be high and dry."

He turned his back on them to stare like a connoisseur at the painting in front of him, which by fortunate coincidence was of a large naked Renaissance lady, a flowing landscape of fleshy curves. She reclined on a chaise longue, her back to the gallery, a sunlit Italian city visible through a balcony behind her.

Opened as part of the 1901 Glasgow International Exhibition, Kelvingrove Art Gallery and Museum was a vast towered sprawling structure on the banks of the River Kelvin, built in what the architects claimed was the Spanish Baroque style, not that anyone would have known the difference. The museum was the last place in which a street bookie like Bosseye would be caught touting for business— the perfect location for the detectives to meet their reluctant informer. Dreghorn made sure the only other visitor in the gallery, a well-dressed older woman, was out of earshot, then he and McDaid stepped forward, hemming Bosseye in. "Has someone threatened you?"

"No, but, I'm in dangerous territory, know what I mean. Not your usual wee neds."

"Big neds, then?" McDaid teased.

Bosseye glared at the big man, although his bad eye also seemed to be perusing the painting on the wall over McDaid's shoulder. "Big enough to call themselves respectable," he said, giving the gallery another furtive once-over. "Teddy Levin." He paused for effect. "That's who your man Geddes owed money to."

"You think Teddy Levin is respectable?" asked McDaid.

"Do you have anything on him? Ever had him banged up in a cell? No, it's easier picking on harmless souls like me."

Dreghorn frowned at his partner.

"Theodore Levin," explained McDaid, "owns the Gordon Club, haunt of high heid yins from the Corporation, the Merchant's Guild, the legal profession. And the underworld."

"Some of your lot, an' all," Bosseye added accusatorily. "Propping him up quite nicely."

"He runs a number of legal businesses," McDaid continued, "but the story is, he's also one of the city's biggest bookmakers—present company excepted—moneylenders and brothel keepers. Keeps it all at arm's length, though, makes sure there's no direct connection to him."

"Well, your dead body used to be a live one at the Gordon Club. Regularly. Lots of important people there to act the big man with, but you've got to keep up with them—horses, the boxing, roulette, cards. Expensive, if you're no' on a winning streak."

"And Geddes wasn't?"

"Started becoming a problem in the last year or two. Teddy gave him a bit of leeway at first because of his family connections, but they didn't seem to serve him very well. The losses kept coming, the payments got smaller and the debts got bigger."

"Big enough to get him murdered?"

"People don't get murdered around Teddy Levin. They get clumsy, become forgetful, know what I mean? Fall down the stairs after one too many, slip under a tram on a foggy night, leave the gas on. Any eejit can commit a murder—it takes brains to commit an accident."

McDaid widened his eyes, impressed by the observation. "That's almost philosophical."

Dreghorn said, "So he usually prefers something more subtle than slitting your throat and throwing you in the Clyde. But what if he wanted to send a message to everyone that owes him money?"

"They already get the message, loud and clear, believe me."

"Where are you getting it from?"

"One of the bouncers at the Gordon likes a bet but can't afford the stakes. He likes a chat too, and I let him think I'm impressed by the glamour of his job, though all he does is stand outside in the pissing rain most of the time. I give him the odd tip to keep him sweet, 'cos sometimes he has interesting tales to tell."

McDaid went to say something, but Bosseye started backing away. "Uh-uh, I've said too much already. Last thing I want is to start getting accident-prone myself." He pointed at them. "It'll be on your heads if I do."

Dreghorn and McDaid watched Bosseye walk away, taking care not to make eye contact with other gallery visitors, then realized that the older woman was standing next to them. They nodded politely, embarrassed that, with all the artistic gems on display, they'd seemingly stopped to appreciate a big bare bahookie.

"Bottoms are quite fascinating, aren't they?" she mused. "At a certain angle, they almost look like a smile . . ."

21

In America, Roosevelt remained ahead in the polls, now planning to drop any commitment to the League of Nations and promising a "new deal for the American people." In Germany, the National Socialists, the Nazis, already the largest party in the parliament, were about to fight the second election of the year, driven by their leader Adolf Hitler's relentless invective of hatred, bigotry and violence. In Italy, Benito Mussolini was strutting around like some resurrected Roman emperor, proclaiming that Fascism was the universal movement of the age and boasting, somewhat fatuously, of his country's military might. In Russia, Joseph Stalin was revolutionizing the nation with his egalitarian Five Year Plan, although rumors of state torture, forced displacement of people and famine were beginning to surface. In Britain, the Government of National Unity was anything but unified, and Ramsay MacDonald had abandoned the Ten Year Rule, which decreed that Britain need not prepare for another war in that period, following Japanese military aggression toward Shanghai.

And in Glasgow, Bonnie Archie McDaid had just rooted out the cause of all the world's ills: "Mustaches."

Dreghorn, driving, tried not to take the bait. Failed.

"Hitler—mustache," McDaid expounded. "That wee man's nursing one big grudge against the world, and if we don't watch out, we're all going to know about it."

Dreghorn nodded; no argument there. He turned the car onto Gordon Street and drew to a halt on the opposite side of the road from their destination.

"Stalin—mustache," McDaid continued.

"No' signing up for his communist utopia, then?"

"Too good to be true, if you ask me. Something sinister about him. If you had to pick a bad yin out of a line-up, my eye'd be on him."

"Gentleman Mac—mustache," said Dreghorn, getting out of the car. "So, he's a nasty piece of work as well?"

"Sometimes a lame duck's just as bad." McDaid sighed in disappointment. "And he might be more interested in the 'Gentleman' part than the 'Mac' part, these days."

"Mussolini—no 'tache."

"Aye, but he's baldy," McDaid said as if it was explanation enough and started to cross the road. "Too baldy."

Dreghorn was about to respond, his exasperation at boiling point, but a bulky form in a bowtie blocked his way.

"Members only, pal."

Despite being chosen for his size, the doorman was clearly intimidated by McDaid, who had a good couple of inches on him in every direction. But he stuck to his guns.

Dreghorn flashed his warrant card in the man's face, wondered if he was the one who'd blabbed to Bosseye. The man flicked his eyes to the card, his lips moving as he read. Then he jerked his head reluctantly toward the stairs. "On you go, I suppose."

The Gordon Club was on the second floor of number twenty-five, a stoic Georgian edifice, its air of respectability enhanced by the Girl Guides Association headquarters housed on the floor below. Girl guides and gangsters; it was like some witty ditty from Noël Coward.

The entrance was subtle, trying hard for tasteful. A stair runner, the carpet thick and soft, drew them invitingly toward the second floor, the walls a warm plum color that wouldn't have been out of place at Kelpie House. It was too faint to hear from the street, but as they neared the top, music, chitchat and the tinkle of glasses drifted toward them. Rare sounds in the Depression, ones that you wanted to soak up.

McDaid groaned, "More bloody jazz."

The door opened onto a thick lush velvet curtain, the same color as the walls. "Fancy," said Dreghorn and swept it aside.

Light dazzled them at first. They stepped out of the glare, their eyes adjusting, feeling disoriented and exposed. Beyond the door, the lighting was dimmer. A clever ploy, giving staff and clientele the chance to identify newcomers, judge whether they were worth consorting with or best avoided.

A young woman in a uniform just on the tasteful side of French Maid offered to take their hats and coats and asked if they'd like a table or would prefer to sit at the bar.

The atmosphere of the Gordon Club was that of a post-Prohibition Hollywood lounge bar, minus sunshine, palm trees, healthy complexions and silver-screen stardom. Glasgow was home to over a hundred and ten picture houses, often two or three to a street, which were packed to the gunnels every night. So it was only natural that the great and the good—in their own eyes at least—would seek to emulate Hollywood's international glamour. Compared to the Empire Bar, the Gordon Club was an impressive establishment, but William Powell and Myrna Loy weren't likely to roll up any time soon to share cocktails with city councillors, corporation bureaucrats, minor criminals or the president of the local Masonic Lodge.

The floors were polished wood, the bar long and curved, with the largest array of drinks that Dreghorn had seen outside of the Astor House in Shanghai. Booths lined the mirrored wall opposite the bar.

On the other side of the bar, diners sat at tables in front of a small stage, where a singer was doing a passable version of Cole Porter's "Love for Sale." She did little to disguise the Glasgow in her accent, which, to Dreghorn's ear, added an angry, bitter edge.

The detectives handed the girl their hats, said they'd be happy at the bar and ordered drinks so expensive it almost brought a tear to McDaid's eye. "Hope this is on expenses," he said, sipping his whisky sparingly.

The club was busy. Groups of suited men sat in the booths or milled at the bar, laughing and joking, already well-oiled though it was still early. Waitresses sashayed among them, smiling with sweet insincerity at their repartee. Couples took up the other tables, mainly older men with younger women, some of whom looked timid and self-conscious, others bold and brassy, wrapping their dates around their little fingers.

"A lot of lassies in here," noted McDaid. The pubs he was familiar with were bastions of manhood. Any woman entering put her reputation at risk, unless she was there to chase out her husband.

"Are you suggesting," Dreghorn asked, "that these young ladies might have some ulterior motive for smooching with these baldy old bawbags?"

McDaid raised his glass in an ironic toast to a sharp-featured man at a nearby table. The man frowned, but reciprocated, obviously not recognizing the detective.

"The defense lawyer for those wee shites I was at court with last week," McDaid explained. "Sleekit wee shite himself."

Dreghorn wasn't surprised. So far he'd spotted a couple of lawyers he'd encountered before, reporters from the *Daily Record* and *Glasgow Herald,* and politicians he recognized from photographs in those papers. It was exactly the sort of place Charles Geddes would have gravitated to.

A woman was walking toward them, blonde, older and more

business-like than the waitresses, her dark suit the height of elegance beside their uniforms. The band had gone up-tempo with "It Don't Mean a Thing (If It Ain't Got That Swing)," but the clientele were still at least two drinks ahead of them.

The woman introduced herself with a smile that didn't quite reach her eyes. "Kitty Fraser, gentlemen. Do you have your membership cards with you?"

"Right here." Dreghorn handed her his warrant card. "We'd like to speak to Mr. Levin."

"I'm not sure he's here tonight. I could make an appointment or have him contact you. Can I ask what it's about?"

"Not here? So he wouldn't be the fellow you were just talking to? The one who told you to sashay on over here?"

Flustered, she glanced involuntarily at the booth she had come from. It was too far to see clearly the features of the man sitting there, but although he made no gesture that Dreghorn could see, Kitty Fraser obviously read the signs. "I'm sorry, we're a private members' club and value discretion, so we have to be cautious. Mr. Levin invites you to join him for a drink."

"Delighted to," said Dreghorn.

"Try and stop us," McDaid added.

She led them to the booth, gestured for them to sit, and asked if they wanted the same again.

"On the house," the man stated. A hauf and a hauf and a pile of newspapers, local and national, rested on the table before him. *The Times* of London was open at the financial pages. "What can I do for you, officers?"

"Officers?" Dreghorn repeated. 'Is it that obvious or do you have some reason to keep an eye open for the polis?"

The man smiled. "Short of tattooing Mr. Sillitoe's new tartan across your foreheads, there's not much more you could do to advertise the fact."

Another of the chief constable's changes had been to add "Silli-toe's Tartan," a checkered band of black and white squares, to police uniforms to make officers more easily identifiable. Quickly deemed a success, there was talk of introducing it nationwide.

"The size of you, the air of intimidation, the suspicious looks you dished out when you came in, the cheap suits . . ." The man noted McDaid's glance at his and Dreghorn's clothing. "No offense, quite the opposite. I prefer my lawmen poor—poor and honest."

"Unlike club owners," said Dreghorn.

Theodore Levin was small, but like a dancer or a fighter, not small like the stunted hunger-shrunken forms that filled the streets and factories. Even Dreghorn, possibly the shortest officer on the force, was above the average height of the working-class civilian population. Levin was younger than Dreghorn expected, too young to have fought in the war, so he didn't have the haunted look of that generation. No, despite the charm, exquisite tailoring, and pencil mustache, he had the air of a predator, confident in his power, wait-ing patiently for the leaders of the pack to grow old and weak so he could strike.

"No apology about that; I work hard for my money. And while I might not be above telling the odd white lie, I'm not a criminal." Levin smiled, innocent as a babe.

"No one said you were, Mr. Levin," McDaid said. "Guilty con-science?"

"Far from it." He leaned forward, pointed out some of his cus-tomers. "David Ross, councillor at the City Chambers, seat on the Police Committee, if I remember correctly. Sir Hugh MacDonald, owner of Denny's Shipyard and Marine Works. Albert Campbell, on the board of Courtauld's. Donald Ramsey, assistant editor of the *Evening Times*. You think they'd associate with anyone disreputa-ble?"

McDaid made a show of looking at the men Levin had singled

out, two of whom were in the company of young women. "Here with their wives?" he asked bluffly.

"I wouldn't know," Levin answered. "Or care. People's affairs are their own concern. They don't come for choir practice and confession. Is this a shakedown, gentlemen?"

'Is that no' something the Blythswood Ladies' Club offer?" Blythswood Square, just off Sauchiehall Street, was one of the city's more notorious red light districts.

"You'd know better than me. I've never been that desperate."

"No," said Dreghorn. "Shakedown's something they say at the pictures. In gangster films."

Levin touched his whisky glass as if contemplating a chess move. "I already have friends in the Glasgow Police, but if you're interested in membership, I'm sure I could offer a discount."

"Would that get us through those doors your bouncers are keen to keep closed?" Dreghorn motioned with his eyebrows toward a door on the stage side of the bar, where a doorman was refusing entry to a couple who had tired of the band, nodding toward the detectives by way of explanation.

Levin didn't look round. "If you like spending time in broom cupboards and empty offices."

"So we wouldn't find any untoward activities taking place through there—back-room gambling, roulette tables, cards, or beds for your poor overworked members to lie down on for a wee bit of relief."

"Sordid imagination you have, inspector. If that's what police work does, you should consider another occupation."

"You don't mind if we take a look, then?"

"Wouldn't dream of trying to stop you, if you've got a warrant. If not, then, no." Levin shook his head sadly. "I can't have my customers embarrassed or disturbed by you barking up the wrong tree. You're welcome to come back tomorrow, when we're less busy. Be happy to give you the full guided tour then."

"By which time you'll have cleared everything out."

"Again, all in your imagination, inspector. Was there something else?"

"Charles Geddes," Dreghorn said. "You know him?"

Levin tapped a finger to the paper he'd been reading, which had run the story that morning. "The fellow you pulled from the Clyde? No, I don't think so."

"Sure about that?" McDaid set his elbows on the table. "We heard he was a regular."

"No, I'm not sure. I try, but I don't know everyone."

Kitty Fraser returned with their drinks, and Levin gave her a sidelong glance. "Kitty, is Charles Geddes a member here?"

"Aye, he is." She nodded gravely. "Terrible business, what happened to him. Seemed like a nice man. Always tipped well." Her voice tailed off as if ashamed that was how she judged the man.

Levin seemed surprised, but he also seemed like a good liar. "Did I know him?"

"You might have met him. He was a lawyer, something like that. He sometimes came in with clients."

Dreghorn gestured for her to sit down. "When did you last see him?"

"I don't know, a few days ago."

"He's been dead a few days. How long before that?"

She rolled her eyes up, counted the days. "Last Friday. He was with a young lady."

"Had you seen him with her before?"

"Once or twice, maybe, but it's hard to be sure. Mr. Geddes—well, he often came in with women, not always the same one."

"Did you get her name? Any of their names?"

The naivety of the question amused her. "No, but I don't think it'd have done you much good if I did. Some of the men who come here—" Levin gestured for her to speak freely. "They're not always with their wives. They're with their secretaries or girlfriends, their mistresses, if you want to be all Mills and Boon about it. They don't always offer names, or, if they do, they might not be their real names. You learn not to ask."

Dreghorn thought for a moment, thanked her for the drink and her time. She smiled and nodded, stood up to leave, said to Levin, "Mr. Logan wanted a word, when you've got a chance."

"I'll join you in a minute, we're almost finished here." Levin looked at Dreghorn expectantly.

The detective took his time, sipped his whisky. "No gambling of any sort on your premises, then?"

"It's illegal, inspector."

"Charles Geddes' family seemed to think he had gambling debts."

"More fool him. Never rely on luck, that's what I say."

"What about your other members—any gamblers or bookies among them? Maybe he got in with a bad crowd."

"There's no bad crowd in here." Levin had done well, but now Dreghorn saw the first flash of menace in his eyes. "I wouldn't allow it. It's my club, my crowd."

"And very impressive it is too." Dreghorn knocked back his whisky. "Just like the Copacabana."

"Been there, have you?"

"Only in the newsreels." Dreghorn stood up, McDaid following.

Levin insisted on walking them to the door, all trace of hostility gone; he seemed almost sad to see them go. Excitement sparked through the club as they passed, customers leaping up to greet him, shake his hand, slap his back, keen to show how close they were to him.

Despite his obfuscation about Geddes, he seemed to know every other member, asking about their families, offering business advice, making jokes about drunken revelry at the last Hogmanay party, complimenting the beauty of their female companions. He made a couple of introductions to the detectives, eliciting perfunctory acknowledgments and platitudes about what a good job the police did. Levin was oleaginous in the way he moved smoothly from one table to another, charm personified.

Dreghorn knew the club owner was showing them the influence he had, the power he held. He recalled the flare of violence in Levin's eyes, and couldn't help wondering if this show of power was intended to scare them off, or was a challenge for them to try and bring him down.

The bouncer gave them the bad eye as they left, but in the history of dirty looks they'd received it ranked pretty low.

"Levin's young to be doing what he's doing," Dreghorn said as he got into the car. "Could be a front, I suppose."

McDaid slammed the door. "Seemed pretty gallus to me, the wee nyaff. No' the type to take orders from somebody else."

Dreghorn looked up at the club, the windows frosted for privacy. "He's not got much heft to him. He'd need to be sharp as a tack to hold things together."

"Or a loonie. Short loonies are always the worst." McDaid looked pointedly down on Dreghorn. "And what did I tell you?" He tapped his upper lip. "Teddy—mustache!"

Dreghorn allowed the big man his moment of triumph. A car had pulled up across the road. A man and woman emerged, the man slipping his arm around the woman, directing her toward the Gordon Club. Dreghorn watched as the doorman nodded at the man and waved them in; a regular.

"Think there was something going on between him and Geddes?" McDaid became serious again.

"He's a good liar if there was, but he was a wee bit too quick to deny any knowledge of Geddes. The way he was cozying up to his other customers, how likely do you think that is?"

McDaid tried to stifle an almighty yawn. The big man had been working long hours and hadn't seen much of his family since the Geddes case dropped into their laps. Dreghorn sometimes overlooked the fact that other officers had wives and weans, lives outside of work.

"Take the car back and get yourself home, big man. I fancy a walk, clear my head, maybe have a quiet dram somewhere less hoity-toity."

McDaid frowned. "You're sure that's all there is to it?"

"You want to take me back to the station and grill me?" Dreghorn already had the door open. "I'll be home within the hour."

McDaid looked unconvinced, but started the engine anyway. Dreghorn slapped the roof as he drove off, watched the car turn onto Buchanan Street and disappear from sight, then crossed the road back to the Gordon Club.

"Members only," the doorman said.

Dreghorn shot him a withering look. "You're a tryer, I'll give you that."

Slipping past the curtain again, Dreghorn removed his hat slowly, concealing his face until he was past the spotlit entrance. "The bar again," he said to the same woman before she could ask.

The hat maneuver hadn't fooled Teddy Levin, but it wasn't intended for him. He intercepted Dreghorn at the bar. "Forget something, inspector?"

"Just went off duty. Wondered if that offer of a drink still stood?"

Levin's eyes warned that it might be dangerous to accept as he spoke out of the side of his mouth to the barman. "Whatever the man wants." He nodded at Dreghorn. "Enjoy your night, inspector. No dancing on the tables."

Dreghorn ordered a large malt, loosened his tie, and undid his top button. The woman he'd seen outside sat alone at a booth, glancing around nervously, careful not to catch anyone's eye. The man who'd accompanied her was nowhere to be seen, in the toilet or hidden among customers at the bar. Dreghorn sipped his drink, savored the sweet burn, as he walked toward the woman.

"Are you all right, hen? You look awful lonely, there by yourself. How about I join you for a wee bit, keep you company?" He was already sliding into the booth opposite her.

"No, I'm fine; I'm here with someone." Her eyes searched the club nervously. "He'll be back any minute."

"He'll no' mind." Dreghorn gave her his best smile. "I get on with everybody."

Up close, she was younger than he'd assumed. Seventeen or eighteen, and pretty, with a vulnerability that would make some men want to protect her, and others take advantage.

"The lady's with me, pal." The voice boomed harshly above them.

Dreghorn glanced up, said, "I think 'pal' might be pushing it."

The man stiffened and drew back on seeing Dreghorn's face. He managed not to drop the drinks he was carrying.

Dreghorn gestured at the seat beside the girl. "Don't be shy, take a pew. It's Bell, isn't it?"

Arthur Bell, the bell-ringing house father from Trinity Village, lowered himself slowly into the booth. He was wearing a dinner suit, the bow-tie slightly askew around his thick neck. It might've looked good on some bright young thing but it made Bell look like an over-the-hill bouncer who'd picked it up in a pawn shop.

"Some place, this," said Dreghorn. "You must be doing well for yourself."

"You and all."

"Guest of the management."

"We live quietly at Trinity, frugally. When I visit the city, I like to come here. For the music, you know. A wee treat."

Onstage, the band was delivering a version of "Body and Soul." The singer didn't look like she'd gladly surrender either.

"What about you, miss? You like the music?"

She made a face and shook her head, her first flash of personality.

"Maybe I should go, leave you both alone. Two's company and all that."

"Oh no, we're not courting or anything like that. Mr. Bell's a friend. He's helping me out."

Dreghorn leaned forward like a sweetie wife eager for gossip. "Where did you meet? How do you know each other?"

"From Trinity," the girl said, biting off her words as Bell pushed forward, crowding her, placing his elbows on the table.

"Are you no' a bit old to be in care?" Dreghorn asked.

She hesitated, and Bell interjected, "She's a patient at the hospital." She flinched, shame in her face. "TB. Poor lassie's been there for months. Touch and go for a wee while, wasn't it, hen? But you're on the mend now."

She nodded, smiled weakly.

Dreghorn smiled back, reassuring. "Well, you wouldn't know it; you're looking well now. What's Arthur doing for you? You said he was helping you."

"Why are you asking me all these questions?" She looked from Bell to Dreghorn, unsettled.

"He's a polisman," said Bell disdainfully. "Can't help himself."

"Sorry, force of habit. If you don't watch it, you start seeing criminals everywhere."

Bell sighed. "I'm one of the few people at Trinity who can drive, so I help out with transport when I can—family visits, picking people up from the station . . ."

"Taking consumptive patients out dancing? Plying them with drink? Unorthodox treatment, Doctor Bell."

'Is this our girl?" Kitty Fraser was standing at the end of the table. "It's Rose, isn't it? Rose Laing?" she asked. "I'm Mrs. Fraser, but you can call me Kitty. What do you think of the place?"

"It's wonderful." Rose seemed comfortable for the first time, enthusiastic. "Dead glamorous."

"Well, we try. Still here, inspector?"

Dreghorn raised his glass, toasting her powers of observation. "Mr. Bell and I encountered each other recently. Only polite I say hello. You know each other?"

"Rose is here for an interview. Well, a wee chat to see how we get on—like a house on fire, I'm sure."

"To work here?"

'As a waitress, maybe, though the customers can be a bit cheeky— you have to be friendly but firm, so they don't get any ideas. We also own a few cafés in town, so that's another possibility. Would you like to come with me, Rose? It's quieter in the back office, we can chat there."

Bell stood up as enthusiastically as Rose. "Some people I need to talk to."

Rose smiled at Dreghorn as she joined Kitty, leaving him seated alone. He made a mental note to look into Bell's background, check if the man had a criminal record.

"These poor girls," Kitty said. "They suffer so much in hospital, away from their families, losing their jobs because they're sick for so long. We like to help out if we can, get them back on their feet."

Dreghorn said, "Teddy's a real saint."

"He's no' as bad as some." Her accent slipped momentarily, but her smile and poise quickly returned. "Another one, inspector?"

"Think I've had my fill." Dreghorn stood up, downed his whisky. He tipped his hat to Levin as he left, but received no response.

He could have caught a tram to the West End but chose to walk, welcoming the rain. He thought about Rose's nervousness, the way she'd flinched at the mention of the hospital. About Bell's smug hostility and the flash of pragmatic honesty in Kitty Fraser, how it made her seem strangely familiar. And about Teddy Levin, with his king-of-the-castle confidence.

None of it seemed right, but then, the world hadn't seemed right since he was sixteen years old. And then only because he didn't know any better.

Back home, he lay awake, waiting for Mrs. Pettigrew to chap his door. She didn't.

22

SATURDAY, 8 OCTOBER 1932

The search of Lockhart's yard had led to nothing but blind alleys, dead ends. All those interviewed claimed they hadn't seen Geddes there in over two years; indeed, managers had been instructed to deny him entry, which corresponded with what Isla had told Dreghorn.

DC Brian Harvie's despondency on his return from the yard had nothing to do with a lack of progress. A pot of paint had fallen—or been given a helpful nudge, knowing the popularity of the police since the Red Clydeside strikes—from a scaffold. The pot missed Harvie, but the explosion of green paint didn't, spattering his best suit in what looked like patterns of shamrocks.

"If only it had been orange, to match your temperament," McDaid quipped, receiving a two-fingered thrust in response.

Geddes' neighbors revealed little new information. One woman had spoken to him on the day of his murder; she distinctly remembered because he had complimented her on the new hat she was sporting as she took her poodle to the Botanic Gardens for the little tyke's morning walk. Another neighbor seemed to recall seeing Geddes leave Number 10 as he drew the curtains for the evening, but couldn't swear to it.

The Dunoon police, whom Dreghorn had contacted after the Lockharts' interview, had been in touch to confirm that the *Lion*

Rampant, the yacht Rory captained on his America's Cup bid, had indeed arrived at the Royal Clyde Yacht Club on 5 October.

WPC Duncan visited Geddes' city-center office and interviewed Miss Hastings, his secretary. The young woman was distraught, and Duncan suspected that her relationship with her employer might not have been strictly professional, although the secretary had nothing but praise for the Lockhart family. Mrs. Geddes had offered her three months' wages to wind up office affairs and promised sterling references to help her gain future employment.

The secretary compiled a list of Geddes' clients, accompanied by the relevant documentation, case files, and bank statements, reluctantly handing over the latter because they showed how much he relied on his wife's money to keep the practice afloat. So far Duncan had uncovered no illegal activity or criminal connections. Something did intrigue her though.

"Geddes' appointments diary," she said, flicking through a large hardback book as Dreghorn leaned over her shoulder. She stopped at a particular page, ran a finger down the entries.

"Most of the appointments are written by Miss Hastings, listing the client's full name and details of where meetings are due to take place. But here, on the night before his death, Geddes made his own entry, and it's a little vague."

Geddes' hurried scrawl read "M. R.," followed by a hand-drawn arrow to the initials G. C. and the number 7.

"Miss Hastings confirmed that G. C. stands for the Gordon Club. She claimed she has no idea who M. R. is, and I think I believe her. If you flick back through the diary, there are quite a few entries from Geddes himself, always just the bare bones—initials and times, nothing else."

"Assignations with women," Dreghorn mused. "Or meetings with clients whose identities he wanted to remain secret for some reason."

"That's what I thought, sir. And if you look at today's date . . ."

Dreghorn read, "M. R. at Miss C.'s. One p.m."

"Miss C.'s is Miss Cranston's Tea Rooms, Miss Hastings said."

"A real Stab Inn, that." McDaid was leaning against the desk opposite, a cheeky grin on his face. "Big-time criminals only."

Dreghorn gave his partner a rueful look. "Then you'll no' fancy a spot of lunch there."

The big man, always hungry enough to eat a scabby dog, came off the desk to remonstrate, but Dreghorn had already turned away. "WPC Duncan, how would you like to join the plainclothes division for the afternoon?"

Tea rooms, the politeness and absolute propriety of them, always made Dreghorn want to behave disgracefully. He especially disliked Scottish ones, with their shortbread and scones, and the twee image of dreamy tartan-clad romanticism they promoted, noble lairds and bonnie lassies, hills and glens and lochs. None of which had anything to do with the city outside, most of whose inhabitants couldn't afford to step inside such an establishment.

Ellen Duncan seemed rather keen on them, though. She'd told him her first name and chatted away ten to the dozen from the moment they arrived. Stepping out of uniform into civilian clothes, it was as if she'd divested herself of the reserve she maintained at the station. She also had little hesitation in ordering the most expensive cream tea when Dreghorn told her it was on expenses.

The only time her reserve returned was when, recalling the inspector's hand on her arm a few days earlier, he asked what it was like working with Strachan. She responded with a quick, overly dismissive "Oh, fine!" and asked Dreghorn if he wanted more tea.

She lived with her parents in Dennistoun, loved police work and was especially admiring of the detective division, she revealed. She was sure it was only a matter of time before there were women detectives. Women had a different view of the world to men, were more insightful and compassionate, less blinkered. They would be a major boost to the force. Dreghorn didn't disagree and said nothing to discourage her, but he knew how deeply prejudice ran in the force. Tough enough being a Catholic, even what the priests called a lapsed one, let alone a woman.

Ellen's eyes fell upon the last scone on the cake stand—Dreghorn's, if things were divided fairly. He nodded for her to help herself, and then glanced at the door. They'd informed the manageress that they were on official business and she'd agreed to signal when Geddes' lunch companion arrived. It was a long shot; Geddes' death had been in the papers the previous day, but Dreghorn couldn't discount the possibility that whomever he was due to meet might have missed the news. He only hoped the manageress didn't give the game away. She was flushed with excitement, as if she'd been plunged into a suspense thriller by Gaumont's wunderkind director Alfred Hitchcock, alerting Dreghorn with an alarmingly well-telegraphed shake of the head as new customers arrived.

As it was, Dreghorn recognized the woman the moment she walked in. He didn't know why, he just knew. He'd already alerted Ellen before the manageress directed the woman toward Geddes' table.

"Excuse me, miss, you're meeting Charles Geddes?"

The woman looked up from her menu, surprised to see Dreghorn and Ellen. She nodded, said yes, her voice warm and soft.

"You haven't heard, then?" Dreghorn continued.

"I'm afraid we have some bad news, miss. Do you mind?" Ellen was already starting to sit, her face kind, concerned. Dreghorn was pleased she didn't wait to follow his lead, impressed that she was already forming a connection with the woman. Compassion—maybe there was something to it.

He pulled over another chair as Ellen said, "Mr. Geddes was

killed a few nights ago. I'm Constable Duncan; this is Inspector Dreghorn. We're investigating his death. We found your details in Mr. Geddes' appointment book."

The woman seemed scared, as if wondering where the next blow was coming from. "What do you mean, investigating?"

"He was murdered," Dreghorn said.

"No." Tears welled up in her eyes. She tried to blink them away.

Ellen placed a comforting hand on the young woman's arm. "What was your relationship with Mr. Geddes, Miss . . . ?"

"Molly. Molly Raeburn. My father died a few months ago. Charles—Mr. Geddes—was the executor of his will."

"Why meet him here?" asked Dreghorn. "Wouldn't his office be more appropriate?"

Molly Raeburn shook her head innocently, and Dreghorn realized how young she was, eighteen at most. "We weren't discussing business; my father's affairs are mostly done with. I suppose we've— become friends."

"Mr. Geddes had a lot of friends, Miss Raeburn." Ellen drew back her hand. "For a married man."

"Oh no, we weren't—nothing like that. He's been helping me with—well, everything, really. Charles was my father's lawyer; he helped with the funeral arrangements, tying up my father's affairs to make sure there weren't any problems for Mother and me. He was advising me on what to do with the money Father left."

"If you don't mind, what was your father's name, and what business was he in?"

"Eric, Eric Raeburn. A bailie with the Corporation."

Dreghorn nodded; bailies were civic officers within the Corporation, influential and imbued with a degree of legal authority in areas such as transport, housing, and licensing.

"We weren't rich, but he had some investments, properties that he rented out. I didn't know what to do, so Charles was helping me work out what was best." A pause. "And I liked him. He treated me fairly, not as if I was some naive young girl who needed her hand held or was scared of the big wide world." She drew a breath. "Where . . . ? I mean, how . . . ?"

"He was found in the Clyde on Monday morning."

"God. He was drowned?"

Dreghorn shook his head, watching her reaction. "No. I'm afraid we're not releasing any more details than that at the moment."

She bowed her head as the tears came again, fumbled with her handbag. Dreghorn handed her a napkin. She gripped it in her hands, but didn't raise it to her face, letting the tears run. "I'm sorry. My father, now this—" She smiled weakly, displaying a vulnerability that would no doubt have appealed to Geddes almost as much as the money she'd come into.

Dreghorn felt Ellen looking at him, checking, perhaps, if the same appeal held for him. "Are you courting, Miss Raeburn?" he asked.

"No." Shy, almost coquettish.

"No former boyfriends that might have been jealous of your relationship with Mr. Geddes?"

"I told you, it wasn't like that."

"Who might have got the wrong idea, then?"

"No. I'm training to be a teacher. Between that and caring for Father—he'd been unwell for some time—there hasn't been time for romance."

"No thoughts of it with Mr. Geddes?"

He expected a touch of indignation, but she thought sadly for a moment before answering. "He was married, but he said that he and his wife were separated, that she no longer loved him. In another time, another place, who knows?"

For a moment, they were an island of stillness among small talk and clinking cups and saucers. Another dead end.

"I'm sorry about your father, Miss Raeburn," Dreghorn said, "and for the questions we had to ask you. My card. If you recall anything about Mr. Geddes that you think might be of help, please get in touch. If you wouldn't mind giving Constable Duncan your details, we'll leave you to your lunch."

"I don't think I'll be staying," Molly said, taking Ellen's notebook and pencil. Dreghorn felt a pang of sympathy as he watched her write. Molly Raeburn was about the same age as Rose, the girl with Arthur Bell the previous night, but had an easier life ahead of her, even if it didn't feel like it at the moment. The sympathy faded as he thought of Bell, his hand lingering and possessive on Rose's back as he directed her toward the Gordon Club.

Molly handed the notebook back to Ellen and extended her hand to Dreghorn.

"I'm sorry I couldn't be of more help. Pleased to meet you, despite—" She left the rest unsaid as they shook hands, nodded perfunctorily at Ellen and headed quickly for the door, upset by the attention.

Ellen suddenly leaped to her feet, rushing back to their table, where a waitress was about to clear away their plates.

"Thanks, but we're not finished yet." She shielded her half-eaten scone from the waitress's attentions, and took a bite, jerking her head after Molly Raeburn as Dreghorn joined her.

"If it's all right with you, sir, I'd like to do a bit more digging. Not as innocent as she seems, if you ask me. Did you see the looks she gave you?" Ellen fluttered her eyelashes exaggeratedly. "Butter wouldn't melt."

"It's possible she may just have found me devilishly handsome."

Ellen almost choked on the last of her scone. "If I disagree, sir, will it harm my chances of promotion?"

He laughed. "Not with me, constable; an attitude like that's exactly what you need. And if you pounce on criminals the way you did on that scone, we'll have the city cleaned up in no time."

McDaid looked as though he'd been toiling away in a steamie instead of the squad room; shirt buttons undone, tie hanging like a limp noose. Paperwork had that effect on him. He greeted Dreghorn and WPC Duncan like a man who'd lost the will to live and told Dreghorn that Isla Lockhart wanted a word with him. Urgently. Her words.

"Couldn't you have handled it?" said Dreghorn. "She likes you."

"Oh, no! Only Inspector Dreghorn will do, thank you very much."

Dreghorn slipped his hat back on and drove to Great Western Terrace. He was surprised when Rory Lockhart answered the door. "She's given the staff the afternoon off, and Nanny's taken Catriona to the Botanic Gardens," he said. "I was on my way to the yard and dropped in to see my niece. Thought I'd better stay—Isla's found something."

Dreghorn didn't even have a chance to say hello. Isla, pacing the floor, nodded sharply at the table as he entered. Two photographs lay there, face down.

"Look at them!" she raged. "If he wasn't dead already, I'd bloody well kill him myself!"

The first photo showed a ruddy-faced middle-aged man, naked from the waist down, a shirt and waistcoat still covering his portly upper torso. He looked almost surprised to find a woman on her knees before him, performing fellatio, as lawyers would describe it in court, a term Dreghorn's younger self had thought had something to do with opera. The man's features could be clearly seen, though Dreghorn didn't recognize him.

The couple stood by a large bed, the room decorated like a layman's idea of a French bordello, mirrors and erotic paintings on the walls, lush velvet replaced by tartan.

Dreghorn had been expecting worse. Since photography was invented, it had been used to capture people fucking and to fuck them over. In Shanghai, with its different zones of international jurisdiction, foreign nationals fell victim to kidnap and blackmail all the time, lured by opium and the promise of exotic sex. Considerably more sordid than what he was looking at, although he understood Isla's outrage.

"Do you know the man?" he asked. Isla shook her head as if it was a ridiculous question.

"To be honest," Rory said, "I was surprised it wasn't cheeky Charlie himself. You think they're of an artistic nature, or for more nefarious purposes?"

"Offhand, I suspect Rudolph Valentino here doesn't know he's got an audience. It's set up so that his face is visible, but the girl's isn't."

In the second picture, the action had moved onto the bed, the woman now straddling the man who, inexplicably, still wore his socks and garters. The woman's face remained unseen. No accident, Dreghorn figured. He could see a crescent-shaped mark on her arm, just below the shoulder. A scar, maybe, although it could have been a trick of the light.

"Where did you find them?"

"I didn't," Isla said. "Catriona did. Stuffed inside that raggedy old bear you pulled out from under the bed. *Mummy, Mummy, look what I found!*"

"She'll be all right," said Dreghorn. "She's too young to understand."

"Oh, you're an expert in child psychology, are you? I know she won't understand, but she was disturbed, I could tell. That bastard. His own daughter! No, *my* daughter! He doesn't deserve to be called her father. From now on, he's nothing to her. Don't even mention his name." She took a deep breath, gestured for Dreghorn to sit down. "Do you think he took these himself?"

"More than likely paid for them to be taken, or acquired them from a third party. What he was doing with them is the bigger question. Maybe he was up to something, using them to his own advantage in some way. If we can identify the man, we might have a better idea."

Isla stepped past Dreghorn, her leg brushing his knee, and sat at the other end of the sofa, a gap between them. She sighed deeply. "Do you think they had something to do with his death?"

"Highly bloody likely, I'd say," Rory exclaimed. "I told you it was too soon to come back here. What if the killer's looking for them?"

"I've had the locks changed," Isla said. "We're as secure as we can be. And James has arranged for police patrols to check on us."

"I don't care if the Gordon fucking Highlanders are barracked outside, you're coming back to Kelpie with me." For the first time since meeting Rory again, Dreghorn caught a glimpse of the steely officer he'd served under.

"No, I'm not."

"What about Catriona?"

"We're perfectly safe. We have staff and we're closer to the police in town than we are out at Kelpie."

"Then I'm moving in here with you."

"And who'll look after Daddy?"

"Please, the old bastard's indestructible. He'll outlive us all."

Dreghorn reached for the photos, suddenly tired of Lockhart family squabbles. "I'll take these for the investigation." It wasn't a request.

Isla got to her feet. "What kind of man could leave filth like that in his own home, among his daughter's toys?"

"A desperate one, maybe," Dreghorn said. "Or a clever one. We didn't find them."

"Cunning would be a better description," Isla said bitterly.

Dreghorn said goodbye; he'd be in touch if there was any news. He tucked the photographs under his arm as he walked down the steps to his car and didn't look back, though he knew they were standing at the window, watching.

McDaid had undergone a transformation, from grumpy Mr. Hyde to cocksure Dr. Jekyll whose God complex was in the ascendant. He was balanced on the rear legs of his chair, feet crossed on his desk. The pile of papers had been reduced to a paltry few sheets, the rest miraculously transported to the desk Ellen Duncan now sat behind.

"Solved the case, big man?" Dreghorn asked.

McDaid swung his feet off the desk. "Just found out that somebody knows more than they're telling. Remember wee Teddy saying that he didn't know Geddes, or that they'd maybe just met in passing?"

McDaid turned the papers so that Dreghorn could read them. He tapped a finger beside a name on the first document, an invoice from Geddes to a client. "Three months ago," he said, "Geddes handled the purchase of some commercial property in Shawlands for a company called Claymore Holdings. Now, I rang up what's-her-name, Geddes' secretary—"

"Miss Hastings," Ellen said.

"That's the one." McDaid nodded. "I asked if she knew what the properties were being used for. Aye, she did. A new branch of Universal Stores, not long opened—the same Universal Stores as those two menodge clowns the other day. Now, they were a couple of rank bad yins, and I figure whoever they work for is as well, so I did a bit more delving. I asked Companies House in Edinburgh for the registered address of Claymore Holdings. Cathedral Street, same premises as Universal Stores in the city center. WPC Duncan kindly checked the land records for me. Claymore Holdings owns the entire building."

Ellen flicked through the top papers of the pile on her desk. "And quite a few others as well, commercial and residential, and scores of tenements in the East End and the South Side."

"Own the houses they live in, sell them the things they need to live," said Dreghorn.

"Not only that," said McDaid. "Claymore owns a number of bars and cafes, including the Lomond Tea Rooms chain, and our new favorite haunt the Gordon Club. I got heavy-handed with the lad at Companies House, told him I was on the verge of cracking a murder case and if he didn't give me the names of all those on the board of directors at Claymore, he'd be guilty of obstructing the course of justice and would face the full wrath of the law. Any of them jump out at you?"

McDaid pushed his notebook toward Dreghorn. Among a short list of names that he didn't recognize, one was written in larger letters than the others: Teddy Fucking Levin.

'Is that his real middle name?" Dreghorn asked.

"All right, lads?" McDaid said. "Been duffed up by any old ladies lately?"

Brodie and Jessop, the menodge men they'd encountered earlier that week, had been leaning against the bonnet of their Austin Twenty, smoking and eyeing up women walking past on their way through George Square. They hopped to their feet in alarm as Dreghorn and McDaid strode toward them.

"Stay there looking bamboozled," Dreghorn growled. "Your boss'll be out to hold your hands in a minute."

First, they had driven to Universal Stores in Cathedral Street, which was closing for the day. The shop-floor staff admitted to hearing of a Mr. Levin who worked upstairs but claimed never to have met him.

From there, they drove down to Gordon Street, where the Gordon Club was preparing to open. The girl who met them at the entrance said they were expecting a busy night as there was some big do on at the City Chambers. Mr. Levin was attending, she said, but it was by invitation only.

"Don't worry," McDaid told her, "we're champion gate crashers."

Neither Dreghorn nor McDaid had been inside the City Chambers, towering above the north end of George Square, but they succeeded in not looking awed by the granite pillars in the reception hall, the Carrara-marble central staircase that led to the upper floors, the gold-leafed walls and ceiling, and the great stained-glass dome overhead. If the Gordon Club was a paean to the new glamour of Hollywood and the silver screen, the City Chambers was a testament to an older world, to the money, the power that builds cities and bends men to its will.

McDaid gave Dreghorn a cynical sidelong glance. "Good to themselves, aren't they?"

A huge mosaic of the city's coat-of-arms was set into the floor at the entrance, bearing the legend: *LET GLASGOW FLOURISH.* Dreghorn wondered if it was an order or a plea.

They didn't have to ask for directions, as the noise of the shindig could be heard from upstairs. They took the stairs quickly, Dreghorn jogging to match McDaid's stride.

The Banqueting Hall on the second floor was vast, the walls adorned with frescoes depicting a history of Glasgow that the majority of its citizens would never see. The room was lit by vast electric chandeliers that hung from the ceiling—"electroliers," they'd been called when first installed. A band was playing somewhere—not jazz, McDaid was pleased to note, but something refined, classical.

The guests were all in evening dress, so if Dreghorn and McDaid stood out as policemen at the best of times, it was even more apparent now. The event, they learned later, was in honor of the Merchants' and Tradesmen's Guilds and the good work they carried out in the city.

They moved slowly through the guests, not removing their hats, their eyes scanning the faces, drawing cold disdainful glances in return. McDaid spotted Levin first, nudged Dreghorn. Levin was with a group of older men, but seemed to be the center of attention, mentor instead of student, making comments that reduced the others to helpless laughter. He looked in their direction as the laughter continued. His expression didn't change, but he gave an almost imperceptible shake of his head, as if warning them off or unable to believe that they'd dared to come here.

"Teddy," said Dreghorn.

"You're sure you want to do this here?" Levin asked considerately, only their best interests at heart.

"If you'd care to accompany us, there're a few questions we need to ask you."

"I don't care to, not at the moment."

"Shouldn't lie to the police in the course of a murder investigation, then."

"It's rude. And an offense," McDaid raised Levin's arms into the air, started a body search.

"Excuse me, gentlemen," Levin said breezily to his companions, "there seems to be some sort of misunderstanding here."

A crowd was forming, voices raised in protest; it was a scandal, an outrage, an abuse of power, the chief constable should hear of it.

McDaid's eyes lit up as his hand fell upon something in Levin's inside pocket. He removed it, pressed a button. The click of the switchblade, glinting in the electrolier light, silenced the chorus of disapproval. McDaid feigned shock. "Wouldn't have thought you'd need to bring your own cutlery to a do like this."

Levin was unperturbed. "If the police did their jobs properly, honest citizens wouldn't be scared to walk the streets or feel the need for protection."

"Exactly," said Dreghorn. "That's why we're taking you away."

Levin stiffened as McDaid pulled his hands behind his back and cuffed them together, not necessary, perhaps, but another affront. As they led him away, the great and good of Glasgow society quickly stepped aside, as if fearing contamination.

"Congratulations, you two know how to fuck things up for yourselves," he said as they descended the stairs. "Those people back there own the city. Those people own you."

"Then we've done them a favor by pointing out a sleekit wee shite like you," said McDaid.

"Not how it works, big man. I speak their language, play the same game. It's not me you're humiliating; it's them. I don't give a fuck what anybody thinks. All you've done is show disrespect to people who can destroy you—not with a gun or a knife or anything like that, but with a signature or a word in the right ear."

They had reached the bottom of the stairs now, footsteps echoing on cold marble.

"Just remember, it didn't need to be like this." Levin stopped, looked at Dreghorn. "You're marked men now."

"You might have a few marks on you yourself by the time we get to the station." McDaid clapped a hand on Levin's shoulder and propelled him through the swing doors, his face and upper torso careering off wood and glass. He staggered as he came out onto the street. The menodge men rushed forward, but a glare from Levin stopped them in their tracks.

"Get me Garrison!" he snarled.

23

"Get me Garrison!"

The cry went up whenever a gang leader was arrested for a slashing, stabbing or, best of all, murder. Or when a big-money bookie's luck ran out, or a renowned safe cracker landed behind bars, facing a lock he couldn't blow.

"Get me Garrison!"

Whenever a randy aristocrat forced himself upon one of the household staff, believing it was his God-given right, and she decided to press charges, the ungrateful little tart. When a drunken businessman ran down a wee lassie in his Rolls-Royce and didn't stop, thinking her pals wouldn't be sharp enough to memorize his number plate.

"Get me Garrison!"

Whenever a worker in the shipyards or the pits was crippled in an accident and dared to challenge his bosses' generosity by suing for greater compensation than the paltry sums they offered to keep his family alive.

"Get me Garrison!"

George Garrison was the premier defense lawyer in the west of Scotland. He preferred the term "premier" because it took longer to say than "best," especially when delivered with the rolling "r"s of the Scottish tongue.

If you wanted to extricate yourself from trouble with the law, then you went to George Garrison and Associates. Not "Partners," because no other lawyer deserved equal billing.

The police detested Garrison because he made them seem like bumbling PC Plods during cross-examinations that had juries roaring with laughter. Procurators Fiscal loathed him for having their prosecutions thrown out of court or guilty verdicts diminished to a humiliating degree. Prosecuting lawyers feared the seductive charm he oozed toward the jury and the punishing articulacy with which he demolished their arguments. They called him the Devil's Advocate, which merely played to his ego and further enhanced his reputation.

Even his clients grew to hate him, for the price of evading justice was considerable. Once money ran out, businesses, cars, and houses were all collateral that Garrison was willing to accept. Whatever the verdict, George "Did You Shag His Wife An' All?" Garrison was the real winner.

He entered Central Police Headquarters behind a policeman escorting a surprisingly pretty young prostitute by the arm. The prostitute, half-cut, looked at Garrison with unsteady eyes and blew him a kiss. Watching from behind his desk, Shug Nugent fancied that the lawyer, a preternaturally tall figure in a navy pinstripe suit, gave her a cheeky wink in return.

Garrison placed his hat on the reception desk, stood like a man waiting to be taken to the best table in the restaurant. "I believe you have a client of mine in your cells, Sergeant Nugent."

"And who would that be, Mr. Garrison?"

"No games, please; I've got theater tickets for this evening. Theodore Levin, a respectable businessman whose doorstep your colleagues should never have darkened."

"I'll have to check the charge-sheets," Nugent said, making no effort to do so. "If you'd like to take a seat."

"I'll stand, thanks. I believe you keep them under the counter."

Garrison's cold glare would have intimidated a seasoned court-room prosecutor, but Nugent's countenance was so fierce he could have outstared a Trafalgar Square lion. The lawyer allowed himself a small smile. "I could get you off a charge of murder, sergeant. No jury would have the balls to convict a face like that."

"Especially not if you were the victim, sir."

"Something funny, Mr. Levin?" McDaid asked. "You were giving us a wee fly smile there. You find being a suspect in a murder case amusing?"

"Absurd, not amusing. I was just thinking how embarrassed you'll be when you realize you've arrested the wrong man."

"Who said you were under arrest, Mr. Levin?" said Dreghorn. "You're just helping us with our inquiries."

"Nice of me."

"Where were you on the night of October the second?" Dreghorn asked again.

They had already been through the rigmarole, but Levin betrayed no hint of annoyance or impatience. Keep at you until you slipped up, the story changed, the details wavered—he knew their racket well.

"I don't know," he said. "Most likely at home with the wife, in the club, or en route from one to the other, with my driver and a couple of the lads."

"Not keen on your own company, are you?" said McDaid. "Always like to have someone around."

"Plenty of opportunity for alibis, then," Dreghorn said.

"I'm a busy man." Levin shrugged apologetically. "And it's not an alibi when it's the truth."

Dreghorn nodded at the switchblade on the table. "So, if we have the blade analyzed, we won't find traces of blood on it."

"Only mine, maybe. Cut myself the first time I opened it." Levin looked sheepish; it didn't suit him. "Stupid of me to carry it, but I've got a nervous disposition. Lots of robberies in town. And the horror stories you hear about these razor gangs. Makes you scared to walk the streets. Isn't someone meant to be doing something about them?"

Dreghorn placed his elbows on the table. "Tell us about Charles Geddes again."

"There's nothing to tell."

"Then why did you pretend you didn't know him?"

"I don't know him. If people say I've met him, fair enough, but I don't remember."

"You don't remember someone as well-connected as Geddes?"

"Couldn't have made much of an impression." Terse, irritation beginning to bite.

Since arriving at Turnbull Street, Levin had been polite and co-operative, as though he mildly regretted the oblique threats he'd made as the detectives escorted him from the City Chambers, while imparting little or no information. Possibly their attempt to humiliate him had struck a nerve, and now—in an interrogation room with bare floorboards and nicotine-stained walls, a world away from the City Chambers—he felt that remaining calm and composed would have been the better strategy.

"We found a number of invoices for legal services from Geddes to Claymore Holdings," Dreghorn stated. "Your company."

"Speak to my accountant, then."

"You had no contact with him during the work he did for you?"

"I delegate to trusted associates."

"You don't seem the trusting sort to me."

"People do have to earn my trust."

"And if you break that trust, you end up in the Clyde with your throat slit?"

"The papers might call you the Untouchables, but we're not in

Chicago." Levin leaned forward as if about to make a confession. "If someone crosses me, I get the lawyers onto them."

Suddenly a voice boomed from the corridor, rich and authoritative, "Has he been charged?" Levin gave the door an I-told-you-so glance.

The door flew open and George Garrison swept in like a man who'd risen from his coffin to feed on the blood of innocent virgins. "Not another word, Teddy."

"It's all right, George. Just helping the police with their inquiries."

Garrison placed his hands on Levin's shoulders with avuncular concern. "I'd expect nothing less from a law-abiding citizen such as yourself." He glared at the detectives. "Would one of you clowns care to explain the nature of these inquiries?"

Deputy Chief Constable McVicar entered the cell in Garrison's wake, summoned urgently from home, a cozy cardigan over his shirt and tie. McDaid squirmed like a man trying to conceal that he'd just sat on a pin cushion.

"I'll have your badges," Garrison threatened, "for harassment and abuse of police power. Mr. Levin informed me that he's already spoken with you and offered his full cooperation. What breathtaking feat of detection have you since undertaken that gives you the right to manhandle my client and humiliate him in front of his peers?"

"Your client withheld information in a murder investigation." Dreghorn quickly detailed the links they'd uncovered between Levin and Geddes.

Garrison snorted and harrumphed throughout the explanation as if playing to the cheap seats, shaking his head and rolling his eyes in disbelief. "If you think any of this constitutes just cause or is evidential in a court of law, inspector, then you must have acquired your sheriff's badge in a lucky dip." He became serious. "Do you intend to charge my client?"

Levin flicked his eyes toward Dreghorn with lazy confidence.

"Not today," the detective said.

Garrison waved flamboyantly at the door. "Then you're free to go, Mr. Levin. And if you take my advice, you'll give serious consideration to suing the Glasgow Police for harassment, defamation of character, and potential loss of earnings due to the damage they may have done to your business reputation through their outrageous behavior."

Levin stood up slowly, straightening the wings of his bow tie. "Thank you, Mr. Garrison, I might do just that." He stopped in the doorway. "It wouldn't be for myself, you understand, but there are plenty of charitable institutions in the city that would benefit from an injection of funds."

He and Garrison stepped out into the corridor as if Dreghorn and McDaid were the prisoners and visiting hours were over. As their footsteps died away, McVicar addressed Dreghorn contemptuously. "I warned Sillitoe that he was giving you enough rope to hang yourself. I didn't think you'd have the ingenuity to drag the entire bloody department to the gallows with you!"

24

McVicar had done his best to reprimand them for their treatment of Levin, but despite polite acknowledgment that perhaps they could have handled things better, they were far from penitent, convinced Teddy knew more than he was saying. Deep down, McVicar probably agreed, but was playing the politician and had little regard for Dreghorn and McDaid at the best of times.

When Dreghorn arrived back at Mrs. Pettigrew's, she informed him rather coldly that a Mrs. Geddes had telephoned. Typically, Dreghorn hadn't given much thought to his relationship with Mrs. Pettigrew, not wishing to entertain the prospect that she might end up caring for him more than he did for her. Or vice versa.

Dreghorn returned Isla's call, and she reminded him that they had engagement that night. He tried to talk her out of it, saying again it wasn't a good idea, but she wouldn't take no for an answer.

So he washed and shaved—cold water at that hour—and put on his best suit, which was not that different from his worst. He lit a cigarette and stepped outside to wait. He was trying for discretion, but Isla sounded her horn as she pulled to a halt and cried, "Taxi for Inspector Dreghorn!" The curtains behind him twitched and he knew Mrs. Pettigrew was taking it all in.

The drive to Trinity was enjoyable and relaxed, Dreghorn glad to at least have the illusion of stepping away from police work, and Isla happy not to be the grieving widow, caring mother, devoted daughter or hard-headed businesswoman.

"I never feel I have to act the lady of the manor with you," she said.

"That's because I'm so far down the pecking order you don't have to. You and I were never meant to rub shoulders."

"We did more than rub shoulders, James." Isla kept her eyes on the road ahead.

"Did we? Not sure I remember. Long time ago."

"Of course you don't," she said, not so much humoring him, as roasting him with sarcasm.

"Peace" and "Hope" materialized briefly, then disappeared just like the real things. "Love" flared forlornly as the headlights of Isla's car flashed over the street sign, and quickly vanished.

"I've always thought the street names a little self-defeating," she said. "Guaranteed to make the children practice the exact opposite of what's preached to them."

"Not just the weans," said Dreghorn.

"You're already a lost cause." Isla nodded at the glove compartment. "The hip flask's in there. Help yourself, you might need it."

"With you to keep me company? Never."

Isla had been sipping from the flask when he'd first got into the car, ostensibly to keep the cold at bay, but also, she claimed, to stave off boredom; the Trinity fund-raisers were interminably dull affairs.

"Oh, I'll be on my best behavior. Grieving widow, remember? I'll spend the entire evening batting away condolences." She gave him a soulful, sincere look, said, "Oh, thank you, thank you *so* much," and then brightened. "How was that?"

"Heart-breaking. Though having me along might raise a few eyebrows."

"You're my knight in shining armor. My husband's murderer is still on the loose. I could be the next target. You're only doing your duty."

"Except I'm not on duty." He removed the hip flask, shook the contents, which were already getting low. "And if I have too much of this stuff, it might be me you need protecting from." He immediately regretted the comment, but her eyes danced mischievously.

"Promises, promises, inspector."

Light flooded from Summerton Hall's grand windows, spotlighting the expensive cars outside. Isla had blocked a couple of vehicles in, but didn't seem to care; she headed straight for the entrance. Two older pupils opened the doors and offered them a printed schedule of the evening's events. Another pair of smiling pupils opened the doors into the main hall. The guests were gathered with their backs to Dreghorn and Isla, listening to the children's choir singing "Faith of Our Fathers." An insensitive choice, Dreghorn thought. Faith in their biological parents was probably in short supply among most orphans.

Miss Taylor, the headmistress, was stationed on the perimeter of the crowd, alert for new arrivals. She spotted Isla and whispered to the man beside her—Alasdair Dalrymple.

Dreghorn offered to fetch some drinks, and moved off before Dalrymple, turning obsequiously to Isla, saw him. He skirted the crowd, heading for a makeshift bar tended by some fresh-faced youths, and ordered a large whisky, and a sherry for Isla. The choir weren't bad, if you liked that sort of thing. At school, Dreghorn's singing voice had so impressed teachers that they'd told him just to mouth the words silently like a ventriloquist's dummy.

He knocked the drink straight back, ordered another, and scanned the crowd. The guests weren't far removed from those he'd seen at the City Chambers, confident in their wealth and influence, but also keen to be acknowledged for their compassion and generosity.

Just as the choir finished with a crescendo, on the opposite side of the hall, towering above the other guests, he recognized the patrician profile of Chief Constable Sillitoe, in full uniform, cap tucked under one elbow as he clapped.

"Who invited you?"

Dreghorn turned to face Arthur Bell, the older man's cheeks flushed with alcohol. "No guest list's complete without me, Arthur," he said. "How's Rose?"

"Who?" Too innocent to be true.

"The lassie you were with at the Gordon Club."

"Oh, aye. Fine, far as I know. Why?"

"Polis. It's my duty to be concerned. She looked as though she was recovering well. From the TB."

"On the mend, all right. Poor lassie's been through a lot."

"So much so that the sanatorium up the road had never heard of her. Watch out, you're dripping all over the place."

Concern had passed over Bell's face, but he recovered, passed his glass to the other hand and shook off the beer that he'd spilled.

"Dropped in there on my way here," explained Dreghorn.

He had asked Isla to pull into the sanatorium as they neared the village. She waited in the car while he went in, producing his warrant card at the reception desk. He kept the details vague, but said that there'd been a family emergency and he needed to speak urgently with one of their patients, a Rose Laing.

The receptionist had frowned, said the name wasn't familiar; patients were usually long-term, so the staff got to know them. She checked the admissions book, but there was no Rose Laing listed. Perhaps there'd been a mix-up?

"They said she wasn't a patient, Arthur. Never had been."

Bell was flustered. He sipped his beer to try and hide it, looked over his shoulder toward Dalrymple, who was still currying favor with Isla.

'Is she a pupil here, Arthur?" The edge to Dreghorn's voice was unmistakable.

"No!" Outrage, but maybe also a bit of relief. "Want to come with me? We'll go through the school register right now."

"So why were you lying? The receptionist suggested that maybe she was at the maternity hospital instead. Similar addresses. Sometimes the post gets mixed up. Is that it?"

"Mr. Bell?"

Bell broke away from Dreghorn's gaze, as Dalrymple and Isla approached. The Director nodded politely at Dreghorn and addressed Bell: "Arthur, could you make sure everything's in order for the prize-giving?"

"Of course, sir, right away." Bell gave Dreghorn a dirty look as he hurried off.

"Good to see you again, inspector," Dalrymple said. "I've been chatting with Mrs. Geddes and feel that we may have got off on the wrong foot when we last spoke. No excuse, but I was in the middle of an important appointment when you arrived. My mind was all a-flutter. If you're still conducting your investigation, I'm happy to help in any way I can. A young woman at the maternity hospital, wasn't it, who put her child up for adoption . . . ?"

Dreghorn rattled off the details as if on the parade ground: "Sarah Hunter. Date of birth, the twenty-eighth of April 1899. The baby was born on the second of June 1914. It's an inquiry, not a fully-fledged investigation as yet, but more information would certainly be helpful."

"I'll gather together the files and we can arrange an appointment sometime next week." Dalrymple smiled, looking to Isla for approval. "Regarding the details of the adoption, there are obviously rules and regulations, so we need to maintain an element of discretion."

"Inspector Dreghorn is the most dedicated policeman in Glasgow," Isla said, "and I speak from experience. He keeps us safe in our beds from all sorts of cut-throats. He wouldn't cause anyone harm. Unless they deserved it."

Dalrymple, slightly taken aback, glanced at Dreghorn. "The child would be an adult now so it's possible she may have wished to contact her real parents. It's often the case, even in happy adoptions. That would make it easier."

"I don't intend to cause any upset to anyone," Dreghorn said. "Just the opposite."

"You're not the only police officer we have here tonight. Chief Constable Sillitoe is also a guest."

"Spotted him, aye," Dreghorn said. "I'll pop over and say hello." When hell freezes over. He could have kicked himself for not considering that his boss might have been invited. Sillitoe had taken a house a couple of miles away in Kilmacolm, and was exactly the sort of august personage Dalrymple would have courted. To Sillitoe, refusing a cause like Trinity, and the opportunity to inspire its morally impressionable young charges, would have been a dereliction of duty. He would, however, regard Dreghorn's decision to escort Isla as questionable, to say the least.

Dalrymple made earnest apologies—he was expected to mingle with the other guests—and wished them a good evening.

Dreghorn said, "He's changed his tune."

"I was singing your praises." Isla raised her glass in a toast. "I also mentioned that in the current economic climate, Lockhart's might have to review the scale of the donations it makes to charities like Trinity."

"Cunning." He clinked his glass against hers.

"So, your boss is here. The great gangbuster."

"He gives out the orders. Muggins here does the busting."

"I'd like to meet him."

"Oh, he'll be delighted to see us together." He nodded toward the stage, where Miss Taylor was beckoning to get Isla's attention. "You're wanted."

"I'm presenting the prize for General Excellence." She drained her glass, flashed a self-deprecating smile. "Hardly the expert. There's music afterward. Do you dance?"

"As if I had chewing gum stuck to my feet."

Dreghorn figured another drink might not be the best idea, but fetched himself one anyway, and kept out of Sillitoe's sight for the duration of the prize-giving. Using surveillance training to avoid your boss—there was a first time for everything.

He made small talk with pupils and other guests, asking subtle questions about Trinity and its staff, but gleaning nothing scandalous or suspicious. Isla raised laughter and applause from the crowd with a brief speech, and was positive and encouraging toward the winners, making him wonder which was the act, that or her cynicism. After the ceremony, a band of older pupils started up. Expecting a ceilidh or something traditional, he was surprised to hear them play "I've Got You Under My Skin."

Isla asked, "Are you dancing?"

"Are you asking?"

"Telling."

Another bad idea, he thought, but he'd already taken her hand and was stepping onto the floor. They were shy in each other's arms, the sudden closeness dissipating their earlier cockiness. Tentative smiles when they met each other's eyes, then quickly looking elsewhere—in Dreghorn's case, straight into the eyes of Percy Sillitoe, which were far less friendly.

The chief constable was dancing with his wife, his stern gaze following his detective like an outraged owl's. Dreghorn nodded casually and twirled Isla away in an attempt to escape Sillitoe's attention. The song ended and Isla excused herself, heading for the lavatories, only to be waylaid by an older lady, who oozed sympathy but darted a suspicious glance at Dreghorn.

"Dreghorn." The voice, quietly authoritative, had the perfect pronunciation of a BBC announcer.

"Sir," he answered before he'd even turned around. "I wasn't expecting to see you here."

"I'm sure you weren't." A wig and gavel couldn't have made Sillitoe more judgemental. "Your dance partner seems familiar."

"Miss Lockhart," said Dreghorn. "I mean, Mrs. Geddes."

"An attractive woman."

"If you say so, sir."

"You think it's proper for the officer in charge of a murder investigation to be seen in public with the victim's wife?"

"Mrs. Geddes was afraid to attend on her own. Her husband's killer hasn't been apprehended yet."

"You're on duty then, part of a bodyguard detail?"

"Not officially, sir."

"There's no such thing as unofficial duty on my force, Dreghorn. Only duty." He waited as Dreghorn acknowledged his words with a grave nod. "This business with that chap Levin—McVicar thinks you overstepped the mark, disgraced the department."

"Teddy Levin knows more than he's saying," Dreghorn said firmly. "I was just trying to rattle him."

"You didn't succeed, by the sound of things. Even if you're correct in your suspicions, such actions could jeopardize proceedings in the long run. Consult me first next time. And I'd like a progress report on my desk first thing on Monday morning."

Dreghorn sensed Isla coming up behind him. She extended a hand. "Chief Constable," she said respectfully.

"Mrs. Geddes," Sillitoe shook her hand, bowed his head reverently. "I'm extremely sorry for your loss. Rest assured we're doing everything in our power to bring the perpetrator to justice."

"Thank you. Your officers are a credit to you, especially Inspector Dreghorn. I've been on edge since my husband's death, but I didn't want to let the charity down, so I convinced him to accompany me tonight. The inspector did argue against it—"

"Not strongly enough. But I'm sure he'll return you safely to your daughter while the night's still young. She'll be missing you. And her father, of course."

"I should be getting back to her. I've been trying to put a brave face on it, but"—she gestured at the revelry around them—"it's all a bit too much at the moment."

Sillitoe agreed sympathetically and Isla moved off to say her goodbyes.

"Dreghorn."

"See it through, sir?" Sillitoe's family motto, the phrase with which he habitually dismissed his officers.

"Don't be facetious, inspector. On this occasion, I'd doubt the wisdom of that advice. Remember you're a police officer, first and foremost. I don't expect you to aim for sainthood, but I do expect you to exercise due care and respect toward those you're sworn to protect. Especially those who might be suffering confusion or fragility after being touched by the hand of crime."

"Sir." Dreghorn lowered his eyes from Sillitoe's withering stare.

The chief constable's voice softened a little. "You're too good an officer to be simply banging heads together, Dreghorn. You have more to offer your city. So does McDaid. Although right now I can't help thinking you're the one that needs a knock on the head. Bring you back to your senses." The voice hardened again. "Straight home with her. And straight home with yourself afterward. Understand?"

Isla was talking to another well-wisher when Dreghorn stepped outside, her attitude to the woman warmer than to some of the others that had approached her.

Isla turned to him. "James, this is—"

"Inspector Dreghorn and I have met before," Kitty Fraser said, whether embarrassed or amused it was hard to tell.

Dreghorn tipped his hat. "I had to ask Mrs. Fraser's employer a few questions recently."

"Employer?" Isla glanced from Dreghorn to Kitty.

Kitty smiled patiently. "It's what everyone thinks. An easy mistake, I suppose, attitudes being what they are." She met Dreghorn's eyes. "I don't work *for* Mr. Levin; I work *with* him. We have business interests in common."

"Mrs. Fraser is one of our patrons." Isla laid a hand on Kitty's arm. "She owns the premises that houses our secretarial school in the city center and leases it to the Trust free of charge."

Kitty patted Isla's hand as if it was the least she could do. "It's a shame you're leaving just as I'm arriving." She gave Dreghorn a pointed look. "Mr. Levin encountered a few problems earlier this evening and I had to hold the fort at the club for a while."

Dreghorn smiled. "If there's anything I can do to help Teddy out?"

Kitty squeezed Isla's hand as she stepped away, gave Dreghorn another smile that didn't reach her eyes. "Oh, I think you've done enough already, inspector. Good night."

"Where are we going?"

"A short cut. See, we're in Love already."

Glancing out of the window, he saw the Love Crescent sign fading into the night. Isla had driven off in the opposite direction to the one from which they had arrived. Eventually, she slowed the car to a halt.

They were parked outside Trinity Church, the lights of Summerton Hall no longer visible, the music hardly audible.

"All those caring faces back there," she said, staring at the windshield as if the energy was draining from her. "All their kind comments. Most of them looked down on Charles when he was alive, but now it's, 'Oh, what a tragedy,' 'Such a lovely man.'" She laughed bitterly. "One woman could hardly stop crying. I'm sure he slept with her."

"Sometimes the truth blurs, the dead take on a new life," Dreghorn said. "Makes it easier for those they left behind. Whatever else, he can't hurt or embarrass you anymore."

"He never did. Didn't hurt me, didn't anger me, insult me, shame me, didn't do anything." She looked at him. "What's worse—if you hate, or if you just don't care?"

Dreghorn had no answer, wasn't sure there was one. She smiled sadly.

"Your chief constable didn't seem particularly pleased to see you there with me."

"Probably thinks we're at it."

"*At it!*" she repeated in delight. "Romantic." She turned to face him, drawing her knees up, snuggling into the seat; he could hear her stockings rasp silkily against each other. "How much don't you remember?"

"Every kiss, every caress, every—" He stopped himself. "You?"

"It's as if it never happened. Could all have been a dream."

Later, he told himself that he could have stopped it, should have pushed her away, but in truth he didn't know who moved first, just that his lips were on hers, his hand under the fur of her coat, on the flowing silk of her dress, on the flesh underneath, her body arching toward his.

25

SUMMER 1914

The training camps were organized twice a year, winter and summer. For the next six months Jimmy made sure he won every bout he fought, so he didn't forfeit his place. His amateur stock was high, and there was talk of him turning professional in a few years with Sir Iain's financial backing.

He tried not to think too much about Isla Lockhart, but for all his good intentions his heartbeat quickened when he saw her again, though that may have been because the encounter very nearly killed him.

The coaches had sent them all on a cross-country race. Jimmy was one of the leaders, only a couple of runners ahead of him, the majority trailing behind. Emerging from the forest path onto one of the muddy roads used by the keepers, he was startled by the sound of a horn blasting. A bright red Argyll Flying Fifteen was racing toward him, the man in the passenger seat waving urgently. Jimmy's alarm was tinged with short-lived elation as he realized Isla was driving, laughing madly, with Rory beside her, trying to seize control of the steering wheel.

Jimmy dived to the side, landing on the grass verge. The wheels narrowly missed him, and he glimpsed the personalized ornament on the bonnet—a horse or a kelpie—as he rolled into the ditch beside the road. He lay still, breathing heavily, glad that it was summer; in winter, he'd be soaking in icy water. The car didn't stop, the sound of the engine fading into the distance. He hadn't expected Isla to swoon or throw herself into his arms, but he'd hoped for a look or maybe a smile, not that she'd almost run him over and not even notice.

He clambered out of the ditch as the other runners bounded past, leaving him last, and told himself he was nothing more than a dare to Isla Lockhart, an impetuous flouting of the rules to annoy her parents. She'd quickly forgotten everything, which was exactly what he should do.

The next day, still smarting, Jimmy was happy to lose himself in exercise. Throwing combinations into the heavy bag, he didn't notice Rory enter the gym in dark trousers and shirtsleeves, more casual than they were used to seeing their patrons dressed. He nodded greetings, watched the fighters at work, inspected their techniques.

"Time I tried my luck, I think," he said as he came to Jimmy.

"Sir?"

"A spot of sparring. I didn't bring gloves, but I assume you've got spares."

Robertson appeared from the other side of the heavy bag, stopped it swaying. "Sorry, sir," he said. "It's not allowed."

"Not allowed by whom? My family owns these facilities, so I imagine if I want to use them . . ."

"Aye, sir, but I suppose what I mean is that I don't think it would be right."

"I can judge right and wrong for myself, sergeant. Gloves, please."

Rory stripped off his shirt, tossed it over a stool. He was slim and long-limbed, glowing with health, muscled in the manner of a rugby player or rower.

"Dreghorn?" He grinned.

Before Jimmy could answer, a voice called out, "I'll give you a go, sir." Charlie Currie was already in the training ring, ready to spar. He smiled, banged his fists together. "No bother."

Jimmy glared at Currie; he liked Charlie well enough, but knew he had a touch of the bully in him. Rory didn't notice Jimmy's concern, or chose not to.

Training ground to a halt as Rory sprang into the ring. No one seemed comfortable with what was happening other than the two opponents, who touched gloves and started circling each other. Rory skipped and danced faster; Currie stayed calm, stalking patiently. Rory threw a couple of jabs. Currie soaked them up easily, but nodded as if impressed. "Good one, sir," he said.

Rory was a passable boxer, top of his class at Fettes. But Currie was tough, hardened by years of manual labor, driven to use the noble art to change his life, to escape.

They hadn't long started when Sir Iain arrived with Captain Ross. There was a brief kerfuffle between Ross and Robertson, who shrugged helplessly; what else could he have done? Sir Iain left them to it, moving ringside. Currie glanced warily at the elder Lockhart.

"No favors in the ring, Currie," Sir Iain ordered.

"No fear of that, Sir Iain." Currie went on the attack, stinging jabs at first, gradually flowing into combinations to increase the pressure. If Rory dodged or blocked one punch, he was inevitably caught by the follow-up. His counterpunches grew wild, telegraphed.

Soon Rory was bleeding from his nose and mouth, one eye swelling. He was game, though, rejecting offers to finish the bout with an angry swipe of his glove. Even Currie, hardly a sympathetic soul, was growing reluctant to carry on, looking to his trainers for advice, receiving only animosity in return for taking things too far. As he glanced at them, Rory caught him with a solid cross that caused a couple of onlookers to cheer in support.

Incensed, Currie spat blood onto the canvas and retaliated, steaming in with a flurry of blows. His defense long gone, Rory took two good shots to his head and was already going down when a third connected. Toppling backward, one arm hooked over the middle rope, he landed in a crooked sitting position, legs splayed out straight.

Robertson nodded for Jimmy to help Rory to his feet. Later, he put it down to his imagination, but he could have sworn Rory was smiling.

Sir Iain gripped his son's arm as Jimmy helped him down from the ring. "What did that prove?" he hissed. "You're not one of them. They don't want you to be." He glanced at Jimmy, who pretended he couldn't hear, tightened his grip. "Never give up your advantage. Never give up your power."

At the summer ceilidh that evening, Currie was acting the big man, strutting around making sure the Kelpie staff knew he'd belted their lord and master, as if he was some working-class hero battling for their rights. Divisions had opened up between the squad, some siding with Currie, others thinking he'd gone too far—there was nothing honorable in humiliating an unfairly matched opponent. Currie caught Jimmy's eye a couple of times, held the look provocatively, and raised a bottle of beer in salute. Jimmy didn't return the gesture, which he knew would irritate Currie, who always wanted to be liked.

Eventually, Currie crossed the dance floor. "Have you got a problem with me, Jimmy?"

"You could've gone a bit easier on him. Rory's all right."

"Rory, is it? What, you and him the best of friends? Who says I didn't go easy on him? If I'd gone for it, he'd be deid right now."

"Aye, right," Jimmy said. "Forgetting I've been in the ring with you? To be honest, he didn't give you a bad fight."

Currie laughed as if admiring Jimmy's spirit, reached into his pocket and drew out his cigarettes. "Fag?"

"Got my own, thanks."

Currie shrugged as he popped a cigarette in his mouth. "Maybe you're the fag."

"What?" The band had started up a new tune; Jimmy had to strain to hear.

"Maybe you're the fag. That's what Rory and his like have in their posh private schools—fags. Younger pupils that act like tea-boys for them, polishing their shoes, making their beds, warming the bog seats, maybe even"—Currie made a motion with his cupped fist—"giving them a wee wank round the back of the bike sheds." He lit a match, the flare glinting in his eyes. "Is that what you do for him?"

Jimmy knocked the match out of Currie's hand, said, "I'll warm your face, you prick."

"Go ahead, then. Any time."

Jimmy glanced around; dancing couples whirled past, other revelers laughed and drank and ate. "Outside," he said.

The night air cleared his mind, cooled his anger. Gravel scrunched under his feet as he decided they'd gone far enough and turned. A few of the other athletes had followed them out. Jimmy slipped off his jacket and threw it to one of them. Currie drained his beer and tossed the bottle into the darkness. Jimmy raised his guard.

"We're no' in the ring now, yah eejit!" Currie grunted and sliced a kick between Jimmy's legs.

Jimmy twisted desperately, taking the brunt of the blow on his hip—not ideal, but better than having his testicles crushed. He staggered and fell, saw the worn sole of Currie's boot coming down. He rolled back, felt the shudder as Currie's foot stamped into the ground.

He scrambled away, arse scraping the gravel, trying to find space to regain his footing. Currie followed like a striker chasing the ball, ready to boot it into the back of the net and win the game. Jimmy realized his head was standing in for the ball.

His shoulders came up against something solid. Currie grinned as he saw his chance, swung his foot. No grace or finesse—a toe-basher, they'd have called it on the terraces. Jimmy threw himself flat, the kick passing over him, Currie's foot smashing full force into the corner wall of Kelpie House.

"Fu-fu-fuck!" Currie cried, hopping back, injured foot in the air, arms flapping dementedly.

Jimmy rolled to his feet, driving his elbow into Currie's groin. He stepped back as Currie crumpled in on himself and shoved, sending him sprawling.

He was drawing back his foot for a kick of his own when he heard a dog barking. "You lot!" a voice challenged, one of the gamekeepers probably. "What're you up to?"

Jimmy and the other athletes started running for the house. He looked back after a few steps; Currie was still curled up on the ground, hands cupping his groin. Jimmy rushed back and hauled Currie to his feet. They stumbled toward the kitchen doors, catching a glimpse of the dog, and were laughing together as they slammed the door shut on its frustrated barking.

Currie's arm was around Jimmy's shoulder as they entered the hall and each grabbed a beer, joking about how hopeless their scuffle had been and bonding over their narrow escape from the Hound of the Lockharts. Jimmy was on his second beer, Currie pointing out the lassies they'd got off with the previous year, when he realized he'd mislaid his jacket.

He stepped outside gingerly, expecting to be savaged by an angry hound, and crept back to the scene of the fight. No sign of the jacket. "Shite!" Against his mother's advice he had borrowed the suit from his Uncle Joe, who fancied himself rotten in it, although it looked better on Jimmy. There was no way he could afford to buy a replacement.

"Scandalous."

He jumped, looked in the direction of the voice, and saw a dark shape leaning against the wall. A red dot flared, giving a glimpse of Isla Lockhart's features, and then faded as she removed the cigarette from her mouth.

"Language like that could corrupt an impressionable young lady," she said.

"If I see any around, I'll be sure to start talking proper. Nice jacket, by the way."

"This old thing?" She gave a playful twirl. "Just something I found lying around." His uncle's jacket was too big for her, but she still looked good in it. She thrust her hands into the pockets and skipped around him.

"Brawling in the grounds. Not the best way to repay my father's hospitality."

"You were out here?" He was embarrassed that she'd seen him scrabbling about on his backside, but at least he'd won, if either of them had.

"I came to see the ceilidh—our dances are more formal, much less fun. I popped outside for a cigarette and next thing you and your friends trooped out. Didn't even notice me. I had a ringside seat. Your opponent—was he the one who beat Rory black and blue?"

Jimmy didn't confirm or deny it. "How is your brother?"

"Fine. Seems rather pleased with himself actually."

"He shouldn't have done it."

"I imagine the temptation to bash the boss's son on the nose was too hard to resist." She treated him to a wry smile. "You taught him a lesson though."

"I meant Rory. He should never have got into the ring with Charlie."

"Obviously not, but"—Isla shrugged—"fathers and sons. Always trying to live up to each other. You know how it is."

Jimmy smiled sadly. "No' really."

"Oh, I'm sorry." It was the first time, he thought, that she'd spoken without a sheen of sarcasm. "He died?"

"Might as well have done. Last heard of in Australia, but that was years ago. I don't really remember him. My ma brought us up on her own."

Isla slipped an arm through his, and they strolled away from the house and through a gate onto a path he didn't know existed. It wound down through woodland, with large flowering shrubs and bushes on either side that were exotic to his eyes—azaleas, witch hazel, heather, and thistles, Isla pointed out, when he asked.

"I know what thistles are!" Jimmy exclaimed. "And heather."

The sun was setting through the trees ahead, painting the Clyde in warm pink hues, softening their view of the world, as they talked about their lives.

"After the summer, I'm going to Brillantmont. It's a finishing school in Switzerland." The prospect intrigued her, but she wasn't overly thrilled. "The usual story—pack them off to become young women, then marry them off to some supposedly eligible bachelor who'll increase the family's finances or prestige. Look how well it worked out for Mummy and Daddy."

Jimmy didn't think life at Kelpie House looked too bad, but made no comment. If Sir Iain and Lady Jane didn't get on, the place was big enough for them never to have to see each other.

"I'd rather stay here and go into the family business like Rory," Isla continued. "It's what Mummy would like too, but Daddy outright refuses to buck tradition. Another victim of my gender—but not for long." A look of quiet determination. "Mummy and I are suffragettes, you know."

In March that year, Isla and her mother had helped smuggle Emmeline Pankhurst—"hidden in a laundry basket!"—into St. Andrew's Halls in Glasgow, only just escaping when the police broke up the meeting and arrested Mrs. Pankhurst. After Brillantmont, Isla planned to throw herself into the cause.

Jimmy nodded encouragingly—as if he'd given it any thought—then joked about wearing lederhosen and yodeled like a screeching cat. She laughed, nudged his ribs, and warned him to be quiet.

"Ouch!" he yelped exaggeratedly. "What is this—kiss, cuddle, or torture?"

"What's that?"

"Kiss, cuddle, or torture. You didn't play it at school?"

"Rory went to Fettes, but I was educated by a governess called Miss Kirkland. She would never tolerate such frivolity."

"Lads and lassies go into separate teams and take turns chasing each other. When you're caught, you get asked, 'Kiss, cuddle, or torture?'"

"And what did you choose?"

"Torture every time." His eyes hinted that he might have changed his mind since then.

"I like the sound of that. I'd be good at torture." She darted forward, attacking his torso with ticklish pinches. He laughed and yelped and pretended to try and fight her off.

"So, what would you choose?" he asked.

"You'll have to catch me to find out."

She laughed and ran along the path, which curved into the trees ahead. The path led onto a stretch of shoreline that Jimmy hadn't seen before—a natural deep-water inlet, sheltered by trees; a private harbor for the Lockhart family during the milder summer months. A large two-story boathouse stood as close to the river bank as the tides allowed, the walls painted a blinding white, not an ideal color for Scottish weather. A veranda ran the length of the building, giving wonderful views of the Clyde. The balcony windows were dark, but he imagined an opulent entertaining space inside, like some gentleman's club. The barn-like doors on the lower floor opened directly onto the shingle. Through the windows he could see the racked-up shapes of sculls and rowing boats.

A jetty protruded into the river, a small motor boat and a large sleek yacht moored to it. Jimmy recognized the name—the *Quentin Durward,* Sir Iain's pride, in which he had raced to victory in many competitions. The ships built in the yards were breathtaking in their own right, but the *Durward* was a thing of real beauty. The entire harbor was beautiful, part of a world that wasn't his. He felt like an interloper, out of his depth, and for the first time felt a slight chill in the air.

A mischievous stifled giggle reached him. Jimmy caught a glimpse of Isla behind one of the veranda support pillars and lunged, but she was too fast, darting out of reach. She ran onto the pier, thought better of it, and started back, but Jimmy was blocking her way, crouched like a goalie awaiting a penalty.

She feinted to one side, and then ran the other way. Jimmy hooked an arm around her waist and held her tight. She struggled wildly, both of them laughing, but eventually relaxed. He shifted his grip, grasping the lapels of his uncle's jacket, and stared into her eyes.

"Kiss, cuddle, or torture?" he whispered.

She didn't answer, just moved closer, until their lips touched.

They kissed and touched and talked and laughed for Jimmy didn't know how long, covered by his uncle's jacket and cuddled on something called a chaise longue that they'd dragged out onto the veranda from the boathouse. In the distance they heard voices, car doors slamming, and engines starting up. The ceilidh had come to an end; the lads would be heading back to their dormitory, the Lockhart household to their beds.

Isla sat up, concerned. "We should go. People will be looking for me."

"When do you leave for Switzerland?" he asked. "I could get a train to Largs on my day off. We could have ice cream, or something like that . . ." Even to an optimist like him, it didn't sound a tempting offer, not to someone who had a yacht at the bottom of her garden.

"Term starts at the end of the summer, but my mother's threatening a grand tour of Europe together before that." She caught the disappointment on his face and swung her leg over his hips, straddling him. "Why? You won't care; you'll be too busy traveling the country, running around with gangsters' molls and those girls who walk about the ring in their knickers, holding numbers above their heads."

"Ya dancer! I'm going up in the world, then."

She punched his shoulder in mock outrage, left her hand there as they gazed at each other, and then leaned in to kiss him again.

As it was, Isla didn't go to Brillantmont after the summer, and Jimmy visited Europe before she did. A few weeks later, on 4 August, 1914, Britain declared war on Germany, and Joe Dreghorn, queuing to enlist, sniffed suspiciously at his lapel and wondered why his best suit smelled of expensive scent.

26

He woke more content than he had been in a long time, until he realized what had caused him to stir. The sound of Catriona Geddes playing in her bedroom, two doors down from where he lay naked with her mother. He felt a flood of shame, swore silently at himself.

For once, he wished he had drunk more so he could blame the alcohol, but he'd been in control of his actions as much as anyone could be. Worse, he knew he'd do the same again. Wouldn't think twice.

Isla was still asleep, turned away from him. His mind flashed back to the previous night, to their frenzied stripping of each other, her lean body in the dark, his mouth on her nipple, his tongue trickling down her belly. He'd gasped as he came and was breathing hard afterward. She'd shushed him, stroking his chest until he fell asleep, saying, "There, there."

He inched up carefully. The bed didn't creak, neither did the floorboards. Obviously in a different league to what he was used to. He gathered his clothes, heard Catriona's sing-song voice again, and dressed hurriedly. The situation was uncomfortable enough without being discovered naked by a six-year-old as she popped in to say good morning to her mother.

He shoved his tie in a pocket and carried his shoes in one hand, recalling the echo of the polished wooden hallway he had to cross before reaching the front door. Slipping on his jacket, he removed his notebook and pencil, wrote, "Sorry. Duty calls," tore out the page and left it on the bedside table. The door made a small noise as he opened it, but there was no movement from Isla. For a moment, he wondered if she was feigning sleep to avoid any awkwardness.

Heading for the stairs, he had a cautious peek through Catriona's half-open bedroom door as he nipped past. The girl was arranging dollies and stuffed toys around a miniature table and chairs, ready for breakfast.

He crept down the stairs, spying his coat and hat on the rack beside the main door. He made it across the hall without a sound and was reaching for his coat when a voice said, "You weren't as quiet as this on trench raids, sergeant."

Rory Lockhart was seated in the drawing room with a ringside view of the tiptoeing detective, his face bright with knowing humor. He was dressed in a silk dressing gown and pajamas, a pot of coffee on the table, that morning's *Glasgow Herald* open on his lap.

"Morning, sir," Dreghorn said. "You're an early riser."

"I like to see the world before everyone else does. Got into the habit when we were in France."

"I didn't know you were here."

"If Isla won't return to Kelpie, then I'll stay here until this is resolved. Means I get a chance to spoil my niece. Coffee?" Rory topped up his own cup. "I'll call for a fresh pot."

"Thanks, but I can't stay."

Rory nodded at the hallway. "Funny, what you were doing. If you were a woman, they'd call that a walk of shame."

"I wouldn't."

"Nor me. But that's because we're open-minded men of the world. We've seen enough to know what matters." He savored his coffee, met Dreghorn's eyes. "We should talk."

* * *

Our Father, Who art in heaven, Hallowed be thy name . . .

Other than funerals, it had been years since Dreghorn had attended Mass, but the words were still there, ingrained like rings in the trunk of a felled tree.

The exterior of Sacred Heart Church on Old Dalmarnock Road was as blackened as any tenement, but inside the walls and barrel-vaulted ceiling were bright with fresh paint, the gold of the tabernacle gleamed, and the pale morning sunlight, filtered through the Diocletian windows, took on a magical quality.

Dreghorn had sneaked in toward the end, drawing disapproving glances from the more devout worshippers. "Peace be with you," he said with a beaming smile, extending his hand to a particularly recalcitrant couple as he sidled into the pew after a halfhearted genuflection.

The priest raised the host and then the chalice, blessed the bread and wine as the body and blood of Our Lord Jesus Christ. As a child, before his First Holy Communion, Dreghorn had been eager to know what the body of Christ would taste like, imagining a rush of goodness through his body. That it was dry, papery, and tasted of nothing was a huge disappointment.

Dreghorn scanned the faces of the congregation as they queued to receive communion and returned to their seats. He saw the woman he was searching for and watched until she reached her pew, memorizing her clothing and gait to help spot her later.

He was the first out of the service, crossing the road to the tram stop and smoking a Capstan as the church emptied. The woman chatted briefly on the steps with other parishioners, said her good-byes, and walked off. He crushed his cigarette underfoot and jogged after her, making sure no other churchgoers were within earshot before calling out, "Miss Hunter? Excuse me, Miss Hunter!"

She stopped and turned with a small sigh. "Not for a wee while," she said.

Dreghorn tipped his hat, pleasantly apologetic. "Sorry, Mrs. Docherty, I know. Just wanted to make sure it was you." He flashed his warrant card to identify himself.

"If you're looking for my brother, you're barking up the wrong tree. We don't speak much these days."

Janet Hunter, Billy's older sister, had married young in an attempt, it was said, to get away from her father. Her husband Patrick Docherty was respectable and hardworking, a good father to their children and someone any man would be proud to call a brother-in-law, apart from one thing—he was a Catholic. Understandably, given his standing in Bridgeton society, Billy Hunter didn't offer the union his blessing. The rumor was that early in the relationship Billy and Peter MacLean had given Docherty a hiding to warn him off, but the incident only drove him and Janet closer together. Billy and his father refused to attend the wedding. To add insult to injury, Janet embraced the Catholic faith, and in the twenty-odd years since had been a regular at Sacred Heart.

"It does have something to do with Billy," Dreghorn admitted, "but not in the way you think. Mind if I walk with you?"

"It's a free world, mostly." She started on her way again, pace brisker. "You must be keen. It's not often your lot darkens the doorstep of a Catholic church."

"I'd call myself an optimistic atheist more than anything, these days, but technically I'm still a Tim." He shrugged as she gave him a look of disbelief. "It's no' exactly the sort of club you can get out of once you're in." She laughed, and he asked, "Are you going to see your mother now?"

Her smile faded. "What if I am?"

"It's not just you that I want to talk to."

"Is that Catholic with you?" The voice was strident, but not without affection.

"She means Pat; they actually get on all right, but . . ." Janet said softly as she unlocked the door, then raised her voice to answer, "No, a different one today."

Dreghorn removed his hat as he followed her inside, his shins colliding almost immediately with the bed that was set up in the center of the room, claiming most of the available space. Janet and Billy Hunter's mother Margaret was propped up by pillows, a walking stick beside her on the candlewick bedspread. Her frame was frail, but the eyes were bright and curious. Janet gestured at Dreghorn as she skirted the bed. "Ma, this is Inspector Dreghorn, a policeman. He wants to have a chat with us."

Margaret's gaze became fierce. She snatched up her stick, would have prodded Dreghorn painfully, if he hadn't stepped out of range. "Away!" she cried. "I'll take my stick off your head! Always after my Billy, so you are."

Dreghorn raised his hands as if at gunpoint. "No' the day, Mrs. Hunter. I come in peace, cross my heart." He glanced at Janet, nodded as she smiled and mouthed, "Tea?"

Margaret lowered the stick, but kept a firm grip on it. "Thought you said he was Catholic?" she snapped.

"He is," Janet answered.

"And a polisman?"

"Aye," she said over the sound of the tap as she filled the kettle.

"In the name o' the wee man." Margaret shook her head in outrage, gave Dreghorn a long, hard stare. There was a glimmer of recognition. "You were with our Rab in the war, one of Jock Dreghorn's boys. Right bastard, that yin."

"So they say." He looked around, detected a faint smell of urine from the commode in the corner. "It's not Billy I'm looking for," he said. "It's your daughter."

Janet and her mother glanced at each other, wary.

"Your other daughter—Sarah."

The name jolted Margaret. She struggled to speak, a lump in her throat. Janet went to her mother, throwing Dreghorn a look of bitter accusation.

"Where is she?" Margaret whispered. "Is she all right?"

"That's what I want to find out," said Dreghorn. "I've been asked to look for her."

"By whom?" Janet had a hand on her mother's shoulder.

"King Billy himself."

"Why does he want to do that?" Margaret seemed to shrink with age as she spoke. "After all this time?"

"Says it's for you, that you deserve to see your daughter one last time."

"I'm no' deid yet!" A spark of defiance, fading quickly. "She could be on the other side of the world. I wouldn't blame her. I ruined that poor lassie's life. That's all she was—a wee lassie."

Janet squeezed her mother's shoulder to quieten her. "What's Billy told you, then?" she asked.

"That Sarah's been missing for the best part of twenty years. That she got herself into trouble with a lad and that you convinced her to give the baby up for adoption. Billy was in jail at the time and you didn't say anything because you didn't want to worry him."

"Why would he ask you to find her? You're no' exactly best pals, I'm guessing."

"Better the devil you know. It's what I do. And we were in the war together."

"That bloody war!" A reason, an excuse she'd heard all too often.

"He didn't want me to talk to you on my own, but I thought it might be best, in case you hadn't told him the truth, the whole truth, and nothing but the truth."

Margaret bristled. "You think I'd lie to my own son?"

Dreghorn folded his arms. "If he was already in Barlinnie Prison for assault, you might. Billy's got a temper. No telling what he would do if he heard someone had done the dirty on his wee sister—lose the head and go for another prisoner, attack a guard? He might have killed somebody, ended up at the wrong end of the long drop." His blunt reasoning silenced them. "Aye, I think you'd lie to him if you had to. And it might be an idea not to let him know I was here. The long drop's still looming."

Janet sat on the bed and squeezed her mother's hand. Dreghorn let them think for a moment before continuing. "Billy said you refused to talk about it. Said that Sarah was meant to go to Trinity, but ran away the night before she was supposed to leave. None of you have seen her since. He was determined to track her down when he got out of jail, but the war happened and he was shipped off to France." He watched their reaction. "Except, I don't believe she'd risk the baby's life by running off. And I don't believe you'd let your daughter, your wee sister, go through something like that on her own."

Margaret looked him in the eye. "She did go to Trinity. We just didn't tell Billy."

"I know. I've been there. I'd like to know what happened afterward. I know it's painful, but Billy won't rest easy."

"She had the baby, the second of June 1914, at a quarter to six in the morning. I refused to see her. I couldn't. If I had, I wouldn't have been able to—" There were tears in the old woman's eyes, thoughts of how different things could have been. "Sarah begged me, but I said no. I think that broke her heart."

"Giving up the baby broke her heart," Janet said. "We thought we were doing the right thing. I'd have taken the wee lamb myself, but—"

"You couldn't," her mother said.

"I was expecting my first at the same time, and Patrick was out of work," Janet explained. "Sarah was still at Trinity when I had my baby. God knows how that made her feel—seeing me watching our wee yin grow up, all the while knowing she had to give her own away. Maggie. She called the baby Maggie. I suppose whoever adopted her would've named her something else."

"What do you mean—she was still there?" Dreghorn asked.

"She worked at Trinity for a year or so, helped with the laundry— big job, all those kids—and worked some days in the grocer's."

"You're sure? They never mentioned it to me."

"We visited whenever we could, got the train to Kilmacolm. If it was just Ma, she'd meet Sarah there in the Cross Cafe. If it was me, I'd walk from there to Trinity."

"They told me they liked to break up mothers and children as quickly as possible where adoption was involved. Kinder that way, they said."

"They made sure a certain distance was kept, but no, she could see Maggie. Why would she torture herself by staying otherwise?"

Margaret gave a little sob. Janet slipped an arm around her shoulders. Dreghorn could now see how frail the older woman was, clinging to life. He felt like an intruder, a ghoul, hated himself for dredging up their pain.

"What happened in the end?" he asked.

"Prospective parents would come to see Maggie." Margaret's voice was weak. "Well-to-do couples. Sarah saw them sometimes. She wasn't supposed to but she knew when visits were happening, so she'd hide and watch. Eventually, someone wanted Maggie and it was all arranged. They never told Sarah who, just told her to say her goodbyes."

"Trinity said that after the birth, Sarah went back to her family. As far as they knew."

Janet said, "I went to be with Sarah on the day of the adoption, but the train was jiggered, so I arrived late. Maggie had already left with her new mother and father, they told me. Sarah was gone too; they didn't know where. Or care.

"In the early hours of the morning she'd been caught trying to run off with Maggie. Lucky they hadn't called the police on her, they said—for trying to keep her own baby!" Then her voice lost its anger, became forlorn. "We never saw her again." She turned her head, kissed her mother on the temple.

"You've no idea where she went, what happened to her?"

Janet shook her head, said nothing. Margaret stared straight ahead, lost in the past.

"What about the father of the child?" Dreghorn asked. "Could she have gone to him?"

"She never told us who the father was, and believe me, we asked." Janet stood up, weary of Dreghorn's presence. "Whoever it was must've known something was going on, but he never came forward, so he couldn't have been up to much."

"You must've had your suspicions. A lad she went to school with, someone from the neighborhood?"

"I drove myself mad trying to work out who it might be, but she wouldn't say. She was a good girl, but back then she was always eager to please. She was the only one who could calm my da down when he was mad with the drink. Not that he was any softer with her than Billy or me. Hit the roof when he found out she was expecting and refused to have anything to do with her at Trinity. The bairn would've been just another life to make a misery, though he wasn't well by then."

"When did he die?"

"In the September. Lung cancer." Janet saw the suspicion on Dreghorn's face, shook her head vigorously. "No, no, nothing like that; he never—" She glanced at Margaret and gave a nod toward the door. "My mother's getting tired and I've no' even made her breakfast."

Dreghorn suddenly felt as if the room was shrinking to make him seem a threat. He thanked them for their time, apologized for upsetting them, and headed for the door. Janet followed him out on the landing and shut the door so her mother couldn't hear.

"I loved my sister," she said. "And I miss her every day, but I wouldn't bring her back to this." She gestured at the walls around them, the neighborhood beyond. "If I found her—or someone else did—I'd tell her she was well out of it. Do you understand?"

Dreghorn nodded, murmured a sheepish goodbye as she stepped back inside and closed the door. Outside, he stopped on the pavement, fixed his hat on his head. Gray clouds were slowly smothering the sunlight, threatening rain. *Back then,* Janet had said in reference to her sister's character, which implied that Sarah Hunter's nature had changed over the years, and that Janet had more recent experience of it than she admitted.

He darted across the cobbles in front of an approaching tram, its bell ringing to signal a stop. He tipped his hat to a young lady waiting for another tram in the opposite direction. She raised an eyebrow as if to say he should be so lucky.

27

MONDAY, 10 OCTOBER 1932

Expecting a humdrum day of paperwork and investigative frustration, Dreghorn left Mrs. Pettigrew's early and put in a good hour at the police gym—circuits, skipping, speed-bag, heavy-bag—before work. Normally, he and McDaid trained together twice a week, but he was restless, his mind full of thoughts of Isla.

The rest of his Sunday had been uneventful. Leaving Bridgeton, he just managed to arrive in time to meet his mother outside the Kelvin Hall for their weekly stroll through Kelvingrove Park.

"Look," he said, "wore my Sunday best for you."

"More like Saturday night's leftovers." She turned her cheek for him to kiss. "Otherwise, you might have had time to go home and shave."

"Hey, who's the detective here?" Dreghorn had said, slipping his arm through hers.

At Turnbull Street, he scrawled out the report Sillitoe had demanded and gave it to a secretary to type, fully aware how sketchy it was. Instead of charting progress, it highlighted how far they were from identifying, let alone catching, Charles Geddes' killer.

He telephoned Trinity first thing but was told that Mr. Dalrymple was at a meeting with the school's trustees—would he like to leave a message? Dreghorn said he'd call back. His background check on Arthur Bell had been similarly fruitless. Bell had served as a corporal in the Cameronians' 2nd Battalion during the Second Boer War, stationed at the notorious Irene concentration camp where one of his duties was the photographing and cataloging of Boer women and children imprisoned in horrific conditions after the destruction of their homes by the British. Unorthodox qualifications for looking after orphaned children, perhaps, but not against the law.

McDaid approached, nervously holding a brown envelope containing copies of Geddes' pornographic photographs.

"What if I get run over by a tram or something, and they find this on me? I'll never live it down."

Dreghorn surveyed McDaid's monolithic build. "If a tram runs into you, I'd be more worried about the passengers." He nodded at the door. "Chop-chop."

As McDaid trudged off, the telephone rang. Dreghorn reached for it, expecting Dalrymple, heard Shug Nugent's distinctive dour tones. "There's a party brewing at Bridgeton Cross. PC Stewart called it in."

"Surprisingly conscientious of him."

"Must be worried, out there all on his lonesome. Can't do his usual and hide in the pub pish-house with Sillitoe in charge. Says Billy's gathering the troops, giving them a talking-to."

"I'll spread the word. Have a couple of Black Marias standing by in case we have to send in the heavy mob."

The phone rang again as soon as he'd hung up. *You're popular the day, James,* he thought. It was Isla Lockhart, bright and bubbly: "Nanny's taking Catriona to Kelpie House to see her grandfather, though to be honest, it's the horses she's more interested in. Staying overnight. I did have an engagement this evening, but it's been canceled, so I'll be on my own. I think I might need a little protection, don't you?"

"What about Rory?" Dreghorn recalled the awkward encounter with his old captain.

"Won't be back tonight either. That's why he suggested taking Catriona to Kelpie."

"I don't think it's a good idea."

"Yes, you do. And so do I."

Dreghorn said nothing, remembering his last glimpse of her naked back as he slipped out of bed while she slept. There was a smile in her voice as she said, "I'll expect you about eight," and ended the call, confident he wasn't going to protest any further.

"If only you'd won the gold. You could've been like Victor McLaglen with the write-ups I gave you. Or your man Weissmuller, beating your chest and running about the jungle in tartan trunks. From Olympian to purveyor of filth, that's one mighty fall."

Denny Knox keeked inside the envelope again. "Jeez, my glasses are steaming up."

"Since when did you pitch your tent on the moral high ground?" McDaid moved the envelope away from the wet rings left by Knox's beer glass.

"Hey, I work for the *Express* these days. Quality news only, thank you very much." Knox sipped his beer, as if all their gabbing was giving him a real drouth. McDaid wasn't fooled; he knew Knox had turned to alcohol while working as a war correspondent on the Western Front. Still a respected journalist, he hadn't crawled completely into the bottle, but certainly kept it half full. "So, what's this about?" he asked.

"Might be nothing, might be crucial evidence. Hard to say until we know a bit more."

"Evidence in what?"

"An important case. Not at liberty to say any more."

Knox's spectacles balanced precariously on the tip of his bulbous nose. He pushed them up over his eyes, focused sharply on McDaid. "You and Dreghorn are on the Geddes murder, aren't you?" He didn't wait for an answer, removed the photographs from the envelope, and examined them closely, sensing something bigger.

"I'd like to be in that fellow's shoes," he said, "or his socks at least. He's kept them on, see? Why would you do that?"

"You don't recognize him, then?"

"Not offhand, but the resources of a national newspaper are at my disposal." He looked around to make sure no one was eavesdropping. They were in the Express Bar in Albion Street, a watering hole for reporters from the *Scottish Daily Express* offices next door, as well as rivals from the *Herald,* the *Citizen,* and the *Times,* all ready to stab each other in the back, albeit with fountain pens rather than blades. "What's in it for me?"

"If you can supply names and any other information about the lovebirds, the story's yours."

"Exclusive?"

McDaid nodded.

"Who's that coming from?" A note of distrust.

"Me and Jimmy."

"That's not going very high. If this is something to do with Geddes, your bosses might cover it up to save the Lockharts the embarrassment."

"They might, but we're men of our word, you know that. It's a big story. Might even be a book in it."

Archie McDaid had first met Denny Knox when he was covering the 1924 Paris Olympics. Knox had followed the pipe-playing wrestler's progress through the games and liked to claim credit for being the first person to describe him as "Bonnie." They maintained contact afterward when Knox dropped sports reporting in favor of the crime beat. He was forever threatening to write a book about some scandal or other—the incompetence of officers during the war, corruption and graft in the Corporation, the bigotry and sectarian divisions that split Scottish society, the Catholic Church's protection of priests accused of molesting children. But McDaid suspected that, thanks to a combination of alcohol and impatience, he would never do it. He was better at writing short angry articles that infuriated the elite. Pressure had frequently been put on editors to keep Knox on a shorter leash, but the reporter was like a terrier—warning him off just increased his ferocity.

"Buy me another pint and I'll see what I can do." Knox slid the photographs back into the envelope.

"Wouldn't a half be more sensible? It's no' even dinner time."

"Not when you're paying."

McDaid harrumphed and lumbered to the bar, delving into his pocket.

"Get me a pie while you're there," Knox called after him. "Like you said, it's nearly dinner time."

Ellen had hoped the look of polite disdain she'd afforded Dreghorn as he'd tipped his hat to her was convincing, not tinged by the surprise she'd actually felt. The last thing you expected when on undercover surveillance was for your superior officer to draw attention to you. She was beginning to realize that a mischievous humor lurked beneath the inspector's taciturn exterior. After all, it was a Sunday morning and neither of them was in uniform—what could be more natural than a gentleman saying good morning to a pretty girl? Even if she did say so herself.

She'd already allowed one tram to pass by and had thought it would seem suspicious to do so again. Fortunately, Janet Docherty had emerged about ten minutes after Dreghorn. Even if Ellen hadn't recognized her from the inspector's description, the woman's anxiety betrayed the fact that she'd just enjoyed a visit from the police.

As she turned into Dalmarnock Road, Ellen had risen from the bench as if to stretch her legs, then crossed the road and followed.

She'd been wary when Dreghorn had asked what plans she had that Sunday—fending off advances was something she'd become casually adept at, although Inspector Strachan's subtle persistence unnerved her—never overtly sexual, as if he only had her best interests at heart. Fortunately, Dreghorn seemed to genuinely appreciate her talent for police work, and there was no hint of impropriety. There was a degree of irregularity in what he was asking, and he'd been sketchy about why she was shadowing Janet Docherty, giving her a line about having to follow hunches in an investigation, "even if they don't always play out the way you want."

He'd apologized for ruining her day off and promised he would record it as overtime so she'd at least benefit financially. Otherwise, she was to give him her report on Monday.

Now Dreghorn was seated at his desk, staring at the telephone receiver as if it was a hand grenade and he couldn't remember if he'd pulled the pin or not.

"Is everything all right, sir?" she asked.

"Oh, aye, happy days are here again." He hung up. "How did you get on yesterday, constable? Any trouble?"

"None at all, sir. The suspect left the address at eleven hundred hours—not long after you. She seemed agitated."

"I sometimes have that effect on people. She didn't see you?"

"If I was some big lummox of a policeman, I'd have stuck out like a sore thumb. I pretended I was window-shopping or on my way to meet my beau. She even held the tram for me on London Road— saw me running for it and asked the conductor to wait—otherwise I might have lost her. I just smiled and thanked her.

"She disembarked at Central Station and I continued my surveillance." Ellen paused, wondering if her choice of words bordered on the melodramatic, but Dreghorn waved for her to continue. "I stayed one behind her in the ticket queue so I'd overhear her destination—Bearsden. And I sat in a different carriage on the train.

"At Bearsden, she walked to Boclair Road—a nice neighborhood, townhouses, lots of trees, plenty of privacy—and rang the doorbell of number fourteen. She looked ill at ease. The woman who answered seemed shocked to see her, but they obviously knew each other. The woman invited Mrs. Docherty in, but she refused. They had a heated argument. Mrs. Docherty kept pointing at the other woman, as if accusing her of something. Sorry, sir, I was too far away to hear anything. If I'd tried to get closer, I'd have been seen."

"You did well, constable."

Ellen nodded, pleased. "They talked for a few minutes before Mrs. Docherty stormed off. I heard the other woman shout after Mrs. Docherty, then slam the door. I ran hell-for-leather but I realized I couldn't get to the end of the street before Mrs. Docherty reached the pavement and would have been able to see me, so I ducked behind a parked car.

"When she was almost level with me, I scooted round the other side of the car and watched her through the windows until she turned the corner. I thought I'd be pushing my luck if I kept following her. Just as well there weren't any polis around—I'd have been arrested for acting suspiciously. Is something wrong, sir?"

Dreghorn was smiling. "I'm breathless with excitement. John Buchan couldn't have told it better."

"Was I trying too hard?"

"Top of the class, constable."

"I checked the Council records." Ellen flipped open her notebook. "The house is registered to a Catherine Fraser."

"Blonde hair, early thirties, about your height? Attractive, but a wee bit hard-faced?"

"Could be her, aye." She consulted her notebook again. "I thought it was unusual that a woman was the sole owner, so I checked back further. The previous owner was her husband John Fraser; the deeds passed to her on his death. The name sounded familiar, so I checked criminal records—"

"Johnnie Fraser, the Who's Who of hoors?" Dreghorn said.

Ellen nodded. Until his death a few years earlier, Fraser was the biggest purveyor of prostitutes in Glasgow, operating a tiered network that respected the class system—backstreets and single ends for the regular punter, posh West End townhouses for the upper echelons.

Dreghorn stood up, grabbing his hat. "Told you, constable, hunches don't always play out the way you think they will—Catherine Fraser works with Teddy Levin, our main suspect so far in Charles Geddes' murder. Maybe we should have a word, eh?"

"You want me to come with you?" Ellen forced the grin off her face.

"I could ask some big lummox of a policeman, if you'd prefer? We're not short of them."

Ellen shot to her feet. In the car, Dreghorn was silent; the last thing he'd expected was for Ellen's surveillance of Janet Docherty to throw up a possible connection to Geddes. With a new married surname and the adoption of a pet form of her middle name, it seemed Sarah Catherine Hunter had become Kitty Fraser. Hiding in plain sight.

He sensed Ellen looking at him. "Thanks for giving me the chance, sir," she said. "It doesn't happen often."

"No? Inspector Strachan seems fond of you."

"Too fond."

"Maybe he's being protective, thinks of you like a daughter."

"Aye, right. He already has two daughters."

Dreghorn became serious. "If he's pestering you, Ellen . . ." He was aware the word seemed inadequate.

"It's not so much that, it's— He's careful. Anything he says could get taken two ways, as if it's all in your head. But it's not, it's—" She shook her head, uneasy.

An alert came through on the radio, ordering all available officers to an incident on Norman Street. Ellen seemed grateful for the interruption. Dreghorn changed direction and turned on the bell. "I'll take you back to the station," he said.

"You'd be wasting valuable time, sir—simpler if I came with you."

He threw her a stern glance and accelerated. "All right. But you stay in the car."

28

In the midst of the stramash, it was virtually impossible to tell Billy Boys from Norman Conks. The police could identify each other— the regular constabulary by their uniforms and the plainclothes officers by their size, suits, and batons—but the rest was a melee of punching, kicking, slashing, and stabbing. Shouts of rage and pain were punctuated by the sound of smashing bottles hurled from tenement windows or deliberately shattered to create blades.

Reports had been received that morning of the Billy Boys massing in larger numbers at Bridgeton Cross. Such gatherings were more common prior to their regular Sunday church parade, when they would march up Poplar Street and down French Street, a circuitous route to the Church of Scotland, but one that allowed them to circle the mainly Catholic Norman Street with the enthusiasm of an Apache war party surrounding a wagon train.

Billy Hunter liked to think of himself as a master tactician, a general leading a well-disciplined army. Emboldened perhaps by the recent arrest of the Norman Conks' leader, Bull Bowman, for allegedly cracking someone's skull with a pick-shaft, the Billy Boys went on the march just before eleven. Today, instead of dispersing at the Church of Scotland, they veered straight into Norman Street.

And merry hell broke loose. Again.

Dreghorn twisted a Conk's arm up his back and used him as a

battering ram through the scrum toward a Black Maria parked like a barricade across one end of the street. Another police van was similarly positioned at the other end, hemming in the battling gangs.

"Lovely day for a barney, sir," a young constable said, unlocking the doors. The van was half full already, a tableau of battered faces from both gangs blinking in the light as the doors opened. It was impossible to keep them separate, and conflict could well erupt again inside the vans, but at least it was contained. One prisoner made a lunge for the doors, but Dreghorn shoved his captive into the man, knocking his arse back onto the narrow bench. "Play nicely," he warned, slamming the doors shut.

McDaid marched into the brawl as if the road ahead was clear all the way to Loch Lomond and he had the entire police band marching in procession behind him. He pulled a man around and hit him on the turn, sending him sprawling onto the cobbles. The man's opponent stared up at McDaid, a perfect invitation for a straight jab that put him flat on his back.

He carried on without breaking stride, knocking gangsters down right, left, and center. He rarely hit anyone more than once and didn't waste time looking back. A couple of enterprising officers followed in his wake, manhandling his dazed victims to the waiting police vans. When they were later questioned in court, the prisoners' testimonies invariably ended, "Then Big Bonnie Archie hit me, and I don't remember anything else."

It was far from a fair fight; the self-styled gangsters were mostly small and malnourished, though the weapons they carried ruled out sympathy. McDaid remembered Chief Constable Sillitoe's first address to his officers, his blunt comments about "the strong arm of the law" and the use of force.

Occasionally, McDaid worried about the undoubted talent he

possessed for meeting violence with violence. Returning home after work he had to pause to make sure it wasn't a bitter, angry policeman who stepped through the door, but a loving husband and father.

McDaid's children would never fear him. They would wrestle him to the floor and make fun of him as a blundering big bear. They would cover their ears and run away laughing when he played the bagpipes. But they would always be safe when he was around. He would make sure of it. They were still too young for the gangs to be a danger or a temptation, but that wouldn't always be the case, which was why McDaid had volunteered without hesitation to join Silli-toe's crusade.

A Billy Boy was swinging frenziedly at a group of Conks with a German cavalry sword, lifted from some battlefield by an older rela-tive and stolen or passed on with pride. McDaid flung an arm around the swordsman's neck in a chokehold.

At least his violence was under control. He remembered the look on Dreghorn's face when he'd burnt Tam Bryce's hand with the kettle, and thought of the war, when battles had raged for days; sol-diers living and breathing death, forced to become both more and less than human.

McDaid's war had been with the Black Watch, fighting the Turks in Mesopotamia and the biblical heartland of Palestine—corpse-cold by night and hellfire-hot by day; sieges, sandstorms, and brutal, bloody hand-to-hand combat. Amazingly for a target his size, he came through with only minor injuries, no bullet or bayonet wounds, but was struck down and nearly killed at war's end by Span-ish Flu. In Glasgow, the schools were closed, the streets sprayed with disinfectant, and people had hid behind masks or smoked furi-ously, believing that tobacco fumes killed the germs.

McDaid felt the swordsman go limp. He lowered the semi-conscious man gently into the arms of the constables behind him as another wee nutter, not even carrying a weapon, charged, yelling,

"You and me, big man!" McDaid grabbed him by the throat, heaved him off the ground, and held him overhead, noticing a twinge in his back as he did so—that didn't used to happen. Then he hurled the wee man, still croaking insults, into the thickest part of the brawl, bringing down six or seven men.

In his head, McDaid heard the cheers of the crowd as he won bout after bout on his way to the 1924 Olympics. Still got it, he thought, ignoring the temptation to wince and rub his back.

Dreghorn strong-armed a Billy Boy past him. "Showing off again, big man?"

The race through the streets, alarm bell ringing, had been exhilarating. Female officers rarely embarked on duties outside the station and it was the first time she'd been at the scene of such a disturbance—a full-scale riot, almost.

The hullabaloo reminded Ellen of the cheering at a football match, but with an extra helping of venom and the crash of shattering glass. Women and children leaned out of the windows yelling abuse, cheering encouragement, throwing bottles and rotting vegetables, and emptying chamber pots. One woman, carried away, hurled an entire chanty into the crowd.

Watching through the windshield, Ellen realized she was rocking back and forth with excitement, exactly like her father when he listened to boxing on the wireless.

A Billy Boy came bolting in terror through the scrum with a Norman Conk barreling after him, a bloodstained pick-shaft in his hands. The first man stumbled and fell onto broken glass. The Conk swung the pick handle, bringing it down on the Billy Boy's back as he struggled to rise. Ellen looked around; no police nearby. The pick-shaft pummeled the fallen man again.

A full-size police truncheon, not one of the short batons issued to plainclothes officers, lay on the backseat. "If anything happens,"

Dreghorn had said as he left the car, "there's always that. Don't be feart to use it." She hefted the weight of it in her hand.

Female officers weren't allowed to make arrests, weren't supposed to even leave the station except to offer comfort and compassion on bereavement duty. The furor, if she was injured, would have serious ramifications. None of which she thought about as she leaped from the car. All she saw was the bloodstained pick handle, breaking bones, pulping flesh . . .

She shouted a warning, not sure if her voice would be heard above the chaos. The Conk turned, his savage expression spattered with blood. "A woman polis?" he said, flabbergasted. "That's below the belt, so it is. I'm no' here to batter some wee lassie."

As he lowered the pick handle, Ellen gave him an appreciative smile, then swung the truncheon into his right kneecap with all her strength. He yelped, the leg buckling under him, and crashed to the pavement beside the man he'd been beating seconds earlier. Ellen rolled him onto his front, twisted an arm behind his back, and drew out her handcuffs.

"And they say chivalry's dead, eh?" she said. "You'd make your mammy proud. Well, apart from the attempted murder . . ."

"Hey, you!" Dreghorn shouted. "Throw that bottle and I'll come up there and chuck you out straight after it," he threatened.

The twelve-year-old, leaning out of a third-story window, an empty Tizer bottle held above his head, froze. A flurry of thoughts passed across his face before sticking on self-preservation and getting money back on the bottle. He closed the window surreptitiously, as if hoping his change of heart wouldn't be noticed.

Dreghorn slipped the baton back into his inside pocket, flexed his other fist, the knuckles scraped from a bicycle chain that had whipped around his forearm. The sleeve of his jacket was torn and covered in oil. The riot had been broken. The Black Marias were jam-packed and the cobbles carpeted with broken glass, dropped weapons, spattered blood, and the odd prone body.

He saw WPC Duncan scurry back into the radio-car, and sit there smiling innocently as if she'd never left it. He was about to say something when Billy Hunter and Peter MacLean sauntered round the corner into Norman Street.

"No' like youse two to miss a party." Dreghorn nodded at one of the vans as its engine started. "Sure we can find room if you don't mind squeezing."

Hunter looked around in mock surprise. "Has there been some sort of disturbance, inspector? Wouldn't know anything about that." The smile in his eyes said otherwise. "Peter and me are just out for a wee constitutional, know what I mean?"

"Clears the cobwebs," MacLean agreed.

"We'll be getting on our way, then, seeing as you've got it all in hand." Hunter signaled MacLean to walk on, but held back himself. He glared at Dreghorn, eyes cold and hard as a razor.

"Told you no' to go near my ma without me," he said. "Think you can come into Brigton and I'll no' know about it?"

Dreghorn arrived at Isla's forty-five minutes later than she'd said, a tiny act of rebellion that she hadn't noticed in the slightest. She offered to have one of her staff mend his torn sleeve, but he declined. She asked if he was hungry—the cook had made something that sounded French—but he'd had a fish supper in the pub with McDaid and Ellen Duncan, who initially resisted joining them until they convinced her that she'd earned it.

"Wouldn't mind a drink," he said.

Isla invited him into the drawing room and he flopped onto the couch, suddenly exhausted. He closed his eyes, took a deep breath, forced them open again. "Sorry, you'll think I just came round for forty winks."

She handed him a drink and smiled. "I hope not." She eased down beside him, tucked her feet under her. "Tough day?"

It tumbled out of him, the whole story—pressure from his bosses, the run-around from Dalrymple, a potted history of the Billy Boys and Norman Conks, the epic street fight. He omitted any details relevant to her husband's murder but was surprised how much he'd opened up. So was she.

"It's a different world," she admitted.

Dreghorn laughed, sipped whisky. "A wee bit."

"Just my luck. Keep going at this rate and you won't be around much longer either." She met his eyes, but then looked away self-consciously. It was the first time either of them had mentioned anything resembling a future together. But she recovered well. "Good that you and Sergeant McDaid are out there though, looking after things." She raised her glass in a toast. "Glasgow salutes you."

He returned the toast. "Dear old Glasgow town."

Isla laid down her glass, took his hand, and kissed his grazed knuckles. "Is that any better?"

"It's a start."

She moved closer, her leg touching his. He cupped her cheek in his palm, slid his fingers into her hair, and kissed her. Breaking contact only to switch out the lamp, they stayed on the sofa, urgent and hungry, not even bothering to undress. They lay there afterward, bathed in the warmth of the fire. Eventually, Isla sat up, took Dreghorn's hand, and led him upstairs.

29

Dreghorn was used to communal showers from his barracks days and the police gym, but a shower for a single household, large enough to hold someone McDaid's size and taking up the best part of a bathroom, was something new entirely. An obscene luxury compared to tenements where scores of tenants shared barely working lavatories, and tin baths were painstakingly filled with water heated on a range for whole families to dip into one after the other. After a day of fighting and a night of passion, though, he set aside his working-class outrage and decided to indulge himself.

The pipes groaned at first like some great stirring beast. The water flowed hot and powerful and he counted off the stings and aches of his injuries: the bruised cheek where McDaid had accidentally whacked him; the burn on his right hand; the grazed knuckles of his left; his cock raw and tender, though that one wasn't unpleasant.

When he'd awoken, Isla was already on her feet, slipping into a silk robe. She asked what he'd like for breakfast; her cook would prepare it.

"Thanks. But I've got to get to work."

"Love them and leave them, inspector?"

"Far from it, there's nothing I'd like better, but—" He took her hand as he stood up. Even with her makeup smudged, her hair messy, she'd never seemed so beautiful. Beautiful and real.

"We can't do this anymore," he said. "Not just now, with the investigation. Rory saw me leaving the other morning."

"Rory doesn't care. He's the least shockable man in the world."

"No, but I do. When the case is closed, I'll be yours to do whatever you want with."

They stood in silence. Her eyes promised nothing. He went to kiss her, but she stepped back, said, "You've got work, remember?"

So Dreghorn had trudged off to the shower, trying to convince himself he was doing the right thing. His mood had darkened further as he remembered his encounter with Billy Hunter. In a roundabout way, although large-scale gang fights were a regular occurrence, yesterday's violence was down to him, a reprisal for approaching Margaret Hunter.

He pretended he didn't hear the door opening behind him, whistled a carefree tune as he washed. He pictured the robe sliding off her body, sensed her stepping into the bath. Her breasts pressed against his back. She whispered in his ear—something about testing the strength of his resolve—and curled her arms around him, reaching down.

Not very resolute at all, it turned out.

McDaid sniffed loudly, tracking a scent that led to Dreghorn.

"You smell nice."

"Don't I always?" Dreghorn asked. "I like to make an effort for you."

"Fine, if you like whisky and fags. But today there's an intoxicating new aroma wafting around you."

"Different soap."

"You're strictly carbolic. New bedroom and bathroom more like. I'm a detective, remember?" He puffed exaggeratedly. "It's like a tart's boudoir in here."

"Blending in nicely, then, aren't we?" Dreghorn nodded through the windshield.

They were parked on the opposite side of the street from Kitty Fraser's unfeasibly grand residence, 14 Boclair Road, far enough away not to arouse suspicion. It was late afternoon; they'd spent the morning in court, giving evidence in the murder trial of Thomas Bryce. The more sensational aspects of the case had captured the grubby attentions of the tabloids, while the broadsheets were in attendance to weave the tragedy into the wider tapestry of Glasgow's social deprivation.

The evidence against Bryce was damning. He refused to meet anyone's eyes and shifted uncomfortably throughout the trial, as if already feeling the noose around his neck. If he'd cried, "Get me Garrison!" no one had cared enough to listen, for his court-appointed defense was lackluster. Sadie and Ally Reid testified that Bryce had confessed his crimes to them and that, far from helping him escape, they were merely plying him with alcohol to get him so stocious that he wouldn't cause trouble when they handed him over to the police. "A citizen's arrest is what we were making," Sadie claimed. "Tried to tell them that"—she pointed accusingly at Dreghorn and McDaid—"but would they listen? Wallop you first and ask questions later, that's their game." Sentencing was expected at the end of the week.

An overweight man in a tailor-made suit emerged from Number 14, crossing the road to the car parked in front of them. He became aware he was being watched as he unlocked the door. Dreghorn tipped his hat. McDaid gave him a cheeky wink. The man's sated expression paled into panic. He clambered into the car and drove off. The detectives had already taken his number.

He was the fourth gentleman caller since they'd started their surveillance. In addition to being registered in Kitty Fraser's name, the

premises were also listed as a guesthouse. The guests were numer-
ous, but didn't appear to stay very long.

"It's a knocking shop," McDaid said, about ten minutes later than
Dreghorn had expected. "A posh knocking shop." He looked around
at the houses, far bigger than anything he'd ever be able to afford.
"So, what are we doing here? Sightseeing?"

"You're the detective."

McDaid took a deep breath. "Charles Geddes was murdered. We
know, or suspect, that he owed Teddy Levin money, gambling debts
more than likely. Also that his practice wasn't doing well. Catherine
Fraser works for Teddy, supposedly as the manageress of the Gordon
Club, but we suspect—the magic word again—that she's also in
charge of running prostitutes for him and his clientele. Now it appears Mrs. Fraser is also the owner of a high-class brothel out here in
sunny Bearsden. All of which amounts to . . ." McDaid shrugged,
mystified.

"You're forgetting," Dreghorn said, "Geddes had photographs of
a risqué nature in his possession, which may or may not have played
a part in his death. How did he get hold of them? What was he planning to do with them?"

McDaid nodded at Number 14. "You think he was involved with
this hanky-panky?"

"Just asking questions. Getting answers is the hard part."

"Like playing darts blindfolded, but hoping you'll hit the bulls-
eye."

"That's police work for you."

Dreghorn had the key in the ignition when McDaid pointed through
the windshield. "Hold on a wee minute—is that a polis car?"

"Well," Dreghorn said, "we saw a priest going in there earlier, so
why not another of our moral guardians? Might explain why none of
the neighbors have complained."

They had been there for three hours now, the light beginning to fade. The police car stopped right outside Number 14, bold as brass, a uniformed officer behind the wheel. Two passengers got out. One stood tall, smoothing down his mustache with a thumb and forefinger; the other hunkered beside the driver in a simian crouch to say something, then straightened up, removing his hat and running fingers through thinning hair. Strachan and Orr.

"They *could* be here to make an arrest," McDaid said.

Strachan didn't knock when he reached the door, but walked in as if he owned the place, Orr swaying as he followed. Dreghorn figured that they'd been drinking.

There was movement at the window of the ground-floor reception room, a female form closing the curtains, although they were too far away to identify her. Shortly afterward, two upstairs lights went on.

Within minutes, the driver's head was nodding as he struggled to stay awake. He soon gave up, tipped his head back against the seat, and pulled his hat over his eyes.

"Five minutes to nod off," McDaid said. "Dedication like that makes you proud to be a polis."

"Suits us, the now." Dreghorn opened his door.

"Whoa, where do you think you're going?"

"Shush. You'll wake Sleeping Beauty."

He closed the door quietly and peeked through the open window at the sleeping policeman as he crossed the road. In a less salubrious area, someone would lean in and nick his helmet. Dreghorn was tempted. He gave the front door a business-like rap and tipped his hat at McDaid as he waited.

A young woman in a maid's uniform—a real maid's uniform, not the saucy postcard equivalent—opened the door. The smile froze on her face as she recognized him; whatever greeting she'd been taught to give curdled in her throat.

"Evening, Rose. It is Rose, isn't it?" It had been four days since he'd sat across from her and Arthur Bell in the Gordon Club. "Probably not the sort of work you were expecting."

Lost for words, she glanced at a doorway to the left of the central staircase.

"Mrs. Fraser's in there, aye?" he asked.

"Do you have an appointment, sir?"

"Don't need one. She'll be delighted to see me. Ray of sunshine, me."

Dreghorn brushed past and pushed open the door she'd been trying to guard. The sitting room was large and tastefully furnished, not in the same league as Isla Lockhart's but exactly what you'd expect the upper middle classes to favor, apart from the two scantily clad women seated at a round card table. One was dressed as if she couldn't decide between Wild West or Moulin Rouge, and the other wore suspenders, French knickers, and a long diaphanous robe. A wireless sat on the table between them, tuned in to what sounded like *Children's Hour,* of all things.

"Very educational," Dreghorn said. "Lady Jane will be turning in her grave."

Kitty Fraser, seated on the sofa, the top buttons of her blouse undone, tossed aside the magazine she was reading and rose wearily to her feet. "Inspector."

"Polis are like trams—you wait ages for one, then three turn up at the same time. My colleagues are upstairs, then? They've been daft enough to leave their motor parked outside."

Kitty nodded at the whores, who got up and left, neither bothering to switch off the wireless.

"How long before they're back down?"

Kitty glanced at the clock on the mantelpiece, surprisingly relaxed. "Orr always finishes first, but then sits around for ages to make everyone think he lasts longer. Swears the girls to secrecy, but"—she smiled—"there are no secrets here. Strachan will be another five, ten minutes. The girls never speak about him. I think he scares them. Not that he's hurt anyone, or ever been less than polite." She watched as Dreghorn paced the room. "Why, do you want a shot, inspector? On the house. I'll call the girls back in. Take your pick."

"How about you? Or that poor girl who let me in? Grooming her to go on the game, are you?"

She shook her head with a touch of anger. "This isn't the life for Rose. She's here, earning a wage, until our new tea room opens in Paisley; she'll work there. I don't force anyone into this."

"The choices they've got, you probably don't have to."

"I didn't make the world the way it is. You've never paid for a woman, not even in the war?"

Dreghorn looked away from the knowing amusement in her eyes. A brown envelope rested against a vase of fresh flowers on a coffee table, the flap bent backward, giving a glimpse of a thick bundle of notes inside.

"What do you want, inspector?" Kitty Fraser asked coldly.

"The truth." He hadn't expected it to sound so insignificant. "Confession's good for the soul, so the priests used to tell me."

"The truth is, men are quite happy to use women however they like, if they can get away with it. They come here because they like the lies as much as the sex, like to pretend that they're getting fucked because they're wonderfully attractive, not because they're paying for it. What sort of truth do you want?"

"The sort that leaves a man floating down the Clyde with his throat cut."

"I had nothing to do with Charles Geddes' death."

"But you knew him more than you've been letting on."

"Not really."

"He came here, though? His sort of place, I'd have thought."

Her eyes flicked toward the clock. "He didn't need to; he was attractive to women. But he seemed to like the simplicity. A quick shag, then back to the wife. Enjoyable company on the surface, but I don't imagine he was a very nice man."

"Nicer than whoever took a blade to his throat." He paused, letting the tick of the clock play on her mind.

"You'll find it more awkward than I will when they come down, inspector."

"Not when I tell them how much information you've been giving me about their off-duty shenanigans. This is a house of lies? I can tell a few too."

She glared at him. He heard movement upstairs, raised an eyebrow.

"Geddes had photographs hidden in his house, dirty pictures with men like the ones who've been streaming through your door all day, and young lassies not too far removed from the two sitting over there. Do you have cameras hidden around this place, Mrs. Fraser?"

"Some clients might like a photo."

"Souvenir for the wife and weans?"

"To wank over in their offices," she said with a venom that tarred the entire male species. "Or when the lady of the house and the little darlings are tucked up asleep in bed." The clock ticked. "I've no idea how he got hold of them. Or where they came from."

"So you'd have no objection to me looking at your rooms to see if they match the photos?"

"They're occupied at the moment."

"It's all right, I'm not shy."

Laughter upstairs, the clump of shoes being dropped on the floor.

"I know you get some of these girls from Bell and maybe Dalrymple at Trinity. I saw Bell bring Rose to the Gordon Club for your inspection, remember? Was Geddes blackmailing them about that? Or was he targeting you and Teddy?"

"You think Alasdair Dalrymple's capable of murder?"

"Teddy is. And I think Arthur Bell is. He served in the Boer War, ran a concentration camp for Boer women and children, beat them, starved them, locked them in a stockade to roast in the afternoon sun . . ."

When she didn't comment, Dreghorn started to open the door, but stopped and said, "I could just tell your brother where you are, Sarah."

He heard her sudden intake of breath. She was standing bolt upright, the color drained from her face, fear in her eyes. She tried to speak, couldn't. It was the first time he'd seen her control slip.

"Janet came here on Sunday. I had her tailed all the way from Bridgeton, you were seen opening the door to her." He had no more patience for argument or denial.

She looked around as if suddenly lost, trapped in an alien existence.

"Billy'll be pleased to see you. It's amazing you've been in Glasgow all this time and never bumped into each other. Different circles, I guess."

"Bastard!"

"All I want is for you to tell me what you know. No more stories."

A door opened upstairs. Floorboards creaked. A fist thumped on another door. Strachan's voice boomed, "Stop farting about, Graham! We know you shot your bolt ages ago."

Kitty tried to push Dreghorn into the corridor. "All right, but not now."

"When?"

"Tomorrow, come back tomorrow. Now go!"

Dreghorn took his time, turning up his collar, putting on his hat, the voices and footsteps growing louder. He saw Strachan's feet at the top of the stairs as Kitty pushed him into the garden and closed the door.

Strachan's driver was still asleep as Dreghorn went past. He quickly crossed the road and slipped into the passenger seat of the radio-car beside McDaid. They watched as Strachan and Orr emerged, illuminated by the light from the hallway. In contrast to Orr, tie askew, shirt tail hanging over his trousers, Strachan was as immaculate as an undertaker. He slipped the envelope of money Dreghorn had seen in Kitty's parlor into the inside pocket of his coat as Orr opened the car door for him. The constable woke with a start as Strachan slammed the car shut.

Dreghorn and McDaid prepared to duck out of sight as the other police car started up, but the constable executed a three-point turn and drove off in the direction they'd come from.

"I've a taste in my mouth only a dram will get rid of," said McDaid.

30

But McDaid was forced to forgo his dram when they returned to Turnbull Street.

"Sorry, big man," Dreghorn said. "Prior engagement."

McDaid was huffy about it, suspecting Dreghorn was slinking off to see Isla Lockhart. "She's the wife of a murder victim, Jimmy."

"Who said I'm meeting a woman?"

Dreghorn frustrated the big man further by offering no explanation beyond a cheeky tip of the hat as they parted. He walked briskly along Argyle Street, ducked through Central Station onto Gordon Street, and crossed the road to the Grosvenor Restaurant, where Rory Lockhart had suggested they meet for dinner, implying that they had important matters to discuss. Information that would be helpful to the case, Dreghorn presumed.

They made small talk at first, Dreghorn entertaining Rory with darkly comic tales of his days in the Shanghai Police. Rory returned the favor, focusing on the years he'd spent in Hollywood, where he'd laughed his way through a couple of screen tests, partied with Greta Garbo, Joan Crawford, and Douglas Fairbanks Junior, and slept with supposedly rising starlets whom he'd never subsequently seen on the silver screen.

Dreghorn only intended to have one course, but after a Martini in the bar beforehand thought *To hell with it.* He had cullen skink to start, one of his favorites. For his second course, he went for Beef

Wellington. Rory ordered a bottle of Chateau Petrus 1929 which, Dreghorn had to admit, wasn't bad. He decided to have Baked Alaska afterward.

The conversation finally came around to things more personal.

"My coming home was always on the cards," Rory explained. "My father would've liked me ensconced within the business years ago. In his current state of health, I can't shirk my responsibilities any longer. Shame Isla wasn't born a boy; she's far more adept at business than I am, but *c'est la vie*. I've told him I'll run things into the ground within weeks, but he refuses to see sense."

"Business'll be booming again. The Depression can't last forever."

"Mine will. Accountants, shareholders, politicians, unions." His eyes closed and his head flopped to one side with a great narcoleptic snore.

Dreghorn laughed.

Rory smiled. "I was serious when I said you should come and work for us. Don't see why I should suffer alone. And it'd be less dangerous." He gestured at the fading bruises on the detective's face.

"Doing what?"

"Unrest is in the air—Labor party, Communist party. We need someone to root out troublemakers, organize strike-breakers, keep the unions in line."

"I thought you liked to use Billy Hunter for that sort of thing."

"At that particular point we needed work to continue or there might not have been any jobs left for them to strike over," Rory said. "I've nothing against Hunter himself—a good man to have under your command—but an association with his organization?" He shook his head. "So what do you say?"

"Thanks, sir, but I don't think so. I've been on the other side, re-member? If I was still there, I'd probably be one of your troublemak-ers."

Rory laughed. "Either way, the offer's open." He drained his glass, raised an eyebrow. "Perhaps I should've got Isla to ask you."

"What do you mean?"

Rory seemed to enjoy the edge in Dreghorn's voice. "Just that she might be more persuasive. She'd be better running things than me, but it's not that kind of world, is it? I'll make sure she's closely involved in the day-to-day stuff, though. I'd be mad not to. Better judgment by far. In most things."

Dreghorn finished his wine, said nothing. An attentive waiter refilled their glasses. Dreghorn didn't touch his. "You wanted to talk, sir," he said. "Something about the case?"

"Not at all. That's your field of expertise. If you've information you wish to share, it's at your own discretion. We trust you. That's why my father requested your involvement."

"Your father?"

"He respects you. Always did."

"Aye, right."

"It's true." Rory's eyes softened to what Dreghorn took as a patronizing degree. "And I wanted to give you my blessing."

"For what?"

"You and Isla."

"Wasn't aware we needed it, sir."

"For Christ's sake, stop calling me sir. You don't. I was being facetious. I'm saying you don't have to hide anything from me."

Dreghorn said, "There's nothing to hide."

"Whatever you say, inspector. I just wanted you to know it doesn't matter to me. Life's short. We know too many people who learned that the hard way. I said the same to Isla." A sanguine smile. "She was even ruder than you."

To finish, they had cheese and biscuits with port, then retired to the smoking lounge for brandy and cigars. Dreghorn puffed a couple of times to light up and sat back in his armchair, the buttons of his waistcoat straining, stifling the urge to break wind.

"No wonder you lot get gout," he said.

Rory blew smoke rings at the ornate ceiling. "Rather that than rickets."

"At least you've got a choice in the matter."

"You might think that, but I'm as much a prisoner of my background as you are of yours. Possibly more."

"Most people would happily swap cells with you."

Rory nodded bitterly, stared into the fire that blazed in the hearth. "It's not easy to lead men to their deaths," he said. The words hung in the air like ghosts, clung like cigar smoke. They hadn't spoken about the war yet, but it was there of course. It always was.

"Some people didn't find it too hard," said Dreghorn. "Some people were fuckin' geniuses at it. Especially the ones behind the lines, sticking pins in maps and moving us about like pieces on a chessboard. You were one of the good ones, sir."

"Good and bad didn't come into it, Dreghorn. We did what we had to do."

"Most of the time, maybe."

Rory stared at Dreghorn, wondering if his words held a hint of accusation. Dreghorn didn't clarify it one way or another.

"I was surprised at you, becoming a policeman," Rory said. "Why? All those rules and regulations. Wouldn't have thought you'd find them easy to follow. Not after the war."

Dreghorn blew smoke onto the burning tip of the cigar, heard it crackle, the taste suddenly acrid in his mouth. "Because I've seen the alternative," he said. "I've *been* the alternative. We both have."

Rory raised an eyebrow as if that was something he hadn't considered. "I wondered if you'd got a taste for it during that business with—what was his name?"

Dreghorn knew immediately. "Currie."

"Currie, yes. You were the one who tracked him down, brought him back. Almost got arrested for desertion doing it. He was a friend of yours?"

Dreghorn raised the brandy to his mouth. But it smelled sweet and sickly. He lowered the glass without drinking. "Up to a point."

"Then you know all about leading men to their deaths."

"He didn't go that easily. Took a bit of persuasion."

"Poor bastard. Hard to feel anything but sorry for him, even after what he did."

The world seemed to have shrunk until it was only them and the blazing fire. Dreghorn almost jumped when someone across the room laughed raucously and called for more whisky.

"You must see quite a bit of Hunter these days."

"Too much," Dreghorn said.

"He's certainly earned himself notoriety in recent years."

"He had that before the war. You just didn't move in the right circles."

Rory laughed. "You don't find it strange, old comrades now on opposite sides?"

"Billy'd argue we always were."

"A man of strong principles, passionate beliefs. There's something to be said for that, surely, even if you don't agree."

"Sometimes, I wonder how much of it's taking a loan of all the numpties and nutters that follow him. Makes him the big man in Brigton, gives him power and authority that he wouldn't have anywhere else."

"I hear he drills his troops as if they were a real army."

"Oh, aye. Left-right, left-right, about turn. And finish with a hearty rendition of 'God Save the King.' Maybe you had more of an influence than you think, captain."

"Hardly an honorable claim to fame."

They finished their brandies, knocking them back.

"I thought about contacting him," said Rory. "A social call, not what we were talking about earlier."

"And?"

"I thought again." Firelight danced in Rory's eyes. "One for the road?"

31

1914-1917

War is a barrage, an endless bombardment. Shells, bullets, bayonets. Charges, retreats, stalemate. People, places, faceless enemies. Terror, pain, grief, relief. Screams, laughter, aching silence. Orders, orders, orders. Reload. Start all over again.

It changes time, stretches fleeting moments of peace and happiness, or compacts entire lifetimes into one single screaming moment of bloody death. War steals the past, making it seem so far away that it must surely have happened to someone else. And it takes the future because there is none. The moment is everything. Everything is now.

Basic training is an adventure, like one of Sir Iain's training camps, though without the attraction of his daughter. Jimmy joins his Uncle Joe in the Gordon Highlanders Clydeside; a Pals' Battalion, though pals is taking it a bit far, as they're Tims, Proddies, Eyeties, Jew boys, Lithuanians, the whole melting pot, and would be barneying in the street if they weren't now barracked together, part of the military machine.

Malky Clarke is there, as is Charlie Currie. And Rab Hunter. They've hardly seen each other since the razor incident, but Jimmy's got a reputation now—boxer and patter merchant—while Rab wilts in his brother's shadow.

Jimmy makes his life hell for the first few weeks, then finds Rab greetin' one day, because his da's just died. Jimmy says he's sorry.

"He was a cunt," Rab says. But it doesn't stop the tears.

After that, they're almost as friendly as Jimmy is with Charlie Currie, though you wouldn't want Charlie going with your sister, roving eye that he has—and hands, if he gets the chance. It's a laugh, not like going to the dancing with your mates, but a lark all the same. And they'll be back by Christmas—everybody says so.

Then they're shipped to the Somme. The barrage begins. And doesn't stop.

Jimmy learns fast, soaking in the sights and smells and sounds of the battlefield. He recognizes the hacking cough of Mills bombs and German stick bombs, the shuddering boom of mortars, the metallic clanging of 5.9 howitzer shells bursting in re-echoing volleys, the roar of a Maxim machine-gun as you go straight toward it over the top.

He becomes inured to blood and gore, can pinpoint wounds and the weapons responsible with unnerving accuracy. His nostrils are quick to detect the slightest whiff of gas or of a decomposing corpse disinterred by shelling after months underground.

He fires fifteen rounds a minute from his Lee Enfield Mark III, but quickly realizes that the bayonet is unwieldly in close combat, best used for toasting bread and opening cans. Like most soldiers, he favors improvised clubs—knuckledusters or a sharpened spade.

He's glad of his pals to begin with, the camaraderie and familiarity. They anchor his sense of dislocation among the ruins and craters, festering pools and sucking mud, tree stumps and body parts. Then they start dying. With each of them, a piece of him goes.

His Uncle Joe is shot in the face as they go over the top in another doomed push, his jaw hanging off. Jimmy holds it in place with his hands until the medics arrive. Joe survives, but will never speak properly again. Jimmy's mother sends him letters, saying how the doctors are working to build Joe a new jaw with clay and copper. It gives him nightmares—the image of his gloriously garrulous uncle turned into some life-size child's doll.

Rab Hunter is blown apart when German forces storm the fire trench and grenadiers hurl their bombs into the dugouts. He sits against the trench wall, tries to gather his spilled intestines back into his stomach.

"Fuckin' hell, Jimmy," he says. "Fuckin' hell." Jimmy, buried fast under the collapsed dugout ceiling, watches him die. It seems to take forever. He regrets the hatred he'd once felt for Rab, wishes he could take it back.

Captain Ogilvy, their commanding officer, dies in the same assault, though no body is found when the Germans are repelled. Jimmy returns from hospital on the same day as Ogilvy's replacement arrives.

Captain Rory Lockhart, uniform immaculate, but with cuts and bruises on his face from having been caught in the Quintinshill rail crash, news of which has only just reached them.

Gallusness is good to have, but easy to take too far. When Captain Lockhart inspects the troops, Charlie Currie is cocky, rather than respectful. In private, he lets it be known that he knocked their new captain on his arse back on Civvy Street. Nothing is private in the trenches.

They're back at the reserve lines when Lockhart orders Jimmy and Currie to the officers' dugout. He aims his pistol at Currie's head as they walk in and pulls the trigger. The hammer clicks on an empty chamber, but Currie pales anyway. No mean feat. It's winter in the trenches and he's already as peelie-wallie as a ghost.

Their eyes meet. No words are spoken, but Currie steps out of line no more. Becomes a model soldier. Yes, sir; no, sir; three bags full, sir.

* * *

"We are all standing at the edge of the grave." Captain Lockhart addresses his troops on the morning of the first push he has been part of. They've had a tot of whisky to steady their nerves and the allied cannon have stopped their barrage, a clear signal to the Hun that they're coming.

"Some of us fall in. Some of us step in. Some of us are pushed. But it's waiting for us all," he continues. "Today, tomorrow, there's no escaping it. How we face it is what's important. Don't let me down. Don't let yourselves down."

With that, he's first up the ladder, first to face the enemy guns. Every time he goes over the top, he returns without a scratch.

Captain Lockhart volunteers them for a trench raid to gather intelligence on enemy positions. He leads them, faces blackened, out into no-man's-land under cover of darkness. It's a success—no casualties, and they disable a machine-gun emplacement, kill its crew without a sound, and bring back an officer for interrogation. Ten minutes alone with the captain and he reveals everything. The brass are delighted. Good show, they harrumph over brandy.

More raids, more silent kills, more sabotage, more intelligence gathered that seems to make no difference. The captain seems to live for the hunt, stalking enemy soldiers as if he's back at Kelpie and they're his to do with as he wishes. On one mission, Jimmy is confronted at gunpoint by a sentry. Before the soldier can speak, Lockhart emerges from the night and slits the man's throat from behind, then stares at Jimmy with a wolfish smile and a mocking salute.

Their success earns them a fearsome reputation and a name—the Black Squad, a reference to their shipyard profession, even though there's precious few of that original squad left. The Black Squad. Jimmy finds it distasteful, but others revel in it. He wonders if Lockhart is more at home in the desolation of no-man's-land than behind the lines, where some semblance of civilization still exists.

Jimmy is made sergeant. Not that he wants the authority, argues against it even, but the captain tells him he has no choice. He goes on leave with the promotion hanging over him, heading to Albert, three miles behind the Somme front line, with Charlie Currie.

They get drunk, visit the brothels, get drunk, visit the brothels again. Jimmy tries to picture Isla as he thrusts himself toward a fleeting release, but it shames him instead of thrilling him, makes him sad. Finally, at a loss, they wander the remains of the town.

On top of the basilica of Notre Dame de Brebières is the Leaning Virgin. Originally named the Golden Virgin, it was tilted almost horizontal when the church was struck by a shell in January 1915.

"Look, she's trying to kiss me," Currie says.

"Trying to stick the heid on you, more like," laughs Jimmy.

They find a shell-hole that leads to underground tunnels dating from the thirteenth century, according to the madame at one of the brothels. They light the way with matches, but don't go far. Currie jokes that they could hide out the rest of the war here. With their luck, Jimmy tells him, the Leaning Virgin would fall on the shell-hole and trap them there for good.

After that, they get drunk and visit the brothels again. Currie, uncharacteristically reflective, asks, "Do you sometimes think you don't know yourself anymore? Sometimes I look in the mirror and it's me, but it's no' me."

Jimmy feels the sergeant's stripe that will soon appear on his shoulder. "Don't talk shite, Currie. Anything that's no' you would be an improvement."

Billy Hunter is among the next group of reserves that arrive from Britain, granted early prison release, rumor has it, on condition he sign up for King and Country. Jimmy hasn't seen him since the Ballater Street slashing. There's no recognition in Hunter's eyes, and little acknowledgment of Jimmy's stripes.

"Tim?" Hunter asks.

"Jim," Jimmy answers.

"Funny cunt, eh?" Hunter's eyes smiled. "Fair enough. Long way from home. Just point me in the direction of the bastards that did for my brother and we'll get along fine."

Jimmy thinks he's seen it all—gone beyond being shocked or sickened. He's wrong. She's lying naked in the attic bedroom of the brothel, blood everywhere. He knows her. He's been with her. He's ashamed he can't remember her name.

Charlie Currie was her last customer. Gone now. Bits of his uniform scattered around the room.

Captain Lockhart places a hand on Jimmy's shoulder, says that they're due back at the front and will have to leave Currie to the Military Police. Jimmy knocks his hand away, storms into the night. He tears through the drinking establishments, or what passes for them in wartime, and confronts local black-marketeers and criminal types that might be willing to aid a deserter for a price. Nothing.

The sun's rising when he stares up at the Leaning Virgin. He swears she's leaned further over to stare at the shell-hole and the darkness within.

Jimmy doesn't even need a torch for the tunnel. Currie has gathered debris and lit a fire, and he sees it flickering after a few steps. Currie leaps to his feet as he approaches, the bayonet in his hand. The blade has been cleaned. "It wasn't me, Jimmy," he says, a tremor in his voice.

"Then why run? What're you hiding down here for?"

"I don't know—I was scared. I woke up and the poor lassie was just lying there, and we were covered in blood. I was—"

"Was what?"

"I was roaring drunk. I don't know what happened. I don't remember."

"Don't know who you are anymore? Don't know what you might do?"

"I didn't mean it like that. It wasn't me, Jimmy. I wouldn't have hurt her."

"You going to stab me as well, Charlie?"

The blade is almost touching Jimmy's stomach. One thrust is all it would take. Currie's hand trembles. He breaks down and falls to his knees, swearing that it wasn't him. Jimmy gently takes the blade from his hand.

One thrust is all it would take. Instead he slips an arm around Currie's shoulders, lets him weep.

It's hardly a trial. A British soldier has murdered a French citizen. In the climate of fear and suspicion that war breeds, even among allies, justice has to be seen to be done. The military tribunal finds Currie guilty of murder. The sentence is death by firing squad.

Jimmy wants to believe that Currie didn't do it, couldn't do it, but the barbarity of the battlefield has atrophied his faith in humanity. He curses himself for not having been there, as if that would have made any difference, for accompanying Captain Lockhart to the officers' bordello. "Privileges of rank." Not that the other officers welcomed him.

Currie asks to see him on the morning of the execution. They stand awkwardly in the cell as the time approaches. "When you get home, go and see my family, will you?" Currie asks, eyes shining with tears. "Tell my mammy I didn't do it. Tell her it's all a mistake."

Jimmy barely nods.

"You believe me, don't you?" Currie pleads as they take him away. "You believe me, don't you, Jimmy?"

Jimmy stands at the rear of the firing squad. Somewhere in the walk from the cell to the courtyard, Currie has regained his composure. He stands tall and proud, as if back in the ring, waiting for the judges to declare the winner in a contest rigged in his opponent's favor.

He stares at Jimmy as the captain readies the squad.

Dreghorn stares back.

He doesn't flinch as the rifles fire.

32

It's misty tonight, observed the wee old woman in the jazzy head scarf that he helped off the tram on Great Western Road. He asked if she'd like him to make sure she got home safely, but she said she only lived a stone's throw away.

"And, here"—she elbowed him in the ribs—"I might no' let you go if I got you hame."

"Chance would be a fine thing," he said, acting flattered. She whooped with scandalized delight, chuckling as she waddled off.

Misty was putting it mildly. Murky was more like it—a deep dank fog choked with the smoke of thousands of tenement chimneys. The ghostly orbs of the streetlamps did little to pierce the gloom, and the one consolation was that strangers were as shocked by your sudden sinister appearance in the swirling fog as you were by theirs.

Dreghorn had stayed longer and drunk far more than he'd intended, unwanted memories surfacing on the journey home. Live your life and don't give a damn was Rory's attitude. There were worse philosophies, Dreghorn had to admit, thinking of pointless deaths and wasted lives. And of Rory's sister—the girl she'd been when they first met, the woman she was now.

The only other time he'd drunk wine in such abundance was as a private in the army, when they'd liberated a stack of bottles from the cellar of a bombed-out chateau, and tanned them the night before the first big push he'd been involved in. Bad idea. Hangovers and machine-gun fire don't mix.

Later, Dreghorn would make excuses that the wine was responsible for allowing the bastards to get the drop on him. He could handle beer and spirits with the best of them, but the effete intoxication of wine obviously blurred the senses more.

They must have been waiting somewhere around the start of Hamilton Park Avenue, for he was already halfway to Mrs. Pettigrew's when he sensed their presence.

Footsteps. Two men. Keeping pace. Trying not to alert him. He didn't look back. Let them think they had him. He felt the detective's baton in his inside pocket bounce reassuringly against his chest and undid the buttons of his coat for easy access.

Then two more men materialized in the murk ahead, one stepping from a doorway, the other emerging from behind one of the few parked cars in the street. No random mugging, then. Premeditated. Two at the front, two at the back, cutting off any escape. He thought about Shanghai, the things he'd learned—fight dirty, kill or be killed—and wished the weight in his coat was that of his old service revolver.

The two at the front walked steadily toward him, confident in their power. One wore a fedora, the other a bunnet low over his eyes. Scarves covered their lower faces, concealing their identities like bandits in a Western at the Gaumont. The footsteps of the two behind him speeded up.

Dreghorn lunged forward, and threw a straight jab into the vulnerable flesh of the first man's throat. The man gagged, staggered backward. Then he drew the baton and swung in one movement, breaking through the second man's guard and striking him across the cheekbone, his head snapping to the side.

An arm snaked around Dreghorn's neck from behind, pulled him back tight against the third attacker, big and solid. A bad move: it left the detective's hands free.

Dreghorn jabbed the baton over his shoulder, missed and shifted his aim. He swung again, felt the point of the baton connect with something soft, an eye socket he hoped. The arm around his neck loosened and he head-butted backward, smashing the crown of his head into the man's face.

He broke free, but the fourth man grabbed the back of his collar and pulled him off-balance. A fist thumped into his right kidney, a hard, sharp punch, a knuckleduster or roll of coins gripped in the palm. Dreghorn crumpled sideways with the impact, leaving himself wide open for the first man, recovering, to hit him with a right cross.

The fourth man pushed him into the railings that separated the townhouses from the pavement, whipped the coat from Dreghorn's shoulders, used it to pinion his arms at the elbows, then spun him back round to face the others. Another cross, a left this time, then four hooking punches, rapid-fire, into his gut, though they hadn't reckoned on the hearty meal he'd eaten. His insides erupted in pain. Bile and acid churned, flooding his throat and mouth. He heaved up his dinner, heard it spatter on the pavement, followed by an agitated scuffle of feet.

"Aw, gie's a break! Watch the fuckin' shoes."

There was laughter among his attackers. The man holding Dreghorn relaxed his grip, said, "Here, you hold him. I want a go."

Dreghorn shrugged free of his coat, but his legs gave way. He broke his fall with his palms, gasped for breath, the taste bitter in his mouth. His mind cleared a little. One of the men loomed over him. "Up, you prick."

Hands gripped his shoulders, pulled him upright. He threw out a short jab, weak but well-aimed more by luck than design. His fist struck the man in the balls, eliciting a grunt of pain and sickness. As the man doubled over, Dreghorn swept an arm around his legs and lunged, bringing him down heavily. That was as far as his strength went, though. He flopped on top of his attacker, swung a punch that wouldn't have dented a pillow.

The others laughed, one of them crying out, "Watch it, Davy, he's going for a legover." The voice seemed familiar.

"Wheesht!" Another voice, threatening and serious. "Nae names."

One of them kicked him in the ribs, once, twice, with steel toe-capped boots, and the breath whooshed from his body, winding him. Dreghorn rolled to the ground, lay still, the cool wet of the pavement strangely comforting against his cheek.

"Right, that's enough," one of them said, not out of compassion, but keen for things not to escalate to a murder charge.

Another voice hissed accusingly, "Is it fuck enough! Nearly took out my eye, the bastard."

Hands gripped his collar and hair, hauled him to his knees. His lungs started working again, the explosive intake of cold air snapping his eyes open. He saw the bars of the railings immediately ahead of him. Beyond that he saw lights behind the curtains of the nearest house, and briefly wondered why no one had intervened. This wasn't the sort of neighborhood in which street fights took place. Maybe that made it easier for them to mind their own business.

The hands pulled him back, about to smash his face into the railings. Dreghorn gritted his teeth, braced himself for the impact as best he could.

It never came. There was a small delicate sound, like fine silk tearing, and something misty and warm spattered his face. The hands released him. A voice howled in pain and terror. Hard to believe such a small sound could cause such distress, but it happened again, followed by another, even more chilling shriek.

Dreghorn slumped against the railings, his vision blurring. Feet scuffled in panic on the pavement. One of his attackers bellowed a warning, but there was an edge of uncertainty, of fear to it. Dreghorn could only see shapes in the fog, like a shadow play he'd seen once in Shanghai. One shape moved gracefully, elegantly, reaching out to caress the others, which staggered and lurched and cowered in response. Footsteps on cobbles, exhalations of pain, and incoherent curses, gradually receding. Among it all, he realized, there was another sound, a carefree whistling to accompany the shadow dance. He recognized the tune as the darkness took him.

> *Hello, Hello, we are the Billy Boys,*
> *Hello, Hello, you'll know us by our noise . . .*

33

"To say you've got a face like a well-skelped arse would be a compliment."

It wasn't so much the words that brought him back to life as the tone of gleeful amusement. It took an age to open his eyes, as if some joker had welded them shut, but Dreghorn was pleased that they did open and hadn't swollen over "like a pair of dug's baws," as Dougie McGinn, his old boxing trainer, would've said. Raising his head, he was less pleased to see Billy Hunter sitting in the armchair by the window, smoking.

"Found these in your pocket." He rattled Dreghorn's packet of Capstans. "Didn't think you'd mind, seeing as I did you a wee favor out there."

"Clean out my wallet as well?" Dreghorn croaked. It sounded like he'd been gargling with gravel.

"No' enough there to make it worthwhile."

Hunter nodded toward Dreghorn's left. Wincing, the detective looked round to see his wallet lying open on the bedside cabinet, his warrant card removed and laid on top. He was in his room at Mrs. Pettigrew's, splayed out on the bed where Hunter had dumped him like a sack of coal. So far, he had only raised his head from the mattress. Now he had to be a real hard man. And sit up straight. Pain clawed its way across his torso as he forced himself up. He felt like he'd been used like the ball in an Old Firm match.

"Might be an idea to stay put," Hunter advised. "You took a few good shots. Lucky I was passing."

"Passing? Right. How much did you see?"

"Most of it. I was already waiting across the road when they turned up. You did all right. Didn't want to jump in too soon in case I hurt your pride."

"Considerate of you. Know any of them?"

Hunter stubbed out his cigarette. "You've had a few too many dunts to the head if you think I'd blab. Shouldn't be too hard for you to recognize, though." He reached into his pocket, drew out a cut-throat razor, flicked it open, the blade red with blood. "I left my signature on them." He stood up, stepped toward the sink, and rinsed the blade. The water flowed red, then pink, and then clear, all evidence washed away.

Dreghorn asked, "How'd you find out where I live?"

Hunter gave the razor a shake, clicked it shut, and dropped it back into his pocket. Dreghorn didn't really expect an answer. Sillitoe was making strides, but the Glasgow Police Force was still an institution in which a bribe or an appeal to religious sympathies could go a long way.

He tried another tack. "How did you get me in here?"

"Chapped the door and apologized for the lateness of the hour. The lady of the house was most understanding. Disapproving, till she realized it wasn't bevy that had laid you low. Well, not entirely. She'll be up any minute. Fetching some tea. Biscuits too, hopefully. She was upset at the state you were in. You must be a good tenant. Unless there's a bit more to it than that . . ."

There was a knock at the door. "Inspector Dreghorn?"

"Mrs. Pettigrew." Dreghorn forced himself to his feet, using the bedstead for support. It creaked loudly in protest. For a moment, he thought it was his body.

"Better let yourself in, hen," Hunter said. "You'll be waiting donkey's years for Jimmy to get there."

Mrs. Pettigrew entered, deftly balancing a tray in one hand. She crossed the room quickly, giving Dreghorn a stern look. "You should be in bed, inspector."

"He was waiting for you to tuck him in," said Hunter.

She ignored his innuendo, placed the tray on the table beside the armchair. Despite the hour and the circumstances, she'd brought teapot, strainer, cups and saucers, and a plate with both Penguins and Jaffa Cakes. Standards had to be maintained, no matter what. Dreghorn hoped he hadn't bled on the carpet on the stairs.

"A doctor is what he needs." She clamped her hands on Dreghorn's shoulders and sat him firmly back down. Somehow, he managed not to yelp in pain.

"Worse than it looks." He smiled weakly. "I'll be right as rain in the morning."

"You'll be dead on your feet." She returned to the tray, started pouring tea. She had been in bed when Hunter had battered the door, pulling a dressing gown over her nightdress and reassuring the other tenants that nothing untoward was going on as she hurried to answer. The belt had loosened, showing a little of her chest as she bent over.

"It's terrible what this city's coming to," she observed. "Who knows what they'd have done if your friend wasn't there to help? I don't know, all that trouble in the East End, the razor gangs . . ."

"Oh, aye," Hunter's eyes danced with delight. "Some rank bad yins out there right enough."

Mrs. Pettigrew tightened her dressing gown and nodded coldly at the table. "There's milk and sugar on the tray." She wetted a tea towel under the tap and dabbed at Dreghorn's face. The towel came away pink, dotted with dried blood.

"Sorry," he said sheepishly. "I try not to bring my work home with me, but didn't have much choice tonight. If it's any comfort, it's linked to another case I'm working, not gang-related."

He could see in her eyes that something had changed. Their relationship, such as it was, had shifted gears, sliding back to strictly professional, and he figured that he'd be needing new digs sooner rather than later. Dreghorn may have been an amusing devil's advocate among her little company of poets, artists, and intellectuals, but Billy Hunter was the devil incarnate. The detective's job, exciting in an abstract way, had suddenly become a harsh bloody reality.

She folded the towel neatly. "You still need to see a doctor, if you ask me."

"I'll pop into the Police Surgeon first thing, get him to look me over."

This didn't satisfy her greatly, but it was concession enough. She looked at Hunter, pushing an entire Jaffa Cake into his mouth with the devotion of a novice nun receiving communion from the Pope himself. "Inspector Dreghorn needs rest and recuperation. I trust you won't keep him too long."

Hunter spoke through a full mouth. "No, just a couple of things to chat about."

She gave Dreghorn a last look as he murmured heartfelt thanks, and left, closing the door without a sound.

"Fine-looking woman," Hunter said. "I'd be in there, if I was you."

Dreghorn grunted, got to his feet again, and stepped to the mirror. Not a bonnie sight, but it could've been worse. There'd be more bruising and swelling in the morning, but he was used to that. He tasted blood as he probed with his tongue, but found no loose teeth. He stripped off his shirt, gently pushed at his ribs through his simmit. Nothing broken, he reckoned, but difficult to say for sure. He thought about the marks on Charles Geddes' corpse. A professional beating. Not unlike the one he'd just received.

"We had a deal, Jimmy." No humor in Hunter's eyes now.

"Thought you trusted me, Billy."

"Up to a point. You're still a polis. And you're a Tim."

"Only on paper. When it comes to religion, I spat my dummy out a long time ago. One side's as bad as the other."

"You're kidding yourself, man." Hunter shook his head, marveling at Dreghorn's naivety. "All that shite runs deep—cut you to the quick and you'll bleed shamrock green. Like I said, we had a deal."

"No deals, Billy, not with you. I said I'd do what I could. And I am. Nothing's changed there."

"How do I know that? I've no' seen hide nor hair of you."

"Drop into the station for a blether whenever you want. The door's always open. Might lock behind you, though."

"Fuck off."

They stared at each other. In the street, with an audience, there'd have been no turning back, but here, in a West End bedroom with tea and biscuits on the table? Dreghorn laughed, gestured across the room as he sat back down on the bed.

"There's whisky and glasses in the dresser. Help yourself, if you want a dram."

Hunter weighed up the pitfalls of accepting hospitality. "You want one?"

He didn't, but, "Fuck it, aye. It'll either kill me or cure me."

Hunter got the whisky, made a face at the quality of the brand, and poured as Dreghorn talked.

"First, I checked the births register for Glasgow around the time you said. No mention of a Sarah Hunter anywhere, which meant she either got rid of the baby through some backstreet butcher, the child didn't survive, or she went further afield, somewhere she wasn't known—less of a scandal. There was nothing listed in the stillbirths register, so I checked records for Paisley and Renfrewshire, and found a birth registered to her at Trinity Maternity Hospital."

"Trinity?" Hunter handed Dreghorn his dram. "She never went; she ran away."

"I've seen the paperwork: a baby girl, born on the second of June, 1914, no complications, both mother and child healthy."

"You think my ma and my sister would lie to me? I told you no' to go near her if I wasn't there."

"If I hadn't, we'd have got nowhere. And they did lie—to protect you, more fool them. Twenty years is a long time, Billy. Sometimes memories play tricks on people. They end up believing what they want to believe. Or they might've been scared of what you'd do. You were in the Big Hoose, after all." The glass felt heavy in the detective's hand. Everything suddenly seemed heavy. "The baby was put up for adoption. Poor lassie; no' an easy thing to do, give up your wean. After that, Sarah went back to her family as far as Trinity knew."

Hunter knocked back his whisky in one gulp. "So, how do you find her now?"

"I'm working on it." Dreghorn sipped his drink, coughed as it burned down through him.

Hunter didn't appreciate the vagueness of the answer, but didn't push it. "What about the wean?"

"Adopted within a year or two."

"By who?"

"Don't know. Confidential information."

"You're a polis. You can find it out."

"Not without good reason. Maybe not even then. It's a different area of law."

"A dying old woman who's never seen her grand-wean—you don't think that's reason enough?"

"It's not up to me. The girl, Sarah's daughter, she's got new parents, a new family. She might not even know she's adopted. You can't just go trampling over other people's lives, Billy."

The fire in Hunter's eyes warned that he could do whatever the fuck he wanted. "Maybe I should go and see these Trinity folk, have a wee word."

"Flashing your razors in a village full of vulnerable orphaned children? Brilliant idea. Go to the top of the class." Dreghorn noticed he was slurring—alcohol and fatigue, hopefully, not concussion.

Hunter looked at the empty glass cradled in his hand, aggression fading. He sighed and got to his feet. Dreghorn did the same, stiff and awkward, like a scarecrow trying to uproot itself from the earth.

"I can see myself out," said Hunter.

"Just in case you get lost on the way."

"Scared your fancy woman might be waiting to catch me unawares on the way down?"

"No fears."

They didn't speak further as they left the room, Hunter skipping down the stairs like Fred Astaire, Dreghorn as stechie as a cowboy who'd been in the saddle for a week. Hunter waited with exaggerated patience for Dreghorn to open the main door, then trotted down the steps into the thick dark murk.

Dreghorn said, "One thing, Billy. If I find your sister—and it's a big if—whatever happens is up to her. If she doesn't want anything to do with you, it ends there."

"Gentleman Jimmy Dreghorn." Hunter cocked his head like a man who'd just seen the catch in a contract but couldn't help admiring it all the same. "Remember, that was a posh doing you got earlier the night. Some folk out there wouldn't leave you looking half as good."

34

THURSDAY, 13 OCTOBER 1932

Dreghorn lost a day, signed off work against his wishes by Willie Kivlichan, whom Mrs. Pettigrew had contacted when he was slow to regain consciousness the Wednesday morning after the attack. He had awoken to find McDaid waiting to take a statement, slurping tea and polishing off the biscuits Billy Hunter had left.

"You're going nowhere, wee man," McDaid said. "Doctor's orders."

Dreghorn had blinked in and out of consciousness when Kivlichan examined him, not that he could remember. He'd taken a bad beating but sustained no serious injuries. Before leaving, McDaid said, the doctor had noted the similarity to the assault on Charles Geddes.

"We must be pissing off the right people," Dreghorn said.

"Speak for yourself. Everybody loves me."

Dreghorn groaned as he tried to sit up, pain scuttling across his torso.

McDaid gave him a scornful look. "Away, you big jessie. Never had your ribs cracked before?"

"Like a xylophone played with a sledgehammer a couple of times."

Despite the sarcasm, he appreciated the slow burn of rage in the big man's eyes as he recounted the previous night's events.

Normally the police rallied around when one of their own was injured, but Dreghorn's precarious position as the first Catholic inspector in town afforded him as many smirks as sympathetic nods when he returned to work on Thursday. Not that he had time to do much more than flick through the messages and reports on his desk before leaving for court. Thomas Bryce was being sentenced that morning.

Sillitoe cut an impressive figure as he stood to attention in the dock. He spoke eloquently about the dangers of gangsterism and the corrosive effects of alcohol and violence, inciting a frenzy of activity in the reporters' notebooks. Dreghorn didn't doubt the sincerity, but he'd heard the speech before, albeit with a few tweaks and splashes of local color; Sillitoe regularly took the stand to condemn underworld figures and encourage judge and jury to impose the harshest punishments.

Peggy Bryce, the marks of violence all but gone from her face, showed little reaction throughout, drained perhaps by the heartbreaking testimony she'd given earlier in the trial. Dreghorn had nodded to her once or twice, but received no response. Alan Kerr, a few seats away from his sister, stood and yelled at his brother-in-law, "Hanging's too good for you, yah bastard!" before being pulled back down. Lizzie Logan was there too, but whatever bond she and Dreghorn had shared as the ambulance men carried out the tiny corpse was gone.

The press box was full, pencils scribbling in notebooks, recording events with various levels of gratuitousness, the broadsheets from the heights of moral superiority, the gutter press living up to their name with all the sordid details but none of the stark sadness. Among them, Denny Knox made a show of not catching McDaid's eye.

A glance at the public gallery showed more empty seats than

usual. Gang members usually turned out in force when one of their own was in the dock, a menacing show of support that often had prosecution witnesses retracting statements or being struck by sudden amnesia. A crime as monstrous as Bryce's, however, earned enmity and disgust from all sides. After he had spoken, as Bryce was taken down to the cells and the jurors left the court to deliberate the verdict, the press flooded toward Sillitoe. He cut them off with a curt "After sentencing, gentlemen," and nodded for Dreghorn and McDaid to accompany him outside.

The entrance stairs to the High Court were crowded with lawyers, clients, court clerks, reporters, and ghouls whose idea of entertainment was listening to prosecutions in public galleries. Sillitoe marched across the Saltmarket onto Glasgow Green.

"Courts and morgues," he said, "never the most inviting. Good to get some fresh air."

Dreghorn agreed, lit a cigarette, inhaling deeply. In the distance, he could see the grand McLennan Arch standing over the Charlotte Street entrance to the Green.

A light rain was falling. Sillitoe tested a few drops on his face. "Drizzle?"

"Not even that, sir," McDaid answered. "It's just spitting." Sillitoe filed the term away, eyed Dreghorn. "You don't look too bad."

"Fairly well turned out yourself, sir."

Sillitoe didn't react, the sarcasm either over his head or beneath his notice. "I hope you got in a few licks of your own."

"Not as many as I'd've liked."

"Any idea who they were?"

"They kept their faces covered, didn't say much. Add that to the fog . . ." Dreghorn shook his head. "They chose their moment well."

"You don't think it was a random assault, then?"

"It was me they were after all right."

"Related to any of your cases, do you think?"

"Wouldn't rule it out, sir."

"Anything else of note about them?" Sillitoe glanced back at the court when Dreghorn shook his head. "At least you'll get your conviction today. I expect a severe sentence."

Dreghorn preferred not to attend trials if he could avoid them. All too often court proceedings were a bitter disappointment. Many officers could shrug off bad verdicts philosophically, but in Dreghorn they festered, especially when the accused flashed a triumphant grin or gave him the two fingers on receiving a lenient sentence. He said, "Wish I shared your confidence in Scottish justice, sir."

Sillitoe gave him a wry smile. "We can but do our best, Dreghorn. Sometimes the rest of the world has to catch up."

It didn't take the jury long to reach a verdict. A court official called them as Dreghorn finished his cigarette. Sillitoe gestured for his detectives to lead the way. "The moment of reckoning."

"Thomas Ian Bryce, it is the sentence of this court that you be taken from this place to the prison of Duke Street, Glasgow, there to be detained until the twenty-ninth of November next and upon that day, within the said prison of Duke Street, Glasgow, between the hours of eight and ten o'clock, suffer death by hanging."

Thomas Bryce didn't break down as the judge banged his gavel; he froze, his eyes glassy, as if rigor mortis had already set in. The wardens had to prize his fingers from the edge of the dock. In the expectant hush that followed, the judge reached under his desk for the black tricorn cap, and placed it on his head with the solemnity of the Reaper before completing the sentence: "This is pronounced for doom."

After Bryce had been led away, the reporters again converged on Sillitoe. He was open and magnanimous, praising judge and jury for their wisdom and high moral standards, his officers for their dogged investigative prowess, and the victims for their bravery in the face of overwhelming pain and loss. At the periphery of the throng, Denny Knox sidled up to McDaid, asking if the sergeant would be good enough to confirm a few facts. They compared notebooks, pencils in hand. Sillitoe finished with the reporters, refusing further questions, and approached Dreghorn. "Well done, inspector, a good verdict. You're satisfied? Faith rekindled?"

"Doesn't change the fact that it happened, sir," Dreghorn replied. "Doesn't change much of anything." It would have been easier to play along with the success, but the forlorn figure of Peggy Bryce being led away by relatives lingered with Dreghorn.

"Oh, but it does. It gives them pause, Dreghorn. It makes criminals fear for their lives. It hammers home exactly what they risk forfeiting if they break the law. If this verdict results in one less killing, one less assault, then it's a victory."

In Dreghorn's experience, people in the act of murder rarely paused to consider the consequences of the fatal blow, but he nodded anyway. "Sir."

The chief constable announced with a sigh that he had to attend another "riveting" meeting at the City Chambers. Dreghorn declined the offer of a lift back to Turnbull Street; it was good for them to be seen straight back on the streets after a high-profile trial like Bryce's.

He waited until Sillitoe was out of earshot, then asked McDaid, "If Denny Knox was checking facts with you, why were you the one writing in your notebook?"

"Turn left here."

"We're not there yet—it's up here on the right."

"Left. Now."

Dreghorn detected a low sigh as McDaid spun the wheel, turning off St. Andrew's Drive onto Terregles Avenue. Knox and McDaid's "comparing of notes" had been a ruse, allowing the reporter to pass on the identity of the man in the pornographic photographs discovered in Charles Geddes' house. Knox had the photo McDaid gave him blown up by a staff photographer whom he trusted. The new image focused on the man's face, cutting out the scandalous details to preserve Knox's potential exclusive. Knox had shown the photo to fellow reporters and was surprised when recognition came from one of the political journalists rather than the crime-beat hacks.

Eric Raeburn, recently deceased, had been a bailie for the Corporation, who served on the housing, public assistance, gas, transport, and shipbuilding committees. Not a "high heid yin" as such, but definitely someone the business community would wish to keep in with. Raeburn had worked in the City Chambers, traveling in from Pollokshields where he lived with his wife and daughter.

Counting down house numbers as they drove, Dreghorn noticed two figures, bunnets pulled low, on the corner of the road opposite Raeburn's residence and decided on a sudden change of course.

One of the men, leaning against a lamp post, flicked the dowt of his Woodbine into the road with a shower of sparks. The other took a final draw of his own and launched it further than the first, extending his arm like a boxer throwing a jab. He laughed triumphantly, raised two fingers to his companion, then saw Dreghorn coming toward them. He nudged the other man and they started walking briskly in the opposite direction, only to find McDaid sauntering toward them. The older of the two turned to Dreghorn with a rueful smile.

"Loitering with intent, Peter?" said Dreghorn. "A petty charge like that on your record would be an embarrassment."

"Away," MacLean said. "We just stopped for a gab."

"Aye, no law against it, is there?" The second man was Andrew Caldwell: assault, breaking and entering, drunk and disorderly.

"No, but there is a law against breaking into law-abiding citizens' houses and robbing them blind." McDaid halted behind Caldwell.

"No idea what you're talking about, officer." MacLean was enjoying the innocent act.

"You weren't casing these houses, then? Checking out the locks, timing the owner's comings and goings?"

"I'm affronted, Archie. Is that what you think of us?"

"It's a wee bit out of your way," said Dreghorn. "So what are you doing here?"

"Just walking. No' much else to do these days."

"Is that all right?" Caldwell thrust his head forward. "It's a free world, you know."

Dreghorn ignored Caldwell, addressed MacLean. "Back to Briggy, quick march, no more argy-bargy."

Dreghorn and McDaid stayed where they were as the Billy Boys strolled away, Caldwell giving them fly peeks over his shoulder.

"They're spreading," McDaid said.

"Like a rash," Dreghorn agreed.

They crossed to Raeburn's house, with its gate and well-tended front garden, and rang the doorbell, which chimed gaily. Molly Raeburn answered the door, her welcoming smile sliding into surprise when she saw Dreghorn. He introduced McDaid and told her he had some more questions. She stepped forward, pulling the door over behind her, her voice hushed. "I'm not sure what else I can tell you, inspector."

"This involves your father, so we'd like a word with your mother as well."

A woman's voice called out, asking who was at the door. Molly hesitated before answering, "We'll be there in a minute, Mother." Biting her lip, she motioned them inside. As he passed, she laid her hand on Dreghorn's arm, smiled tentatively. "Mother doesn't know

I'd been seeing Charles. She wouldn't approve. Will you have to tell her?"

Dreghorn patted her hand, his tone avuncular. "No promises, miss, but we'll be discreet."

Mrs. Raeburn was on her feet when Molly led them into the lounge, dressed all in black, her hair pulled up immaculately in a style that made Dreghorn think of prim Victorian ladies, although she could only have been in her forties.

"Inspector Dreghorn, Sergeant McDaid; we're investigating the murder of Charles Geddes." She shook his hand, maintaining contact only for as long as politeness dictated, and gave a single nod of her head. "Shocking," she said. "My heart goes out to his family. He was a great help to Molly and me."

She gestured for the detectives to sit down, and told Molly to fetch some tea and biscuits. But Dreghorn declined, saying they didn't want to take up too much of their time. "I understand Mr. Geddes acted as your solicitor when your husband passed away. Who recommended him to you?"

"No one. It was all arranged in advance. My husband, Eric, had been unwell for some time. Angina. A weakness in the heart. I imagine he wanted to spare us unnecessary complications in the event of his death." She turned to Molly, smiled sadly. "Typical, thinking of us instead of himself."

"Did Mr. Raeburn use Mr. Geddes for any other legal business?"

"We own some properties which are rented out. Mr. Geddes handled the conveyancing and the leases for the tenants. Beyond that, I couldn't be sure. We had a very traditional marriage. I ran the household"—she looked around proudly—"while Eric took care of everything else." She forced a smile. "Is there some irregularity in my husband's affairs?"

McDaid was bluffly reassuring. "Purely routine, ma'am; we're questioning all of Mr. Geddes' clients as part of the investigation.

Sometimes, you never know what details may prove relevant. We're trying to build a picture of the victim."

Dreghorn nodded. "Do you know where your husband and Mr. Geddes met?"

Mrs. Raeburn perched primly on the edge of the seat, almost painfully upright, as if she'd put on her dress without removing the coat hanger. Dreghorn noticed Molly adopt an identical pose, a demurer attitude than that of the confident young woman he'd met a few days ago.

"I was there," Mrs. Raeburn said, with an unreadable glance at Molly. "It was at Trinity."

"Trinity?" Dreghorn kept his voice matter-of-fact. "The orphanage?"

A single nod. "At an event to celebrate former pupils who had made something of themselves and become prominent members of society."

"Mr. Raeburn was brought up in Trinity?" asked McDaid.

"Until the age of fifteen, when he secured a junior position with the Corporation. His mother died when he was young and his father couldn't cope, or so the story went. Eric had no interest in learning about his blood family. The staff at Trinity, his house mother and father, they were his family as far as he was concerned. Until we came along, of course."

She smiled at Molly, though no affection rose to her eyes.

"Who introduced them—your husband and Mr. Geddes?"

"Oh, I can't recall, inspector. We attended a lot of functions with Eric's job. Mr. Geddes' references and credentials were impeccable, the work he did with charities such as Trinity, his family background . . ."

"You mean, by marriage, with the Lockharts?"

"Oh, yes. We've met Sir Iain on a number of occasions, even attended dinners at Kelpie House. A magnificent home. Have you been?"

"A few days ago," said McDaid. "Different circumstances, though."

The gravest of nods. "Of course." She looked at her daughter. "Actually, Molly, I'd like some tea. All this talking, you know. Would you be so kind?"

"Of course, Mother. Change your minds, gentlemen?" Molly smiled at the detectives, who declined again, and left the room.

"A sweet child," Mrs. Raeburn said tolerantly. "An orphan herself, also from Trinity, but she doesn't know. So young at the time that we thought it best. Even if Eric and I had been able to have children, he would've still wanted to adopt, to give someone else the chance he had."

The detectives made appropriate noises. Dreghorn leaned forward, elbows on his knees. "Mrs. Raeburn, did your husband seem worried in the weeks or months leading up to his death?"

"About his health? He was quite sanguine about it really."

"No, other matters. Something that might've been preying on his mind?"

"I don't follow, inspector." Her body seemed to grow even more upright.

"Did he say anything about being put under pressure or threatened, forced to do something he wasn't comfortable with? Inside or outside of work?"

"He had a very important job and took it very seriously, but I can assure you Eric would never be party to anything illegal or improper. Has someone made allegations against him?"

Dreghorn glanced at McDaid, whose expression was impassive. He slid his hand under his jacket, tapped the edge of the photo tucked into the inside pocket, changed his mind and removed his hand.

"Some of Mr. Geddes' other clients are less than reputable, shall we say?" he said. "With someone in your husband's position, we have to check that there are no compromising connections."

She took a long breath, exhaled equally slowly. "On Corporation business my husband occasionally encountered corruption in other individuals, and crude attempts to influence his decision-making from politicians and so-called businessmen, but he rose above such behavior. You have a word for it . . . ?"

"Graft," McDaid growled.

"He was offered bribes, golf club memberships, admittance to the Freemasons. He"—her voice rose—"always turned them down; I can assure you of that." She paused to let her sincerity sink in. "Was something like that involved in poor Mr. Geddes' death?"

"We have to look into everything, Mrs. Raeburn, leave no stone unturned." Dreghorn smiled, stood up. "Thank you for your time; you've been most helpful. We're sorry for intruding."

Returning, Molly quickly set down her tray and led the detectives out, closing the door firmly behind her. "Have you made any progress in your investigation, inspector?" she asked.

"That depends," Dreghorn said. "Have you remembered anything that might be useful?"

She laughed, a frivolous suggestion, and nodded back toward the lounge. "Did she say I was adopted? Father told me years ago, but didn't want her to know that I knew. She acts like it's a secret in some gothic romance, but you'd be surprised how many people she tells." Her smile became self-deprecating. "I'm the cross she loves to bear."

Dreghorn didn't know what to say. He gestured at the bay window as they stepped outside. "While we're here—nothing to be alarmed about—but you should speak to your mother about getting extra locks fitted to the doors and windows. There've been a few housebreakings reported in the area. Best not to take chances."

35

"It's a cause that's close to my heart. Hard enough for a woman to make her way in the world before the Depression, let alone now."

"You don't strike me as one for causes."

"No? Maybe you're so used to looking for the bad in people that the good escapes you."

Dreghorn considered her response, shrugged with his eyebrows, not entirely denying it.

A telegram from Kitty Fraser had been waiting when he returned to Turnbull Street, asking to see him that evening. Before driving to Bearsden, he had looked up the address of the Jane Lockhart Educational Trust in Renfield Street, across the road from where the new Paramount Cinema was being built. He had pretended he was interested in enrolling his niece in evening classes as a birthday present and had been given a brief tour, looking in on rows of young women hammering diligently and determinedly on typewriters. Regular courses were available, he was told, the majority of students being subsidized by the Trust. He saw nothing suspicious, nothing to suggest that it was anything other than a charitable institute for underprivileged women, though he had still questioned Kitty Fraser's involvement.

"Does Isla know what you and your girls do for a living?"

"She knows that we believe in the same things, that I have a share in Universal Stores and co-own Lomond Tea Rooms, that I have commercial and residential property. As for how I got them?" A nod toward the bedrooms upstairs. "If you think she'll be appalled, then tell her, but my 'girls' are exactly the sort of people she set up the Trust to help—the sort of women her mother fought for."

She set down her cup and saucer with a loud chink, daring him to disagree. So far, everything had been very civilized. Dreghorn had been shown into the parlor by Rose once again and asked if he wanted tea or coffee. Kitty had joined him and sat demurely at the opposite end of the sofa, maintaining an air of respectability for some invisible chaperone.

Dreghorn said nothing; they both knew the Trust wasn't his real reason for being there.

"How do I know I can trust you?"

"Be nice to say because I'm a policeman, but considering who you were entertaining the other day . . ." Dreghorn smiled cynically. "Afraid you don't really have a choice. Tell me what you know or you'll be enjoying a Hunter family reunion."

"You bastard."

"It's not me, it's the city."

She stared at him defiantly, sighed. "You're right—Arthur Bell sometimes recruits girls for us."

"From Trinity?" Dreghorn slipped out his notebook, snapped it open.

Kitty paused warily as his pencil hovered above the page, then nodded. "From the women who put up their babies for adoption in the maternity hospital. Sometimes from among pupils who've reached the age of consent."

Dreghorn tried to keep his expression emotionless.

"Some of these women have no lives to go back to. Or were shoved out to whore on the streets by their husbands in the first place," Kitty continued defensively. "And the orphans? They can only stay at Trinity for so long. The school tries to find them jobs, but there's a depression on—no jobs for adults, let alone children. What about the ones they can't help—what chance have they got?"

Dreghorn raised his eyes toward the rooms above. "This is giving them a chance?"

"Better than some. I was one of them."

He stopped taking notes and looked at her.

"Arthur approached me a few days after I'd had my baby. Some of the nurses give him tip-offs about patients whose prospects are— less than rosy, shall we say? He was friendly, helpful, brought me flowers, wasn't threatening at all."

"Charmer."

"I'm only telling you what it was like. Was he taking advantage? Of course, but he seemed kind, and kindness was in short supply at the time. He introduced me to a woman—Auntie Agnes, we called her—who said she could help. Room and board in return for 'favors' for nice men. By nice, she meant wealthy, respectable."

"Like all those nice men traipsing in and out of here? Should put them on the honors list."

"Some of them already are."

"This woman, Auntie Agnes, she worked for Johnnie Fraser, the brothel king? Your husband?"

"Not then, he wasn't, but aye. Agnes looked after us, kept us in line if she had to. I didn't meet Johnnie for a few months, but I could tell he took a shine to me. I must've impressed Agnes too—when she became too ill to carry on, she recommended me to take over. Johnnie and I started spending more time together. Eventually, I moved out of a public bedroom into a private one."

"And now you're running the show. Or is it Teddy?"

"We have an arrangement. I help with aspects of his club and he makes sure we're not troubled by unsavory elements."

"Isn't that what Strachan and Orr are for?" Dreghorn asked. "Or are they how Teddy keeps you safe?"

Kitty smiled inscrutably. "More tea, inspector?"

Dreghorn hadn't touched the first cup. "How else is Bell involved?"

"He's not."

"Oh, come on."

"Johnnie was a lot older than me. He and Arthur knew each other from the war in Rhodesia, against the Boers. Johnnie had the gift of the gab; he was clever. Drink, girls, he would procure them for the other soldiers, set up gambling schools, cards, pitch and toss. But he wasn't really a hard man, so he needed help if there was fighting to be done, warnings to be issued, debts to be collected."

"Bell."

"He was one of them. They stayed in touch when they got back. Johnnie had had enough of doffing his cap and yes-sir-ing, no-sir-ing to officers. He decided any business he did under the sun in Rhodesia would be just as profitable in the pissing Glasgow rain, maybe more so. I don't know how the Trinity arrangement came about, whether it was Johnnie's idea or Arthur's. You'd have to ask Arthur."

Dreghorn got to his feet, walked to the bay window and looked out into the street, leafy, quiet and deceptively innocent. He turned back to face her. "These girls—how young does he try to bring you them?"

She gave him a look of revulsion, sickened by the suggestion.

"We both know it happens."

"Not here." Anger in her voice.

He let the tick of the clock fill the room before asking, "What about Dalrymple? Does he know what Bell's up to?"

"I've always suspected, but don't know for sure. I've never had dealings with him, and he's not a customer here. Perhaps he just turns a blind eye. He seems very proper."

Dreghorn nodded; that's what made him suspicious. "Who was Geddes blackmailing? You, Bell, Dalrymple, Teddy?"

"Your coming here is the first I've heard of any blackmail. From the little I picked up, Teddy was unhappy with Geddes, but other than that, I can't help you."

"Unhappy enough to kill him?"

She didn't rise to his probing, in control once again. "You're the policeman."

Dreghorn leaned against the windowsill. "Bell brings you girls from Trinity, though I'm sure you do some recruiting of your own. This is fairly exclusive"—he glanced around the room—"so you cater to a better class of clientele than on the streets. Levin recommends your services to members of his clubs, but he makes sure they're people who can be useful. They think Teddy's their friend, that he's discreet, so they drop their guard along with their breeks— and you photograph their shenanigans for posterity. I'd love to see their faces when Teddy invites them into his office for a private drink and then slaps them across the face with their dirty deeds."

He thought for a moment, lit a cigarette. "It's not money he's after, though—it's power, influence. From the looks of the Gordon Club, he must have half the Corporation in his pocket. But somehow Geddes got hold of these photos and tried his hand at blackmail. We could've told him that was a bad idea, but Geddes was a gambler, thought he could win, even when there wasn't a chance in hell."

"Again, inspector," Kitty stated, "I'm not involved in any blackmail schemes, though I suspect my husband may have dabbled, years ago now. After his death, I discovered false wardrobes and transparent mirrors in a couple of our premises that could have concealed an observer—and Arthur does have some knowledge of photography. I had them taken out immediately. If Teddy fancies himself as an extortionist, you'll have to speak to him. I've always advised him that it's best to build on trust, not mistrust."

Stalemate. Dreghorn pushed himself off the sill and sat in the armchair opposite her. "Why didn't you go back to your family?"

She hugged herself, rubbing one arm as if her clothing itched unbearably. "They wanted to send me away. My da said he wouldn't have it in the house. He died the September after the baby was born, but my mother still sided with him, even though she'd felt the back of his hand more than any of us. She said she was ashamed of me. Billy? He was in the Bar-L—what could he do? Rab? He was a waste of space, pretended it didn't happen. And my sister was too busy trying to get away herself."

"What about the father?" Dreghorn asked.

She blinked, surprised to find tears in her eyes. "He wasn't around anymore."

"Who was he?"

"No one." Her eyes warned that he'd asked more than his share of questions.

"I'm sorry. Can't be easy to give up your child." A stupid thing to say, just meaningless words.

"It was one of Arthur's incentives when he first mentioned Auntie Agnes. That he'd let me see my baby while she was at Trinity, give me news of her once she was adopted."

"Did he keep his word?"

She nodded stiffly. "When Johnnie died, he even told me where she lived, who'd adopted her, what her new name was. He must've trusted me; probably thought I was hard enough not to care by that point."

Or was trying to keep in with you, Dreghorn thought, as you'd just inherited Fraser's illicit empire.

"I think she's had a good life. I'm not even sure she knows she's adopted. Arthur says there haven't been any inquiries from her. I suppose that must mean she's happy."

"I'm sure it does, aye," Dreghorn agreed. "She must be a young woman now."

"Eighteen." The weight of the years was in her voice.

"Have you seen her?" he asked softly.

"Used to go and watch her over the years, make excuses to be in the area. I'd see her going to school, skipping out the door, going for walks in the park or having an ice cream in a cafe with"—her voice caught—"her new ma and da. I used to make up little plays in my head, chance meetings on a tram, in a shop, where she'd know me as soon as she saw me. But we never did meet. I never went near her. Just watched from a distance."

Dreghorn thought it was the saddest thing he'd ever heard.

"The last thing I want is pity." She glared at him. "Especially from you, Inspector High and Mighty. You're working for my brother. How noble's that?"

"It was a deal with the devil, but seemed worth it at the time. If it's any consolation, it shows how far he was willing to go to find you. The Billy Boys wouldn't be happy about their gaffer hobnobbing with the polis."

"How long's he been looking for me?"

"All his life, the way he talks. But your mother's not well."

"I know. Janet's told me."

"He says he'd like her to see you one last time. Says she keeps going on about ruining your life." Dreghorn shook his head. "I can't believe you've managed to avoid him—or anyone you knew—all this time."

"Would you recognize yourself from twenty years ago? I was a child then, a waif from the slums. I'm a different person now. I talk, walk, dress, wear my hair differently. Don't think there haven't been moments when my heart was in my mouth—a face in the street, a voice that might have been familiar.

"I've had the odd stare, but then they've shaken their head and dismissed the thought. In the early days, I used to live in fear of someone I knew walking through the door, but Johnnie was always keen to"— a sarcastic edge—"keep out the riff-raff. And I avoid the

East End like the plague. I stay in touch with Janet, but we always meet elsewhere."

Her eyes became distant, the past creeping in. She blinked, then was back with him, accusing, "Will you tell him you found me?"

"Not if you don't want to be found. I warned him of that."

She didn't seem convinced. "He won't like it."

Dreghorn, weary, said, "Billy's got a big long list of things he doesn't like. He'll have to live with one more."

36

"Red sky at night, shepherd's delight."

"That's not the sky." Dreghorn accelerated, foot to the floor, barely caught the sound of McDaid swearing as the engine roared. The orange glow vanished as the road dipped, then reappeared, flashing in and out of sight between the trees as they approached Trinity Village.

McDaid had waited in the car in case his presence caused Kitty Fraser to clam up. Dreghorn had crossed the road and driven off as if to face the devil, quickly explaining what she'd said about Bell and Dalrymple, but not mentioning her relation to Billy Hunter.

Dreghorn took the corner onto Faith Street at speed, braked hard as the headlights illuminated figures in the road ahead, so engrossed in what they were watching that they hardly noticed the police car. He hit the horn to clear the way, startling them.

The village was in uproar, every inhabitant on the streets, by the look of it, milling around in fear and confusion, teachers and house parents trying desperately to gather panicking children into groups. Staff from the sanatorium and hospital were also attempting to help, carrying smaller children in their arms, yelling instructions at older pupils. The children were in their nightclothes, the orange glow washing over them.

One of the townhouses was ablaze; a window shattered with the heat, spitting sparks and shrapnel through the air, echoed by a chorus of screams. Leaping out of the car, Dreghorn realized it was Dalrymple's house, where they'd spoken on his first visit. He pushed through the crowd, identifying himself as a police officer, McDaid following.

A tall willowy woman in a nightdress and unbelted dressing-gown stood on the lawn, bewitched by the flames, features reddened by the heat. It took Dreghorn a moment to recognize her—Miss Taylor, the head teacher who'd given him a tour of the village.

The flames roared, and burning timbers cracked like breaking bones. He shouted, "What happened?" above the noise. She stared strangely at him, not quite there. He gripped her arms, shook her until some semblance of awareness returned to her eyes, and repeated the question. She shook her head, couldn't find the words. He tightened his grip, making her flinch, asked where Bell and Dalrymple were. She stammered that she didn't know.

"Have you rung the Fire Brigade? The Fire Brigade!"

She pointed vaguely into the village. "We have a fire wagon here. Some of the men have gone to fetch it." Almost an afterthought: "Mr. Bell is in charge in the event of a fire, but no one's seen him."

Dreghorn released her with such force that she staggered backward. He glanced around. A tapestry of firelit faces stared back, filled with fear and uncertainty. A young woman, a teacher presumably, approached tentatively.

"Miss Taylor," she said, "I can't find Morag Gilmartin. All the other children are accounted for, but there's no sign of her."

"Take the register," Miss Taylor advised, as if it was the solution to everything.

"I have. She's not here!"

"Miss!" A girl clutching a menagerie of soft toys stepped out of line. "Miss, Mr. Bell came for her. It was after bed-time. He told the rest of us to get to sleep."

The crackling of the flames suddenly grew louder. Dark smoke billowed into the air, smothering the stars in the night sky. A couple of rooms were still dark, but the rest were fierce with flames. Somewhere round the back, out of sight, another window exploded like a shotgun. A red glow pulsated through the cracks between the roof tiles as the fire spread into the attic that ran the length of the house.

Dreghorn and McDaid looked at each other, thinking of another child they'd been too late to save, and ran for the house, the roar of the flames filling their ears, heat prickling their skin. Dreghorn grabbed the door handle, ignoring the burn of the metal. Locked. He looked at McDaid; the big man was already charging with a bear-like growl. He drove his shoulder into the wood, smashing the door open, and recoiled, hacking and coughing, staggered by the wall of heat that surged out, searing their eyeballs, singeing their hair.

The hallway was so far untouched, but filling with smoke. Dreghorn struggled to remember the layout of the house. Dalrymple's office was to the left; he had no idea what lay to the right. He slapped at the wall for the light switch. Nothing happened, the electrics shorted by the blaze. He motioned for McDaid to check on the right, then crouched low, trying to see through the smoke. Flames flickered ahead, spreading around the doorway of Dalrymple's office. Dreghorn pressed his back to the wall to keep his bearings and inched along, knocking paintings from their hooks. Coughs racked his body, every instinct telling him to run.

Opposite him, just before the office, was a large reception room. Smoke billowed from the open doorway. He shrank back as he passed, paintwork bubbling and bursting on the wall behind him. Flames filled the room, consuming the furniture. The corridor separating the rooms was not yet alight; had the blaze somehow started in two separate locations instead of spreading from a single source?

He was buffeted by another blast of scorched air, dry and choking, as he kicked open the office door. The heat was too great to get any further than the doorway.

One wall was completely ablaze from floor to ceiling, Dalrymple's extensive book collection now tinder for the fire. Dreghorn tried to make sense of what he could see. A shape on the floor, in front of the fireplace, materialized into the limbs and torso of a body, flesh and clothes blackened beneath a rippling sheet of flames.

The heavy curtains were ablaze, a shattered window at least sucking out some of the smoke; a chair, the one he'd sat on, overturned on a burning rug; the safe, open, flames licking the insides, papers turning to ash. Dalrymple's desk was a solid block of fire and behind it, seated upright as if about to interview him for entry to hell, another burning corpse. He could make out the spidery shape of Dalrymple's spectacles, still clinging primly to the man's cooked flesh, the lenses shattered, melted eyeballs bubbling in their sockets.

Dreghorn heaved and retched, but nothing came up. The bookshelves collapsed with a groan, spilling their blazing contents over the floor, sparking debris rising in a cloud. His vision swam and he gasped for air. The smoke was thicker now. Disoriented, he began to panic. There was a great crash from somewhere and fire spilled from the reception room into the corridor, igniting the runner-carpet, but also showing him which way to go. His wheezing, rasping breaths were almost as loud as the fire. Shielding his face with his forearms, he ran blindly into the flames.

McDaid had forgotten the missing child's name, so was forced to bellow, "Little girl! Where are you, little girl?" like some marauding fairy-tale giant, which would surely only terrify her further. He had thrashed through a number of rooms, first kicking open the door to a boot room, then tearing through the kitchen. He smashed windows with the legs of a chair as he went, in an attempt to clear the air. Not that it made much difference; most of the smoke was in his lungs.

He entered a bedroom, dropped to one knee and looked under

the bed, momentarily glad of the marginally fresher air near the floor. He yelled for the girl again, voice spluttering, growing weaker. He hauled open a wardrobe door, tore hanging clothes free of the rail. Nothing.

He burst back into the corridor, looked back in the direction he'd come from. The fire was creeping into the hallway now, burning debris falling from above as the ceiling weakened. He yelled Dreghorn's name, could hardly hear his own voice above the roar of the fire.

One more room to check. He threw open the door. The master bedroom, he assumed, bigger than the last one. His next attempt at a yell emerged as a hoarse, dry croak. The rest of his body felt like it was going the same way, shutting down, giving up. He looked under the bed. Again, nothing. It was an effort to get back up. He picked up a chair, lumbered to the window and smashed it with a couple of thrusts. It was all he could do to stop himself climbing out into the clean, cold, fresh air outside. He leaned heavily on the chair as he set it down, looking around.

Was that a whimper he heard?

Overhead, the ceiling paint was blistering. In one corner, above a double wardrobe, fire was breaking through, plaster and wood smoking and smoldering.

He staggered to the wardrobe. Locked. Fiery rain fell from above, spattering onto the wardrobe roof, catching in the brim of his hat; he could smell the wool burning. He grabbed both sides of the wardrobe, gave it a shake. No sound, but it was inordinately heavy; more than clothes inside.

He launched a kick at the center of the doors, between the keyholes. The wood buckled and splintered. He dug his fingers under the edge of the door, tore the whole thing free, hurled it across the room. The wardrobe was almost collapsing. He braced it upright, swept aside clothing. He was working by touch alone now, blind in the smoke. He felt around frantically, touched hair slick with sweat, a soft cheek, a child's shoulder. He crouched, scooped up the limp and lifeless girl, and headed for where he thought the door was.

There was a sound like the world was splitting apart; something struck his back as the ceiling collapsed. He stumbled, but kept going, bouncing off the doorframe into the corridor. He ran as best he could, but his steps were heavy, the air like hot sticky tar. He saw nothing, heard nothing, his entire world shrunk to the tiny form in his arms.

Hands gripped his shoulders. He thought he heard a familiar voice. "You're on fire!" He tried to shrug the hands away, but their grip was strong, insistent. Cold air as painful and shocking as the heat of the fire struck him, froze his lungs. He kept going for as long as he could, then fell to his knees. Something like a beating of wings struck his back. The little body remained still in his arms. The hands that had grabbed him tried to wrestle off his coat. He resisted at first, but then let them slip one arm off, then the other, still holding the girl close. A burning bundle was tossed to the grass beside him; his best coat, he realized.

He touched his head to the girl's, whispered everything was all right, that she was safe now. His voice rasped, almost failed. She could have been one of his own—older than Hamish maybe, but younger than John. You're all right, now, hen. Wake up, please.

He became aware of someone kneeling before him. A woman, nurse's uniform, eyes urgent but kind in the firelight. She extended her arms. It took him a moment to understand what she wanted. He passed the girl gently but reluctantly to her. She scuttled backward on her knees and laid the child on her back.

McDaid hunched forward, forehead touching the cool wet grass. He breathed deeply, the world seeping back in. The Trinity fire wagon was there now, men unrolling the hose, running toward the fire. Dreghorn was on the ground beside McDaid, retching with the dry boak like a cat bringing up a fur ball, his face streaked black as if he'd just emerged from a shift down the pits. He had guided McDaid and the girl to the front door, ripped off the big man's coat before it burnt through to his skin.

The nurse was pounding on the girl's chest with all her strength. He wanted to tell her to stop, that the poor wee thing was too fragile. Then she leaned down and covered the child's mouth with her own, breathed for her. She rocked back on her heels, breathing hard, checked her patient. Nothing.

She pummeled the girl's chest again, lips moving silently as she timed the movements. She inhaled deeply, bent forward for another attempt at mouth-to-mouth resuscitation. After a moment, the girl spluttered into life, chest heaving as her lungs sucked in air, limbs thrashing. She hadn't regained full consciousness, but was breathing again at least. The nurse lifted her from the ground into a gentle hug, murmured words of comfort, and gave McDaid a look of relief.

From the sounds coming out of him, McDaid wasn't sure if he was laughing or crying.

37

FRIDAY, 14 OCTOBER 1932

Larger fire engines arrived shortly afterward, along with police officers from the local stations, but Dreghorn immediately took charge. Greenock and Port Glasgow were the nearest conurbations, but he insisted that the fire was linked to an ongoing investigation and should remain under the jurisdiction of the Glasgow Police. If that seemed irregular to the newcomers, none of them had the nerve to argue with the detectives, who looked as though they'd been to hell and back.

Once the fire was extinguished, Dreghorn arranged for the corpses to be transported to Glasgow City Mortuary for examination and identification. The children were taken to the dining hall to be fed cocoa and biscuits, and kept there until the bodies were removed. Then they were allowed to return to their houses, though few would sleep without nightmares. Makeshift beds were made up in the gym hall for those who resided within sight of the still-smoking ruin.

Dreghorn ordered Miss Taylor to compile a list of all Trinity staff, including doctors and nurses from the hospital and sanatorium, and any visitors to the village that day. If the fire was suspicious—and Dreghorn would have bet a month's wages to Bosseye that it was—then police interviews would be conducted as soon as possible.

They waited until the ambulance carrying the bodies had set off for Glasgow before returning to the car. A second, larger fire engine had arrived from Greenock, and the firemen were going through safety checks before investigating the cause of the blaze. Dreghorn gave their captain a card, asked him to call as soon as they reached a verdict. They sat in the car for a while, silent and bone weary, before Dreghorn started the engine. McDaid tapped out a message to Turnbull Street, requesting that the police surgeon make his way urgently to the mortuary. Within minutes of sending it, McDaid had nodded off, head resting against the passenger window.

Dreghorn drove straight to the mortuary, arriving at the same time as Doctor Kivlichan, the corpses already inside. It was morning now, but still looked like night, as if the sun was reluctant to rise over Glasgow's blackened sprawl. He closed the car door gently, leaving McDaid asleep inside.

A full post-mortem would have to wait until formal identification, but a preliminary examination could be undertaken. Unable to stomach the sight and smell of the bodies again, Dreghorn sat in the office while the doctor scrubbed up and went to work, nursing a cup of tea and wishing it were something stronger. His throat felt like he'd been gargling with razor blades and cheap whisky. He lit a cigarette and was racked by a coughing fit that felt like his insides were coming apart.

Willie Kivlichan entered the office as Dreghorn was in full flow. "If you're trying to wake the dead, you're in the right place."

Dreghorn raised a hand in submission, and crushed the cigarette into the ashtray on the doctor's desk. The doctor had undone his top button and pulled out the crucifix he wore around his neck as if to ward off evil spirits. He tossed a set of handwritten notes onto the desk, opened a drawer, and pulled out a bottle of Johnnie Walker and a glass. He emptied the remains of Dreghorn's tea into the wastepaper bin and poured them both healthy measures of whisky.

"Bit early, don't you think?" the detective croaked.

"You look as though you need it."

"What's your excuse?"

"Some bastard dragged me out of bed to look at two burnt corpses."

"Could've been worse. There was almost a wee lassie with them."

Morag Gilmartin, ten years old, had been taken to hospital, but hadn't fully regained consciousness. As his head had cleared, Dreghorn was horrified to recognize her as the girl from the playground on his first visit to Trinity. She would live, but the doctors were concerned at the amount of smoke she had inhaled. If her brain had been starved of oxygen for too long, there could be permanent damage.

Dreghorn remembered McDaid's words a few hours earlier, as he'd staggered to his feet, the fire still raging: "What the fuck were they doing with a wee lassie locked in a cupboard, Jimmy?"

Dreghorn had said nothing; there was no answer.

Kivlichan knocked back his drink and poured another. "You wanted me to find evidence of foul play over and above the fire."

"I wanted you to check if it was a possibility."

"You'd be disappointed if it wasn't." Judgment or accusation, it was hard to tell.

"Surprised." Dreghorn had never seen Kivlichan so serious before. Perhaps the duties of a police surgeon required him to contemplate aspects of human nature at odds with the Hippocratic Oath.

"Nothing on the smaller corpse, the one you said was seated," Kivlichan continued with a sigh. "At least nothing I can detect at the moment. The post-mortem might reveal something."

"That's Dalrymple, the least likely of the pair to offer any resistance. The other one?"

"Difficult to find, but . . . there's damage to the esophagus consistent with some heavy pressure applied to the throat, a chokehold, perhaps. And there's a two-inch incision on the back, under the bottom rib, and, I'm assuming, traveling diagonally upward into the heart. Can't say how deep until we perform the post-mortem, but a serious injury and, I'd say, expertly done."

"Could it be the same weapon that was used to kill Charles Geddes?"

"Possibly."

"So, theoretically, a perpetrator may have murdered or seriously injured at least one of them before setting the fire, hoping it would destroy the evidence?"

Kivlichan nodded. "A body is completely incinerated after two hours at the constant high temperatures of a crematorium. A structural fire might burn hotter for a short while, but not long enough to destroy the body, and you can usually differentiate between tears in the skin caused by flames and those caused by weapons. Only an expert would know that, though."

Dreghorn's mind flashed back to Trinity, to the flames that had blocked the corridor, his reckless run through them. A few more minutes and it would have been him served up on the slab, roasted to perfection. He sipped whisky to chase away the thought. Kivlichan finished his in another single gulp, reached for the bottle again.

"Drunken diagnoses don't go down well."

Kivlichan stared defiantly at Dreghorn for a moment, then relaxed, put the bottle down without opening it. "I hate fires. They stay with you in a way other deaths don't. Give me a good stabbing or shooting any day." He sighed. "Some of the first injuries I treated were burns. Horrific stuff, men scarred for life, disabled . . ."

"At the front?"

"I was at Quintinshill. On the first train."

"Christ!"

Quintinshill, a desolate stretch of railway in the Scottish Borders just north of Carlisle, was the site of Britain's worst rail disaster, recalled by survivors and witnesses with the same sense of horror as the Great War or the Spanish flu epidemic that followed.

At 6 a.m. on 22 May 1915, a glorious summer morning, a train carrying five hundred soldiers, half of the 1st Battalion/the 7th Royal Scots, left Larbert Station in Stirlingshire, bound for Liverpool, where they would travel by ship to the Dardanelles, their ultimate destination the killing grounds of Gallipoli. The majority of them were asleep, after spending the previous night mobilizing for the journey. Well aware that they were heading into battle, they nevertheless felt safe on home ground. Spirits were high.

At Quintinshill, signalmen James Tinsley and George Meakin were changing shifts. Across from where they chatted in the signal box, a local stopping train had been temporarily shunted to the southbound mainline to clear the northbound line for a couple of Glasgow expresses. This placed it directly in the path of the troop train.

"I just forgot," Tinsley said tearfully during the trial afterward, in which he and Meakin, broken men, were found guilty of culpable homicide.

The troop train struck the local train at eighty miles per hour. The front carriages derailed, shooting over the locomotive of the smaller local train. Wreckage was strewn across both railway tracks. The carriages of the troop train were wooden, the majority lit by gas cylinders suspended beneath the floor. The impact crushed the carriages, compacting 215 yards of train into just 67 yards, every carriage filled to capacity with human beings. Fire erupted immediately, as burning coals from the locomotive tender ignited gas leaking from the ruptured cylinders.

Thirty seconds later, the second northbound Glasgow express, whistle shrieking as the drivers tried desperately to stop, plowed into the twisted wall of blazing wreckage. Two hundred and twenty-five lives were lost, all but twelve of them Royal Scots, the rest passengers and workers on the express and local train. Another 191 soldiers were injured, along with 55 civilians.

"It was as if God had reached down, picked up a piece of the war, and dropped it onto Bonnie Scotland like a big fucking hand grenade to make sure we all knew how hellish it was," said Kivlichan.

Dreghorn finished his whisky. The doctor pushed the bottle over to him.

"I was lucky," he said. "I was close to the rear, in one of the few carriages that didn't have gas lighting. I was asleep for the first collision. Woke up being wrenched all over the place, as if the world was turning upside down, bodies and luggage flying everywhere. A soldier beside me had his leg trapped. I tried to pull him free—told him to shut up with all his screaming—but it was jammed fast. There were screams everywhere, not just him. And you could hear the carriages creaking and the hiss of the gas, the whoosh of the cylinders going up as the fire shot along the train. Through that, I heard a whistle, getting louder and louder, and I realized there was another train heading for us. Some poor bastards staggered out of the wreckage only to go under the wheels of the second train. I tried to run, but the boy with his leg stuck wouldn't let go of me." He looked at Dreghorn, shame in his eyes. "I drew my foot back to kick him off, and then the other train hit . . .

"When I came to, I was halfway down an embankment by the tracks. There was burning grit in my hair and I shook it out." He ran a hand through his hair. "If I ever go bald, my skull's all divets and craters, like the surface of the moon." The humor was forced. "The boy who'd been trapped was beside me, his leg torn clean off, and his neck broken. He was lying on his belly, but his head was twisted back to front, still staring at me.

"I climbed back to the top of the embankment. It was chaos. Trains piled on top of each other, carriages crushed or overturned, fires everywhere, the walking wounded staggering around, hundreds of men still trapped. Officers were trying to impose some sort of order, but it was impossible.

"I was covered in burns and cuts and bruises, but nothing serious, so I tried to help as best I could. I'd only just qualified as a doctor, but had never seen or imagined anything like that. There were men missing limbs, soldiers trapped in the wreckage, some of them in burning carriages, watching the fire creep closer, no way to free them . . ."

Dreghorn said, "I heard officers shot their own men."

At first Kivlichan didn't seem to hear, but then he nodded gravely. "When they ran out of bullets, they used their bayonets—thrusting and stabbing to end things as quickly as possible. It was either that or let them burn to death. Some were so badly injured they wouldn't have lived. I tried to concentrate on the ones who could be helped. We found medical supplies in one of the rear carriages. I pumped a good few full of morphine to take away the pain, at least, but there was no saving them. I lied, though, told them they'd be all right, then sent them to oblivion." He was silent, drained, tried to form a self-deprecating laugh. "Sorry, I shouldn't go on about it. You've seen your fair share too."

Dreghorn brushed the apology aside as he picked up the bottle. "A long time ago." He nodded back at the mortuary, with its tiled floors and drains that made it easy to wash away the blood. "You're up to your elbows in stuff here that none of us could stand. Only natural it builds up inside you, makes you think."

Kivlichan watched the detective pour a drink. "There's more," he said. "I've never spoken about it. I don't know if anyone has. Some things . . ."

Dreghorn drank, waited.

"Afterward, when we gathered the bodies together, there were some with bullets in their heads whose injuries didn't warrant it.

Shrapnel wounds and broken bones, but nothing life-threatening. With medical treatment, they'd have survived."

"In a situation like that, it must've been hard to know who could be saved and who couldn't. All too easy to make a mistake."

"That's what I told myself then. It's what I tell myself now. But a perfect shot to the head of each of them, time and time again?" Kivlichan shuddered. "I can't get away from the thought that maybe they weren't all mercy killings. What if some of them were deliberate? If you ever wanted to get away with murder . . ."

"Any reason to think that? Suspicions about who was responsible?"

"No. Nothing like that."

"It was only officers who did the shooting, so that might narrow it down, though they do like to look after their own. Recover the bullets, and ballistics would be able to identify the weapon, but . . ."

"It was chaos, Jimmy. Over two hundred people dead, almost the same number again injured, the survivors heading toward certain death at Gallipoli. You can't blame the top brass for not wanting to hear what I was saying. They swore me to secrecy, promised that the matter would be looked into, but I doubt it was. I never heard anything more about it." Kivlichan took a deep breath. "Maybe you're right. Maybe it wasn't deliberate. Whoever pulled the trigger might've thought he was doing the right thing. With all the blood, it would've been hard to tell, especially without medical training. It's not something anyone should have to do. If you've gone that far, how can you ever come back?"

Dreghorn said nothing, remembered Rory Lockhart aiming his pistol at Charlie Currie's head not long after Quintinshill. He felt uneasy, something cold growing inside.

"Sorry," Kivlichan said, "I push it to the back of my mind, but whenever I have to deal with a burns victim, it all comes back." He stood up, fingering the crucifix at his neck as he steeled himself for the world. "Sometimes, it makes you wonder why you keep believing."

Dreghorn didn't respond.

"You don't go to Mass anymore?" Kivlichan asked. "Communion, confession?"

"If you ask me, all the shite he puts us through, God's the one who needs to confess."

McDaid was awake when Dreghorn returned to the car, a sooty smear on the window where his head had rested. Dreghorn told him about the knife wound and Kivlichan's experiences at Quintinshill.

"You can aye rely on the Doc to cheer you up," McDaid said.

Dreghorn asked if McDaid wanted to go home and get cleaned up before they carried on.

The big man shook his head. "I've been nursing my wrath for long enough."

38

Rain was flowing in rivulets down the windshield. Through it, they saw a car draw to a halt on the other side of the road, outside the Gordon Club. Two forms emerged from the front, one larger than the other, both bending against the stinging wind and rain.

The police car stank of smoke and fire, singed hair and clothes. And charred flesh, cooked almost to the bone, although Dreghorn knew that was his imagination, the stench seared into his memory from last night. And other nights.

Their hands and faces were blackened, streaked with soot and sweat like soldiers camouflaged for a trench raid, their suits ragged and burnt. Suddenly, the law seemed very far away.

"I'll take the big yin; you take the wee yin."

McDaid glanced down at Dreghorn. "Sounds like a good deal."

They stepped out of the car, slamming the doors behind them. No time or patience for stealth, not now.

Jessop, the smaller of the pair, spotted them first, and called a warning to Brodie, who was at the back door, taking instructions from the passenger.

Brodie smiled scornfully. "Fuck," he said. "It's the Robertson's Golly and his pal." A square of medical gauze was taped to his cheek—the sort of thing you might have to wear if Billy Hunter had taken a razor to you on a foggy night.

"Cut yourself shaving?" Dreghorn asked and charged, crouching low. He drove his shoulder into the car door, slamming it shut on Brodie, who wheezed as the impact forced the breath from his lungs, his ribs cracking.

Dreghorn straightened, but kept one hip hard against the door, trapping Brodie upright. He smashed his elbow into the man's face, felt bone crunch. He drew his arm back and struck again, once, twice, three times, Brodie's head flopping back and forth, face spattered with blood. He stepped back, swept Brodie's limp body aside, and slid into the car.

He heard the tell-tale click above the sound of the door slamming. The flick-knife was at his throat as he turned to face Teddy Levin, the tip of the blade touching his carotid artery. Levin was trying to remain composed, but his lips were parted, his breathing excited, a cruel fire in his eyes. This was the real Levin, the gangster, the backstabber, ruthless and vengeful. A small thrust, a quick slash and Dreghorn's blood would shower the interior of the car like the deluge outside. And he could see Levin wanted to do it; it was all he could do to stop himself.

"You're fuckin' mad," Levin said.

"You're fuckin' making me mad," Dreghorn told him.

The car shuddered violently, and the blade pricked Dreghorn's neck, drawing blood. Jessop was sprawled unconscious on the bonnet of the car; his face mashed against the windshield like a champion gurner's, rainwater running over him.

McDaid got into the driver's seat with his usual gracefulness, slammed the door shut, juddering the car again. Levin's control was impressive, the blade barely nicking Dreghorn a second time. Blood trickled down the detective's neck, under his shirt collar.

"Go ahead," Dreghorn said. "You're down for three murders already. Might as well go for broke."

"You'd be doing me a favor," McDaid chimed in. "He's been nipping my heid for weeks." He gave Levin a look of murder. "Then I could reach over and rip your head straight off. Save the hangman the job."

Levin shook his head. "What're youse two on about?"

"Charles Geddes," Dreghorn said.

"Him again? Gets around, for a dead man."

"Must be inconvenient for you."

Levin shrugged with his eyebrows. "Nothing to do with me."

"Says the man holding the knife to my throat."

"You attacked me, maybe killed my two assistants. How was I to know you were the polis in among all the confusion?" A pause. "*Three* murders—who else am I supposed to have killed?"

"Alasdair Dalrymple, Director of Trinity Village, and Arthur Bell."

"Bell, I know. He comes to the club. Dalrymple? Uh-uh. They're dead?"

"Burnt alive," growled McDaid. "It's a miracle a whole village full of kids didn't go up in smoke with them. I carried out one wee lassie . . . They don't know if she'll make it."

"Tragic, but accidents happen."

"That's what somebody's hoping we'll think. But me and Jimmy are naturally suspicious."

"Fire's your pal if you want to cover something up," said Dreghorn. "Given long enough, it destroys everything—evidence, bodies. But Trinity has its own fire wagon. Basic, but it does the job. The fire was put out quicker than whoever set it expected."

"How do you know it was started deliberately?"

Dreghorn glanced at the blade against his neck. "Because someone put a knife in Arthur Bell's back."

"Not an injury commonly associated with being caught in a fire," McDaid pointed out.

Levin thought for a moment, then lowered the knife and eased back in his seat. He didn't fold the blade back into the handle, keeping it ready. Dreghorn resisted the urge to raise a hand to the cut on his neck.

"So," Levin said, "what're you trying to say?"

"That you're fond of accidents."

"Having them?"

"Arranging them."

"Ever thought that whoever told you that might have an axe to grind? I'm a successful businessman. A lot of sad cases out there hate me because of that."

Dreghorn said, "You run whores through your club—cozy wee rooms through the back where your members can slip away to—and have a network of brothels in the South Side and the West End. Fancier than some maybe, but still knocking shops."

"Vivid imagination, inspector." Levin smiled politely. "All conjecture without evidence. Slander even. And inadmissible in court, Mr. Garrison would say."

"Indulge my fantasy," said Dreghorn. "Feel free to chip in, if I'm straying from the point."

"All right, speaking hypothetically . . ."

"Jings," said McDaid. "All these big words."

". . . you run the clubs and the gambling, Catherine Fraser runs the brothels, and you share legitimate businesses like Lomond Tea Rooms, which you can also funnel illegal profits through," Dreghorn continued. "Arthur Bell supplies some of the girls. I saw him bring a lassie to your club for her to interview. Very professional. She's kind to them, like a mother hen with her chicks, but whatever way you look at it, chicks eventually get slaughtered.

"Now, I don't know if he gets his eye on some of them when they're children, makes friends, gets them to trust him till they're older. Wouldn't surprise me. I do know he targets unwed mothers who give birth in the maternity hospital at Trinity. Some of them aren't much more than children anyway. Maybe he coerces them, or maybe they're desperate enough no' to need much persuasion." The old anger was in his voice now. "They've not long given birth. They're giving up their babies for adoption. They've shamed their families, who want nothing to do with them. And here's Uncle Arthur, offering to help them earn a wee bit of money to get back on their feet. He dangles their children in front of them as a little extra incentive, says he can get access to them at the school, or help keep tabs on them after they're adopted."

McDaid's bulk seemed to grow, blocking out Jessop's squashed features on the windscreen. "They're just lassies," he said, "scared and vulnerable. They've given up something they love, or had it taken away from them. They probably hate themselves for it. And then bastards like you get a hold of them, take advantage. No' anymore. It stops here."

Levin tightened his grip on the knife. "Wag the finger all you want, big man," he snarled with disdain. "It'll never stop, because there's one thing in this world that'll never change: Men want to shag women. And a lot of them are more than willing to pay for it, some highly respectable—wife and weans and a good job. That might offend your God-fearing teuchter sensibilities, but it's the truth. Would you rather they were getting humped up back closes and alleyways, where any wee ned or old drunk can stab them or slash them or give them a good kicking if he doesn't feel like paying? Or would you prefer they were somewhere safe and warm; inside, off the streets, where there's people looking out for them, protecting them?"

McDaid rolled his eyes at Dreghorn. "We've got it all wrong. Send the King a telegram—medal for Teddy!"

"Nothing you're saying amounts to murder," Levin pointed out.

Dreghorn leaned an elbow on the back of the seat, stillness at his core, the tripwire taut. "Illegal, though. Scandalous too. The bigwigs and high heid yins that favor your club wouldn't stick around for long if it came out, even if they weren't the ones doing the shagging."

"If it was true." Levin's denial seemed less firm than before. "Where's Geddes in all this?"

"Geddes has a high opinion of himself, likes to think people jump to attention when he's around, likes to charm women into bed with all his big talk. He's an important man of the world, a winner. Which is why he's no' happy that you've got him in your pocket."

"How's that?"

"The invoices he sent Claymore Holdings. None of them were paid. There are no corresponding sums of money paid into his bank account. You were using him to do free legal work—interest on the debts you hold over him."

"Through this gambling ring I run, in addition to being the god-father of Glasgow whoredom?" Levin shook his head in disbelief.

"Somehow, Geddes learned about the arrangement you have with Bell. He's a gambler; he likes the odds, and he sees a way to get you off his back and make some money on the side. He blackmails you: cancel his debts or he'll reveal the whole sordid story. He demands a little extra on top for the inconvenience you've put him through. He's got photographs, can prove what's going on.

"Do you consider paying him off? No chance. You know that won't be the end of it. He'll be back for more. That's what blackmailers do, that's what gamblers do. So you weigh up the odds and decide he's better off dead. Not just him, Bell and Dalrymple as well. They know too much, especially if they've all been keeping records of your business. They could turn against you too. Or be turned against you. Wouldn't it be handy if they all went up in smoke together?"

After a moment, Levin looked out at the rain. Whether he was thinking, or just making them wait, Dreghorn didn't know.

"It wasn't me he was blackmailing." Levin faced Dreghorn again. "And I didn't kill him. Or Bell and Dalrymple. They're nothing to me." He gestured with his hand like a puff of smoke.

Dreghorn shared a glance with McDaid, reluctantly acknowledging the air of truth in Levin's voice.

"The other stuff," said Levin. "If you want to be bloody-minded, go ahead and arrest me, but you'll be on a hiding to nothing. Protection, friends in high places, call it what you want; I'm no' going to jail anytime soon."

"Because you're paying off Strachan and Orr? We saw Catherine Fraser pass them an envelope."

Levin tutted, disappointed that they'd think him so crude.

Dreghorn smiled bitterly as light dawned. "You've not just got them in your pocket; you're an informant as well. Nice one. Keeps the streets clear of your rivals. Just them, or does it go higher? I noticed McVicar was keen to get shot of you when we brought you in."

Teddy smiled inscrutably. "You've been talking to Kitty, aye?"

"If anything happens to her . . ." Dreghorn warned.

"I'll be as annoyed as you. Fine woman. We work well together. No complaints. But she wasn't always at the top of her game. Started off at the bottom, on her back—a few other positions as well. She must've been good, though, because she married Johnnie Fraser. Johnnie ran these houses of ill repute that you think I've got something to do with. He died of a massive stroke a few years ago, and Kitty decided to carry on the business herself, which she'd virtually been doing anyway. But the vultures started circling. Everybody thinks whores are easy money."

"And you were the biggest vulture," McDaid stated.

"She came to me," Levin tapped the tip of the blade against his own chest. "Recognizes a gentleman when she sees one. She runs things the way she wants, and I make sure no one tries to muscle in on her. Her girls stay safe. Well, safe as they can be. Men are bastards.

You ought to hear the stories she tells." He glanced from Dreghorn to McDaid. "Any arrangement that procured girls from Trinity was between Kitty and Bell. Might even have been on the go when Johnnie was still alive. Geddes might have found out about that, but it's nothing that would've given him a hold over me. He'd have got his arse skelped if he tried it. If you want to find out who he was blackmailing, I'd look a little closer to home. His home."

"The Lockharts?" There was an edge to Dreghorn's voice, as if it was something he'd secretly suspected.

"Geddes wanted to be a man of substance, but deep down he knew he wasn't. What he didn't like was other people knowing it as well. Old Man Lockhart thought he was a parasite and treated him accordingly, cut him off from business affairs, refused to pay off the debts he racked up."

"Which is why Geddes ended up owing you money."

"He said he'd be able to pay back everything he owed, but that he needed a little breathing space to set it up. He claimed he had something on Lockhart, something that the old man would pay handsomely to stop coming out. And keep paying. Money, property, company shares, it could all be ours, he said, if I agreed to hold off on his debts for a few weeks."

Dreghorn remembered the beating Geddes had received a week or two before his death. "You agreed, but had those two gorillas give him a hiding . . ."

"Objection, your honor, wild speculation on the part of the prosecution."

". . . just like somebody tried to do to me the other night."

Levin raised an eyebrow innocently, news to him. "The way you go around harassing folk, I'm surprised there's no' a queue all the way down Sauchiehall Street."

"What did he have on Lockhart?"

"No idea. Might not even have been the old man. Might have

been that war hero son of his. Or the daughter—she's fond of you, I hear." Levin shrugged. "Geddes wouldn't tell me. Kept going on about knowledge being power and all that shite. Didn't stop him ending up dead."

"You're saying Lockhart had him killed."

"Objection, your honor, putting words into the witness's mouth. I'm saying there are people out there with a stronger motive than me. A reputation like the Lockharts' might be worth killing for."

He returned the blade to the handle with a deft click and dropped the knife smoothly into his inside pocket. He smiled. "Happy families, eh?" he said.

39

"The coalman usually delivers at the back."

Her smile would normally have charmed him, but now it seemed cruel, superior. She stepped aside to let him in. He stayed where he was, in the rain.

"James, what happened to you?" Concern now, or a convincing stab at it.

"I was at Trinity."

"Oh God, the fire. I heard about it on the wireless. Are you hurt? Don't just stand there, for heaven's sake, come in."

Isla reached for his arm, but he avoided her touch. Rainwater dripped from his coat onto the polished parquet floor.

"You're soaked. Please, go through, warm yourself by the fire."

"I've seen enough fires for one day."

He walked into the drawing room: the blazing hearth, the abundance of seating, the paintings on the wall, the enormous bay windows, the luxury, all seemed obscene to him now. This was no more his world now than it had been when he'd been in Sir Iain Lockhart's office as a fourteen-year-old boy. He caught sight of himself in a mirror. That boy was long gone.

"Sit down; you look exhausted." Isla followed, but kept a wary distance. "I'll tell them to bring some tea. Or maybe some soup?"

"Nothing."

"Was anyone hurt? They didn't give many details on the news . . ."

"Arthur Bell, one of the house fathers, and Alasdair Dalrymple, were both killed. Archie was lucky. Just made it out."

His gaze was making her uncomfortable. She glanced away as if searching for the right words. "That's terrible. Those poor men . . ."

"They weren't saints. And at least one of them was dead before the fire started. Murdered, just like your husband. Nobody's innocent here."

She stepped closer, took one of his hands. "James, you're scaring me. You need to rest. Lie down upstairs, sleep for a while, then we can talk."

He shook his head, his smile as sour as bile, and placed his other hand over hers, rubbed them together. She pulled away, her hands smeared with soot and grime. He reached out, caressed her cheek with more pressure than was comfortable, dirtying her face. She slapped his hand away and stepped back. "What are you doing?"

"Showing you what it's like to get your hands dirty, because you never do, do you? You, your father, your brother—you all lead charmed lives, or so we all think." Dreghorn paced the room. "But maybe the family that has everything just has more to lose than the rest of us. How far would you go to keep it?"

"If you have something to say, inspector, please do us both a favor and get to the point. Life suddenly seems too short to waste any more time on you."

"Your father's been bankrolling Trinity Village for years, noble philanthropist that he is." He paused; she acknowledged his words with an angrily raised eyebrow. "Alasdair Dalrymple and Arthur Bell have been pimping out girls from the school, and young unmarried mothers from the maternity hospital, supplying them to Teddy Levin to use as whores in his clubs and other establishments. You know, the ones your husband was a member of."

"That's ridiculous."

"Wish it was. But it's true. Straight from the gangster's mouth, though I doubt he'd admit it in court. And it could be worse."

"It's already despicable, if it's true. How could it be worse?"

"We found a little girl, not much older than your Catriona, locked in a wardrobe in Dalrymple's bedroom. Archie got her out, but it's touch and go. We don't think whoever set the fire knew she was there, but . . ."

"My father donates money to Trinity for the good of the children. If Bell and Dalrymple were engaged in criminal activity, it has nothing to do with him."

"Of course not. Pillar of the community. Everyone respects him, from the Lord Provost down to the welder's apprentice in the yards. Except for your husband. No love lost there. The photographs you found? The woman was a prostitute; the man was high up in the Corporation. I'm surprised you didn't know him. The sort of man who could be very useful—especially when you've got pictures of him having his cock sucked by some woman who's definitely not his wife."

Isla met his eyes again; she wasn't shocked by his crudeness.

"We suspected Geddes was trying to blackmail Levin," Dreghorn continued, "but he wasn't. He wanted Levin as an accomplice, for protection probably. But where did he get the photos? Who else might benefit from the leverage photos like that would give them? And how would Geddes get his hands on them? He wasn't a criminal, not really. Where would he find them?" Dreghorn spread his arms, encompassing the world around him, the world of the Lockharts. "Maybe they were right under his nose. Who, above all, would Geddes have liked to kick in the teeth?"

"You're trying to implicate my father?"

"He's one of the most powerful men in Scotland. But times are changing; there's a depression on. I've seen how ruthless he can be."

"Maybe he just saw through you, realized you didn't deserve the faith he put in you. He's in a wheelchair, inspector. He's virtually a cripple."

"There are others around him."

"You'd better arrest me, then; I'm the one who's been handling his affairs. Maybe I stabbed Alasdair Dalrymple in the back."

"No, you've got other ways of influencing the investigation."

She slapped him. He didn't flinch, so she swung again, balling her fist, hitting him in the mouth. He caught her wrist on the third swing, letting her know that he could easily have stopped the others.

"Get out!" she hissed.

He released her, spat a mouthful of blood into the fire. It sizzled. He stopped at the door, didn't look back. "Tell Sir Iain we'll be dropping in for a chat."

"Get out, you bastard!"

40

SATURDAY, 15 OCTOBER 1932

Dreghorn slept for twelve hours straight, sprawled on the bed only half undressed. When he woke, there was an imprint on the sheets, as if someone had drawn an outline around him and shaded it in with charcoal. It took almost as long to clean the bath as it did to scrub the ingrained soot from his body. He heard Mrs. Pettigrew moving around the house, wondered if she'd offer to scrub his back. She didn't.

He and McDaid met in the Rialto Café and wolfed down enormous breakfasts. McDaid was put out that Dreghorn even managed to devour his clootie dumpling, which he usually deposited on the big man's plate.

They pushed through the throng of reporters gathered outside Turnbull Street, saying nothing. The papers had reported the Trinity fire, the deaths of Alasdair Dalrymple and Arthur Bell, and the rescue of Morag Gilmartin. They lauded the heroic actions of DI James Dreghorn and DS Archibald McDaid, who'd risked their lives to save the child.

Questions were raised, however, about the reason for the officers' presence at the scene. No answers were forthcoming in Chief Constable Sillitoe's statement. His officers' conduct was above and beyond the call of duty; thanks to them, an even greater tragedy had been averted; fire investigators were working to ascertain the cause of the blaze; and further information would be released in due course.

The preliminary fire report, read out to the detectives gathered in the Murder Room, confirmed Dreghorn's suspicions. The fire was started almost simultaneously in Dalrymple's office and the reception room. Burning coals and logs had been shoveled from the hearths onto the carpet, furniture, and curtains. The arsonist had then escaped, stealing Dalrymple's house keys and locking the door. No witnesses. A porter at the hospital had reported seeing car headlights traveling away from the village at the appropriate time, but was too far away to recognize the vehicle or read the number plate. There had been no scheduled visitors or official appointments that day.

The victims were incapacitated before the fire was set, in Bell's case possibly already dead. They would know more after the postmortem. Formal identifications would take place later that day. Dalrymple's sister was traveling down from Dunblane, and Bell had a wife in Paisley—from whom he was separated but not divorced—listed as his next of kin in school employment records.

"What about the wee girl?" Ellen Duncan asked. "Did the killer know she was in there?"

"We're proceeding on the assumption, no," said DCI Monroe, "but we can't rule anything out. We're arranging interviews with the staff at the village, and some of the children if necessary. If there's abuse of any kind whatsoever involving the pupils, then someone must have known, or at least had suspicions."

Strachan smoothed his mustache with thumb and forefinger. "Locked in the headmaster's cupboard? Pretty strong punishment for not doing your homework."

"Is this the same perpetrator as the Geddes murder?" DS Tolliver asked, unlit pipe jammed between his teeth.

"We're running about like headless chickens, getting nowhere," said Brian Harvie. "Is Teddy Levin still a suspect?"

Strachan shook his head dismissively. "Teddy might turn a blind eye to minor infringements or cut the odd dubious business deal, but he's not Al Capone. And he's been useful to the police on more than one occasion."

Dreghorn agreed. "We had a word with Levin yesterday. He might know more than he's saying, but I don't think he's our man anymore."

Strachan's mustache bristled at Dreghorn's sudden familiarity with the club owner. Dreghorn met his gaze, but gave nothing away about how much he knew.

"He claims Geddes approached him with the photographs," Dreghorn carried on, "not in an attempt to extort money, but to get him to become a partner in whatever scheme Geddes was cooking up. Honest citizen that he is, Teddy turned down the offer in the strongest possible terms and advised Geddes not to embark on such a crooked path."

"Did he give any indication who Geddes planned to target?" Monroe asked.

"No. Someone wealthy, important." Dreghorn ignored the flare of suspicion in McDaid's eyes. "Maybe more than one person."

"No, no, no, you've got it all wrong," Orr waved his arms as if trying to clear the air of midges. "This is about revenge. If someone'd been fiddling with me when I was a wean, I'd come back and make sure they fuckin' paid for it when I was grown up. How many children have gone through that orphanage over the years?"

"We can't discount that possibility." Monroe nodded at Strachan. "Boyd, you and Orr look into it. Examine the records of pupils who have passed through Trinity during Bell and Dalrymple's tenure, and check for subsequent criminal records. Wouldn't necessarily be a sign of guilt, but it might give some indication."

"Sir." Strachan glowered, unhappy about being sidelined from the main investigation.

Dreghorn spoke to McDaid as the meeting broke up. "Before you say anything, I'm not doing anyone any favors. I didn't mention the Lockharts because I don't want any interference from the high heid yins. We keep it between ourselves until we've got hard evidence that nobody can argue against."

He neglected to mention his confrontation with Isla, which he now regretted. If there was some conspiracy among the family, his recklessness may well have alerted them. He thought about her as he put on his coat, about her father's angry scrawl and Rory's drunken musings a few nights earlier.

WPC Duncan was seated at a desk, Strachan leaning over her from behind, uncomfortably close, pointing out something in the files before her.

Dreghorn said, "Ellen, may I have a word? Something I'd like you to look into . . ."

"Sir." She sprang dutifully to her feet, pushing her chair back. The corner caught Strachan in the groin, causing him to wince audibly.

"Oh, sorry, sir!" Dreghorn caught the glee in her voice.

Tedium ruled the day; a mass of interviews, reports, and witness statements, none of which led anywhere. Dreghorn accompanied Arthur Bell's estranged wife and Alasdair Dalrymple's sister to the formal identifications but gleaned little information from them.

After the Boer War, Bell took to the drink and was impossible to live with, his wife said. When he was offered the position of house father at Trinity, she refused to join him. They stayed married, though; she didn't want the stigma of a divorce. He enjoyed life at Trinity and sometimes sent money, out of guilt for the way their marriage turned out, she thought. Dalrymple visited his sister twice a year, when he would stay at a local guesthouse. He doted on his nieces and nephews, though his conversations were often rather too highbrow for them.

Dr. Kivlichan had been informed of the identifications, but couldn't perform the post-mortems until the following afternoon. More waiting. More frustration.

Returning to the Murder Room, Dreghorn found Ellen Duncan on the telephone. She shook her head. Nothing to report. Tension was high, the workload increasing with no conviction in sight. Dreghorn was on the verge of suggesting that he and McDaid pay Boss-eye or Denny Knox a visit in the hope of shaking something loose when his telephone rang.

Shug Nugent, more respectful than usual: "Inspector, there's a lady at the desk asking for you. Says she witnessed an abduction."

"I'll send Ellen down to talk to her."

"No, sir, she insists it has to be you. She's in quite a state. Says you know her. A Mrs. Fraser, Catherine Fraser."

"In quite a state" was not a phrase Dreghorn would have associated with Kitty Fraser, but Shug's description was accurate. She was disheveled, her hat missing, strands of hair falling across her face. Her clothes were splashed with mud, her palms scraped, a tear in one stocking. She was fearful, more than when Dreghorn had threatened to reveal her whereabouts to her brother, and her eyes were red from crying.

"Mrs. Fraser," he said discreetly. "Sergeant Nugent said something about an abduction. Is one of your girls in trouble?"

"No, not one of them. It's— She's—"

"It's all right, take your time." He placed a supportive hand on her arm. "This woman who's been abducted, do you know her?"

She gave an uncertain nod.

"What's her name?"

"Molly. Molly Raeburn."

Dreghorn gave no hint of recognition. "That's better. And Molly's a friend of yours?"

"She . . ." Dreghorn could see a lifetime of lies in her eyes, a wall that was crumbling. "She's my daughter."

"She ran out into the street. I went after her, but the owner blocked my way and I lost time paying the bill. It was pouring with rain, hats and umbrellas everywhere, a bunch of Old Firm fans on either side of the road, shouting at each other."

Dreghorn nodded; both teams were playing that day.

"It took me a while to spot her. If she hadn't left her umbrella in the café, I'd never have seen her. She was quite far along, where Sauchiehall Street meets Rose Street. It was hard to see, but it looked as if she was talking to a couple of men, arguing. One of them grabbed her, forced her into a car. I tried to open the door, but it was locked. Molly looked out at me. She was terrified."

"Did you see the men?"

Kitty shook her head. "All I saw was her."

"Kitty, I need you to think, concentrate. You still saw them, even if it was out of the corner of your eye. Were they tall, short, well-dressed, shabby?"

"They were wearing suits, not expensive ones, and bunnets pulled low to hide their faces."

"Not the type that usually own cars, then. What happened next?"

"They drove off. I ran beside them, rattling the door handle and banging the window. I even jumped onto the running board, but it was wet, and I slipped and fell into the gutter." She looked at the stains on her clothing as if taking them in for the first time, and then reached into her handbag, pulled out a crumpled scrap of paper. "But I got the number."

Dreghorn snatched the paper from her, nipped out and passed it to McDaid.

"Aye," McDaid grunted. "Though the car's more than likely stolen."

After her revelation about Molly, Dreghorn had taken Kitty to an empty office rather than an interrogation room. Keeping it simple at first, he'd drawn out the basic details he needed to start making inquiries. Kitty and Molly had met at 3 p.m. in the Rhul Tea Room, Sauchiehall Street. At around 3:30, the exchange had become heated. A quick phone call to the establishment confirmed the argument. Molly had stormed out, whereupon unidentified assailants had forced her into a car. Now, as Ellen laid cups of tea in front of them, Dreghorn backtracked.

"So Miss Raeburn is your daughter, the one who was adopted. Did she know?"

"I told her today."

'Is that why she ran off?'

"She was upset. It was a shock, I suppose."

"You've no idea who the men were, or why they wanted to kidnap her?"

She shook her head.

"Were you lying when you said you'd never spoken to her, just watched from a distance?"

"Does that matter? Shouldn't you be out looking for her?"

"You have to tell me everything you know." When she still hesitated, he said, "We know she was involved with Charles Geddes, Catherine. We know that her adoptive father is the leading man in Geddes' photographs. So why contact her now?"

"I was scared for her. Geddes brought her to the club a few times. He introduced us, would you believe that? Obviously she had no idea who I was, but I recognized her right away. I was horrified to see her with him, but of course I had to be the perfect hostess. I didn't know he was involved in anything dangerous at the time, I just—"

"Didn't think he was ideal suitor material."

She looked at him to gauge if he was being sarcastic, seemed surprised by the sympathy in his eyes. "When Geddes went to the gents," she continued, "I tried to warn her. She claimed that they weren't going together. Her father had died a few weeks earlier and Geddes had been helping Molly and her mother with legal matters." Kitty's face softened. "She seemed so innocent. Not something I see much of these days."

"Me neither."

The rest of the story tumbled out of her. "The thought of him hurting her was too much. I did what I told you I dreamed of. I made sure we accidentally bumped into each other, and suggested we go for afternoon tea. We got on well and I suggested we meet again. We became friends. She said I was like the big sister she never had. She talked about how she and her mother never really got on. Called herself a Daddy's girl. Whenever I asked about Geddes, she'd change the subject or brush it off, as if he wasn't worth talking about. And then he was murdered."

"Did you speak after that?"

"She was upset; but more than that, she seemed scared. After her father died she went through his things. In a case in the attic she found photographs of him with another woman—not holding hands or walking in the park. There were other things, threatening telegrams. Someone had been blackmailing her father with the photos. Not for money, for influence, forcing him to do them favors through his position at the Corporation. But Eric Raeburn had kept a diary, meticulously recording everything he'd ever done for them. She showed the material to Geddes—the family solicitor, after all— and he said he'd deal with it. He promised that her father's name and reputation wouldn't be dragged through the muck."

"Did she show you any of it?"

"No, she'd given it all to Geddes for safekeeping. This was before we'd spoken. When you told me about the photographs, I realized that Geddes had got them from Molly, and that keeping them safe was the last thing on his mind."

"Would've saved a lot of trouble if you'd mentioned it at the time," Dreghorn said.

"I was trying to protect her."

"You didn't think that whoever killed Geddes might try and track down the original source of the photographs?"

"I wasn't thinking straight." He could hear the agitation in her voice. "Did Geddes really think he could extort money from Teddy and get away with it?"

"We're not sure Levin was the intended victim, not now. What happened when you met Molly? Did you tell her all this?"

"I told her that, after what had happened to Geddes, I thought she might be in danger, and that we should go away somewhere. She was confused. Why would I want to go away with her? 'Because I'm your mother,' I said."

Kitty paused, slow tears in her eyes. She shook her head as Dreghorn offered her a cigarette. He lit one for himself as she started talking again. It sounded, sadly, as much like a confession as any other he'd heard.

"Once I started, I couldn't stop. I told her everything in one great breathless rush, as if I couldn't get it out fast enough. About Trinity. About how giving her up was like giving away a part of myself. About finding out who adopted her—I didn't tell her how—and watching her grow up, sometimes walking so close that I could've touched her, but never did. About how seeing her happy broke my heart even more, even though it was all I wanted for her."

"How did she take it?"

"Well, I didn't expect her to jump up and hug me. She was shocked, speechless to begin with. We were both crying—heaven knows what the other customers thought."

Molly had taken Kitty's hand across the table and smiled through her tears. She had known she was adopted since the age of sixteen. She sometimes wondered about her birth mother, but had enjoyed a happy, contented life with the Raeburns. She reassured Kitty that she had no reason to feel guilty or ashamed. She hoped they could be friends; they *were* friends. She squeezed Kitty's hand and they both laughed, glad of the release.

"I told her, 'I wanted to keep you so much.' But it was impossible. My age, our poverty, the shame my family said it would bring on them. And my father, he was a brute, he"—she unbuttoned the right sleeve of her blouse, started to roll the cuff up her arm with angry jerky movements—"I showed her. I showed her what he was like, what he did."

Dreghorn's unease grew with each turn of the cuff.

"When I told my family I was expecting, my mother was doing the ironing. My da took it off her, gave her a wee kiss on the head, grabbed my wrist, and pulled my arm flat across the kitchen table. He said, while I was burning and squealing, that if I didn't get rid of it he'd *beat the little bastard out of my body.* I couldn't bring her home after that, could I?"

Dreghorn didn't answer, stared at the white puckered skin, the curving V-shaped indentation on her bicep. The same scar was on the arm of the girl in the photograph with Eric Raeburn, the girl he, like Molly, now recognized as Sarah Catherine Hunter. The revelation would have shattered Molly Raeburn's world. Mother, father, whore, adulterer; unimagined ghosts of the past suddenly given flesh.

"She started gasping for air and holding her chest, as if she couldn't breathe. I thought she was choking and jumped up to help, but she gave me a look of . . . revulsion. She got to her feet so quickly she overturned her chair and ran out, knocked a tray out of a waitress's hands. I don't know what happened. One minute we were touching, holding hands, the next—" Kitty stared at him. "What's wrong? Why are you looking at me like that?"

Dreghorn didn't have the heart to tell her.

* * *

The car was found on Dumbarton Road, Clydebank, opposite the John Brown Engineering Works, abandoned, Dreghorn suspected, in an area where the kidnappers wouldn't be known. It had been stolen in Rutherglen the previous night, and its owner, Andrew Patterson, a baker with a small chain of shops, had reported the theft first thing that morning. There was no sign of Molly Raeburn.

Dreghorn and McDaid drove out to Clydebank, where the young constable who'd found the car stood guard. He pointed out that the keys were in the ignition; it was a miracle the car hadn't been stolen a second time, or vandalized. Motor vehicles were the preserve of the wealthy, fair game for a bit of destructive fun if parked in the wrong area.

Dreghorn brushed the steering wheel for fingerprints, a technique that McDaid avoided because he always ended up looking as if he'd sneezed in a talcum powder factory. All the powder highlighted were smudges, nothing clear enough for identification. The doors, windows, and dashboard were other possible sources of prints, but he'd leave that to the Forensics Department. Checking the back, McDaid reached under the seat and pulled out a woman's handbag. The contents confirmed that it was Molly Raeburn's. There was still money in her purse, ruling out theft as a motive for the abduction.

"You think this has something to do with Geddes, or the fire?" McDaid asked.

Dreghorn leaned an elbow on the open door, stared across the roof at McDaid. Something dark and ominous was forming in his mind, like a zeppelin approaching under cloud cover for a bombing raid, but he couldn't quite grasp it. He shook his head, shrugged.

The whistle shrieked in John Brown's Yard, signaling the end of a shift and taking Dreghorn back a lifetime. Normally, the sound triggered a mad rush of bodies from the gates. Now, it was a skeleton crew at best. Above the yard walls, Dreghorn could see the mammoth unfinished shape of Hull Number 534, the unnamed Cunard ocean liner that was to have been the salvation of the Clyde. Work had been suspended the previous December, plunging thousands into unemployment.

McDaid took the stolen car and they returned to Turnbull Street, where they agreed they needed a dram to soothe their throats, still raw from the fire. Dreghorn returned to the Murder Room for a final check, while McDaid went to Forensics to arrange a thorough examination of Andrew Patterson's car. Ellen Duncan was pacing restlessly in the corridor.

Dreghorn glanced at his watch. "It's home time, constable."

She waved her notebook, eyes wide with excitement. "I was waiting for you, sir." She looked around warily. The Murder Room was empty apart from Strachan, Orr, and DS Tolliver. Dreghorn noticed Strachan watching them, stroking his mustache.

"You asked me to make more inquiries about Rory Lockhart's return to Scotland," Ellen continued. "He said he arrived in Glasgow on the fifth of October after being forced to stop for repairs at the Royal Ulster Yacht Club in Bangor, Northern Ireland, on the thirtieth of September. I spoke to the harbor master of the Royal Ulster on the telephone and asked exactly when Mr. Lockhart sailed the *Lion Rampant* back to Scotland. He said he waved the *Rampant* out on the fifth of October, but that Captain Lockhart wasn't on board."

"What?"

"The *Rampant*'s attempt to take the America's Cup was a co-challenge between the Royal Ulster and Royal Clyde Yacht Clubs. Prior to the race, it set sail for New York from County Down, but Rory joined the crew late, sailing from Scotland, where he'd been visiting his family, on his own yacht, the *Quentin Durward*—which remained berthed at the Royal Ulster all the time he was away."

"And was still there when he got back?"

Ellen nodded grimly. "He set sail aboard the *Durward* from the Royal Ulster on the morning of the first. Alone."

"Two days before Charles Geddes was murdered. He's been lying to us all along." There was no surprise in his voice, only resignation.

"Looks like it, sir. I'm sorry. He's a friend?"

"Never quite that."

Dreghorn entered the Murder Room, thoughts racing, after sending Ellen to fetch McDaid. Strachan blocked his way, said, "You and PC Duncan, thick as thieves."

"Scared we're talking about you, Boyd?"

"Nothing about you scares me."

"You're slow off your marks, then," said Dreghorn. "I saw you, stuffing a wad of money into your pocket after a free shag at Kitty Fraser's. But we all know who it really came from. Teddy Levin, who's so useful to the police, isn't that what you said?"

Strachan raised a hand to halt Orr, who, sensing the mood, had stepped forward. Out of earshot, Tolliver rose from his desk and asked, "Everything all right, lads?" Blessed are the peacemakers. No one answered.

"Your word against ours," Strachan said.

"Your arse. Me, Teddy, and Archie had an interesting chat. You need to start asking exactly who's in whose pocket." Dreghorn glanced at Tolliver, kept his voice low. "Keep your distance from Ellen Duncan. Or I'll spell it all out for Sillitoe."

Strachan's mustache bristled with disdain. "Run to the boss?"

"It's called upholding the law."

"Instead of stepping outside and trying to sort it yourself?"

"Don't worry, that'll come first."

Dreghorn's phone rang. Nobody moved. The ringing seemed to get louder. Tolliver crossed the room and answered. "Mrs. Geddes."

Dreghorn grabbed the receiver, kept his voice businesslike.

"James?" The tremor in her voice put him on edge. "You were right. I found more of them."

"Photographs?"

"Like the ones in Catriona's room, but worse. Much worse. There are children in them, some as young as Catriona. It's . . . *sickening*. The people, I know some of them. I can't believe—" Her voice cracked, and he felt her pain.

Dreghorn turned his back to Strachan, said, "Isla, take deep breaths. Try to calm down. You're doing the right thing calling me. Where are you?"

"Kelpie House."

'Is anyone else with you? Catriona, your nanny?"

"No, I left them in Glasgow."

"Good. Does your father know what you're doing there?"

"He thinks I'm just visiting." She was growing impatient with his questions, eager to tell him more. "It's not just photographs; there're blackmail letters, threatening to expose people for the fucking monsters they are! And other papers, listing who everybody is—what they like. It's—"

"Listen to me, Isla. Gather as much of it as you can, and get out of there. You've got your car, aye?"

She said yes, half listening at best. He could sense the frantic workings of her mind.

"Drive to the Dumbuck Hotel and stay in the bar or at reception, where people can see you. We'll be there soon. Isla, are you listening?"

"Yes!"

"Then do as I say, no arguments. And don't say anything to your father, just tell him—"

"It's not my father. It's Rory!"

41

This time, there was no banter between Dreghorn and McDaid as they drove under the rearing horses. In the darkness, they took on a demonic silhouette, curving into the air like horns.

Isla had not been at the hotel. A flash of identification and a few bellowed questions established that no one of her description had been there. They continued on to Kelpie House, the wind howling in from the Clyde, salt spray peppering the car like bursts of gunfire.

Dreghorn informed McDaid of Ellen's discoveries and Isla's phone call. He spoke tersely of the other suspicions that had been forming in his mind; Charlie Currie's murder verdict and execution all those years ago; the shooting of helpless victims at Quintinshill.

"No' quite the pampered playboy, then."

"Best shot in our regiment," Dreghorn said, swerving to a halt, sending gravel spattering over the front steps. "No' one for taking prisoners either."

He ignored the doorbell, battered his fist repeatedly against the door until the footman answered. They stepped inside without invitation, McDaid flashing his warrant card in warning.

"Is Isla here?" Dreghorn snapped. "Mrs. Geddes?"

"Miss Isla was here earlier, sir." Naseby, the butler, had appeared in the hall, alerted by the commotion. "I'm not sure if she's still at home . . ." His speech seemed to slow in direct correlation to their urgency.

"What about Rory, and the old man?"

Naseby bristled at Dreghorn's disrespect. "I haven't seen Master Rory since yesterday morning. I believe he had business in Glasgow. Sir Iain is in the library, but—"

Dreghorn, already moving, barked over his shoulder, "Check the garage, see if Isla's car's there."

McDaid jabbed a finger at the butler. "Quick march, Jeeves, we're no' fuckin' messing about here."

Sir Iain Lockhart was hunched in front of the fire, the glow of a standard lamp behind him, his shadow cast long and sharp across the floor. The nurse sat on the sofa, reading aloud. She broke off and got to her feet as the detectives strode in.

The old man appeared to be asleep, a blanket tucked snugly around his lower half. Dreghorn tore it free, nearly threw it in the fire. The old man raised his head slowly, met Dreghorn's gaze.

"Aye, me again, you old bastard."

"How dare you?" the nurse exclaimed. "Sir Iain's seriously ill. He's too frail to be subjected—"

"Frail as a navy frigate." Dreghorn pointed at the door. "Out!"

She backed away at the threat in his voice.

"Best do as he says, hen." McDaid was more conciliatory. "We are the polis after all."

She was already moving, promising, "I'm going to fetch some-one," without conviction.

Dreghorn said, "Where's Isla?"

Sir Iain's eyes flicked toward the coffee table.

"Get his crayons, Archie."

McDaid gathered the notepaper and crayons, slammed them onto the old man's tray.

"Where's Isla?" repeated Dreghorn.

Sir Iain clawed at a crayon, wrote shakily: *GONE.*

"Gone where? We know she was here not long ago. Is she with Rory?"

Sir Iain's eyes blazed. The crayon didn't move.

"You don't know? That's not like you, sir. What's wrong, not in charge anymore?"

Sir Iain's hand shook with effort, the crayon digging into the paper: *KNOW EVERYTHING.*

"Aye, so do we—the whores, the photos, the bastards you were blackmailing." He leaned down, gripped the sides of the tray, his forehead almost touching the old man's. "But it's worse than that, isn't it? The children, the orphans at Trinity, you used them as well. And it has to be you behind it, or somebody doing your bidding, 'cos the photos are too old. Rory would have been too young then, though he's in it with you now, isn't he?"

The old man's face was remorseless. *GET ME GARRISON.*

Dreghorn snatched the note before Sir Iain had finished, the crayon leaving a jagged scrawl off the edge of the paper. "Fuck Garrison," he said, and threw the note into the fire.

Naseby was standing in the library doorway, his attitude less haughty than before. He announced that Miss Isla's car was indeed in the garage. He was perturbed, because he was sure she'd left earlier in the evening. He hadn't seen her for at least the last two hours. Around the time she'd phoned Dreghorn.

Dreghorn and McDaid tore through the house, calling her name. If they came up against a locked door, they kicked it open, Naseby running after them belatedly with a large ring of keys.

"We'll find her, Jimmy," McDaid said.

They didn't.

Dreghorn stopped on the landing of the great staircase, leaned on the windowsill. In the distance, across the water, he could see the lights of Port Glasgow and Greenock; the Lockharts had a yard there as well. A ship's horn sounded on the river like the cry of some ancient beast. And, suddenly, he knew.

He jerked his head for McDaid to follow and started down the stairs. As they ran through the hallway, they saw Sir Iain watching from the library, a shrunken figure, sustained by avarice and enmity, flames roaring in the hearth behind him.

Dreghorn remembered the last time he'd come down this path, with Isla's hand in his and the setting summer sun glimpsed through the trees ahead. His companion now wasn't half as attractive, and it was so dark you could hardly see the trees on either side, barely make out their jagged outlines against the stars. The small ornate lamp posts along the route were switched off, the only source of light the torch McDaid had grabbed from the car. The trees creaked and rustled, and Dreghorn noticed how on edge McDaid was. Not that he was skipping gaily himself.

McDaid jumped as something cracked loudly, aimed the torch in its direction.

"I'm the big city detective," Dreghorn said. "You're from the islands. Thought you lot were at one with nature."

"Been gone a long time. And there's no' many trees where I'm from. Nothing grows that tall, the wind we get."

"What's your excuse?"

Before McDaid could respond, something rustled to their right, something moving through the forest. McDaid swung the torch, caught glimpses of gray fur. A deer burst out onto the path a few feet ahead of them, disappearing into the trees on the opposite side. They glanced at each other, aware how vulnerable they were.

"If we had pistols with us," said McDaid, "it would've been venison for tea."

They carried on down the path, which curved as it neared the shore, the lapping of the water now audible. Dreghorn couldn't recall how much further they had to go, but the darkness was becoming less intense.

The trees, landscaped at this point, closed over the path like a tunnel for a few steps and then disappeared as they stepped out into the clearing beside the river.

"Their own private harbor?" McDaid said. "No wonder he could come and go as he pleased."

Everything was as Dreghorn remembered it, though even in the dim light he could see that paint was peeling from the walls of the boathouse, and the wooden jetty was discolored, slick with weed. The windows of the boathouse were dark, no signs of life. On the veranda, he could see the rotting carcasses of the chairs he and Isla had cuddled on all those years ago.

Flickering electric lights hung at intervals along the jetty to make it visible to ships on the river. The *Quentin Durward* was berthed there; a narrow strip of light shone through not-quite-closed curtains behind a cabin window. Boxes and large canvas bags lay on the boardwalk next to coils of rope and fuel drums.

"Someone's getting ready for a trip," the big man whispered.

Dreghorn scanned the harbor again, saw nothing and stepped onto the jetty, McDaid following. The timbers creaked and the wind whistled through the rigging of the *Durward*. The blocky shape of a dredger passed by, causing a wake that spread waves toward them, rocking the boat. As they reached the yacht, Dreghorn thought the river smells took on a fetid air, the depths disturbed.

"Captain Lockhart? Rory? It's Jimmy Dreghorn. We need to talk."

Dreghorn was already climbing aboard. He didn't get an answer. The craft lurched and creaked as McDaid boarded. They shared a wary glance. Dreghorn stepped down onto the stairs that led to the cabin. They were wet and sticky; with what, he couldn't see. The door was secured, but he shouldered it open and threw himself inside, drawing his baton. The brightness was dazzling at first, and he lost his footing and dropped to one knee. Blood soaked through his trouser leg. Behind him, McDaid swore in shock.

Molly Raeburn was looking at him, her brow furrowed apologetically, as if to say sorry for all the bother she'd caused. She looked younger than ever, innocent and out of her depth. Dreghorn recalled her in the tea rooms, bright-eyed and brimming with bravado.

He staggered to his feet, but her eyes didn't follow; they stared at nothing. She was on the floor, sitting upright against the cushioned bench that ran along one wall, as if she'd aimed to sit on it and missed. Her bright flowery dress seemed frivolous, too flimsy for the weather, until he realized that the bursts of color weren't part of any design. They were eruptions of blood. Her torso had been punctured by more knife wounds than he had the stomach to count.

He touched her neck for a pulse, but knew he wouldn't find one. He gently closed her eyelids, more for himself than for her.

McDaid loomed, hunched over in the cramped cabin, ready to tear it apart. "Your man Lockhart," he said. "He's an animal, a fuckin' monster. When we catch him, I'll save the hangman the trouble."

Dreghorn couldn't speak. Inside him was a sense of desolation such as he had felt on the battlefield when an assault was imminent, as if the humanity was draining out of him. Not quite desolation— the old rage was there, and this time he welcomed it.

"We need to go," he said.

"We can't just leave her, Jimmy."

Dreghorn pushed past, said, "She's still warm, Archie. He can't have gone far."

He stepped out on deck, froze. A figure stood waiting on the jetty, hands on hips and one leg raised, resting upon a small object that Dreghorn couldn't make out. It was a pose from a Hollywood swashbuckler, the moment the hero slaps his thigh and laughs uproariously. Instead, the figure brought down its foot as if to stamp on some trapped vermin.

Something clicked in Dreghorn's head, and he saw the wire that he'd missed when he first boarded, trailing over the edge of the yacht and disappearing out of sight in the direction of the engines.

His eyes filled with fire, followed by a white noise that pulsed through his entire body. The deck seemed to rise under his feet, coming apart. A hail of splinters sliced at his flesh. For a moment, he was weightless, and then he was falling.

Falling.

Falling.

Falling.

42

The first thing Dreghorn saw was fear, bright and terrible in Isla's eyes. She was tied to a chair across from him, gagged with a scarf and making noises that he realized were attempts to say his name. He struggled furiously, but his arms wouldn't move, rough-hewn hemp biting into his flesh. He was restrained as Isla was, ropes binding his wrists to the sturdy wooden arms of a chair, his ankles tied hard against the chair legs.

"Archie?" he croaked, then louder, "Archie!"

"Between the devil and the deep blue sea, your friend chose the water." Rory Lockhart gradually materialized from the darkness to stand beside Isla. He smiled coldly. "Sorry, poor show in the humor department."

He was dressed in black—heavy polo neck sweater, woolen trousers, and army boots shined to perfection. His face glistened, camouflaged with oil or boot polish, his hands the same, just like they used to do on trench raids. A bayonet hung in a sheath from his belt. A leather strap crossed his torso, a Lee-Enfield rifle—the soldier's best friend—slung across his back.

"With respect, sir," Dreghorn said. "You're not setting a very good example for the men."

"You think I'm back in the war?" Rory asked. "We might still have it in us, but no. Doctor Freud and his like will have to come up with some new theories for me. Sorry to disappoint you."

"I don't care. Rory, untie us and give yourself up."

"That isn't going to happen."

"Then take that rifle, put it in your mouth, and pull the trigger."

Isla whimpered, whether in alarm or agreement Dreghorn couldn't tell.

"Do the decent thing, old chap? I think I'm beyond decency now." Rory drew the bayonet from its sheath, prompting a further outburst of fearful muffled protests from Isla. Dreghorn didn't break his gaze, didn't look at the blade, tried to ignore the fear that made every nerve and muscle want to twitch and tremble.

Rory examined the blade, turning it as if each side offered a choice. "Remember the first time we talked, after the foxhunt, when I was blooded again? You asked if I was all right. What you couldn't see was that I had my cock in my hand. I wasn't upset; I was excited. By the blood and the smell and the thought that things can die—be killed—so easily." He slid his eyes along the knife to focus on Dreghorn. "I came all over the stable door with you on the other side. You never knew."

For a moment, he seemed to drift away to some dark place inside, then looked at the knife as if remembering its purpose and turned to his sister. She strained against the ropes, rocking the chair, froze as the blade neared her face.

"No!" Dreghorn yelled. "Leave her alone! Don't touch her!"

Rory slid the blade between Isla's cheek and the scarf, taking care not to cut her. The razor edge sliced through silk and the scarf slid off her face.

Isla gasped for air and then screamed, the desperate shriek filling the boathouse. Eventually, the scream became an animal cry of fear and anger. "Are you out of your fucking mind, Rory? What do you think you're doing? Untie us this instant." She had regained a measure of control, speaking as if they were children and a game of cowboys and Indians had got out of control.

For a moment, Dreghorn hoped she'd be able to talk her brother round, but then he remembered kneeling in Molly Raeburn's blood, thought about McDaid floating lifelessly or sunk to the bottom of the Clyde.

Rory said, "I'm saving our family, Isla. From the problem you helped create."

"What are you talking about?"

"He killed your husband," Dreghorn said bluntly.

"He couldn't have. He wasn't even in the country."

"He killed Arthur Bell and Alasdair Dalrymple."

Isla shook her head in disbelief.

"And he killed Molly Raeburn."

"Who?"

"A daft wee lassie lured into playing games she didn't understand. I found her body in his boat."

"The whole world's a game," said Rory, a shifting silhouette in the shadows. "The only way to win is to make your own rules. Did Father say that, Isla? It sounds like him."

Dreghorn's head was clearing, his eyes adjusting to the darkness. They were on the upper floor of the boathouse, the only light coming from the fire Rory had lit. He and Isla sat either side of the hearth. There was a low table between them, a large leather traveling bag upon it. An ammunition belt lay coiled next to the bag like a sleeping snake. He said, "I left word with the Murder Squad, told them everything. Reinforcements are on their way."

"What a thrill it'll be," said Rory, "when they find us all together."

Dreghorn glanced at Isla. She was staring at him, mouth open, in shock. "And someone will be down from the house," he said. "They'll have heard what happened. You blew up your yacht."

Rory gestured lazily toward a telephone that rested on a table in one corner. "I've already spoken to them. Nothing to worry about.

Late-night blasting at Dumbuck quarry. On a still night, you can hear it clear across the estate."

"They'll never believe that."

"After all this time, you still don't understand. I'm their master. They have no choice but to believe me." Rory moved back into the firelight, stood over them like a stern but kindly teacher.

"Rory," Isla's voice rang with emotion. "Please tell me you didn't kill Charles."

His eyes shifted to the dark place. "He didn't think me capable, not at first. He thought I was the person I allow the world to see."

Isla sobbed, almost gagged. Rory touched her cheek, but it was an act. Her grief didn't touch him in the slightest. She jerked away, yelled at him not to touch her.

"Years ago," Rory continued, "when things looked bleak at the end of the war, Father hinted that he had safeguards in place to protect the business—a Pandora's Box he only had to open. I didn't know exactly what until he called me back from America after the race. *PANDORA'S BOX. COME HOME. DISCREETLY.* That was his message.

"I always intended to stop off at Bangor on the way back to pick up the *Quentin Durward*. The fact that the *Lion Rampant* was damaged and had to delay its return for repairs was even more convenient. Everyone would assume I stayed with the *Rampant,* not sailed back secretly on my own. I berthed the *Durward* at the marina—no one uses it when I'm not there—and slept onboard for a few nights. I crept into Father's bedroom when the household was asleep and he told me the whole story in those pithy little phrases of his.

"I sent a telegram to Charles—ostensibly from Father—asking him to come to Kelpie on the Sunday night. I waited outside and stepped into his headlights as he drove through the gates. He was surprised to see me, but I explained that Father had brought me home to negotiate an arrangement with him. I suggested that we go down to the marina because you were in the house, Isla, and surely none of us wanted you to know the sordid details.

"We parked his car out of sight on the gamekeeper's road. As we walked to the marina, he told me what it would cost to keep him quiet. He'd been drinking heavily—shame he didn't crash on the way over. Such a lot of bother he'd have saved.

"I sympathized, asked how he'd come by the photographs and blackmail letters, and he rather foolishly told me about the Raeburn girl. He said he loved her. How ridiculous—her over you? I couldn't have that.

"I pretended I'd forgotten the boathouse keys, but why don't we go aboard the *Durward;* I keep whisky there. I don't remember what else he said. Inconsequential, just like him. All I remember is taking my bayonet to his throat." He looked at Dreghorn. "It took some effort—I was out of practice. I sailed the *Durward* down the Clyde a little way and slipped Charles overboard. The telegram I'd sent was in his pocket, so I burnt it."

"What about his car?" Dreghorn asked.

"I put on Charles's hat and coat and drove it back to the garage at Vinicombe Street. If the attendant saw me, he'd assume I was Charles. It was early morning by then, so I caught a train back to Dumbarton among the workers and then made my way home along the river. No one took any notice of me—it was as if I was one of them." He glanced at Isla. "I'm sorry, truly, but he was blackmailing Father, betraying us. In the war, he'd have been shot for treason, and I'd be given a medal."

"The war's been over for fourteen years," Dreghorn stated. "We're at peace."

"No one's at peace. Are you? Drinking whisky in your shabby rented room, chasing petty criminals to pretend your life has some importance, some purpose. Or you, Isla, with your sham marriages and a daughter who probably loves Nanny more than she does you? Ferguson at least was a better man than Geddes. We used to talk. He confided in me about his impotence."

Isla glanced at Dreghorn, a sad secret revealed.

"All in his head, if you ask me, a result of the war. We chatted on the night he killed himself. I've always wondered if it was something I said." Rory let that hang in the air, then gestured toward Kelpie. "And what about Father, up there in his mock ancestral pile, raging and plotting against the world? Or me—a playboy of the Western world, one of the lost generation, aimless and empty inside, divorced from polite society."

"You're not lost, Rory, you're broken." No accusation in her voice, just anguish. "You have to let us go. You have to let us help you."

"You would too, wouldn't you? I always envied you that—your feelings. I could see them bubbling away in you, but never had them myself. Thank you for all your kindness." He stroked her hair as he would a faithful old pet, then looked at Dreghorn. "Would you help me, inspector?"

Dreghorn nodded. "I know exactly what you need."

Rory laughed; they understood each other. He stepped behind Dreghorn, out of sight.

"How many have there been?" Dreghorn asked.

Rory returned with a chair, set it down between Dreghorn and Isla. He removed the rifle from his shoulder, slung it casually over the back of the chair and sat down to join them. They could have been about to play cards. Or Russian roulette.

"None since the war," Rory said. "Until now. I wore my mask well."

"There were soldiers at Quintinshill. After the crash. How many?"

"You know about that?" Rory was impressed. He thought for a moment. "Hard to say; some of them were genuine mercy killings, some . . ."

"And Charlie Currie—it wasn't him who murdered that woman, was it?" Resignation in his voice. And guilt.

"I crept in on them as he slept, drenched in alcohol, dead to the world. The girl was alarmed at first, but she saw that I was an officer, a gentleman, and became hospitable. *'Vous voyez quelque chose qui vous plaît, monsieur?'*" Rory's voice rose as he mimicked her. "She crossed the room, oh-so-very coy, cupped me in her hand, put her lips on mine—and I slid my bayonet into her heart, held her tight as she died.

"I laid her on the bed, arranged her with dignity. I wiped blood from the knife over Currie, over his shriveled little member, then curled his fingers around the handle. He whimpered, a bad dream, and I almost thought he was going to wake up. But I stroked his cheek and he calmed—'There, there,' I said." He smiled at the memory. "You were dogged in your pursuit of Currie, as if it was a personal betrayal. Shame you didn't have fingerprinting then. Or the inclination to believe him. Always keen to believe the worst in people, even your friends. Maybe that's good in a policeman."

Dreghorn remembered Currie being taken from his cell, the simultaneous shots of the firing squad. Isla was watching him, and he felt a rush of affection for her, the compassion in her eyes. He blinked back tears. He wanted to turn time back, to hold her, to say he was sorry for the harsh things he'd said. He wanted to tell her he loved her.

He said nothing; it would've been obscene in front of Rory. Isla gave a half-smile as if she understood.

She looked at her brother with the same compassion. "You're not well, Rory," she said. "The war did something to you. You're all twisted and torn inside, like barbed wire. Please, you have to let us help you."

Rory shook his head, not unkindly. He placed one hand on Isla's knee, the other on Dreghorn's, squeezed reassuringly. "The war freed me, Isla. It gave me carte blanche to do what I wanted, to taste other lives."

He stared into the fire with unnerving fascination. "When they blooded me that second time, a drop of the fox's blood went in my mouth. Not much, but I saw the world through its eyes, I could taste the fear as the hounds chased it, its exhilaration as it evaded them, only to be scented again later. I saw the hounds cornering me, their fangs coming for me, snapping, tearing . . ." Firelight gleamed in his eyes. "Its death made me feel alive."

Isla stared at him in horror. "Rory . . ."

"All my life, I've been a reflection of others. I laugh when they laugh, cry when they cry, but I never feel those things within myself. Most of my cues, I took from you, my darling little sister. You were always so alive, so full of emotion. I was—" He thought for a moment. "Imagine a ship, a great liner, the flagship of the fleet on the outside. But they forgot to build its insides—the decks, the engines, the crew—so there's a great emptiness at its core. I'm that emptiness. And God help the world, because I discovered how to fill it."

"No, you're not like that." There was hesitancy to Isla's voice, which they all caught, but she pressed on. "You're disturbed, damaged. But you're my brother, and I love you. Now, please let us go."

"I would love you too, if I could, if I knew how. But you're all just things. Men, women, children, police officers, soldiers, workers, all pieces of one great machine. I'm the part that doesn't fit." He sighed as if there was nothing else for it. "The next time was at Quintinshill, but you guessed that, didn't you? There was a boy there, injured, younger than me. I don't think he'd have lived, but it's hard to say. He'd been coughing and there was blood coming from his mouth. I knelt to comfort him, but I couldn't stop thinking about the fox.

"It wasn't a kiss exactly, but it became one. His whole life flooded me." The memory surged through him. "All his experiences, the power of them. We've been lucky, Isla. Privileged. We have everything in a world that has nothing. To experience the opposite—misery and loss, but joy and love too—I drank it all in." His face darkened. "And then I put a bullet through him."

The fire crackled loudly, spitting out embers, their glow fading as they rolled along the floor. Rory turned to Dreghorn. The detective saw the madness burning within him, consuming his being, his reason. It wasn't about protecting his family, if it ever really had been. It wasn't sadism or bloodlust or some taste for killing nurtured by the war. It was something far more warped and twisted and indescribable, both beyond humanity and far beneath it.

"Currie's girl was the same. Her life rushed through me, vivid, visceral—idyllic to begin with. The rhythms of a farm, animals and agriculture, growing and nurturing, reaping and slaughtering. Helping Father in the fields, Mother in the kitchen. A gentle tug on a cow's teat, milk spattering a tin pail. An uncle's hand on her breast, a struggle to get away. A beating from her mother, her accusations dismissed. Lies, lies, lies." Rory was staring into the fire again, almost talking to himself, the lies in his own mind, formed by madness. "Then the thunder of the guns, the start of a never-ending salvo. Soldiers marching by, eyes as heavy on her as her uncle's hands. Animals and crops stolen or butchered and left to rot. A father dead of heartbreak and shame. More men, more hands. No choice. The only way to survive. An existence it was a kindness to end. She was trapped by the war as much as anyone. Used and abused by the likes of your friend."

"Murdered by you." Dreghorn shook his head, thoughts grinding together. "Living their lives as they die? Whatever you believe, it isn't true; it's all in your head. You're mad—you're fuckin' mad! Can't you see that?"

Rory considered Dreghorn's words, then shrugged. "It's real to me, which means, right now, it is to you too."

Dreghorn and Isla stared at each other helplessly. Far out on the Clyde, another boat sounded its horn.

"There were others," Rory admitted. "It was easy on the battle-field, dead and dying everywhere. I think you even saw one. We'd taken a trench and I had blood in my mouth. You asked if I was injured and I said one of the Huns had caught me with the butt of his rifle."

Dreghorn was appalled that he couldn't remember. There'd been too many battles, too much blood. "What about Bell and Dalrymple?" he asked, grasping for rationality.

"They were the only ones left who could hurt us," Rory said as if it was obvious. "Father's not the most talkative these days, so I don't know how he first encountered Bell, presumably through his patronage of Trinity. Perhaps he was a client—Bell was already involved in supplying prostitutes to the great and the good through Johnnie Fraser. I don't know whose idea it was to start blackmailing them, although our father always had an eye for an opportunity.

"They probably didn't imagine that one of their victims would keep the incriminating materials used against him, or catalog the graft and corruption he was forced to engage in. As a bailie, this Rae-burn fellow seems to have been most conscientious.

"Somewhere along the way, Bell noticed that some of their clients had a taste for younger women, the younger the better. He also discovered that his boss, Dalrymple, had similar tastes and coerced him into allowing extracurricular visits to Trinity for 'uncles,' whom they then blackmailed. Fraser had died by this point, ending the use of his brothels for extortion. Dalrymple told me all this after I killed Bell, said that he had been trapped, forced into it. He actually thought he was the victim, although I suspect the girl locked in the cupboard was there for him." He met Dreghorn's eyes, man to man. "I didn't know about her when I started the fire—even I have my limits."

"Did Sir Iain know what you were going to do?" Dreghorn asked. "He was the one Geddes was blackmailing, wasn't he?"

"Father probably expected me to have a quiet word with someone—who'd then have a stronger word with Charles."

"Someone like Billy Hunter."

"I did something similar a few years ago, when the strikes were damaging business. Father was rather impressed. Hadn't thought much of me, until then."

"You did speak to Hunter though. It was his boys who snatched Molly."

"I told him it was an affair of the heart. I'd got her into trouble, but she was refusing my offer to help her do the right thing. They were supposed to frighten her a little and drop her off in the middle of nowhere with a miserable walk home. Then I'd drive along like a knight in shining armor. Billy doesn't know that part. Good man, Hunter."

"Oh, aye, one of the best."

"Only in Glasgow can a compliment sound like a condemnation."

The wind that had been buffeting the boathouse was now joined by rain, great sheets of it spattering the windows. The way Rory was talking, freely incriminating himself, Dreghorn knew that his old captain didn't intend to let him live. Did he plan to kill his own sister too?

"Does Father know about me?" Rory seemed intrigued by the thought. He reached into the bag on the table, removed a handful of photos and shuffled through them, his face a blank. He showed Dreghorn the photos, holding them up one at a time, as if conducting an experiment. "Some of these I took off Geddes," he said. "The others were in Dalrymple's safe. He didn't take much convincing to open it."

Dreghorn didn't hide his anger and revulsion, couldn't if he'd tried, but refused to give Rory the satisfaction of looking away from the sad, frightened little figures, the monsters assaulting them. He stared at the men's faces, tried to burn them into his memory.

Rory then showed them to Isla. She looked away, squeezing her eyes shut.

"Sickened," Rory said. "I know that's how I'm meant to feel, but there's nothing. I used to want a connection, to feel the world the way you do, Isla. But now . . ." He shrugged like nothing mattered. "Father must have seen these. Was he repulsed, like you, or did he just see them as a means to an end?" He flicked through the images without emotion, as a croupier would a set of cards, said almost to himself, "Perhaps he and I are not so different after all."

He tossed the photos into the fire. The images bubbled and distorted, burst into flames. Then he removed another batch from the bag, threw them after the first. He pulled out other documents, some handwritten, others typed. "Blackmail demands, lists of victims and their individual tastes, the positions they held—" He crushed them in his fist and threw them into the flames after the photos. Isla hadn't moved; her eyes were still closed, tears leaking out.

"Doesn't matter," said Dreghorn grimly. "You're finished, whatever you do. They'll hang you. Or lock you in an asylum and burn away your brain. Either way, it won't be enough."

Rory tossed a final batch of documents into the fire, then turned the bag upside down, shaking it to stress its emptiness.

"You might say that," he told Dreghorn. "But it's your word against ours."

Isla opened her eyes as Rory shifted to her side and placed a hand on her shoulder.

"Everyone knows there's no love lost between you and our father," Rory said. "He ruined your boxing career before it had even started, and destroyed your blossoming relationship with my sister.

It's only natural that you'd hate him, and you do have a history of violence.

"You manipulated the Raeburn girl after she came to you with the photos used to blackmail her father. You concocted those ridiculous charges against my father, murdered Charles when he opposed you, murdered gallant sergeant McDaid when he discovered what you were doing, and threatened my sister when she rejected your advances."

Dreghorn said, "You're even madder than I thought if you think Sillitoe will believe that."

"What choice will he have? There's no evidence. There's only Isla and me." His expression became innocent, apologetic. "I'm terribly sorry, your honor, I didn't mean to kill him, but I had to save my sister."

Isla tried to pull away from Rory, but the ropes wouldn't allow it. "You think I'm going to join you?" she said. "Smile and lie as if it's all happy families?"

"It's your duty, Isla. Think of Father and Catriona, if not me." He crouched in front of her, his back to Dreghorn. "I realize you're shocked, upset by my holding you captive, but I had to make you see sense. You've always been the one I look to, but now you have to look to me. Whatever feelings you have, you have to put them aside. You have to be like me."

Dreghorn saw Rory's hand resting on the hilt of the bayonet, felt a slow sickness spreading in his belly. "Isla," he said gently. "Do as he says."

She looked at him in anguish, shook her head, looked lost.

"Isla, please, do as he says."

"See?" said Rory. "James knows what's best."

Dreghorn nodded, felt the tears filling his eyes. She nodded back, blinking away her own tears, then said to her brother, "Go to hell, Rory."

There was a terrible silence, then Rory rose to his feet, blocking Dreghorn's view of Isla. The blade flashed in the firelight, a horizontal slash, and he heard Isla gasp. Blood sprayed over Rory. Dreghorn screamed, lunged forward with all his strength, toppling the chair. He landed hard, temple smacking the floor. Isla's blood showered in hot spatters on his face. He was still screaming, shaking furiously against the ropes, the chair legs drumming against the floor. Isla's feet kicked, her body jerking, until her struggles slowly subsided. Dreghorn strained to look up. Rory was hunched over his sister, hands cupping her face, his mouth pressed against hers, kissing her passionately. Dreghorn closed his eyes, couldn't look anymore.

After a time, Rory pulled away with a great sigh. He fell to his knees in front of Isla, slowly eased himself onto his back and lay beside Dreghorn, his breathing rushed, almost post-coital. Slowly, he turned to look at Dreghorn. There was blood around his mouth, tears of ecstasy in his eyes. "So *alive* . . ." he whispered.

Dreghorn raged at him, a torrent of barely coherent threats.

Rory humored him, listened condescendingly until he had yelled himself hoarse. "I know," he said, nodding like a priest hearing confession. He reached out, placed a hand on Dreghorn's cheek. "I could taste you and her together. She loved you. And she loved me."

Dreghorn jerked his head, shook Rory's hand off. He could feel Isla's blood sticky on his flesh.

Rory rolled to his feet with a dancer's grace, and Dreghorn thought of Isla, sixteen years old, practicing her ballet in Kelpie House while he spied through the window. Rory stretched as if he'd just woken up, looked down on Dreghorn. He crouched, gripped the chair, and heaved the detective upright with a grunt.

Isla's head was thrown back, but her eyes were still on him, staring without seeing, and the wound gaping. Blood was everywhere, sucking at Rory's feet, glistening in the firelight. Dreghorn could feel the spatters on his own face burning like acid, leaving their mark.

Eventually he spoke, his voice quiet. "I'll kill you. I'll fuckin' kill you."

Rory removed the Lee-Enfield from the chair. He aimed the barrel at the detective's chest, then reversed his grip, tossing the rifle into the air as if on parade and catching it again.

"Yes," he said. "You would." And smashed the butt of the rifle into Dreghorn's right hand. Again and again and again.

Dreghorn felt the bones crack, heard them crunch. He passed out when Rory brought the rifle down onto his other hand.

43

Something nudged the base of his spine. Pain pulsed through his hands, shocking his mind back to clarity. He was curled on the floor, his gnarled hands limp and useless, the wood wet and sticky beneath him.

"Attention!"

Rory stood behind him, the floorboards creaking as he rocked back and forth on his heels. Dreghorn had seen him do the same before going over the top, his excitement barely controlled. He shifted onto his back, hands held aloft, but even the air seemed to press in on them, grinding the bones. At least his wrists were intact, undamaged. Bile rose in his throat, and he forced it back down as he glared at Rory, the rifle slung over his shoulder again, the bayonet back in its sheath, blood oozing around it.

"I said—Attention!"

Dreghorn tucked his elbows into his ribs and rolled to his feet, something he did easily in the gym. Now he moved like a dead weight. He swayed, light-headed, wondering when he'd last eaten—a ridiculous concern beside three murders, an explosion, and shattered hands. He glimpsed himself in a mirror on the wall. His face was dark with blood, a mix of his own from a gash on his scalp, and Isla's. His skin was scorched by the explosion. His suit was torn, one sleeve hanging from the shoulder seam, the wool cold and sodden from the Clyde, and his white shirt was brown with mud and blood. He was as camouflaged as Rory. He looked at Isla, took it all in again.

Rory saw something in Dreghorn's eyes, slipped the Lee-Enfield from his shoulder, and motioned at the door, which was now ajar.

The wind and rain almost knocked Dreghorn over as he stepped out onto the balcony. He took the steps drunkenly, bouncing back and forth between the wall and the banister, the wood slick beneath his feet. He managed to stay upright for most of the descent, but his legs gave way as he reached the last step and he toppled. He was almost grateful when the darkness took him again.

Fuckin' hell, Jimmy.

The voice was close to his ear, the speaker's breath as cold as a grave. He'd only lost consciousness for a moment; Rory was halfway down the steps, and the voice certainly wasn't his.

Dreghorn used his elbows to crawl, whimpering with the pain. Ahead, he could see the bow of the sunken *Quentin Durward* protruding from the water beside the jetty. He struggled to his knees as Rory stepped in front of him.

"Remember how you and your friends used to run around in your shorts and vests, as if your lives depended on it? Isla and I used to watch. She felt sorry for you. She knew that one day you'd all be discarded like broken toys."

The wound on Dreghorn's head had opened up again. A film of blood slid over his left eye, and he wiped it away with his sleeve. Rain beat down on his hands, every drop a hammer blow. Rory motioned with the rifle for him to get to his feet. Somehow, he found the strength. He let the rain wash the blood from his eyes, took a few drops on his tongue, savored them.

Rory nodded at the forest and shoreline behind Dreghorn. "A sporting chance, sergeant."

"You think so? Why?"

"I enjoyed sharing a battlefield with you. And despite it all, I'm a gentleman."

"And if I don't?"

"Don't run, don't fight? I'd be deeply disappointed. Don't let me down. Don't let yourself down."

Dreghorn was already backing away. The anger was there now. So was hate. Not that he could do much about it with his ravaged hands. He turned after a few steps and began a weak, shambling run.

"Chop-chop, sergeant! You'll have to be quicker than that."

Was Rory taking aim? Dreghorn would feel the bullet before hearing the shot. Ahead, he could see the path that led back to Kelpie House. A long way in his current condition and offering little or no cover.

"The path?" Rory cried out. "Well, if you want to make it easy for me . . ."

Dreghorn carried on toward the leafy tunnel that led onto the path. Under the canopy of branches, he picked up his pace as best he could. He would be out of sight until Rory passed through the tunnel. He pounded up as many steps as he thought safe, then, hunching over to protect his hands, darted to the right and plunged into the trees, snapping branches, crushing undergrowth, horrified by the clamor he was making. He threw himself behind a tree, pressed his back so hard against it he could feel the ridges of the bark. All around were the sounds of the wind in the trees, creaking branches, raindrops spattering leaves, pounding the path and striking the nearby waters of the Clyde like a waterfall. Enough to drown out the gasps of fear and exhaustion he was trying to suppress?

He imagined Rory scanning the trees, trying to reason out which direction his prey had chosen. Reason hadn't come into it, just desperation. No movement. No sound other than the downpour, now a roar in his head. Was Rory waiting for his nerve to break, ready to fire at the slightest movement?

Dreghorn stared into the darkness. Thick with shapes, it seemed to push back on him. He tried to get his bearings, picture Kelpie House in relation to the marina, remember the routes he'd run as a youth. Something pale and ghostly moved through the trees, beckoning him. He closed his eyes against the sight. *It's not real,* he said silently. Concussion or delirium. Rory was real. The Lee-Enfield was real. That was what he had to focus on.

There was a crunch on the path, a footfall heading in the opposite direction. Dreghorn almost sobbed with relief. He forced himself to wait for a moment, then began moving slowly, elbows at his sides as if covering up in the boxing ring, trying to avoid snagging protruding branches. The ground was muddy, mulched leaves slippery underfoot, and he placed his feet as carefully and quietly as possible.

Making it to Kelpie House was no guarantee of safety. Misplaced loyalty from the servants was liable to throw him straight back into danger. The car keys were still in his pocket, but driving would be impossible with his damaged hands. Maybe he'd be able to transmit a message to headquarters via Morse, though he hoped lack of contact would have convinced Ellen Duncan to send reinforcements. No bells split the air. He was alone. All he could do was keep moving, keep running.

A fallen branch, concealed by leaves, cracked like a rifle shot under his foot. He froze. He felt something in the air to his left. Splinters exploded from a tree ahead. He heard the shot at the same time, the echo dampened by the rain, but still unmistakable.

"Fuck!"

Dreghorn ran, shouldering his way blindly through branches that whipped across his face, and undergrowth that ensnared his feet. The end of a branch stabbed into his right hand and he howled as bile rose in his throat.

There was another shot, the bullet striking the tree he'd just bounced off. He looked back, searching for Rory—a silhouette, a muzzle flash, anything to judge how close he was. Nothing. Dreghorn stumbled on, cursing the noise he was making, trying to grasp fleeting moments of clarity before pain and terror stole them away again. Another shot rang out. He didn't hear the final impact; a good sign, he hoped. Three shots fired so far. The Short Magazine Lee-Enfield Mk III held ten rounds, but Rory would have more ammunition. In his arrogance, he wouldn't expect to need it, but he'd be prepared. And there was the bayonet. His former captain was very fond of the blade.

Dreghorn fell headlong, landed heavily, his chest crushing his hands. He cried out, but the sound was muffled, his mouth pressed into the mulch. He rolled onto his side, glanced at what had tripped him.

Rab Hunter stared back, his peelie-wallie features startlingly white in the dark. He was propped up against a tree the way he had been against the trench wall, his legs splayed out as if to deliberately catch Dreghorn. *Fuckin' hell, Jimmy,* he said. *Fuckin' hell.* He kept staring, unblinking, as if expecting an answer.

Dreghorn couldn't speak. Splinters exploded from the tree, passing harmlessly through Rab. The sound of the gunshot reached Dreghorn at the same time. Rab was gone now, and he saw a movement between trees in the distance, heard the bolt action of the Lee-Enfield as another round entered the chamber.

Rory fired again and, as he scrambled to his feet, Dreghorn felt an impact in his side, spinning him around. Somehow he kept his balance, ran in the direction he now faced, given extra impetus by the bullet. At first, it was like being struck a good body blow, but then the pain became sharper, warm blood leaking over his cold flesh. He kept going, charging through bushes, no longer caring about the noise or the trail he was leaving. He hardly felt the branches and scratches now, wondered if he was going into shock. The new wound was just a fresh stroke on the tapestry of pain his body had become.

Something pale hovered on the edge of his vision again. This time, he looked. Charlie Currie beckoned him with a mischievous smile, a look that always put you on your guard. His battered helmet from the trenches was perched rakishly on his head, but he was otherwise dressed in the white shorts and simmit that they'd sported in the ring. Splashes of blood, black in the moonlight, dotted his vest, the same pattern the bullets of the firing squad had made. He gestured more urgently for Dreghorn to follow him.

That'll be fuckin' right, Dreghorn almost said aloud, veering without hesitation in the opposite direction. Charlie Currie was a gallus chancer who loved nothing more than to drop you in the shite, and that was before the question of revenge from beyond the grave came up. He glanced back at Currie with a cheeky smile of his own, shook his head; Jimmy Dreghorn wasn't that easily caught out.

He took another step and his foot descended into nothingness. His other foot slipped from under him as the earth crumbled and gave way. He lashed out, hooking his left elbow around the trunk of a young tree and landed on his arse, legs dangling. The fall jarred his hands, the pain sharpening his senses. He looked down.

It wasn't a sheer drop, more a steep slope, dotted with small trees and bushes that clung stubbornly to the eroding soil, that rolled down to a narrow strip of shingle along the shoreline of the Clyde. The surface danced with splashes from the rain. Dreghorn struggled to his feet. If he could get to the shore, he would make better progress, perhaps reach one of the communities along the river, but there was no way he could safely navigate the slope in his current state. He lumbered drunkenly through the trees, intending to follow the crest of the hill until it leveled off, but soon lost any sense of direction. His hands grew heavy, swollen, it seemed, to the size and weight of medicine balls. They kept slipping to his sides, and he raised them stubbornly, like a punch-drunk fighter who doesn't know he's beaten.

When he did stop, adrenaline running short, it seemed like he'd run a marathon, though he'd be lucky if it was a hundred-yard dash. He leaned against a tree, listened, but heard nothing. He brushed aside his jacket. Blood oozed from the bullet wound—two holes, front and back. The bullet must have passed clean through, missing vital organs, or he wouldn't still be on his feet. Blood and rain and tears blurred his vision. He shut his eyes against them, suddenly thought that nothing mattered. It would be so easy just to lie down, to close his eyes and let darkness wash away the pain. His legs started to give way. He felt a presence next to him, forced his eyes open.

Isla was leaning against the tree, her head turned to face him, resting upon the rough bark as though it was a pillow. The warmth and affection in her expression brought more tears to his eyes. He raised a hand to touch her, but felt nothing through the swollen flesh, only pain.

"Kiss, cuddle, or torture?" she said, and smiled, but not with her mouth, her throat splitting open wide, wet and glistening in the dark.

Dreghorn tore his eyes away, despair spreading through him like ice. The rain had died to a smirr, accentuating his breath as it misted in front of him. He watched the little particles of moisture, found something fascinating and beautiful in them. When was the last time he'd appreciated life, in all its simplicity, all its complexity?

He thought he saw movement in the trees, too far away to make out clearly, and imagined Rory smiling as he took aim. The head would be the most satisfying shot, but the torso was bigger, a safer target.

Dreghorn pushed away from the tree, stood straight. His legs were leaden and the heart had gone out of him, but if he was going to die, he'd damn well die on his feet. As he spread his arms, he thought of Charlie Currie, his defiance and dignity as he faced the firing squad.

He closed his eyes and waited. He could hear the lapping of the Clyde, gentle now that the rain had subsided, and realized with some surprise that he loved the river, would prefer things to end by the water rather than trapped like some wounded beast in the forest. When the shot finally came, it was from some distance behind him. He almost fell, simply from the shock of still being alive.

Charlie Currie crouched in front of him again, shook his head, mouthed the words *Daft bastard,* and gestured behind Dreghorn the way they did when alerting each other to an enemy presence on trench raids. Dreghorn immediately stepped back against the tree, concealing himself. He nodded his thanks, but the forest was empty once more.

Another shot. Rory firing at shadows. Maybe Dreghorn wasn't the only one seeing ghosts in the night.

The clouds were breaking up, allowing shafts of moonlight to pierce the forest. He saw Rory properly for the first time since the hunt began, the Lee-Enfield held across his chest. He was moving quickly, making more noise than was prudent, confident that he would soon find Dreghorn dead, or dying and pleading for mercy.

He was wrong. Dreghorn was still alive. And didn't intend to give up again. Renewed energy flowed through him, his senses more alert. He counted the shots that had been fired. Seven. Or was it six? He couldn't be sure.

He used the noise of Rory's progress to cover himself, circling the tree, keeping out of sight as his old officer passed by. Rory came to a halt, shoulders sagging in disappointment as he looked down the slope toward the river.

Dreghorn took a moment to get his bearings: pinpointing other trees between him and Rory that offered cover; the proximity of the slope down to the Clyde; a broken branch that lay against the trunk by his feet.

He kicked the branch away from the trunk. It didn't go far, vanished with a disappointing rustle into bushes a few feet away. But it was enough. Rory spun, aimed, and fired at the shuddering bush almost in one movement. Dreghorn emerged from the other side of the tree, sprinting madly in Rory's direction. He didn't look, but could feel Rory swinging the rifle after him, calculating for a moving target, pulling the trigger.

He hit the next tree at full speed, as if attempting to knock it down. Pressed against the bark, he felt the bullet thud into the opposite side of the trunk.

One shot left. Unless he'd miscounted. All too easy.

He feinted left, darting out to give Rory a target, then diving back behind the tree. The shot grazed the trunk as he moved, sending splinters into the side of his neck.

Empty. Unless he'd miscounted. Dreghorn rolled around the curve of the tree and charged.

Rory cursed as the rifle clicked on an empty chamber. He reached into his pocket, came out with a five-cartridge loader. There were maybe twenty-five yards between them. Soldiers were expected to fire fifteen rounds a minute and Rory was well able to match that. But the war was years ago. How practiced was he now? Their eyes met briefly as Rory slid the bullets into the magazine, tossed aside the loader, closed the bolt action, and fired.

The blast was deafening as Dreghorn, pushing aside the barrel, plowed into Rory. The charge knocked Rory off his feet and they crashed into a bramble bush at the crest of the slope, Dreghorn on top, trapping the Lee-Enfield against Rory's chest. He reared backward and drove his elbow into Rory's face, pain flaring in his hand. The bush collapsed under them and they crashed down the slope, still struggling, until a collision with a tree stump separated them. Dreghorn caught chaotic glimpses of the sky, the river, Rory's flailing limbs, then blackness again.

He came out of it like a drowning man breaking the surface. He was on his side, facing the Clyde, head resting on wet shingle. Rory was a few feet away, up against a fallen tree trunk, eyes closed, face twisted in pain. The Lee-Enfield had landed just out of his reach. Dreghorn scrambled toward it on his knees, hooked his left hand under the strap, whimpering as his knuckles scraped the ground, and staggered unsteadily to his feet. He heaved the rifle toward the river, and saw it splash into the water.

The captain's eyes were open, searching. Dreghorn took a couple of steps, kicked Rory in the face with so much force that he lost his balance and crashed to the shingle again. Stupid. Too wild. Too angry. Too late now. He could hear Rory getting to his feet, spitting blood. Dreghorn did the same. It felt like he was climbing a mountain, and seemed to take as long.

They stood, swaying, staring at each other. Rory smiled, his teeth red with blood, his hand curled around the hilt of the bayonet.

Dreghorn charged again, driving into Rory's stomach, but he was too weak. The captain held him in place, and drove his knee into his side, right on the bullet wound. As he crashed onto the shingle, he saw Rory leaping after him, the bayonet raised. Dreghorn jammed his forearms under Rory's wrist, stopping the blade inches from his face. His arms and shoulders burned, the muscles straining as the blade hovered between them. He tried to buck Rory off, roll away, but the captain was too heavy. The bayonet came closer, and Rory's breath was on his face, hot with excitement, expectation. Dreghorn's arms were shaking uncontrollably now, his strength failing. The point of the bayonet pricked his cheek, just below his right eye. He heard animal noises, realized that he was making them.

The captain shushed him like a scared child. "There, there," he said. "There, there." And pressed harder on the knife.

Dreghorn felt the blade slide through his flesh, boring into his cheekbone, felt it creak under the pressure. He screamed, a great roar that filled his head, trying to block everything out.

The weight suddenly lifted, and the bayonet sliced his cheek as it clattered to the shingle by his ear. Dreghorn opened his eyes, raised his head.

Rory was on his knees, making little gasping sounds, eyes wide. A thick arm was wrapped around his neck.

Dreghorn didn't look away, stared straight into Rory's eyes as fury slipped slowly into fear and horrified helplessness. His head made a sudden, awkward jerk to one side as his neck snapped with a surprisingly gentle crack. The corpse was tossed aside with disdain, landing face down on the shingle beside Dreghorn.

Archie McDaid, almost black with river mud, dropped to his knees, looking like some behemoth risen from the deep.

"No' so fuckin' bonnie now, am I?" he said.

"You look beautiful to me, big man," said Dreghorn, but the words were lost among blood and tears.

44

Police bells sounded as McDaid removed his sodden jacket and placed it under Dreghorn's head; reinforcements arriving when they were no longer needed. He fished around in his pocket, drew out an Acme Thunderer whistle and blew with all his puff. Other whistles sounded in response. Soon torch beams were approaching through the forest, policemen cursing as they lost their footing on the slope.

Ellen Duncan was with them, insisting on being there despite regulations; no one else knew the full circumstances. She crossed the shingle faster than the male officers, knelt beside Dreghorn and stared at McDaid in horror.

The big man was slumped on the tree trunk, Rory Lockhart's corpse at his feet. "Don't worry," he said. "Looks worse than it is."

Ellen nodded dubiously, then barked orders to call an ambulance with an authority the arriving officers didn't dare question, woman or not. Then she asked, "What happened?"

McDaid opened his mouth to speak, realized he couldn't put it into words yet. All he remembered was Dreghorn yelling a warning, the explosion, and then recovering consciousness on the shore. The blast had thrown him into the river, but the current had presumably carried him back to shore, depositing him directly under the jetty, where he had lain out of sight for God knows how long. Hard to believe he hadn't drowned, the amount of water he'd coughed up.

"There are two more bodies down there," he said, nodding toward the lights of the marina. "You might need divers. One's in the water, the other's in the boathouse."

He shut down after that, staring at Dreghorn's shivering body, hardly noticing when someone draped a blanket over his shoulders. He only spoke again when the ambulance men turned up with stretchers. The first two rushed to Dreghorn, the second pair stared at McDaid, appalled by his size.

"It's all right," he said. "I'll walk."

It wasn't the closest hospital, but under the circumstances they took the detectives to the Royal Infirmary in Glasgow. McDaid had suffered burns to his face and neck, and countless shrapnel wounds, mostly minor. The left side of his chest was one massive bruise, the ribs cracked or broken, presumably from a flying collision with the side of the boat or jetty. One of his eardrums was ruptured, he was told, which might affect his hearing later.

"What?" he said to the doctor; the old ones are the best. At first he shrugged off the injuries, but was then floored by an unforgiving fever and chest infection thanks to having swallowed half the Clyde.

Dreghorn drifted in and out of consciousness during the ambulance journey and slept for the better part of sixteen hours after treatment. As he'd surmised, the bullet wound hadn't caused serious injury, though he'd lost a dangerous amount of blood.

His right hand was set in plaster. The doctors were hopeful, but it was badly broken and they warned he might not regain full use of it. Rory had done a less thorough job on the left hand, which was badly bruised, knuckles staved, fingers out of joint, but largely intact. He flirted with the pretty young nurse tasked with feeding him, but McDaid could tell it was forced; he could see the pain and sadness in his partner's eyes every time she laughed. Isla Lockhart would never again laugh like that.

* * *

That first night, lying in darkness listening to the sounds of the hospital, McDaid asked, "How could he do all that, Jimmy? That lassie, his own sister?"

"He was brought up to think he ruled the world, with armies of workers and servants. They blooded him with an animal that had been hunted and torn to pieces for sport, and he liked it. At Quintinshill, he executed men—some dying, some not—and he liked it. He went to war, where you can kill anyone you want if you've a mind to, and he liked that too. When it was over, they sent us all home, thank you very much, to live our lives as if it had never happened. And he didn't like that." Dreghorn stared at the ceiling. "Fuck knows, Archie. Doesn't matter now. What matters is that you stopped him. And he won't do it again."

McDaid didn't answer, not believing it any more than Dreghorn. They hadn't stopped anything, just blundered in at the end. Death after death after death. Dreghorn felt nothing for Geddes, Bell, and Dalrymple, but Molly Raeburn and Isla Lockhart especially haunted him. If he hadn't confronted Isla like some petulant schoolboy and accused her of complicity, she might still be alive.

He lay awake for the entire night, scared of what he would see if he closed his eyes.

The Corporation splashed out on a private room for its "heroic" officers, more to curtail press access during convalescence than for their comfort. The revelation that Rory Lockhart, playboy heir to a shipbuilding empire and one of the city's finest sons, had committed at least two murders was a scandal of seismic proportions, not least because it appeared to implicate members of the Corporation itself, albeit indirectly.

The newspapers were covering the story in detail, delving into the backgrounds of the Lockhart family and the murder victims, but

Sillitoe kept his statements brisk—investigations were ongoing and further details would be released if and when it was deemed necessary. This launched a frenzy of lurid speculation, and McDaid could hear Denny Knox gnashing his teeth in the Press Bar because his promised exclusive had so far failed to materialize.

Sillitoe visited as soon as the doctors allowed it. Placing his chair directly between their beds, he informed them that Chief Inspector Monroe would take their statements presently, but that he wished first to go through the details of the case as he understood them, inviting corrections as they saw fit.

On the death of her father, Molly Raeburn and her mother engaged the services of Charles Geddes, solicitor, to deal with Mr. Raeburn's estate. At some point during this process, Molly uncovered compromising photographs of her father as a younger man consorting with a prostitute.

Dreghorn didn't mention that the woman in the photographs was Catherine Fraser.

Blackmail letters and Raeburn's confessional diary accompanied the photos, incriminating Alasdair Dalrymple and Arthur Bell of Trinity Village and bringing to light a disturbing connection to the Lockhart family. Instead of the standard demands for money with menaces, Raeburn was forced to use his position as a Corporation bailie to further the business interests and ambitions of the Lockharts via graft and corruption. The wider implication was that Raeburn was not the only influential figure being manipulated in this manner.

Dreghorn racked his brain for the names he'd seen in the blackmail documents Rory had shown him and gave the few he could remember to Sillitoe, but with the documents destroyed there was no proof.

Instead of informing the authorities, Geddes, who had his own bitter connection to the Lockharts, convinced Molly that they should use the incriminating material against his wife's family, gaining revenge for her father and handsome profits into the bargain. Geddes, however, had underestimated the ruthlessness of his brother-in-law, a man whose very sanity now had to be questioned.

Rory falsified the log of his yacht to make it appear that he hadn't reached Scotland until several days later than he actually did. Whether premeditated or in a moment of rage, Rory murdered Geddes aboard his yacht, and dumped the solicitor's body in the Clyde.

Thereafter Rory, who had picked up a taste for killing during the war, apparently decided that it was safer to get rid of anyone who could incriminate him. He arranged a conspirators' meeting with Bell and Dalrymple, murdered the pair of them, and set Dalrymple's house on fire, hoping the blaze would destroy any evidence of foul play.

Fire investigators discovered that Dalrymple's safe had been opened but was empty. The documents and photos had been removed by Rory, who didn't want to risk anything surviving the fire.

Or he'd taken them to use as leverage, Dreghorn thought, against his father.

"From the account of your witness Mrs. Fraser," Sillitoe continued, "it appears Rory arranged the abduction of Molly Raeburn through a third party, possibly the Billy Boys, whom the Lockhart company have employed for strike-breaking purposes in the past. Do we know who, exactly?"

"They'll be up to their necks in alibis," Dreghorn said. "Probably didn't know what Lockhart was really planning. He as good as told me that."

"Lockhart picked Miss Raeburn up from where he'd ordered them to drop her, took her to the estate, and murdered her aboard his yacht. He then no doubt planned to get rid of the body at sea."

Sillitoe raised a hand to stop Dreghorn interrupting. "The explosives, we've discovered, were stolen from Dumbuck quarry, which adjoins the Kelpie House estate. Lockhart knew how to handle them from the war and from visits to diamond mines in Rhodesia that his father has shares in. Perhaps he intended to destroy the yacht with Miss Raeburn on board, or to fake his own death and escape abroad. I dislike speculation and unanswered questions, but sometimes that's the nature of our job, gentlemen. With the perpetrators and main witnesses dead, we're unlikely ever to know the full details." He raised an eyebrow. "And Lockhart was hardly acting rationally toward the end." He let his words sink in. "Do you agree with my summation?"

"What about Sir Iain?" Dreghorn asked. "This has been going on for years. Rory wasn't behind it initially; he couldn't have been. I don't know when or how deeply he was involved before Sir Iain ordered him back to Scotland, but it was the old man who started it. If it wasn't for his stroke, he might've dealt with Geddes and the others himself."

"Jimmy's right, sir," said McDaid. "Old man Lockhart's sitting up in that big house like the spider at the center of the web, plucking the strands to make us all dance."

Sillitoe looked at McDaid. "Did Rory Lockhart tell you that himself?"

McDaid paused before answering and Sillitoe cut him off. "If you're considering perjury, sergeant, even for the best of motives, be aware that the chain of events on that evening is well established. You were unconscious when the inspector was taken captive."

McDaid remained silent.

"It's your word against his, Dreghorn, and it's common knowledge that there's bad blood between you and Iain Lockhart."

"Nothing that interferes with my duty as a police officer, sir."

"I don't doubt it, but Lockhart has already engaged George Garrison to represent him in the event of any prosecution. You're familiar with Garrison? Without hard evidence or corroboration from other witnesses, he'll wind the jury around his little finger, twisting your testimony to make it look as if you're waging some personal vendetta against a frail old man who's just lost his family."

Dreghorn shook his head. "So, the old bastard gets away with it."

"He's already a prisoner in his own body, Dreghorn." Sillitoe was sanguine. "Whatever time he has left, he'll have to live with the knowledge that he's responsible for the deaths of both his children. No sentence we could hand him would be any harsher." He stood up. "You did well, gentlemen; your city is proud of you."

He lifted his briefcase onto the chair and drew out a bottle of Bailie Nicol Jarvie whisky. He placed it on the table between them with a conspiratorial look. "For medicinal purposes only, you understand."

McDaid tutted. "Matron won't approve."

"As Chief Constable of this fair city, I reserve the right to bend the rules on occasion." Sillitoe glanced at the bottle with an uncharacteristic twinkle of humor. "See it through."

The reward for risking your life in the name of the law wasn't one bottle of whisky, but two. A bottle of Bowmore arrived by special delivery the next day, addressed to both of them. McDaid was impressed. "He's some detective, Percy, to deduce that we'd finish that bottle in a oner. That's why he's the high heid yin and we're the ones getting shot at."

Dreghorn read the card that accompanied the gift. "*A wee thank-you for keeping the streets safe—*"

"That's nice."

"*Teddy Levin.*"

"The cheeky wee shite! I'll smash it over his head."

Neither of them mentioned that Levin's bottle was a more expensive single malt than Sillitoe's blend.

"Mind you," McDaid mused. "Doesn't need to be full to do that."

On the third day, McDaid's family were allowed to descend upon them. The three boys froze on seeing their father swathed in bandages, laid out on the bed like the mummified corpse of Tutankhamen. As they came closer, McDaid sat bolt upright and let out a bloodcurdling roar, causing them to almost jump out of their skins. The big man had dismissed Dreghorn's reservations about the prank, saying, "It'll be a laugh. Mairi'll love it as well."

The two youngest weans burst out crying and ran to their mother, who applauded her husband sarcastically, asking, "Are those bandages there because they removed your brain or your common sense?"

McDaid tousled the boys' hair, apologizing for being a big daft dunderheid. Watching, Dreghorn felt a twinge of envy, wondered about his own life, the decisions he'd made, been forced to make, the chances lost. He thought of Peggy Bryce and the child taken from her, of wee Catriona Geddes, now missing her mother and father. No amount of inherited wealth could change that.

After that, they had a procession of visitors. From work, Ellen Duncan was the most frequent, keeping them updated on the progress of the case, details of new investigations, and general office gossip. The rest of the Untouchables turned up mob-handed, awkward at first because it could easily have been a wake they were attending, but the mood grew raucous once they opened up the beer they'd smuggled in. Deputy Chief Constable McVicar's sense of duty and decorum forced him to visit for all of ten minutes. He said nothing that wasn't complimentary but made it all sound like a reprimand. Of Strachan and Orr, there was no sign.

Dreghorn's mother visited most afternoons and charmed McDaid with her humor, which had grown more askew with age.

Over the years, she had been contacted twice—once during the war, once from Shanghai—with news that her son had been seriously injured. She thanked him for having the good grace to nearly get himself killed closer to home this time, so she could at least visit.

When their visits coincided, she seemed to enjoy the company of McDaid's children more than her son's, taking them to the hospital shop to buy sweets and comics. "That boy has a lovely family," she said pointedly, nodding at McDaid as he kissed the weans goodbye.

"So have you," Dreghorn countered.

She gave him a look from his childhood, the one that said, *Don't come it with me, James Dreghorn, you know what I mean.*

One visit, Dreghorn was moved almost to tears to wake from a nap and find his Uncle Joe sitting alongside his mother. The sculpted copper mask that covered Joe's lower jaw remained frozen, impassive, but his eyes were smiling. In the years following the war, Joe Dreghorn, who had once loved being the center of attention, rarely ventured outside his house, self-conscious of his disfigurement and its effects.

He spoke, the remains of his mouth working behind the mask, the words only partially formed, like someone attempting ventriloquism for the first time.

"I'll *lazy lump* you." Dreghorn's voice cracked at first. "I've been shot, you know."

"And blown up," McDaid said from his bed, "though to be fair, I think I shielded you with my body."

Joe guffawed, gestured at himself; the flesh-hued enamel paint of the mask almost matching his skin.

"It's no' a competition!" Dreghorn said in mock outrage.

When he'd recovered enough to think through everything that had happened, Dreghorn told Ellen to contact Kitty Fraser and ask her to visit him. She was the hidden victim, her pain a secret to everyone but him, and then only because he'd forced the truth out of her. Learning about Molly's death through the newspapers could have destroyed her.

Ellen had visited the Gordon Club first, encountering a charming Teddy Levin. He'd offered her coffee or—despite her being in uniform—"something stronger," and seemed disappointed when she turned him down. He claimed Kitty hadn't been attending business meetings for the last few days. The epitome of innocence, he admitted that he was a little concerned; Kitty had been acting oddly recently and seemed depressed. If there was anything else he could do to help . . .

Ellen had returned to the "boarding house" in Bearsden where she'd followed Janet Docherty. A young maid named Rose informed her that Kitty was unwell and wasn't receiving visitors, but promised that she would pass on Ellen's message.

Dreghorn, sitting up in bed, closed his eyes and sighed.

"Do you think something's wrong, sir?" Ellen asked.

He told her everything: Kitty's real name, the circumstances of the adoption, and her true relationship to Molly Raeburn. McDaid, who deserved to know what he'd nearly died for, was the only other one who knew the full story. Ellen was silent for a moment.

"Dear God," she said. "That poor woman."

"Don't know what you're blethering about," said McDaid. "People pay good money for this and you're getting it for free. You're privileged."

"Feels more like a punishment." Even though Dreghorn raised his voice, the sound of the bagpipes coming to life drowned out the last word.

McDaid stood by the window, blocking the daylight in a fetching tartan nightshirt you could sail the *Cutty Sark* with. He blew into the mouthpiece with a look of intense concentration—constipation, Dreghorn thought—inflating the bag and tuning up before launching into another epic tune.

McDaid had become something of a celebrity during his hospital stay. Early in their recuperation, he had whispered surreptitiously to his eldest boy and next day the bagpipes had turned up alongside the grapes and sweeties. He'd come to an arrangement with Matron; in return for being allowed to practice, he would play short concerts for patients in the public ward—shamelessly handing out business cards "in case your daughter's getting married"—and give lessons in the children's ward. The weans loved having a bash at it, though McDaid complained bitterly afterward about the drool and snotters that clogged up the pipes.

Dreghorn slid farther down the bed, clamped the sides of the pillow over his ears, and counted again the number of days he and the big man had been cooped up together.

To be fair the days were full of banter and bravado. It was at night the demons came out, old and new. McDaid would find Molly Raeburn staring at him whenever he closed his eyes. When he awoke, he was aware of Dreghorn writhing under the sheets in the other bed, fighting invisible foes in his sleep, swearing and sobbing, occasionally saying Isla Lockhart's name.

Neither of them slept well. Neither of them talked about it. It would pass, or they would live with it.

"Will you be all right?"

The doctors had decided McDaid was well enough to be released, but he seemed reluctant to leave.

"I will be once you and that wailing tartan octopus are on your way," Dreghorn replied. Mrs. Pettigrew had delivered clean clothes earlier in the week, but the doctors wanted to keep him in for further observation.

"You know you love it really," McDaid said. "I'll drop in tomorrow."

"Be still my beating heart." Dreghorn shook his head. "Go home, big man. I'm fine."

He wasn't. He paced the room like a caged tiger. He stared out at the city, gray daylight and black buildings, every chimney spewing smoke. He drank the dregs of the whisky.

It wasn't enough.

He looked into the mirror for a long time, thought about what he could live with.

And what he couldn't.

45

THURSDAY, 27 OCTOBER 1932

Whatever loyalty Naseby had possessed was gone. The butler opened the door and stepped aside without protest. "The library," he said.

Kelpie House was dark, silent, and oppressive. The nurse who'd previously defended the old man so vociferously was sitting on a sofa in a reception room adjoining the library, flicking through a magazine and smoking a cigarette. She gave Dreghorn a disinterested glance as he passed.

Sir Iain Lockhart was sitting with his back to the fire, which flickered weakly, as if requiring attention. He looked as though he'd been waiting there since the detective's last visit, the night his son had murdered his daughter. Dreghorn glanced around the room, spotting dust and cobwebs in the dim light, a general air of dissolution. Was there a faint smell of urine coming from the old man?

"Standards are slipping," he stated. "Only one dirty look since I got here, and that was from you."

Sir Iain looked toward the door.

"The hired help? Don't think they're coming. They know it was you. Maybe not your hand on the knife, but you all the same. I think they'll let you rot."

The old man's eyes blazed.

Dreghorn halted in front of the chair, stared down as if at the edge of a grave.

"Whose idea was it? The children, the whores, the blackmail? Did Bell and Dalrymple approach you, or was it all your idea? Did you find out about Dalrymple's tastes, the 'connoisseurs' club' he was running, and decide it could be of use to you? He had a wee lassie locked up in his wardrobe. Rory nearly burnt her alive. Doesn't that bother you?"

Sir Iain swallowed with difficulty, lowered his eyes. Dreghorn tapped his cast against the wheelchair tray like a judge's gavel.

"Uh-uh. There's no turning a blind eye now."

Hate burned fiercely in the old man's eyes.

"That's more like it." Dreghorn glared back. "Or were you one of the fuckin' uncles, popping in to cheer the children up, let them know how much you loved them?" He spat the words. "Is that it? Is that why you bankrolled Trinity all these years? But then, what? Come the war and the Depression, that big business brain of yours started ticking over, working out how you could twist the knife and turn everything to your advantage."

Lockhart grunted in discomfort. Dreghorn looked to the table, where the old man's notepaper and crayons lay.

"You want to say something?"

He grabbed the crayons and paper, slammed them down on Lockhart's tray. It wasn't easy with the cast on his hand, but Dreghorn managed to jam a crayon between the old man's fingers. "On you go, sir. Nice big letters. The word you're looking for is *GUILTY*. Do you want me to start it for you?"

With surprising violence, Lockhart swept the crayons and paper to the floor.

Dreghorn stepped back. "It's funny, when you go into the yard for the first time, all you do is look up—the ships, the scaffolding—

everything dwarfs you, makes you feel small, insignificant. You're just a tiny part of things. But when you called me into your office that first time, I realized you were always looking down, as if you ruled the world. The men, the machinery—it was all yours."

Lockhart was breathing heavily now, sticky lines of spittle forming around the corners of his mouth.

"The workers liked you because you treated them better than other yard owners, but it wasn't because you cared more; you were just manipulating them into working harder. Same when you supposedly brushed aside all the sectarian shite, judged people by their skills and talent rather than their religion. You weren't striking a blow for equality. As far as you were concerned, you were God. It was all yours. You owned us. Build us up, break us down, mold us into whatever you wanted."

The fire crackled as Dreghorn fell silent. He peered into the shadows, then back at Lockhart with disgust. "Didn't work with Rory though, did it? Tried to make him like you, but you created something else entirely. You should've known you couldn't control whatever was in him. Even God gets it wrong sometimes."

Lockhart trembled and jerked, the wheelchair creaking. Mucus bubbled at one nostril, wetting his upper lip. Dreghorn leaned down, hands on the tray. "He took a knife to your daughter's throat. Your fault. He kissed her as she choked on her own blood, said he could taste her life, draining away. Your fault."

Lockhart hacked and coughed, his face reddening.

"Don't worry—my colleague, the big man who came here with me, put an arm around Rory and snapped his neck. Just like that. If I'd known what he was—what you made him—I'd've put a bullet in him back in no-man's-land."

Lockhart's body was racked with pain. His eyes, bulging, never left Dreghorn's; no trace of remorse, no seeking pity.

"Did Rory tell you about Isla and me?" Dreghorn asked. "He wouldn't have been able to resist. Wouldn't have been happy about that, would you? Did your best to stop it last time."

Lockhart's face was turning purple. His good hand clawed at the tray. A wheezing rattle came from deep within his throat.

"What is it? Your heart? Can't be. You don't have one." Dreghorn leaned closer, their foreheads almost touching. "Go on. Fuckin' die."

"Grandpa?"

Dreghorn pulled away from Lockhart. Catriona Geddes stood tentatively in the doorway, holding a sheet of paper. "I've drawn a picture," she stammered.

She looked from Dreghorn to her grandfather, scared, torn between entering the room and running off. She stepped forward slowly, giving the detective a wide berth, skirting around the furniture until she stood beside Lockhart, one hand touching the tray of his wheelchair. The paper slipped from her hand, forgotten, fluttering to the floor at Dreghorn's feet.

He wondered if she recognized him, imagined the sight he presented, the stitches in his cheek, one hand bandaged, a cast on the other, the swollen purple fingers protruding from it. He'd had to slit the seam of his sleeve to fit it over the cast.

Dreghorn picked up the child's drawing, touching in its innocence; a young girl and an old man in a chair outside a shape that represented Kelpie House. Two winged figures hovered in the sky. On one, Dreghorn recognized the pencil mustache of Charles Geddes, and on the other, the sharp angular haircut of Isla Lockhart. He felt a lump in his throat, held up the drawing for Lockhart to see, and placed it on his tray. The torment in the old man's body had subsided, his breath calming, as if the child's presence soothed him.

Lockhart barely acknowledged the picture, his focus on Dreghorn. His mouth twitched with a razor slash of a smile. His eyes fired with triumph. Dreghorn glanced at Catriona, fear and uncertainty in her eyes. He couldn't take it anymore, and turned and walked away.

He paused in the doorway and looked back. The old man's hand had closed over the child's, and the fire was dying behind them.

46

Cheap booze, stale cigarette smoke, and fresh animosity, that's what struck him as he walked into the Mermaid. There were a few smirks at the state he was in, but mainly there was wariness and the odd hint of grudging respect. Not just because of what they'd read in the press, the violence he'd been subjected to, the deaths he'd witnessed.

Usually, he played the game, approached the bar, made barbed comments to gang members he'd arrested in the past. Tonight he walked straight to the snug. No suit, no hat, and murder in his eyes? Jimmy Dreghorn wasn't there on police business.

No one said anything. No one tried to bar his way.

The journey back from Kelpie House had been difficult, not just because of the cast on his hand. A crushing weariness descended as he drove under the stallion gate for the last time. His hands throbbed dully and the cut on his cheek burned like a brand. The wound in his side didn't trouble him too much as long as he didn't bend or twist, although getting in and out of the car was laborious. Twice, he jerked awake, his cast scraping on the steering wheel as the car veered sideways. Fortunately, the roads were empty, the headlights touching nothing but darkness.

"Hell mend you," Matron had warned when he checked himself out against their advice. "Don't come greetin' to me if you're straight back in tomorrow."

He had walked, shakily at first, from the hospital to Turnbull Street. Shug Nugent's normally implacable features had registered surprise. "Didn't know they were letting you out today," he said, as if addressing a convict whose sentence wasn't due to end just yet.

Dreghorn told Nugent he was back on duty and went down to the garage. The radio cars were in use, so he signed out a standard vehicle. Watching him climb gingerly into the driver's seat, the sergeant in charge of the motor pool asked, "Are you sure you're fit to—?"

Dreghorn had drowned out his concerns by revving the engine, and driven off.

Peter MacLean was on his feet and ready for a square go with whoever had dared to enter without knocking. He looked Dreghorn up and down with amusement.

"Glasgow's finest," he said, "have seen better days."

"Fuck off, Peter," Dreghorn said, not stopping. "Fuck off fast."

"It's fine, Peter, on you go," Billy Hunter said. If he took it as a slight to his authority that MacLean was already backing away from Dreghorn, he didn't show it.

Dreghorn sat on the stool opposite Hunter as the door clicked shut behind MacLean. The gang leader was sprawled casually on the battered leather seat in the corner of the snug. Newspapers, playing cards, a bottle of whisky, and two glasses sat on the table between them.

Hunter's eyes smiled. "Somebody's been in the wars." He nodded at Dreghorn's cast as it clunked onto the table. "Again."

Dreghorn picked up the nearest whisky—MacLean's, freshly poured—with his left hand and knocked it back, fueled by the burn.

"Help yourself, why don't you?" Hunter gestured at the rest of the bottle.

Dreghorn stared at Hunter, stripping the layers away. The smile faded from Hunter's eyes. "All that in the papers about Captain Lockhart," he asked. "Is it true?"

"The truth's worse."

There was laughter in the bar beyond, the butt of a joke swearing loudly in retaliation, but it sounded far away, as if they were in their own little world.

"Who did you send to lift her?" Dreghorn asked.

"Lift who?"

"Somebody you could trust, probably. Peter?"

"No idea what you're talking about, Jimmy."

"Molly Raeburn."

"Never heard of her."

"The one Rory murdered, stabbed to death," Dreghorn prompted. "If you've been reading about him, then you know about her. We found the body, me and Archie."

"Poor lassie."

"Something we'll all have to live with."

Hunter displayed no reaction to his inclusion in Dreghorn's statement, the implications it held. "Told you, it's a tragedy and all that, but I don't know her."

"No? I bumped into Peter and Andy Caldwell loitering in the street outside her house a few days before she was abducted."

"Aye? Better call Peter back in, then. What'd he say?"

"Out for an afternoon stroll. Getting some exercise and staying out of mischief."

"There you go. Likes a good walk, does Peter. And if he stopped for a quick fag, well, hanging about street corners isn't an offense. If it was, you'd have half of Briggy banged up."

"Where'd you meet with Lockhart, Billy?" Dreghorn glanced around. "Can't imagine it was here. Somewhere posher probably, you'd be impressed by that. I could ask around a few likely establishments. Someone's bound to remember you lording it up with Rory Lockhart. A right odd couple."

Hunter topped up his whisky, but didn't offer any to Dreghorn. The smile was back in his eyes. Forced now, the detective thought as he reached for the bottle, poured a drink awkwardly with his left hand. He placed the bottle out of Hunter's reach; let his hand linger on it. He said, "I'm not saying you knew what Rory was planning. No' sure he knew himself. You probably thought you were doing him a favor—a romantic fling that was getting out of hand, a girl that was becoming an embarrassment. I'm sure there was money involved too."

"Oh, aye, I'm living it up big-time; the Lockhart family fortune's falling out my pockets." Hunter tapped his trouser pockets to show they were empty, became serious. "I haven't seen the man for the best part of ten years, and even then it was just a bit of business."

Dreghorn didn't seem to hear. "I don't know what you told your boys to do. Put the fear of God into her, tell her to stop harassing Rory or else? Pretty girl. I hope for your sake they didn't feel her up or anything like that. Do you trust them that much?"

Hunter paused before drinking, feigning concern. "Maybe I should get a couple of the boys to help you back to hospital. You look like you need a lie-down, concussion or something."

Dreghorn drained his glass, set it down loudly, like a challenge. "She went to Trinity, you know."

"The lassie you're talking about?"

"She was adopted."

Hunter's eyes narrowed as he considered the change in direction. "At least those two bastards won't be hurting anybody any more. I'd've helped the captain with them, no bother. If the rumors are true."

"They are."

"Bastards," Hunter repeated. "Was she . . . ?"

"Not that we know of."

Hunter raised a toast. "Small mercies." He knocked it back.

"She was adopted when she was two. Nice family, or so it seemed. The father got himself into trouble, though. Prostitutes, blackmail."

"Least he could afford them, with the Depression." Hunter nodded at the bottle. "Hogging that, inspector?"

Dreghorn poured Hunter another drink, then set the bottle back down beside him. Hunter smiled at the detective's precaution, not fully discounting the possibility that Dreghorn intended to bludgeon him with it.

Dreghorn said, "Your sister was at Trinity too. Sarah. She had her baby there."

"So you said." The bench creaked as Hunter leaned forward, the smile in his pupils gone in a blink, replaced with menace. "You found her?" he asked, voice low. "Where?"

"No' as far away as you'd think. It's a small world." He remembered the last time he'd seen Catherine Fraser, a mother torn apart by a missing child, her tough shell shattered. "She doesn't want to see you, Billy. Looked appalled at the prospect."

"It's been a long time, 'course she'll be nervous. Scared, even. I will be too. So will Janet and my ma."

"I warned you it would be up to her. I warned you, and I promised her."

"Fuck your promise." Hunter nodded at the door, the bar beyond. "You think you can make it out of here without telling me where she is? I've got an army out there. The past doesn't matter. She should be with her family. We're the ones that love her."

Hunter's voice had become reasonable, but he was sitting up straight, hands on the edge of the table. His razors were in his inside pockets, and Dreghorn knew how quickly he could whip them out. He sighed, the weariness he'd felt in the car returning, kept his own hand close to the whisky bottle.

"They got her in at Trinity, which was good—outside of Glasgow,

far away from nosy neighbors, and it had a good reputation. Then."
He let Hunter reflect on that. "Everybody expected her to just come
home afterward, pretend it never happened, but Sarah was head-
strong. She got a job at the orphanage, so she could be with the
baby—a wee girl. She called her Maggie after your mother."

No answer.

"Sarah spent about the best part of two years with Maggie before
she was adopted. Must've been murder to watch her being taken
away. A good middle-class family, so she was supposedly going up in
the world. A bright future. I'm sure none of that made it any better."
Dreghorn leaned closer, elbows on the table. "Sarah found out the
name of the family, where they lived. Against the rules, of course,
but we know now that Trinity wasn't as holier-than-thou as everyone thought. She would go and stand outside their house, hoping to
catch a glimpse of wee Maggie. She would follow them when they
walked to school, sit in the pew behind them at church. For years.
Watched her daughter grow up and never said a word. Breaks your
heart, doesn't it? You know the family's name?"

"Don't."

"Raeburn. They changed her name when they adopted her. To
Molly."

Hunter's fingertips were white as he gripped the table, as if it was
the only thing stopping him from slipping into madness.

"Molly Raeburn." Dreghorn pushed one of the newspapers
toward Hunter, a photo of Molly Raeburn on the front page. "She
was your niece."

Hunter seemed to be sucked into the image, his shoulders dropping, head falling forward. Dreghorn stood up, the chair scraping on
the floor, and walked into the noise of the pub. He didn't rush,
moved at his usual pace. He heard his name called, first in a low
growl, then bellowed like a maddened bull.

"Dreghorn!"

He turned as Hunter charged into him, hands clawing at his throat. The collision drove him back through the main door and out into the street. He stumbled at the edge of the pavement and they fell into the road, Hunter losing his grip.

Dreghorn staggered to his feet. He heard Hunter spit, phlegm slapping the cobblestones. The door creaked back and forth frenetically as the Billy Boys flooded out, scuffling to get the best view, shouting bloodthirsty encouragement.

"Gaun yourself, Billy!"

"Get your blades out, Billy!"

"Cut his fuckin' baws aff!"

"Billy?" A woman's voice, quieter than the others, tentative and fearful, but enough to make everyone look.

Kitty Fraser, Sarah Catherine Hunter, as she had once been, looked as though she hadn't slept for days, her hair unkempt; she might even have been wearing the same clothes Dreghorn had last seen her in. Standing by the detective's car, she appeared lost, returned to a world she no longer knew.

"Sarah!" Hunter brushed Dreghorn aside and embraced his sister with the passion of a lover, pressed his cheek again hers.

Dreghorn suddenly realized that he'd known the truth all along, but that his mind had refused to accept it.

"Gie her one for me," one of the younger Billy Boys yelled, only to be urgently shushed by Peter MacLean.

Kitty pulled away, stared into her brother's eyes and said, "She's gone."

"I know, hen, I know." Billy took his sister's arm. "Come on, let's go home. It's time."

She pulled away, distraught. "There's no time left. She's gone. Maggie, Molly, she's gone. I should've told you . . . She was yours—ours—and I gave her away. I gave her away, and now she's dead. He killed her. Lockhart killed her."

"He wasn't the only one." Hunter's voice came from the depths.

"Billy, the lads," MacLean warned.

"No' a word," Hunter stabbed a finger at MacLean. "No' a fuckin' word, right!"

Kitty looked from Dreghorn to her brother. Hunter paced on the cobbles. He raised his hands to his head, fingers clawing at his skull as though trying to tear out his thoughts. Suspicious murmurs coursed through the Billy Boys.

"What do you mean, Billy?" Kitty demanded. "It's nothing to do with you. Tell me it's nothing to do with you."

"I didn't know, I didn't know," Hunter kept repeating, a horrified whisper, rising in volume. "I didn't know!" He grabbed Kitty by the shoulders. "I didn't know who she was. Why didn't you tell me? I didn't know who she was!"

"She was our daughter," Kitty said softly, tears rolling down her cheeks.

Hunter tightened his grip, his body shaking as if he didn't know whether to hug her or hit her.

Dreghorn started to pull him away. "Billy—"

Searing pain sliced across the knuckles of his bandaged hand. He hadn't seen Hunter draw the razors, but the blades were there now, one red with his blood.

Dreghorn recoiled, instinctively raised his guard. He saw madness and murder in Hunter's eyes, and rage.

Hunter came at him, the razors whirling and slashing, almost impossible to see in the dim light of the streetlamps. Dreghorn skipped clumsily backward, blocked a couple of cuts with the cast, the blade scoring deep. He launched a kick at Hunter's groin, but a razor flashed, slicing across his shin. He slammed back against the side of his car. A razor bit deep into his forearm and he jerked the arm away. The other razor slashed at his face.

Then a fist closed around the blade, stopping it.

Hunter turned, moving with a terrible grace.

Kitty stood in front of him, sobbing, her hand dripping with blood. He held the razor above her, trembling with fury. An eerie calm came over her. She tore open her blouse, tipped her head back to show her throat, her eyes never leaving her brother's. It would be a kindness, an end to the pain.

Hunter shook his head, words catching in his throat like fishhooks. He lowered the razor, pressed it to his own throat, started to cut.

Dreghorn charged, slamming Hunter into the car. He cracked Hunter's hand against the edge of the windshield, and the razor slid down the bonnet and skittered across the cobbles. Hunter tried to push him away, but the detective grabbed Hunter by the lapels and pulled him forward into a head butt, smashing his forehead into the gangster's face.

The street was silent, the Billy Boys stunned, trying to take in what they were witnessing, no idea what to do. The only sound was Dreghorn, gasping for breath, almost wheezing.

Slowly, Hunter raised his head. There were tears in his eyes, a terrible understanding of what he'd done, hatred and guilt and self-loathing. A silent plea as well, for Dreghorn to hit him again and again, to beat him senseless, batter all thoughts of his sister and daughter out of him.

Dreghorn swung, wide and powerful, with all his rage, felt Hunter's face collapse, the cast around his hand shatter, and his world disappear in pain.

47

TUESDAY, 1 NOVEMBER 1932

"How's your hand?"

Kitty Fraser glanced at the bandage around her palm as if she'd forgotten about it. Otherwise she was immaculate once more—dressed in her Sunday best, not a hair out of place.

"Almost all better," she said. "Yours?"

"Won't be playing the piano any time soon, but if you've ever heard me, you won't be heartbroken." Dreghorn raised his cast, wiggled his fingers.

They were strolling by the Clyde through Glasgow Green. Outside his house Benny Parsonage was cleaning his boat in the pale sunshine; he nodded to Dreghorn as if approving of the detective's companion.

"I think your friend has the wrong idea," Kitty said.

Dreghorn shrugged. "Benny's one of the good yins."

"Anyone looking would think we're normal. They wouldn't know what we've been through. It's all written inside though. I think that's why I got in touch. There's no one else I can talk to. May I?" She put her arm through his, and smiled sadly. "You know all my dark secrets, inspector."

"Aye," Dreghorn said. "Some polisman. Find out everything, but can't do anything to help."

"You tried." She looked at him. "You know there are rumors about you and Isla Lockhart?"

He said nothing, didn't meet her eyes.

"It's sad," she said. "It's all so sad."

Dreghorn had passed out after bludgeoning Billy Hunter and breaking his hand again. Fortunately McDaid, alerted to Dreghorn's actions by Shug Nugent, had turned up with the Heavy Mob before the Billy Boys got over their shock. The big man had taken Dreghorn and Kitty to hospital for treatment. Billy Hunter was in Duke Street Prison, serving a twelve-month sentence for assaulting a police officer, but nothing more. The sentence in his head would be a lot longer.

Kitty stopped and they turned to look over the water. "It only happened the once, you know, a few weeks before Billy was arrested. And then I tried to pretend it didn't. Until I couldn't any more." She sighed slowly. "What must you think of us?"

Dreghorn said gently, "I think you turned out fairly well, all things considered. Your old man used to terrorize the lot of you—he put a hot iron to your arm. Things like that can't help but throw you together. Comfort, sympathy, love. It's easy to see how things can get confused."

It was her turn not to respond, though her arm remained within his.

"Try no' to go back to your old profession, eh?" he said suddenly. "Stick to the tea rooms—they're all the rage. Find yourself a good man and settle down. Have weans. You're still young enough."

"Are you volunteering?"

They looked at each other for what seemed a long time. Dreghorn broke away first. "I said a good man."

She smiled sadly, slipped her arm free of his, then hugged him and kissed his cheek. "Thank you for trying, Jimmy Dreghorn."

Dreghorn lit a Capstan and smoked slowly as an excuse to watch her walk away. She didn't look back.

He strolled back to the bench outside the People's Palace, where he knew McDaid was waiting, insisting on playing chaperone because Dreghorn "couldn't be trusted with women."

The hunger marchers had reached London, where the Prime Minister had refused to meet them. They had clashed with police outside Buckingham Palace, and with Mosley's Fascists near Trafalgar Square. Giving a speech in Milan, Benito Mussolini had predicted that all Europe would be Fascist within a decade. Dreghorn hoped he was talking shite, but his faith in humanity was at a low ebb.

McDaid was reading the sports pages of the *Record* when Dreghorn sat down beside him. "Jackie Brown beat Perez for the title." He handed Dreghorn the paper. "Normally, I've no time for the short-arse divisions, but well done to the wee man."

Silence for a moment, then out of nowhere, McDaid said, "Mairi and me are thinking of adopting. That wee lassie, Morag . . ."

The nurses had brought Morag Gilmartin, now fully recovered, in to see the detectives while they recuperated in hospital, the visit coinciding with one from McDaid's family.

"Mairi's always wanted a wee girl," McDaid continued. "We carried her out of that fire and—it doesn't seem right to send her back. What're you smiling about?"

Dreghorn felt a rush of affection for the big man. "Mairi's magic—and you don't seem to muddle along too badly. I think it's a wonderful idea."

"No' if you're trying to watch your pennies." McDaid smiled. "What about you?"

Dreghorn pictured Peggy Bryce alone in her single end, Billy Hunter staring at the walls in his cell, Kitty Fraser walking toward an uncertain future. He thought about Isla, felt the ache inside himself. For perhaps the first time, his eyes didn't immediately fill with tears.

"I'll live. Just about."

AUTHOR'S NOTE

"In journalism, just one fact that is false prejudices the entire work. In contrast, in fiction, one single fact that is true gives legitimacy to the entire work. That's the only difference, and it lies in the commitment of the writer. A novelist can do anything he [or she] wants as long as he makes people believe in it."

When in doubt, quote the Nobel Prize–winning author, so I'll shamelessly pounce on those words of wisdom from Gabriel García Márquez to excuse any historical inaccuracies in this novel and the liberties I've taken along the way to serve the story and hopefully make it as entertaining as possible.

Glasgow in the 1930s was, as the saying goes, "no mean city," and the background of poverty, unemployment, discontent, sectarianism, and gang violence in the book is accurate. In 1931, to combat these problems, the Corporation of Glasgow did indeed controversially appoint Englishman Percy Sillitoe (later Director-General of MI5) as Chief Constable, after his success dealing with criminal gangs in Sheffield. His no-nonsense approach to policing and the measures he introduced, such as the recruitment of officers like the fictional Dreghorn and McDaid—essentially the UK's first Flying Squad—are for the most part accurate, although I have allowed radio-cars to patrol the streets a couple of years earlier than they were actually introduced. I have attempted to build Sillitoe's character and speech patterns from his 1955 autobiography *Cloak Without Dagger,* borrowing his family motto *Sileto Teneto Si Leto* for what becomes his parting catchphrase in the book—"See it through."

Sillitoe's squad were named "the Untouchables" by the press. I've embellished this to "the Tartan Untouchables," a suggestion from my partner Deborah that seems to encapsulate the spirit of the book.

Benjamin Parsonage was Assistant Officer of the Glasgow Humane Society from 1918 to 1928, and Chief Officer from then until his death in 1979, whereupon the position was taken by his son George, who patroled the Clyde until his own retirement in 2019. Visit their website—https://www.glasgowhumanesociety.com— for a fascinating history of the Society, the oldest continuing lifeboat service in the world, and an inspiring record of the Rivermen's quiet, undemonstrative heroism. Thousands of lives have been saved and bodies recovered since the Society's founding in 1790.

I discovered Dr. Willie Kivlichan while disappearing down a rabbit hole of research that looked as though it was heading no-where. Amazingly, he really did play football for both Rangers and Celtic before qualifying as a doctor. That was fascinating enough, but to learn that, in addition to his own medical practice, he acted as a police doctor during the period of the book was even better. While, in reality, he wasn't at Quintinshill, he did serve in Africa in the Great War, so I didn't think it was too great a leap of the imagination to have him present at the crash for the purposes of the story.

To this day, the Quintinshill rail disaster remains the worst train crash in British history. That the majority of the victims were young soldiers, killed before they even left home soil, makes the tragedy even more poignant; those who survived were shipped to Gallipoli afterward.

I've largely tried to use real locations where I could, some of which no longer exist, but have taken some liberties with the riverside geography between Glasgow and Helensburgh, and the opening dates of Dumbuck Quarry. Kelpie House is loosely based on Dalmoak Castle, though considerably larger and set in far more expansive grounds. Trinity Village is inspired by Quarrier's Village, the orphan community founded by William Quarrier in the late nineteenth century. The criminal events that occur there are purely my invention, although the Scottish Child Abuse Inquiry concluded in January 2020 that children in a number of institutions, including Quarrier's, suffered physical, emotional, and sexual abuse between 1921 and 1991.

The Gordon Club was a notorious underworld hang-out in 1950s Glasgow, and features in Denise Mina's excellent *The Long Drop*. I may have employed some artistic license to place the same establishment in 1932, but liked the idea of a club acting as a criminal black hole, exerting a corrupt gravitational pull on respectable society over many decades. The strangest things, of course, you can't make up; this den of iniquity really was upstairs from the Girl Guides Association.

The colorfully named gangs listed in the "travelogue" section at the start of the novel all existed—if anything, they're only the tip of the iceberg. Despite the similarity in names, Billy Hunter is not based on the notorious real-life leader of the Billy Boys William Fullarton, who was younger and served in World War II, not World War I, although I have admittedly borrowed Fullarton's penchant for drilling gang members like soldiers on parade and conducting renditions of "God Save the King" at Bridgeton bandstand.

Closer to home, a source of inspiration and research for some elements of the story is the family history compiled by my father Hamilton Morrison. On both sides, my family's connection to shipbuilding goes back several generations. My great grandfather Thomas Mooney lost an eye in a shipyard accident, and, like Jimmy Dreghorn, my paternal grandfather Robert, who died long before I was born, worked as a boilermaker/caulker in black squads in various Clyde shipyards. A fine amateur boxer, winning two gold medals at welterweight in 1921, Robert also fought for a time under the patronage of Sir Iain Colquhoun, 29th Laird of Luss, who ran a stable of athletes not unlike that of Sir Iain Lockhart in the story.

After a period in the Merchant Navy, my maternal grandfather Bill

Gardiner ("Pop," as I knew him) worked in the engine shop of Denny's shipyard for twenty years, where he also first served his apprenticeship before going to sea. Interestingly, to me at least, both were the "eye" men of their respective yards, extracting tiny shards of metal from workers' eyes—a skill I've given young Jimmy in the book. Is this a talent I've inherited? I hope no one ever has to find out!

Looking over my early character notes on Dreghorn, I found I'd described him as a man of "contrasts and contradictions: passionate and romantic, yet cynical and pragmatic when need be; good-humored and possessed of a lust for life, yet brooding and taciturn when faced with injustice; tough, yet tender and caring; patriotic and politically aware, yet distrustful and disdainful of those who hold power; and always punching above his weight." It strikes me now that it's also a pretty good description of Glasgow itself, a city I love, and which never fails to put a spring in my step when I step off the train at Central Station.

I'll finish on one of life's ironies: I once lived in St. Andrew's Square, literally across the road from Central Police Headquarters in Turnbull Street, where Dreghorn and McDaid are based. I had no idea that I would, twenty-something years later, set my first novel there. If I'd known, I'd have been in and out of the place like a peep of gas, soaking up the atmosphere and cataloging every detail. It had long since stopped being a police station by then, but part of it was still in use as some sort of criminal court, which you could have guessed from some of the people loitering outside. To the bold wee ned who, probably straight after leaving court, sneaked into that flat one day and stole my CD collection from my bedroom (while, blissfully unaware, I listened to Isaac Hayes' *Shaft* at full blast in the living-room)—you wouldn't have got away with it if Dreghorn and McDaid were around!

ACKNOWLEDGMENTS

After over two decades as a comic-book writer, I already had a black-belt in self-isolation, but 2020 was the year in which we all got a crash course in that unlikely martial art.

I signed with Pan Macmillan for *Edge of the Grave* just before the country went into lockdown, courtesy of Covid-19. I have yet to meet any of the publishing team in person, but am mightily impressed by their professionalism, passion, and commitment, especially in such challenging circumstances. A big thank you to editor Alex Saunders for believing in Dreghorn and McDaid, and for notes that added extra layers to the story and supporting cast. Thanks also to Charlotte Wright, James Annal, Philippa McEwan, Hemesh Alles, and everyone else involved.

Three cheers for my agent, the indomitable Jane Gregory and her team at David Higham Associates: Camille Burns, Stephanie Glencross, and especially Mary Jones, who helped shape the original manuscript and made me pull up my grammatical socks. Yes, the fight scenes were too long. A nod also to former Jonathan Cape publisher Dan Franklin, who suggested Jane after seeing an early draft.

Last, but not least, to Deborah Tate for her wit, wisdom, passionate support, meticulous research, insightful feedback and for typing this novel from my handwritten pages. Her own interest in Glasgow stems from her mother Elizabeth/Betty's love of the city and evocative recollections of living and working there as a young woman in the 1940s. Without Deborah, this book would be poorer in every respect. Me, too.

ABOUT THE AUTHOR

ROBBIE MORRISON was born in Helensburgh, Scotland, and grew up in the Renton, Coatbridge, Linwood and Houston. On both sides, his family connection to ship-building in Glasgow and the surrounding areas stretches back four generations and is a source of inspiration for the Jimmy Dreghorn series. One of the most respected writers in the UK comics industry, he sold his first script to pub-lishers DC Thomson in Dundee at the age of twenty-three. *Edge of the Grave,* the first Jimmy Dreghorn novel, won the Bloody Scotland Debut Crime Novel of the Year, was shortlisted for the Crime Writers' Association Historical Dagger, and the Fingerprint Awards Debut Book of the Year, and longlisted for the Historical Writers' Association Debut Crown.